SEA AND STARS

Sea and Stars

Kelly Jarvis

Sea and Stars

Excerpts from William Shakespeare's Collected Works

ISBN: 979-8-9923357-3-6 (paperback)

ISBN: 979-8-9923357-4-3 (ebook)

Published by Incantation Press

Cover design and interior formatting by Holly Dunn

For Randy, Keegan, Reilly, and Kasey:
the stars that guide me home

Part One

Isle of Skye, 1847

"...but then there was a star danced,
and under that was I born"
(Much Ado About Nothing)

In the growing shadows of the Cuillin Mountains, the lonely stone cottage looked like it was breathing.

The cold March sky had been crowded with the light of a thousand stars, but now, as the dying night entered its darkest hours, sea mists curled around the cottage like wraiths. Arabella Porter, soaked from her long walk across the moorlands, hurried toward the flickering lantern she had left burning in the cottage window. The unopened letter, the letter which would change the course of her life, throbbed like a beating heart in the pocket of her cloak.

Arabella was the last living member of the Porter family, a matriarchal clan whose history on the Isle of Skye could be traced back hundreds of years. She had been born and raised in the old stone cottage that peered out over the swirling sea, just as all the women in her family had been. Arabella's grandmother, Caitriona Porter, had taught her the art of healing, an ancient wisdom steeped in the secrets of the island, the movement of the seasons, and the favor of the good folk who populated the hills and glens.

The door of the cottage creaked open in noisy greeting as Arabella crossed the threshold and bolted the latch behind her. She draped her cloak over the table and pulled a tinder from the mantle, transferring the flame from her lantern to a few wax candles. Then she bent down to stir the embers barely glowing in the grate. Soon a warm light coated the open room, glinting off the glass bottles lining her apothecary cabinet.

Arabella, alone but for the ghosts who drifted past on dips and swells of firelight, took the folded letter from her cloak and sank into a chair by the hearth. The paper was sealed with wax that had been pressed with the Porter emblem more than twenty years ago. She slid her finger over the smooth design, tracing the familiar spikes and swirls of Scottish thistle which also embossed the silver pendant hanging around her neck. The prickly purple flowers grew in profusion across the island, staining the ground with a violet hue.

Outside, stars shuddered in thick banks of storm clouds rolling in from the sea, and, when Arabella Porter, the last living member of the Porter family, finally released the wax seal to open the letter that would change the course of her life, the lonely stone cottage, which had sheltered her since the starlit evening of her birth, held its breath.

The day had begun in an ordinary way, with a few villagers gathering outside Arabella's door as the sun lifted itself through the layers of a cloudy blue morning. A kettle simmered on the hearth, its cinnamon and clove scent warming the air's chill, but the villagers lingered just long enough to exchange their goods and services for the remedies Arabella pulled from her cabinet. She remembered a time when her cottage had been crowded with women who stayed to gossip and sew after purchasing the Porters' teas and elixirs. Arabella's grandmother and aunts had all been alive then, and Arabella, only a child, would sit in her own little chair by the hearth and practice her stitching while the older women talked. It was in this way she learned the best herbs for heartache and how to heal the scars from burns. It was in those whispered conversations that she learned what little she knew about the mother she had never met.

The Porter Cottage could only be reached by a long trek from the nearest village. It was a pleasant walk in temperate weather, but only the heartiest would venture out in the earliest weeks of spring when snow still capped the Cuillin

Mountains. In the last few years of her grandmother's life when Caitriona's legs had begun to buckle beneath her, Arabella had become accustomed to making house calls and deliveries across the island on her own. This morning, she was preparing to travel to Portree where Fiona McPherson had recently given birth to her second child, when she heard a loud knock followed by the forceful shaking of her cottage door.

Douglas McMillan looked both surprised and relieved when she answered. His gaze fell to his feet. "I didn't know if I would find you still at home." He pulled his hat from his head and looked up with hesitation. "My Mam sent me."

Arabella had known Douglas since they were both children on the island. He and his friends used to toss stones into puddles and laugh when drops of mud splashed across Arabella's dress. "Be gone with you, Douglas McMillan," Arabella had cried one day, hurling a jagged rock at the crowd of boys because she had had enough of their teasing. When Douglas twisted out of the rock's way, his feet slipped beneath him and he fell hard on the ground, snapping his wrist in two. The other boys had scattered, and Arabella had begrudgingly offered Douglas her hand.

"Stay away from me, you little witch!" he had hissed, crossing himself in fear. "You broke my arm!"

"Your fall broke your arm, and it serves you right," she had shot back, though she was sorry for throwing the rock and worried she would be in trouble. She knew Douglas' parents would call on Caitriona to set his wrist.

Although Douglas and his friends had not breathed a word of her involvement with his accident, Arabella had confessed her crime to her grandmother. "Are we—am I—a witch?" she had asked, wondering if her anger at the boys had contributed to Douglas' injury. She had often heard the word *witch* associated with the Porter Clan, though it had always been whispered behind their backs with reverence. Douglas had been the first one to accuse Arabella of being a witch to her face. The word had sounded dark and sharp in his mouth, and it had made her feel ashamed.

Caitriona twirled Arabella's auburn curls, their luminous color the mark of every Porter woman who had ever been born on the island. "Did you transform Douglas into a frog?" she asked. "Or give him a tail? Or turn his tongue blue?"

Arabella had begun to laugh, even as tears slipped from her eyes. The witches in her storybooks were hags who cast curses on unsuspecting villagers. She knew fairy tale witches were not real, but she also knew the Porter women were regarded as practitioners of healing magic. She had listened to her grandmother sing words of comfort to the sick and had watched her aunts brew sweet-smelling balms. She remembered a night when she was very young and, awakened by the haunting sounds of words she did not know, she had wandered outside where she found her grandmother and her aunts swaying together, drawing down the silver light of the moon with their practiced movements. The air had been scented with salt and the night insects had hummed in the bushes and Arabella had thought their dance was the most beautiful thing she had ever seen.

"There's nothing ugly about the word witch until it comes from the mouth of an ignorant man," Caitriona had said, wiping away Arabella's tears, which glistened, wet and slippery, on the crescent-shaped freckle that marked her grandmother's wrinkled palm. "Douglas and his friends are nothing more than silly little boys who make up names for things they don't understand. Now, dry your tears, my child, for one solstice day, not long from now, those silly little boys will all be lining up to pluck your wreath from the river."

The summer solstice, when the old traditions were celebrated, was still the busiest time of year for Arabella. Island maidens would steal away to her cottage under the cover of darkness to make desperate requests for perfumes and tinctures that would bring them luck in love. Long Christianized, Skye continued to celebrate midsummer with communal bonfires, and even the most reverent young women floated wreaths of flowers down the rivers and streams in the hopes of finding a husband.

Now Douglas fidgeted in the silence of Arabella's rundown cottage. He pulled at the patches of his threadbare jacket and absentmindedly ran his hand along the bone he had broken when he was a child. Many of the young men he had grown up with had left Skye, unable to make their livings because large acres of farmland had been repurposed into grazing fields for black-faced sheep. The clearances had sent many crofting tenants to the smoky cities of the Scottish lowlands to work in factories, and some men and women had indentured themselves to wealthy families in the New World. Douglas had stayed on the island to care for his ailing mother who was too weak to make a long journey. He had relocated the two of them to a coastal croft with stony land that was barely cultivable. The damp conditions of their thatched one-room dwelling so close to the water no doubt exacerbated his mother's aching bones.

"I still owe the doctor a considerable sum of money, but my Mam says his medicines make her feel worse. She says your creams must be brewed by the fair folk themselves."

Arabella narrowed her eyes. So, now she was a fairy instead of a witch. Apparently even grown men created names to explain away what they would never understand, an intelligent woman skilled in the art of healing.

The crofter's cheeks tinged red as she continued to stare at him. "The stones on the north side of your cottage are beginning to crumble. I can replace them for you." He swallowed. "Or perhaps I can mend your garden fence before spring?"

If he had not turned his head toward the crooked floorboards in shame, he would have seen kindness soften Arabella's green eyes.

"My fence needs no mending, Douglas, but we can't have your Mam in pain, now, can we?" She buttered a thick slice of brown bread, poured a cup of tea, and bade him sit at her table to eat while she mixed a soothing balm for his mother. It wasn't long before the warmth of the tea eased his wounded pride and they began to laugh, remembering how years ago, a hairy Highland bull, normally a gentle creature, had chased Douglas across a farmer's field until Arabella had distracted the animal with some apples.

The call of a falcon punctuated their laughter. It soared above the cottage in spiraled precision, looking for its mate.

"Do you ever get lonely out here, now that your Gran has passed away?"

Arabella stiffened at his sympathetic tone. Her grandmother had been gone for nearly three months. There had not been many on Skye who could remember the island before Caitriona's birth or imagine it existing after her death. The sight of her grandmother's grey healer's cloak, the color of a winter evening, flapping in the breezes of the village square, had been enough to silence any man who thought to criticize the Porter way of life. Now that the shock of Caitriona's passing was settling in, people were beginning to question Arabella's independence. How would she survive without a husband to care for her, especially now that the governing councils had brought medical doctors to the islands? The old ways would not last; they were more superstition than science. It would be better for Caitriona's only granddaughter to marry and have children, to assimilate into the community rather than reside in her cottage so far away from civilization. Arabella marveled at how quickly the islanders had forgotten that the Porter women had not married for generations, raising their daughters to be strong, free-thinking healers who could take care of others and themselves.

"If I ever do get lonely, Douglas McMillan, I won't be seeking comfort in the arms of the man who is courting Sophie Watson."

He opened his mouth to protest, but Arabella, her eyes now dancing with mirth, didn't give him the chance.

"The two of you will marry in the end," she continued. "She'll birth you seven sons, each one with an appetite even bigger than your own, so save your coins and treat her well."

Douglas smiled with embarrassment at the exaggerated prophecy. He had barely been able to support himself and his mother through last winter's potato blight, but the thought of Sophie birthing his sons made him feel strangely hopeful and alive. Arabella packaged his mother's ointment and lit the tall candle in her window lantern so it would still be burning when she returned home later that night.

"Thank you, Arabella," Douglas said, his eyes cast downward once again as he accepted the package. "I promise to pay you as soon as I can."

Arabella winked as she tossed him an apple. "In case any Highland cows give you chase on your way home," she quipped. Then she grabbed her cloak from its place on the coat rack and, together, she and Douglas closed the creaky cottage door behind them and headed out in opposite directions across the moor.

The Isle of Skye perches off the north west coast of Scotland like a raven returning home to roost, flapping its feathered wings against the Sea of the Hebrides. The island is a wild place, misty and mountainous with tumbling waterfalls, craggy stone formations, and rocky coasts carved by endlessly churning ocean waters, but the moorlands, which stretch from the base of the Cuillin Mountains and roll across the island in great arching swaths, are the wildest places of all. Many travelers, led astray by golden butterflies and meadow pipets, have been lost in the banks of sea fog which roll over the moor hills after sunset, their cries for help eclipsed by the wuthering of the winds.

Arabella had loved the moors ever since she was a little girl. Like other Scottish children, she had been warned to stay away from their running streams and dark lochs where *kelpies* lurked, waiting to drag her down to a watery death, but she had also been taught to appreciate their austere beauty. The moors were more than just barren hills of low growing shrubs cut through with stony paths; they were bowls of light and sound. The droplets of mist which coated the ground made the desolate land alive with an otherworldly glow, and the winds, without any trees to catch and hold them fast, chased each other down the steep slopes and out to the frothing seas, composing sorrowful music that spoke of the oldest magic, violent, brutal, and majestic. Arabella loved to stand upon the gorse in the evening and stare up at the broad expanse of the Milky Way, listening to the sad and lonely songs of the stars.

The moors were the source of Arabella's livelihood. She kept a small garden behind her cottage, growing foxglove and fennel, letting rosemary and lavender bloom in the salt spray, but much of what she harvested for her potions and poultices came from the moors themselves. In springtime she collected clear water from rivulets which wended their way down from melting snows atop the Cuillin Mountains, and in summer she gathered armfuls of purple heather to hang from her rafters, infusing their dried petals into talismans of protection. Autumn found her reaping liquid sunlight from the gold-tipped bracken, and winter left her searching for the bright red glint of cowberries to be rendered into syrups and salves.

Caitriona Porter had taught her granddaughter to read the moors like a book, instilling in her a language of flowers and herbs that was as natural as polite conversation. Arabella remembered how they would walk across the land, hand in hand, as her grandmother taught her to name the local vegetation. Bog myrtle, cottongrass, bell heather, and cross-leaved heath would leap to life as if at her grandmother's call, her words a magic spell that filled the barren landscape with life and color. Back home in their cottage, Caitriona taught Arabella to write, in the old languages and the new, and on rain-swept days when soft skies kept them huddled by their stove, Arabella would trace the names of moor flowers onto the pages of the Porter Family Grimoire, drawing their likenesses beneath the recipes and remedies the Porter women had handed down for generations.

As Arabella set out across the moor to check in on Fiona McPherson, the rolling hills trilled with new life. It was the twentieth of March, the day before the vernal equinox when the earth balanced itself in light and dark. A Highland stag wandered in the distance and clouds of bees droned in the thistles. Fresh gusts of wind brought the scent of new beginnings up from the sea. It was the kind of day her grandmother would have loved, but Arabella, worried about Fiona's new bairn, did not linger to enjoy it.

It was late afternoon by the time Arabella reached Portree, a fishing village with a deep harbor surrounded by high ground and cliffs. The McPherson bairn, a boy with large, clear eyes, was a welcome antidote to the wind-chapped moors. He lay in his cradle, his expression calm and sweet. Arabella brewed Fiona a restorative tea. The woody scent of nettle filled the room.

Arabella had delivered the boy last month, the doors and windows of the home flung open to help the new soul find its way in. At Fiona's request, Arabella had spoken the old words over the baby as he slept. She had lighted a candle infused with sandalwood and sage and moved the flame around him, creating a circle of protection to keep fairies at bay. She had anointed his chest with sea salt and oil to anchor him safely into the world of the living.

The McPhersons, like most families in Portree, would never openly admit to practicing the old ways, but a respect and fear of the fairy world informed their daily lives. Legends were as well-known on the island as bible scriptures, and even Fiona's first child, a precocious little girl only four years of age, could recite the ancient fairy story of Clan MacLeod's Chief by heart. It was said he had fallen in love with a *bean sidhe*, a fairy princess, and that the fairy king himself had presided over their handfasting. The king had refused to sanction a Christian marriage, however, and would only allow his daughter to live with her husband for a year and a day, eventually forcing her to abandon the half-human son born of their star-crossed union. Before she traveled home across the fairy bridge, a crumbling stone arch which still passes over the Bay River in Waternish, the *bean sidhe* wrapped her baby in a shawl spun of fairy silk so he would always remember it was fairy blood which coursed through his mortal veins. Arabella had seen the shawl, now kept in a place of honor at the Castle of Dunvegan, where it is unfurled to protect Clan MacLeod during times of war and famine. Known as the fairy flag, the tattered and frayed shawl remains a symbol of Skye's history, a reminder that the island will always be connected to a primal past it can never fully understand.

Arabella watched the McPherson baby wriggle beneath his blanket. He seemed healthy and strong, but the veil through which he had entered the world remained open, a sure sign she should be cautious. The veil usually closed shortly after a birth, knitting itself together like a healing flesh wound, but Arabella could still feel the gaping passageway between the worlds, tender and porous at its edges. It was this which had drawn her to Portree today, hoping she could intervene if some life-threatening condition, like jaundice or puerperal fever, plagued the baby or his mother.

Arabella had been taught to trust her instincts, for all Porter women were born with a second sight, a curious ability, an unsettling quirk that held them apart from the islanders they served, fairy gifts, their traits were called in hushed tones around the villagers' tables. It was said Arabella's great-great-grandmother had the gift for finding what had been lost, and her great aunts, Una and Aoife, twins born at the stroke of midnight, could detect the lies of even the most skilled deceivers. Arabella had always been able to feel the thinning of the veil between the worlds. Sometimes it was a joyous gift, to sense when new life was determined to break through, to be reminded there was more than earth and sky around her, to know the buds would always return, to know creation would always continue. But other times, when human souls were stuck in the in-between places or when the veil opened to claim those not yet ready to make their final journey, her gift was a painful burden. She had seen the air thinning around her grandmother for years before Caitriona would acknowledge any illness. Arabella had often thought her grandmother's own fairy gift, the ability to speak things into being with her honeyed tongue, had prolonged her stay on earth. Caitriona had simply refused to pass, talking herself into a future that should not have included her, until she was certain her only granddaughter could survive on her own.

Fionna lifted the baby to nurse, smiling down at him as he latched onto her breast and sucked hungrily. Though she looked tired, she was as healthy as her child.

"You've done so much for us already," Fiona said tentatively, shifting her son in her arms. "I know we haven't paid you nearly enough for your services, but our Grandad has been asking for you." It was often this way for Arabella. She would be attending to someone when she was asked to look in on another. Need seemed to cluster in batches on the island.

"He's been languishing for a week now and refuses to be seen by the doctor. Gran says he's been talking to his brother who's been dead these ten years." Fiona wiped a tear from her eye. "It would mean so much to Gran if you could stop by on your way home. He's been so insistent, you see."

So, this was why the veil remained thin. Arabella knew on rare occasions it hovered open over a family to allow old souls to cross through to their eternal rest on the very same passageways created by new souls entering the earthly plane. Hamish McPherson, the baby's great-grandfather on his father's side, was dying.

Hamish was a devout, churchgoing man who had always avoided the Porters, so Arabella was surprised he was requesting to see her. She tied her healer's cloak around her, thankful she had worn it even though the March sun had promised the warmth of spring. Woven of a soft grey wool the color of dawn, the color of twilight, Arabella's cloak was hemmed with a border that ran from the hood down along the full sweep of its base. Each secret space created by the border's decorative stitching had been filled with thistle, rue, and fern seeds, all collected on Midsummer's Eve and crushed to a fine powder. The concoction was thought to gift those who carried it the safety of invisible movement.

Caitriona had helped Arabella weave her first healer's cloak when she was still a young girl, guiding her hands as she spun the wool and harvested the flowers and herbs. Arabella had sewn the decorative border with iridescent thread, carefully pouring her powders into the open spaces on the inside of the hem and sealing them with sturdy backstitches. When she had finished, she had run down to the quiet waters of the nearest loch to test her cloak's abilities, but though she had clasped the garment tightly around her neck and placed the hood over her loose, flowing hair, she had seen her reflection, as clear as day, staring back at her.

"My child." Caitriona's deep laugh had echoed off the water. "Do you think magic works like it does in your storybooks? That you can mumble some words and mix some potions and bend the universe to your will?" She rested her hands on Arabella's shoulders. "True magic is all around us, soft and unpretentious." She gestured toward the loch and Arabella watched as a breeze kissed the surface of the water, obscuring her reflection with rippling waves.

"That isn't magic. That's just the wind," Arabella whispered, though she felt gooseflesh rise on the back of her neck.

"And what is the wind?" Caitriona had asked. "You feel it against your skin though you do not see it with your eyes." Her unbound hair, its auburn color fading into shades of grey and white, moved with the gentle breeze. "And what is the loch?" her voice was soft, like the verse of a poem. "You can circle its shores in under an hour, and yet, if you peer deep into its surface you can see the whole of the heavens in its grasp."

Arabella had leaned toward the water. The wind had relaxed and the misty light of the wet moorlands had risen from the hills around them. Reflected in the small loch's still surface, Arabella saw the fiery sun sparkling on the mountain tops. She saw a white-tailed eagle soar through far-off blankets of clouds. She saw a sliver of the waxing moon, a luminescent sickle in the daytime sky.

"As above, so below. As within, so without. As the universe, so the soul." Caitriona's image had appeared in the water as her melodic voice chanted their family's mantra. The old woman had intertwined their hands and brought them to rest on the center of Arabella's chest. "Do you feel the rhythm of your own heartbeat?" she had asked. "This is the pulse of the heavens. Our hearts, which are so small we might hold them in the palms of our hands, contain the strongest magic we will ever know, and we must learn to trust them." Caitriona's words had poured themselves over Arabella, sticky and sweet. "If you cultivate a meaningful life, your heart's magic will reflect the light of the heavens. There is much in a little, my child, *multum in parvo*. This is the magic and faith we practice."

Arabella had worn her healer's cloak, which matched the one her grandmother wore, each time they were called to help those in need. Although the thistle, rue, and fern seed mixture had not made them invisible, it had allowed the women to move unnoticed among families who were facing their most intimate moments of grief and joy. It was common for their patients, overcome with emotion, to assign credit and blame for life and death upon the Porters. The soft grey wool of their healer's cloaks and the earthy scent of ferns and flowers hidden in the embroidery had protected them, helping the gaze of expectant mothers and ailing elders slide away from the healers, leaving Caitriona and Arabella free to practice their craft, distill their herbs, and recite their words of comfort to quietly help those they could.

Arabella tucked a blanket around the baby and promised Fiona she would look in on her grandparents. Then she turned down Harbor Row, slipping past the brightly painted houses. If the veil was hanging open for Hamish McPherson, there would not be much she could do to help him, but she had made a solemn promise to Caitriona never to abandon her family's healing traditions, and she wasn't going to break that promise.

Hamish McPhearson, whose Harbor Row house looked out upon the dockyard, had been the first man in his family to earn his living on the water instead of the land. His sons and grandsons had followed suit, sailing his small boat down to Glasgow on regular schedules, transporting goods back and forth between the Hebrides and the lowlands.

Margaret McPherson, as short and round as Hamish was tall and thin, led Arabella into the bedroom where her husband lay propped up against his pillows, his skin ashy and grey. Arabella smoothed his sheets and placed her hands over his. He opened his rheumy eyes and moved his lips, but it was a few moments before they formed an intelligible sound.

"Catherine."

It was her mother's name. Arabella had heard the islanders talk about her mother, the wild Porter woman who had broken Caitriona's heart, sailing away to start a new life in America rather than staying on the island to practice her craft. It was said the boat her mother had boarded encountered a fierce storm in the North Atlantic.

There had been no survivors.

Arabella had no memories of her mother. Catherine had left the island shortly after giving birth to her. Those who dared to speak openly of Catherine always mentioned her great beauty, her dancing green eyes and auburn hair, her fairy gift for making strangers fall in love with her. Her death was remembered as a great tragedy for there had been no body to bury, no way for the grieving Caitriona to set her daughter's soul free.

When Arabella was little, she used to pretend her mother had gone to live among the *selkies*, the seal people who swam in the cold ocean waters surrounding Skye, because she had read stories about victims of shipwrecks who had married *selkie* men and lived happily ever after in a kingdom beneath the sea. It was said the human brides would emerge on the beach at the foot of Glen Brittle every seven years to discard their borrowed seal skins and bathe in the fairy pools, sparkling basins of aqua water fed by mountain streams.

Arabella had waited by the fairy pools each full moon of her seventh year, listening for the imagined sound of her mother's voice in the music of the waterfalls cascading through the blue-green light. During the full moons of her fourteenth year, she had diligently searched the grey stones surrounding the pools for seal skins, certain that if she found her mother's pelt and locked it away, Catherine would be forced to return home to their little cottage at the edge of the moors, and Caitriona would be happy once more. By the time Arabella had turned twenty-one, she no longer believed in *selkie* legends, and had it not been for the mournful shadow that passed over her grandmother's face whenever the seas were high, Arabella might have thought she had never had a mother at all, but had descended from the stars that danced in the island mists, birthed into being by her grandmother's honeyed words.

Though his lips were dry and chapped, Hamish waved away the glass of water Arabella offered him. His shallow breath rattled in his throat.

"What can I do for you, Mr. McPherson?" Arabella asked, gently stroking his hand. He did not have long. It would be better for him to gather his children at his side, to sit with his wife Margaret before he lost consciousness and slipped through the open veil.

He pulled himself forward with significant effort and plucked a letter from the drawer of the side table, pressing it into Arabella's hand with a fevered urgency. "Catherine," he said again, the name collapsing into a determined sigh. Arabella looked at the letter, sealed with wax and stamped with a blooming thistle. The yellowed paper was stiff and smelled faintly of mildew. The seal had hardened and cracked. Had Catherine written this letter before she left the island and met her death upon the sea? Why did Hamish McPherson have a letter stamped with the Porter family seal, and why was he so insistent he deliver it to Arabella before he died?

A thousand questions floated through Arabella's mind as the old man fell back upon his pillows. She detected a faint look of relief on his sallow face. He groaned and closed his eyes.

"Mr. McPherson?" Arabella's voice was soft.

There was no answer. Arabella watched his slow, labored breath. His pulse was so faint she could barely feel it beneath her fingers. The light in the room shifted as a cloud passed overhead, carrying the cares of Hamish McPherson's life away from him. Arabella knew he might linger for a few more hours, but Hamish would speak no more.

She tucked the letter into the pocket of her cloak and dropped some leaves of rosemary from her satchel into the basin of water that waited by the bed. She wiped the old man's brow with the scented liquid, hoping it would fill his final moments with sweet memories of the life he had lived, the family he had created. She whispered words of safe journey in his ear, using the old language which sounded rich and sweet, like fairy music. She opened the bedroom window so his soul might find its way out, and she guided his wife to his side, brushing streaks of tears from her full and rosy cheeks. Then she faded into the streets of Portree, her grey cloak disappearing into the evening shadows.

Halfway across the moor, the uneven path lit only by her swinging lantern and the multitude of stars in the sky above, Arabella felt the veil that had been hanging open over the McPherson family begin to close, leaving a faint white scar over the brightly painted homes of Harbor Row.

Now settled in her chair by the hearth, Arabella gripped the letter in her hands, listening. She heard a knife tapping against the kitchen cutting board, the ghostly imprint of a great aunt who had preferred mixing her medicines late in the evening. She heard the creaking of the rocking chair where Caitriona used to knit, spools of soft wool gathered in a basket by her feet.

The night had tipped past its darkest moment, and already the cormorants and red throated divers were stirring in their nests, preparing to fly through the brightening dawn to search for crabs and minnows along the marshy shores. Arabella had been trying to break the seal on the letter for over an hour, but each time she had started to lift the wax from the paper, she had hesitated. She and Caitriona had rarely spoken of Catherine. Arabella had seen lines of sadness and anger on her grandmother's face whenever Catherine's name was mentioned. Now, the part of her that was loyal to Caitriona wished she could throw the letter into the fire and let the mystery of the past burn away. Surely, if her grandmother had wanted her to know more about her mother, she would have spoken about Catherine during the final months of her long illness. But, beneath Arabella's fierce loyalty to the grandmother who raised her was a profound yearning to know the truth.

The paper trembled in her fingers.

"Forgive me, grandmother," Arabella whispered, breaking the seal and unfolding the pages.

The winds stilled. The cottage quieted. Out of the silence, the lyrical voice of Arabella's mother rose from the ink-stained parchment.

My Dearest Arabella,

I do not know if you will ever see this letter, but if you do, please know, my sweet, precious child, that I am sorry.

If you are reading this, fate has thwarted my plans of coming home to you, and you have grown up without me. If my words have found their way to you, then my mother, your grandmother, Caitriona Porter, whose life force seems as permanent and as imposing as the black slopes of the Cuillin Mountains, must have passed through the veil. If you have broken the seal on this letter, you believe you are alone in the world, and all you know of me is that I left you when you were a child, and that there is no hope of my return.

Perhaps I should let you believe, as you probably do, that I never loved you, but nothing could be further from the truth. I loved you the moment I first felt you flutter inside my womb. I loved you when I held you against my chest on the starlit night you were born. I loved you when your tiny fingers curled around mine. I loved you even as I planned to leave you, even as I was forced to imagine a future where I might never see you again.

By now you know all about the Porter Clan, a family of mothers and daughters carved into the history of Skye like the Pictish symbols on the tall stones at Skeabost. We are the healers, the guardians of the old ways, destined to live out our lives in our lonely stone cottage between the moors and the sea. My mother and aunts taught me the craft, passed on to me their knowledge and abilities. I am proud of my Porter name, though I rail against the way it tries to trap me, writing my destiny as if there was no room for my own voice.

As a child I followed my mother and aunts dutifully as they ministered to the sick. I made the poorest of villagers smile with the warmth of my touch. But, while my mother returned again and again to the magic of the island, finding peace in her solitude among the craggy rocks and mountain ridges, I knew I needed more. I wanted romance. I wanted adventure. I wanted to love a man as the moor winds love the hills, with a passionate intensity that unfurls the bracken and makes the heather blush in streams of scarlet flowers.

Your father, a merchant sailor who came to the Isle of Skye from Mystic, Connecticut, is the man who has taught me to love. Even now, as I write to you, I can feel the ache of his absence, for I have not seen or heard from him in almost six months. He first arrived on Skye to negotiate with the landowners and sheep farmers who supplied his company with wool to be sent to the lowland mills in Glasgow for processing before being shipped to America. But, after he met me, his visits to the island were for pleasure, and I often sojourned with him on the mainland as well, showing him the Highland ruins and lochs, teaching him the soft, sweet words of the old tongue. He knew I was pregnant the last time his ship pulled out of Portree Harbor. He promised to come back for us, and while I waited, feeling you grow ever stronger inside of me, I dreamed you might be the first Porter daughter born with her father's features instead of her mother's. I hoped to find in you his warm, dark eyes, his fair hair which shimmers like golden wheat in the sun.

No one knows of my relationship with your father save Hamish McPherson, the owner of the boat who handles his shipping company's regular run from Skye. Hamish had seen your father and I picnicking in the dappled shade of the Portree Forest, and I begged him to keep our secret. Hamish has always been afraid of my mother, as most of the islanders are, but Caitriona is not the only Porter woman born with a formidable gift. I used all my charm to convince Hamish to be our confidant, and he was powerless to resist my request. It is the McPherson boat which ferries me to the mainland now, so tomorrow I can board a ship bound for America. It is Hamish who will take this letter and hold it safe until the day comes you may need it, delivering it to you only if I never return, and only if he knows he has no other choice.

My mother, your grandmother, doesn't know I am leaving the island. Confined by our family traditions, she has never even asked your father's name. Though she rejoiced in your birth, I fear what she might do to your father if she knew I truly loved him and have chosen to leave Skye and spend my life with him. The Porter women do not adhere to the rules of men. The Porter women choose duty over romance. The Porter women raise their daughters alone, never revealing the paternal line. These are the traditions our family has followed for centuries. I hoped to be the one to break them, raising you far from Skye, raising you to know your father and his family, raising you to appreciate the transformative power of romantic love. If only your father had returned to take me away before you were born as we planned, if only I had possessed the courage to seek your father across the sea before my labor pains began, then your life may have been different. But, when you crossed the veil into the world of the living, your green eyes looking up at me, your round head already covered with the auburn curls that are the telltale mark of the Porters, I knew a part of you belonged to the island. I cannot take you away from it any more than I can stay. You, my sweet Arabella, may one day choose to take your place as a healer on the Isle of Skye. I only want you to know it is your choice to make. I only hope you can accept that I have chosen something different.

I do not know if I can find your father. The trip across the Atlantic is said to be treacherous, and America's vast landscapes, thick forests, and endless plains stretch much further than the length and breadth of our small island. To give me courage, I pretend to be the heroine of a fairy tale, setting out to find an unfindable kingdom that lies East of the Sun and West of the Moon. There I will reunite with my lost husband, for that is what your father is to me, though no ceremony has legitimized our union. And while I may not have the friendship of the North Wind to help me on my quest, I have my Porter lineage. My leaving, my rebellion, cannot take that away. My great-grandmother had the gift of finding what was lost, and if our green eyes and auburn hair can be passed down through the generations, then perhaps our other gifts, or at least small shades of them, can be passed down as well. Perhaps one day, our Porter gifts will help you and I find each other again, and the happily-ever-after of my fairy tale will be written in our mother-daughter reunion.

Until then, I know Caitriona will care for you as though you are her own, and in this, I take great comfort. Hamish has promised to let her know when the ship that carries me across the Atlantic reaches America's shore, where your father and I will be safe from her anger and disappointment. I wish I could talk to her. I wish I could feel her arms around me one last time. I wish I could tell her of my plan to return for you as soon as you are old enough to choose your own fate, but I fear her honeyed tongue will speak words that will bind me to the island, and I will wither away like milk thistles in winter, the petals of my soul wilting, one by one, until I am nothing more than a hollowed husk. I have no choice but to go in secret, Arabella, for to stay on Skye, not free, would only absent me more.

It breaks my heart to leave you behind, but I know your grandmother is the only one who can give you the wisdom you will need if you are one day called to practice the old ways. If you are reading this letter, I hope my absence has taught you that, if you choose to heed a different call, it is possible to cut the ancient threads which tether the Porter women to the Isle of Skye. Follow your heart, my sweet Arabella, let it guide you like the North Star guides sailors at sea, and you will not lose your way.

Beautiful though you are, your father did not leave his mark upon you. You do not have his golden hair or his warm, dark eyes. And, although Porter women never reveal the paternal line, I want you to know what no one else on earth, save Hamish McPherson, knows: your father's name is William Stafford. It is only a name, but a name is a powerful thing, a magic spell that casts a light of hope upon our darkest hours, a charm which conjures the peace of knowing exactly who we are. I offer it to you now as a parting token, with the hopes that this name, coupled with our family's ancient gift for finding what is lost, may one day bring the three of us, mother, father, and child, back into one another's arms.

Your Mam,
Catherine

Arabella ran her fingers across the pages. She traced the letters of the names written in her mother's flowing script: *William. Catherine. Arabella.* A tear dropped onto the parchment. The aged ink began to bleed.

Before she read the letter, Arabella had known only that her mother had abandoned her before dying in a shipwreck. She imagined the agony a young Hamish McPherson must have felt when he told Caitriona that her daughter had left Scotland on a ship that had never again reached shore. She wondered if this was why Hamish had always been so afraid of her grandmother. She wondered if this was why he had waited until Caitriona was gone and he was on his deathbed before he delivered Catherine's letter.

Arabella had never dreamed of leaving her home on the Isle of Skye. The ancient art of healing that defined the Porter women resided deep within the island soil. Her maternal family, the long line of mothers and daughters that stretched back across the storied history of the island, had planted its roots in the lonely cottage on the edge of the moors, the fibers held in place by centuries of tradition. Husbands and fathers were inconsequential to the Porters. Even in the long and lonely months after Caitriona's death, when Arabella had struggled to survive on her own, the Porter tenets of female independence had kept her from daring to imagine she might find a living family on her father's side. Instead, she had cultivated her craft, believing she would one day pass her knowledge down to a daughter who would never know her own father, a child conceived of maternal duty rather than brought into the world by a romantic union.

Now, Arabella knew her father's name. She knew the place from which he had come. She whispered the words *William*, *Stafford*, and *Mystic* into the stillness of the cottage, feeling their foreign power on her lips and tongue. If Arabella left the Isle of Skye to find her father, it would be an act of rebellion against Caitriona and the Porter legacy. She remembered the palpable tone of disapproval that had filled the air each time her grandmother had spoken of how Catherine had run away from her family responsibilities. Arabella had always done what Caitriona expected, but now a new hope wrapped itself around her like a warm blanket.

Her father and mother had loved each other. They had loved her. These simple facts changed everything.

It was almost dawn when she fell into a fitful sleep. In her dreams, she heard fairy music beckoning her into the garden where the ghosts of her grandmother and aunts danced, twirling beneath the light of the silver moon. *This is where you belong, my child*, a voice, sweet like honey, echoed in her ear. *Do not forget it is Porter blood which courses through your veins.* But the woodcocks, warbling in the swaying grasses, sang a different tune. *Follow your heart*, they seemed to say as the skies darkened. *You will not lose your way.* Stones began to fall like rain, splashing her dress with streaks of mud.

When she awoke with a start, still in her chair by the hearth, Arabella was certain of only one thing.

She was going to cross the Atlantic Ocean and find her father.

It is not an easy thing to leave a house you love. Each dusty corner holds a memory, each charred mark on the mantle tells a story, each scratch on the floorboards is a record of the shared joys and sorrows that make a house a home. It took Arabella almost a month to extract herself from her regular duties and prepare for her journey, knowing, as Catherine must have known, that she might never return to the Isle of Skye. She wondered how she would make her living in a new country where she would not have access to the cauldrons, tools, and ingredients the Porter women had amassed over hundreds of years. As the day of her departure neared, she folded a few of her favorite dresses and shawls over the Porter Family Grimoire she had packed in the bottom of her traveling case. Its pages were filled with her aunts' recipes, Caitriona's spells and incantations, and the names of Scottish moor flowers, written in the old languages and the new.

She couldn't bear to leave it behind.

Arabella harvested the early spring blooms from her garden and used what was left in her apothecary cabinet to mix and deliver medicines to Mrs. McMillan and her other regular visitors so they would have what they needed in her absence. She inhaled the scent of dried thistle and damp peat moss, wishing she could carry it with her to the New World. She read her mother's letter until she could recite each word from memory. And, when there was nothing left to be done, she placed a bowl of cream on the windowsill in gratitude to the fair folk of the island, an offering and a farewell.

Arabella had never traveled more than a day's walk from her cottage, and she had no idea how she was to manage an Atlantic crossing. She had heard stories of rat infested coffin ships, large vessels that delivered their cargo of North American Timber before packing their empty holds with human souls for the return journey across the Atlantic. In letters dispatched to family who stayed behind in Scotland and Ireland, immigrants described the poor conditions of the crowded ships which were rampant with death from diseases like dysentery and typhus fever.

Not wanting to find herself aboard one of the floating nightmares that left from large ports like Glasgow and Liverpool, Arabella journeyed to Portree in the hopes of finding a merchant ship that would let her pay for safe passage to America. It was a misty April evening when she trudged across the moors with her traveling case, the setting sun tinging the mountain thyme and blooming heather with a rosy glow. By the time she reached town it was dark, and she headed toward MacNab's Inn and Tavern, where local notices and shipping itineraries were posted in the front window. There she learned that *Martha's Destiny*, a three-sailed schooner owned by American investors and captained by a man named Robert Adams, was planning an uncharacteristic detour to Skye after picking up textiles and cork at ports along the mainland coast. The ship was scheduled to collect several dozen casks of Talisker Whisky from the MacAskill brothers' distillery. *Martha's Destiny* would be leaving the Hebrides in late-April, reaching port in New London, Connecticut by early June. Arabella knew little about the New World's topography and she had no idea how much distance lay between New London and Mystic, but if a ship was sailing from Skye to Connecticut, she was determined to be on it.

Arabella booked a room at the inn, hoping to arrange a meeting with the ship's captain who would no doubt dine there while the boat was moored in the harbor and the dockhands were arranging for the delivery of its cargo. MacNab's Inn and Tavern was the hub of Portree, made famous as the site where the rebel sympathizer Flora MacDonald had bid farewell to Bonnie Prince Charles after the Jacobite defeat at the Battle of Culloden. Mr. MacNab was known to play his fiddle into the wee hours of the morning, entertaining what few guests were drawn to Skye by the Highland romances of Sir Walter Scott and the ballads of Robert Burns. Arabella had nursed MacNab's wife through a bout of pneumonia a few years back, and though it frightened him to have a Porter woman staying under his roof, he offered her a bed for as long as she needed it, free of charge.

One evening, a ship's captain and his officers gathered around a corner table, their plates piled high with black pudding, fried onions, and fresh meat and vegetable pies. They clinked their glasses together and tipped their heads back, letting mouthfuls of whisky run down their throats.

"Ach—this is what we've come here for? Give me a glass of ale any day!"

A young man, his whiskers still soft and patchy across his chin, made a sour face. The officers clapped him on the back and laughed. "Just imagine the Scots in America, Billy, who'll gladly give away all their money for a taste of home."

"More like a taste of fire, I'd say." Billy coughed, and the men laughed louder.

The lone woman in the party leaned forward, her hand resting comfortably on the arm of a much older gentleman, clearly the captain. "You're terrible, every one of you," she teased. "Now, leave Billy alone." The captain smiled at her, his thick white beard and gold embroidered jacket bestowing an air of unchallenged authority.

"You heard my wife, that'll be enough," he said. His voice carried a faint trace of brogue. He poured another glass of whisky and the men turned their attention to their food. The captain's wife leaned back, happily tapping her foot to the tune of MacNab's fiddle. Arabella could see she was pregnant, perhaps five or six months along.

Arabella watched as the men continued to eat and drink. She wondered if her mother was right in thinking that Porter women might share shades of their fairy gifts with one another. Could she manifest her mother's ability to charm strangers? Could she let honeyed words drip from her tongue to direct the future as her grandmother used to do? Arabella's heart fluttered as she approached the crowded table and addressed the older gentleman with the gold trimmed jacket. "Excuse me sir, but are you Robert Adams, the captain of *Martha's Destiny*? The ship sailing to New London?"

"Aye, that I am."

"I'd like to pay you for passage across the Atlantic."

Arabella's request was met with uncomfortable silence. Pots and pans clanged in the kitchen. The captain lit his pipe. The rich scent of tobacco filled the already smoky room. He puffed deeply before answering.

"I sail a merchant ship. I transport goods, not people."

Portree was not a large harbor, and Arabella did not know how long it would be until another ship bound for the New World might pass through.

"I've birthed many children on this island," she said, looking at the young woman before turning back to the captain. "I'm skilled in the art of healing. I may be of help to your wife and your crew should anyone be injured or fall ill."

The ship's officers, well-acquainted with their captain's temper whenever anyone other than his adoring wife questioned his position, braced themselves. Like all sailors, they were superstitious, and they did not take kindly to a strange woman speaking of dangers on the high seas as though they were prophecies.

"And what do you know of injuries and illnesses aboard ship, lass?" It was a dark-haired officer who spoke, his voice tight. "Do you intend to curse our journey?"

"No, of course not. I only meant—"

"It's one thing to have our captain's wife on board, but other women will bring nothing but bad luck," Billy said. "My cousin's last voyage nearly ran aground because a lass stowed away in the cargo hold."

"But I—"

"Move along," a third officer barked before Arabella could finish her thought. He pointed toward the door. "We'll have nothing to do with you or your threats."

"Enough!" The captain's tone brought immediate silence to the table. He turned to Arabella, his expression kind but unyielding.

"I sail a merchant ship. I'm not in the business of transporting people."

The young woman leaned forward again, letting her hand linger on the gold bands of her husband's jacket. She had seen a look of desperation in the emeralds of Arabella's eyes, and she had been moved by it.

"Robert, maybe you can make an exception, just this once? I would enjoy a female companion at sea, someone to help me pass the long hours while you sail." She paused to glance at the officers, sighing like a long-suffering mother who loves her children all the more for the trouble they cause her. "And, this might be the perfect opportunity to teach your crew that a woman on board is nothing to fear."

The captain took another swig of whisky and placed his glass firmly on the table.

"Elizabeth, I've made my decision. Don't question me in front of my men."

"Yes, of course, darling. You know best."

She shifted slightly in her chair, letting the folds of her dress fall across the rounded curve of her figure. "I just thought it might be a comfort to have a healer on board," she said softly, "in case the baby arrives early." She looked up at her husband, gently caressing her stomach.

The captain's eyebrow twitched and then steadied. He let out a deep sigh.

Within the space of an hour, he had completed an aggressive inquiry regarding Arabella's reasons for setting sail, confirmed that he had indeed heard of a William Stafford who operated out of Mystic, received testimonials from MacNab and his wife regarding the healing abilities of the Porter family, and offered Arabella a berth and rations in return for her services as a companion to Mrs. Adams.

Elizabeth invited her to join the table and bade the men provide her with food and drink. Billy pulled out her chair while the dark-haired officer filled her glass, and even the captain, at his wife's prompting, gave her a welcoming nod as he added more tobacco to his pipe.

By the time she had finished dinner, Arabella had no doubt that although Robert was the one who directed the actions of his men at sea, it was his wife, Elizabeth Adams, who was the true captain of *Martha's Destiny*.

As *Martha's Destiny* entered the Atlantic Ocean, leaving the islands of the outer Hebrides in her wake, Arabella's relief about securing passage to America dissolved into new worries. The turbulent landscape of the ocean that had taken her mother's life lay ahead of her, and she watched the grey seals gather across the retreating coastline, half-hoping the old stories about drowned women finding new lives as *selkie* brides were true.

"We have a day of smooth sailing ahead," Elizabeth said, her joyful voice at odds with the queasy feeling beginning to simmer in Arabella's stomach. "Let's retreat into the cabin and leave the sea to the sailors."

The sitting room of the captain's quarters was neatly appointed, its wood surfaces polished to perfection, its furniture nailed into place. A pair of hanging lanterns swayed as the ship rolled over North Atlantic waves, casting dancing light across a framed painting of a large house hung on the wall above Robert's desk.

"It's our home in New London," Elizabeth explained when she saw Arabella looking at the painting, "though I dare say, *Martha's Destiny* has been more of a home to us than any house on dry land."

She pulled a tin from a storage drawer beneath a bench, entertaining Arabella with stories about her life at sea as she arranged a pile of biscuits on a tray.

"Robert's first wife passed away ten years ago," she explained. "He has a grown son only a few years my senior. There were some who thought me odd to marry a man old enough to be my father, but Robert is honest and kind. He allows me to accompany him on his travels, which is more than I can say for many merchant captains. I might've wasted away from boredom if I'd been confined to a life in polite society like my mother and sisters." She laughed and poured two cups of ginger tea. "Your stomach will settle if you eat something," she said, offering the plate of biscuits to Arabella. "And you simply must tell me all about your family."

Arabella brought the porcelain cup to her lips and forced herself to swallow. The tea did little to cure her nausea, but sharing stories about her family was medicine for her grieving soul. She told Elizabeth about her grandmother and her aunts. She described the beauty of Skye, the mountains and moors, the pinnacles and waterfalls, the shawl spun of fairy silk that had been transformed into an enchanted flag of protection.

"It's so lovely to have another woman aboard," Elizabeth said as the two of them tidied the sitting room when the tea and biscuits were gone. "The officers talk of nothing but latitude and longitude, and though I'm certain the crew engages in plenty of gossip below decks, they remain tight-lipped around me for fear rumors may reach their captain's ears and get them into trouble."

For nearly three weeks, the ship encountered blessedly mild weather, fair winds and a following sea, which was tamed, Arabella learned from the crew, by the bare breasts of the golden-haired figurehead who graced the prow, but even the measured movements of the waves made it difficult for Arabella to keep her food down. The only relief she found was in walking along the deck, running her hand over the mahogany and white oak railings, gazing up at the towering masts of Douglas fir as Caitriona's old lessons lingered in her ears; *the hawthorn tree is a gateway to fairyland, the rowan tree is an antidote to evil, the elder tree must always be asked permission before you use its flowers and berries in jams or sparkling wines.* Arabella felt a kinship with the wet, salt-encrusted wood of the ship. It, too, had been uprooted and thrown upon the open waters. It, too, ached for the comforting embrace of its native soil.

Halfway through the journey, the morning sun rose bright and red, its rays staining the restless sea the color of blood.

"Red sky at night, sailor's delight," Elizabeth sang cheerily. "Red sky at morning, sailors take warning. Prepare yourself, Arabella. We'll encounter a storm before this day is through."

By afternoon, the water was churning dark blue beneath the slate grey sky. The masts began to creak. The sails filled with the weight of the winds. The ship lurched forward over a large ocean swell, pushing the women, who had been strolling on the deck, off-balance.

Martha's Destiny sailed into a patch of thick fog. Sailors thundered across the bridge in response to the captain's stern calls.

"Perhaps it's time for us to seek shelter," Elizabeth suggested, looping her arm around her companion's waist. Arabella nodded, but her hands gripped the ship's railing, anchoring her in place.

"Arabella?"

"My mother died in a shipwreck," she whispered, looking up at the threatening sky.

Elizabeth placed her hand over Arabella's. "Our ship will not wreck today." She spoke with the confidence of a woman who had spent the better part of a decade at sea. She guided her friend toward the captain's quarters at the stern of the boat and lowered her onto the black walnut bench which ran beneath a wall of square-paned windows. She cleared her husband's desk of his books and charts and tied the storage drawers closed. By the time she finished preparing the room, a driving rain was pelting the glass, its mists blown flat by a countering wind.

"What are you doing?" Arabella asked as Elizabeth tethered her to the bench so she would not be tossed to the floor by the listing of the ship.

"There's no need to fret. Our hold is heavy with cargo, and Robert's crew shall weather us through the storm." Elizabeth's smile was bright amid the gloom of the cabin. "The men will batten down the hatches and strike the topsails. Hold fast and have faith, Arabella. All will be well."

But all was not well, and before nightfall, angry raindrops were driving themselves into the ship like iron nails. The water-logged timbers creaked and groaned. The ocean writhed and heaved like a living thing. A massive wave crashed over the broadside, tipping the vessel until the cabin windows faced the bottom of the black sea.

"Why don't we turn back? Why don't we sail away from the storm?" Arabella's frantic cries were swallowed by the sound of roaring waves as the ship rolled onto its port side once more.

"Robert will reef the mainsails and abandon course!" Elizabeth had to raise her voice to be heard, but her tone remained cheery as the boat returned to an upright position. "He'll have his helmsman sail at an angle and cut the waves with the bow of the ship. We must move through the storm, Arabella. It's the only way we'll survive." She took Arabella's hands in her own. "*Martha's Destiny* is sure and strong; you must believe she and Robert will keep us safe."

Arabella had lived through many vicious storms in her lonely cottage on the Isle of Skye, but there she had been sheltered by sturdy stone and rich, peaty earth. The moor winds may have wuthered down the mountain slopes like phantom spirits marching into battle, but they did not screech like wounded animals or wail like the *Caoineag*, the Highland banshee whose weeping prophesied certain death.

The waves grew larger and angrier, and soon *Martha's Destiny* was surrounded by walls of water forty feet high. White caps thundered across each churning billow like waterborne horses. The ship, its bow pointed toward the wind, was lifted again and again toward the crests of each coming wave, where it would hang, suspended in darkness, until it slammed down into valleys of rushing current and foam on the opposite side.

Water pounded mercilessly against every inch of the ship and Elizabeth, who continued to speak words of comfort as she squeezed Arabella's hand, clutched her bible to her chest, a sure sign that *Martha's Destiny* might need more than Robert's sailing skills to survive the storm. Arabella had never attended church, and she did not know the words to common prayers, but she lifted her face toward the skies and recited a rhyme she had heard Caitriona sing during inclement weather.

Thunder, Lightning, Winds, and Rain
Calm ye now, bring peace again.
By earth, air, fire, and sea,
As I will it, so mote it be.

She repeated the rhyme over and over, in the old language and the new, but the seas continued to roll and heave, so she shut her eyes against the terror of the ocean and tried to imagine the soft violet hue of flowers that drifted through the moors at twilight. If she was going to die in a watery grave between Scotland and America, lost somewhere East of the Sun and West of the Moon as her mother had been, she wanted her last thoughts to be of her island home where the bracken swayed in the summer breeze, where the fairies danced beneath the dappled light of a thousand stars, and where her grandmother's wrinkled hands reached out to smooth away her pain.

Arabella buried her face against Elizabeth's shoulder as wisps of grey and white clouds descended to meet the angry seas below, and the terrible storm churned on without end.

"There now, do you feel it?" Elizabeth laid down her prayer book and stood up slowly as the ship pulled away from the squalling winds which had tossed it through the night. She made her way to the bedchamber where she gathered blankets and a fresh set of clothing for her husband. "The worst is over," she said as far-off streaks of lightening continued to flash in the sky. "The men will be wet and exhausted. They'll need rest." The ocean still swelled beneath them, but its waves had lengthened, and the ship moved over them in long steady arcs.

When the captain finally entered his quarters that evening, he looked tired, but relieved. He pulled his wife into an embrace and spoke tenderly to her, his hand on her abdomen.

"Well, now that the little one has survived his first hurricane, he'll be born with sea legs for sure," he said.

While Elizabeth helped her husband change into fresh clothes, Arabella slipped out to the deck where a golden light blinked on the horizon. The sea flowed gently past the curve of the ship, creating a trail of frothy, white bubbles. A good-natured breeze caressed *Martha's Destiny* as though the heavens had never conspired to sink her. Arabella closed her eyes and inhaled the briny air, listening to the flapping music of the sails.

The ocean stretched itself flat for the next several weeks, and the seasickness that had plagued Arabella since the ship first embarked began to subside. She felt steady as she walked upon the aft deck each evening to watch the sun sink into the western horizon, its rays turning the Atlantic into a liquid field of diamonds. When the far-off lanterns of the stars began to light themselves in the skies overhead, Arabella would repeat the words that had brought her this far, *William, Catherine, Mystic*, an incantation to bring her safely to America's shore.

"It takes a good storm to knock the sickness out of you," Elizabeth said one afternoon as the women mended the sailors' torn shirts and jackets. "Even Robert remembers feeling nauseous before he encountered his first gale." She put down her needle, and a serious look passed over her face.

"Arabella, may I ask you a question?"

"Of course."

"During the worst of the storm, I saw your lips moving as if in prayer. What were you saying?"

Arabella's cheeks warmed at the question, but she looked up from her own needlework to meet Elizabeth's eyes before she answered.

"It was a rhyme my grandmother used to say during stormy weather."

Elizabeth nodded curiously.

"And did you believe your grandmother's rhyme would calm the storm?" she asked.

"Did you believe your prayers would?"

The chronometer fastened to Robert's desk filled the quiet cabin with its whir and tick. Elizabeth reached out to take her friend's hand. "I don't mean to offend you, Arabella, though I do feel I must warn you. Robert is a tolerant man. He keeps his crew under tight control, but we're nearing America's shores, and tolerance on land is very different than tolerance at sea."

Arabella knew many on the Isle of Skye were wary of the old beliefs, but she wondered why Americans, whose very country has been colonized as a religious refuge, would be so suspicious of another culture's spiritual traditions. She had read historical accounts of the Salem Witch Trials, but those had taken place ages ago when people were still frightened by things they did not understand. Surely, America had evolved beyond those ignorant days. A ribbon of pride unfurled in Arabella's chest as she spoke out in defense of her family's legacy.

"My grandmother taught me that words have great power. She taught me to love words. She taught me to trust words. She believed that words repeated with intention could alter and shape the world around us. But there was nothing harmful in the words I whispered during the storm, Elizabeth. I didn't even know I was saying them. I heard them as a child, and they came to my mind to comfort me in a moment of fear."

Elizabeth smiled. "Then your words sound very much like a prayer, and a welcome one at that." She picked up her needle, but paused before resuming her stitching. "I only want you to be careful. America is a dangerous place for a free-thinking woman."

"I thought America was the land of the free."

Elizabeth laughed. "For men, perhaps. Once you find your father, I'm sure you'll be safe and protected." A serious expression passed over her face once more. "Arabella, have you ever wondered why your father never looked for you? If he was a merchant sailor, he should have been able to return to Skye."

Arabella knotted her thread to secure the stitches she had been working on. "Perhaps he thought I died crossing the Atlantic with my mother. Perhaps he was injured and could no longer sail. Or, perhaps he knew my grandmother would never have allowed him to be a part of my life." She folded the mended shirt and picked up another, assessing the tear at the sleeve. "I owe it to myself to find my father, Elizabeth," she said quietly, "even if it turns out he doesn't want to be found."

"Please, Arabella. Just promise me you'll be careful."

"I promise."

In spite of Elizabeth's warnings about life in America, it was an exciting day when the lookout spotted the outline of the New World emerging from the morning mists. Arabella felt the ocean waters relax beneath her as the ship tacked its sails, heading past Block Island and into Fishers Island Sound. Elizabeth pointed out the Stonington Harbor Light and the mouth of the Mystic River as they glided past. She spoke of New London's history with pride, relaying its years of trade with the West Indies, explaining its role in launching attacks on British warships during the American Revolution and the War of 1812, and describing its bustling port, one of the largest whaling cities in the world, its piers packed with taverns and inns, the fermented odor of whale oil mingling with salty ocean air.

Arabella stared at the landscape, so flat and full of thick forests. She had seen nothing but water since leaving Scotland where crags and mountains slid directly down to the seas. She touched the silver thistle pendant dangling close to her heart. The Isle of Skye was thousands of miles away. It was now a part of her past. Her future, for better or worse, was here in this strange New World.

"I don't know how to thank you," Arabella said, when she stepped into the small craft that would row her to shore. She handed Elizabeth a package she had wrapped in paper and bound with twine, bidding her to open it in the sitting room where the two women had weathered the storm, where they had shared their stories, where they had become true friends.

Inside the package, Elizabeth found a baby blanket fashioned from one of Arabella's shawls, the purple wool embroidered with swirls of Scottish thistle. Elizabeth smiled as she unfurled it and read the blessing Arabella had stitched around the blanket's border: *May you always be surrounded by the violet hue of Skye's protection as you sail through stormy seas.*

Part Two

Mystic, Connecticut

"O, that our fathers would applaud our loves,
To seal our happiness with their consents!"
(The Two Gentlemen of Verona)

Mystic, Connecticut, a small New England village as old as America itself, traces its European history all the way back to the seventeenth century, but the Indigenous Pequot, who occupied the area's wooded groves long before settlers arrived, argue it is here, among the eastern white pine and black birch trees of North America, that human life actually began.

According to traditional stories, in the beginning, there were only sea and stars, a dark churning ocean and an endless sphere of sparkling light. Then, a celestial woman fell through a hole in the sky, planting seeds on the back of a turtle and spreading land over the primordial waters, lush, green, and life-giving. The Sky Woman gave birth to a daughter, who in turn gave birth to twins, initiating a sacred chain of creation which would renew itself without end.

Known as great warriors with a deep spiritual connection to earth, air, and water, the Pequot refused to relinquish their cherished homeland, winning every battle against invading colonizers until the night of May 26th, 1637, when an alliance of English, Mohegan, and Narragansett forces, led by Captain John Mason, launched a surprise night-time attack on *Siccanemos*, a settlement located on the western side of the Mystic River. The Pequot men were out hunting at the time of the attack, and Mason's soldiers set fire to the palisade, engulfing the sleeping women and children in flames.

As dawn rose over the terrible night that would be recorded in American history as the Mystic Massacre, Mason and his men hunted down the survivors, executing them or selling them into slavery. They enacted laws to banish Indigenous art and language, but they could not expunge the Pequot presence from the hallowed lands. On dark nights, phantom flames still rage in Mystic, a village whose very name comes from the Pequot word *missi-tuk*: a large river whose waters are driven into waves by winds and tides.

By 1847, Mystic had emerged from its violent colonial past, becoming a noted shipbuilding center that launched expeditions to the Antarctic and the Pacific, its ships returning with enough whale oil to fuel the flickering light of the candles and lanterns illuminating the wealthy homes along its riverbank. But, however cultured the village may appear, the ancient tidal river remains its life blood, its deep blue waters flowing through the heart of its civilization like an artery, its gentle gurgling telling the tale of a landscape far more haunted than it seems.

Arabella stood on a brick pathway, looking at a pair of black painted doors guarding the entrance to William Stafford's home. The home was on Gravel Street which stretched along the western shore of the Mystic River. Stately houses, owned by merchants and sea captains, lined the road in orderly precision, each one larger and more imposing than the next.

Arabella was surprised by how easy it had been to locate her father's place of residence, and she wondered if a small echo of her great-great grandmother's fairy gift for finding lost things had indeed been passed down to her. When she had stepped onto the New London dock, her body still swaying from her long months upon *Martha's Destiny*, she had been overwhelmed by the sights and sounds of the large port city. Sailors of every shade, their bedrolls slung over their shoulders, hurried past. Everywhere was the sound of foreign tongues, barking dogs, and clucking chickens. Spices hung in the humid air like fog.

Arabella's intuition had pointed her past the Customs House and down the busy, cobblestone streets to the Stagecoach Office, where she learned that a coach from New York City would be pulling into New London to pick up mail before making its full stop at The Captain Daniel Packer Inn in Mystic. The swinging motion of the coach made Arabella feel as though she was back on the ocean, and she peered out the windows to steady herself as the horses trotted past swaying marsh grasses and groves of ancient trees, larger than any she had ever seen on Skye.

The Captain Daniel Packer Inn, built in 1756 by its namesake, a square-rigger captain of merchant vessels who had served during the American Revolution, was a welcoming Dutch Colonial building with low ceilings, stone fireplaces, and dark wood beams. Still run by the captain's grandchildren, the inn had been bustling with activity when the stagecoach arrived, the man behind the bar pouring ale and delivering plates of sausages while telling animated stories about his ancestor's ingenuity.

"Before the bridge was built, the captain would transport the stagecoaches and their horses across the river on his rope ferry," he had said, his voice booming over the sound of the crowd as he polished a glass with the cloth hanging from his apron. "Captain Packer loved the inn so much he vowed he would never leave it, even in death."

The other travelers had shivered at the thought of dining in a haunted inn, but the regulars, who were clustered at small tables around the perimeter of the room, and who had no doubt heard the barkeep's practiced tale a hundred times, paid little attention. Arabella had already seen the captain's ghost, wearing his blue cloth jacket and tri-corner hat, standing by the mantle, surveying his customers with pride. Directly above him hung a faint disturbance in the veil. It flickered like a candle flame, a fragile portal between the worlds of the living and the dead.

The captain was a benevolent spirit, and certainly the least of Arabella's worries. Her mother's letter had been more than twenty years old when Hamish had delivered it to her, and she had set out to find her father on a tide of emotion that could not be tempered by reason. Although Captain Adams had recognized her father's name, he had not known much about him, and it was entirely possible that William Stafford had moved or passed away. Her mother had said her father's name was a magic spell, a charm for helping her learn who she truly was, but could a simple name really wield such power? Arabella searched the faces of the regulars gathered around the bar, wondering if any of them might be her father, and when the bartender leaned close to refill her mug with cider, she asked him if he knew where she could find William Stafford.

The bartender turned his full attention to her for the first time since she had entered the establishment. His skin turned a deathly shade of white. "What business do you have with Mr. Stafford?" he asked, and when Arabella did not answer him, he stepped away from her and busied himself with his other customers. A few minutes later, he slipped a piece of paper with the address *15 Gravel Street* written in a thick script into her hand. "Two miles to the North," he said in a hushed tone. "You best get moving if you want to reach your destination before dark."

Now Arabella stood in front of her father's house as a dusky twilight fell around her. Fireflies blinked in the bushes. The clang of hammers rang out from the shipyard across the river. She closed her eyes for a moment and recited the words of her mother's letter. Then she took a deep breath, walked up the brick pathway, and knocked on the black painted doors.

A housemaid led Arabella into a formal sitting room and said she would inform the lady of the house that there was an unexpected visitor. She excused herself with a small curtsy and went to the kitchen to make some tea.

Arabella looked around the room, her eyes drawn upward to the elaborate white molding circling the ceiling. Four chairs, upholstered in a damask print, clustered around a low table covered with lace. The room was papered in a floral print, painted birds perching on the branches.

"May I help you?"

Arabella turned to see a young woman wearing a silk dress gathered tightly at her waist. Her golden hair was pulled into an intricate bun, ringlets framing the sides of her narrow face. Arabella glanced down at her own dress, the tartan pattern worn and faded. She reached up to smooth her unbound hair, which tangled past her shoulders in long, loose waves.

“I’m looking for William Stafford. I was told this is his home.” Arabella’s voice was quieter than she had intended it to be.

The lady of the house let her eyes roam over Arabella’s tattered shawl and muddy shoes. A grandfather clock ticked off the seconds from the foyer. The sound of porcelain teacups rattled in the kitchen.

“This is William Stafford’s home. He’s away on business, so I’m afraid you’ll have to return at a later date if you’d like to speak with him.” She smiled politely, an icy dismissal, but Arabella had not come this far to be turned away.

“My name is Arabella Porter. My mother, Catherine Porter, was a healer from the Isle of Skye. I recently found this letter which she left for me before she passed away.” Arabella pulled the wrinkled parchment from her satchel as though it would justify why she stood in a strange house in a strange country, looking disheveled and out of place. “I’m William Stafford’s daughter,” she explained.

The lady of the house snatched the letter from Arabella’s hand and skimmed its contents. Her lips drew tight.

“I’m sorry, Miss Porter, but there must be some mistake.” She pulled herself up to her full height.

“I am Anne Stafford,” she continued, pausing slightly and staring at Arabella with her full, dark eyes. “And *I* am William Stafford’s *only* daughter.”

It was a testament to Anne Stafford's manners and education that she offered Arabella refreshment after the shock of her unexpected arrival. Anne had known, even as a child, that the marriage between her parents had been one of convenience. She had grown up hearing rumors about her father's infidelity, but what did that matter? Rumors, after all, were not facts, and if her own late mother had turned a blind eye to them, placing the reputation of the Stafford family above any personal betrayals she may have endured, she could certainly do the same. Of course, she had never expected the proof of her father's philandering to knock on the door of their family home and demand an audience.

"I'll write to my father in the hopes of hastening his return," Anne said, vigorously stirring cream into her tea. "You may stay here, and, if necessary, I'll introduce you as a *distant* family relation." She knew rumors would run rampant as soon as her neighbors caught sight of her new houseguest, and she reasoned it would be best to keep Arabella hidden until her father returned. She dropped her spoon onto her saucer with more force than was necessary and took an obligatory sip of her tea. "I'm to be married this summer, and I won't allow a scandal to interfere with my nuptials. After all, we can't be sure your mother's letter speaks the truth."

Arabella hadn't yet spent an hour in her father's home and already she had been reduced to a scandal, her mother labeled a liar. She studied Anne's sharp profile, watching her slender throat constrict as she swallowed a mouthful of milky tea. Her blonde hair and dark eyes matched Catherine's description of William, but she was nothing like the warm, loving father Arabella had been imagining in her mind, the one who had been willing to risk the wrath of Caitriona to spend his life with her mother, the one who would be overjoyed to know that their daughter, at least, was alive. Catherine's letter had painted her parents' relationship as a fairy tale, but maybe it had been something else entirely. Anne was small in stature, but she could not be more than a year or two apart from Arabella. Could William have so easily forgotten Catherine? Or had he already had a wife and daughter when he first arrived on the Isle of Skye?

Arabella had been so focused on finding her father that the discovery of a sister, especially one so close to her own age, was a shock. Her grandmother had been one of seven sisters, born during a time when the island was still rich and fertile with fairy magic. The villagers had nicknamed the sisters the *Pleiades* because they were so often seen walking hand in hand across the moorlands, seven crowns of auburn tresses shimmering in the sunlight like the seven stars which clustered together in the island's winter skies. One of the seven sisters had passed away before Arabella had been born, but the rest had resided in the cottage between the sea and the moors, three of them giving birth to daughters of their own. Arabella had marveled at the way her grandmother and her great aunts could communicate without words, conveying a lifetime of thoughts, feelings, and memories with small arches of their eyebrows and simple tilts of their chins. They bickered often, as sisters do, but any stranger attempting to chastise one soon found himself on the wrong side of all, so fierce was their loyalty to each other. One lonely autumn, Arabella, the only Porter woman of her generation, had woven harvest dolls from stalks of straw, carrying them with her on her childhood adventures, telling them her deepest secrets, wishing she could magically transform them into sisters of her own.

"I'm sure you'd like to rest after your long journey," Anne said, abruptly pushing away her half-filled teacup and rising from the table to escort Arabella to a guest room on the second floor. The air was dusty and stale, so Anne opened a window facing the river. The cool evening, alive with the hum of insects, was at odds with the oppressive heat and awkward silence of the house. "If you need anything, you may call out for my housemaid, Bessie," Anne said, exiting the room. "She's staying with me while my father is out of town."

Arabella breathed a sigh of relief, letting her eyes adjust to the dim light of the lone candle her sister had placed on the nightstand. The room must have been an old nursery where Anne had slept when she was a child. The brass bed was small and close to the ground, and above the chipped mantle was a lithograph of a very young Anne sitting on what must have been her mother's lap. The woman's coloring was drab and far less golden than her daughter's, but they had the same sharp features, the same small frame. Arabella studied the portrait, scanning the veil for remnants of the woman's presence. Anne's mother had likely passed several years ago, but a faint trace of her soul lingered, like a cloud of perfume, the scent half-way between tension and tenderness.

Arabella walked over to the far corner of the room where a wooden dollhouse gathered dust. Three dolls, a mother, a father, and a little girl, sat together on a tiny sofa. Catherine had said in her letter that William had known she was pregnant the last time he had sailed away from Skye, but even in the playthings he had given his legitimate daughter, there was no trace of a sibling to be found.

Arabella ran her fingers over the dollhouse, tracing the layout of the rooms, which were a miniature version of Stafford House itself. She imagined Anne and her mother greeting William in front of the large, black doors at the end of a long day. She picked up the dolls and moved them into the dining room, placing them at a wooden table, a tiny replica of the one she had seen downstairs. She wondered if, during any of the meals her father had shared with his family, he had given any thought to the woman and child he had left behind in Scotland.

She stepped back to survey the whole of the dollhouse. "A home is more than four walls and a roof," Caitriona had always said to her as they roamed through the ancient ruins of castles and abbeys on the Isle of Skye. "A home is a sentient being, like the earth itself, born of blood and story." As healers, the Porters were often summoned into the secret spaces and back rooms of their patients' homes, tasked with discreetly helping those in need, and Catriona had taught Arabella to pay attention to the energies which wafted through the air. "If you listen to the stories a home tells, you will understand those who live within it," her grandmother had explained, "and you must *understand* before you can heal."

Arabella closed her eyes and listened to the stories of 15 Gravel Street. Beneath the buzzing of the insects and the measured gurgle of the river floating outside the window was a far-off sound, sharp and strained. Arabella had noticed the broken light fixtures, the cracked plaster, and the rings of dust on the dented furniture where decorative items had been hastily removed. The sheen of wealth found in the front room of Stafford House was missing from its private spaces, a sure sign all was not as it seemed on the surface. Still, she was surprised by the home's quiet cry of want and need. Even the modest rooms of her father's house were far more opulent than her cottage on the Isle of Skye, a cottage which, for all its own financial struggles, had hummed in contented harmony with the wind-swept moors. Arabella swallowed a lump in her throat as she thought of her abandoned garden and the low banks of clouds rolling in from the Sea of the Hebrides. She lowered herself onto her sister's old nursery bed, her heart aching for the familiar warmth of her forsaken home.

Anne kept a busy social calendar, attending luncheons and ladies' teas, visiting the mercantile and milliner, signing her father's name in heavy credit ledgers whenever she needed to restock her pantry or her closet. She never invited Arabella to join her, but each time she returned from an engagement, she was animated by newfound gossip about prominent Mystic families like the Winthrops, the Denisons, the Stantons, and the Palmers. Arabella listened to her sister's tales of social mishaps with interest, increasingly thankful she had grown up in the black shadows of the Cuillin Mountains with no one to watch her but the fairies.

After several days with no word from William, Anne finally consented to taking Arabella for rides in the family carriage, always in the early morning when they were less likely to run into curious neighbors. Anne wore her hometown as though it were a cloak, showing Arabella the shipyards where the great whaling boats were built, and pointing out the chandlery, the cooperage, and the nautical stores which sold the chronometers, clocks, and sextants the ships' captains needed to navigate the seas.

"My father used to direct all of Mystic's arrivals and departures," Anne said with pride as she and Arabella passed the Alden Shipyard one day before breakfast. "Of course, that was a few years ago, when the Aldens still possessed an admirable reputation." Large buildings sprawled across the shipyard's campus, stretching from the bustling Greenman Avenue down to the wharves that lined the eastern side of the Mystic River.

"I thought our father was a sailor."

"*My* father worked as a merchant sailor when I was a young child, but he made his fortune sending others to sea to do his bidding." She gestured in the direction of Water Street where a far-off row of taverns offered cheap food, alcohol, and female companionship to sailors on shore leave. "Career sailors are unkempt and uncivilized." Her lips twisted in disgust. "Thank goodness my fiancé, Alan, is a gentleman. He's never worked a day at sea, though his family's business investments support several fleets of merchant ships."

One evening, Alan, having heard Anne had a distant family relation in town who might serve as an official chaperone while William was away, sent word he would be joining them for dinner. Anne flew into action, bidding Bessie to roast a chicken and polish the table settings. Then she turned her attention to her sister, pulling her long, wayward hair back into a low bun and throwing one of her own beaded shawls over Arabella's best dress, a simple white linen frock with a neckline too low and a waist too high to pass as fashionable.

"This will just have to do," she said, with a dramatic sigh. "The Newbury family has been waiting for my dowry for quite some time, and I won't have them thinking some poor relation has arrived to take what has been promised to them."

Arabella winced as Anne tugged at one of the stray curls that escaped from her bun. She had not come to America looking for money, and she did not take kindly to Anne's veiled accusation.

"Is it common practice to pay for a husband in America?" she asked, her voice a knot of frustration as she caught her sister's eye in the mirror over the dressing table.

"I suppose they do things differently," Anne spat, "in the Old World."

She stormed out of the room, leaving Arabella to tame her errant hair on her own.

Alan Newbury greeted Anne with a chaste kiss on the cheek and a bouquet of green ivy and myrtle. Bessie arranged the flowers in a cracked ceramic pitcher and placed them in the center of the dining room table. Water trickled onto the faded lace tablecloth.

"Why haven't you used our Waterford vase?" Anne demanded.

Bessie, who had been employed by the Staffords for more than twenty years, clucked her tongue. "I beg your pardon, Miss," she said, a world of meaning beneath her words, "but I wasn't able to find it."

"Well then you must be more careful to put our things back in their proper places."

"Never mind, Bessie," Alan said with a kind smile. "Your cooking smells divine, and I'm pleased to share it with two beautiful women this evening." He raised his glass in Arabella's direction. "To family, however distant it may be."

Alan was every bit the gentleman, impeccably dressed in a tight waistcoat and trousers, amiable in manners and conversation from the first course to the last. "My family has stock in ships that trade around the world," he told Arabella, "but Anne's dowry is necessary for me to finish construction on our new home." He laughed nervously, folding his napkin and placing it over his empty plate. He turned toward Anne. "Have you heard from your father yet? He hasn't responded to my letters."

Anne, her hands clenched tightly in her lap, her food untouched, shook her head. Alan fidgeted in his chair, his eyes flicking over to Arabella before settling back on Anne. "The truth is that my parents are worried the financial negotiations of our union may have changed since your relative came to town, and they would appreciate William's reassurance that all will continue as planned."

Anne, who wore a fashionable silk dress and antique jewelry that looked as if it had belonged to her mother, waved her hand to signal there was no need for concern, but when she turned her face away from Alan, the color drained from her cheeks. Arabella sighed sympathetically. Her own head ached from the tight bun that held her curls in place, and she hadn't forgotten the unfair criticisms that had been hurled at her. Still, Anne was her sister. Of that much, she was certain.

"I'm an independent woman, Mr. Newbury," Arabella said. "I have no claim to the Stafford fortune. I'm trained as a healer and a midwife, and if I stay here in Connecticut, I'll support myself by putting my skills to use."

"Imagine that!" Alan's nervous laughter echoed with relief. "Well, my parents will be happy to hear it, though they'd hardly approve of a lady making her own way in the world. Is that common in Scotland?"

Arabella told Alan stories of the Porter family's independence as he enjoyed two slices of Bessie's blackberry pie. He listened with interest, asking polite questions about her healing knowledge until it was time for him to take his leave.

"My parents are anxious to hear from your father," he reminded Anne when she escorted him to the door and straightened his jacket. He bounded down the brick pathway, stopping once to look back over his shoulder. "I can't bear another delay," he said with a shy smile, tipping his hat in her direction.

Anne closed the door and returned to the dining room. She caressed the waxy leaves of her bouquet.

"Thank you, Arabella," she said.

It was the first time she had addressed her sister by name, but before Arabella could reply, Anne had taken the cracked ceramic vase of flowers and retreated upstairs to her bedroom.

That night, Arabella sat alone in the kitchen at the back of the house, watching the slow progress of the Mystic River. The setting sun glinted off the houses and boats lining the opposite bank. Water gurgled in its river bed, speaking a language Arabella did yet not understand.

A glowing moon rose over the dark purple clouds of twilight in the east. Tomorrow would be the summer solstice. Arabella had already been in America for two weeks. Her heart thumped with loneliness as she thought of the villagers on Skye preparing their bonfire celebrations. Each year, island maidens wove wreaths of twigs, leaves, and flowers into their hair, releasing them into rivers and streams for young men to retrieve. A couple forged by the solstice ritual was considered so blessed that most women decorated their wreaths with telltale signs so their sweethearts waiting downstream would recognize them.

Arabella had heeded Elizabeth's warning to be careful in the New World. She had kept the details of her craft a secret, piously bowing her head whenever Anne spoke of planning her Christian wedding, but tonight was the eve of the solstice, and she longed to celebrate it in the old way.

Thunder rumbled in the distance. Arabella stood up and peered out the window, searching the dusky skies. She had an hour of twilight left. Anne, who had issued more rules about proper female behavior than Arabella cared to remember, would forbid her to leave the house on her own. She would say it was too dangerous for a woman to walk alone at night, but Anne had already gone upstairs to bed, and Bessie was busy with her evening chores. As long as Arabella left quietly and returned before breakfast the next morning, no one would miss her. She lifted her healer's cloak from the hook near the back door and draped it over her shoulders. Then she slipped outside, following the river north toward the shadows of Mystic's untamed forest.

Arabella released the pins that held her bun in place as she watched the Whitford Brook, a small tributary feeding the Mystic River, flow shallow and clear. The air smelled damp with the coming rain. Cicadas thrummed in the trees. She had walked through the woods until she found a quiet clearing where she gathered branches of willow and birch to weave her solstice wreath. She had decorated the twigs with creamy white lilacs and clusters of wild blueberry. Now she placed her wreath gently on her head like a crown.

Arabella had already cast a circle of protection, but a chill ran down her spine as she glanced around the clearing. She would need to remove her clothes before entering the water to perform her solstice ritual, and she wanted to make sure she was alone.

The summer solstice ceremony was sacred on the Isle of Skye. Each year, dozens of sky-clad maidens would walk, hand in hand, toward the flowing waters of the island's streams and rivers, their hair unbound but for the crowns of flowers they carried on their heads. Though a few of the women would giggle nervously as they walked toward the water, most were reverent. They had the comfort of knowing that no man on the island would dare penetrate their ritual space. The men were all afraid of Caitriona.

Arabella kicked off her slippers and lifted her skirts to roll down her stockings. The evening air kissed her exposed skin, whispering its false promise of relief from the day's stifling heat. She looked over one shoulder and then the other, her fingers fumbling as they unfastened the buttons of her bodice. The fabric slipped down to her waist, and she pushed it over her hips and past her thighs, letting it pool at her ankles. She shimmied out of her undergarments and stepped into the moonlight, her skin glowing like milk, the carpet of pine needles soft beneath her feet.

A breeze blew her tangled curls across her back and chest, and she shivered, though the air was thick and warm. She walked toward the riverbank, her breath hitching in shock as the icy water caressed her, rising over her ankles, her legs, her navel, creeping toward her chest as she moved into the center of the stream. When she could barely feel the slick stones of the river bed below her toes, she took a deep breath and sank beneath the surface of the water, letting the current lift her crown of flowers from her head. A moment later she emerged, pushing her wet hair back from her forehead and watching her solstice wreath circle in an eddy before being pulled south toward the Mystic River and the salty embrace of the sea. She followed the wreath's movements until the white flowers faded into the dusky light, imagining their petals floating over the tumultuous Atlantic, carrying her wishes all the way home to the shores of Skye.

Still shivering, Arabella tipped her head back and stretched the length of her body across the surface of the water, letting her unbound chest rise up to greet the moonlight. Her fingers reached down to grasp the slippery rocks at the bottom of the stream so she could float motionless beneath the sky as dark water flowed over the curves of her body. The shrill call of a songbird rang out in the distance. An unseen owl, watching her from the trees, beat its feathered wings.

Arabella looked up at the stars twinkling in the pitch black bowl of the sky. She cupped her hand, scooping their reflection from the water and letting their liquid light trickle over the swells of her breasts. She knew this small New England brook reflected the same stars as the shallow lochs and streams on the Isle of Skye, and she closed her eyes, pretending she was bathing in the starlight that shone down over the moors, her grandmother's vigil keeping her safe from harm. *There is much in a little, my child, multum in parvo. This is the magic and faith we practice.*

An angry yell ripped through the air, and Arabella scrambled upright. She covered her chest with her hands and splashed out of the water, slipping and scraping her knees on the jagged rocks lining the shore. She had just pulled her dress over her head when a large, menacing man stepped through the brush and into the clearing.

He looked at her out of the corner of his eye, and she froze, a deer caught in a predator's sight. He squinted, following a drop of water as it slowly rolled down the length of her neck, over the slope of her heaving breast, and toward the lace ribbon at the top of her still unbuttoned bodice. Then he lifted his eyes to meet hers.

And time stood still.

Anne had warned Arabella never to wander outside the house alone. To journey unchaperoned through town, let alone through the forest, was to court danger. Anne had even gone so far as to tell her Mystic was haunted by a *Dullahan*, a headless demon whose carriage was pulled by six headless horses as black as midnight. If the *Dullahan* found a woman walking alone at night, Anne had said in her spookiest voice, he would douse her with blood still warm from his latest victim and then carry her away so she would never be seen again. Arabella had known her sister was only trying to scare her into staying inside the house, but she had never been frightened by stories. Even now, as she stood barely clothed in the forest, her body trembling in the night air, she wished she were facing a storybook monster instead of a man. At least she would have a chance to bargain with a *Dullahan*.

The man was wearing a flat Irish cap and a white workman's shirt, the sleeves rolled up against the heat of the evening, the linen sticking to the sheen of sweat that clung to his tattooed skin. He had a rifle slung over his broad shoulders, and a hunting knife strapped to his thigh. The hair of his close-shaven beard was so black it looked blue in the moonlight. Arabella bent down and lifted her healer's cloak from the ground, holding it between her body and the intruder. She hoped its hidden herbs would make him glance away from her so she might have the chance to slip into the shadows, but he continued to stare directly at her, his intense, blue eyes moving steadily between her face and the thin, white fabric clinging to her damp figure.

They lingered on the thistle pendant dangling between her breasts.

"Is this yours?" he asked, raising his eyes to hers again as he lifted her solstice wreath in his calloused palm. He must have caught it as it made its way downstream and then followed the path of the river searching for its owner.

She bit her lower lip, wondering if she could outrun him. Her slippers lay on the bed of pine needles behind him. If she ran away from the man, in the opposite direction from which he had come, she might cut her feet open on the forest's rocky path. If she had any hope of moving past him to retrieve her slippers, she would have to catch him by surprise.

"Is this yours?" he repeated, angry she had not responded. His voice was a deep, commanding growl spun from the velvet threads of night.

"It seems to be yours," she said, squaring her shoulders against his authority. The corners of his eyes crinkled in surprise at her bold reply.

A twig snapped in the distance, and the man dropped her wreath to the ground, taking his rifle in both hands and positioning himself between the noise and Arabella. As he searched the tree line for unseen dangers, she glanced up at him. A scar slashed over his left eye, ending just below his chiseled cheekbone. She realized she had seen this man before, working in the deserted Alden Shipyard on a Saturday morning, the large muscles of his back and shoulders straining as he coaxed a heavy piece of lumber into the curve of a ship's prow. She and Anne had taken a stroll to cool themselves by the river's edge because the shipyard had been closed for business. The Alden family, and most of the workers they employed, were Seventh Day Baptists, and they believed that, in the beginning, after God had carved the light from the dark and filled the sea with leviathan, He had taken His rest on the seventh day. Now the Alden family followed suit, closing the shipyard every Saturday so they could gather with their congregation to sing hymns and offer prayers at Mystic's Fishtown Chapel.

The lone man in the empty shipyard had been so completely absorbed in his work that he had attracted Arabella's attention. "What is he doing?" she had asked her sister.

"I certainly don't know," Anne had replied, scowling in the man's direction. "I'm not a shipbuilder." The man ran a hand plane along the curve of the prow, smoothing a rough piece of wood into compliance with his powerful, repetitive movements.

"But, why is he working alone on a Saturday? You said the shipyard was closed for the Sabbath."

Anne had taken Arabella's arm and hurried her along before the man could notice them. "Because he," she said with her nose turned up in disgust, "is a heathen."

Now the scarred man her sister had cautioned her about turned his attention back to Arabella. "What are you doing in the woods at night?" he demanded.

It was more accusation than inquiry, and when she didn't reply, he grasped her arm and drew her closer. "What are you doing in the woods at night?" The heat from his fingers scorched her skin, sending a wave of fire through her wet, chilled body.

"It's not safe for you to be here," he said, pulling her forcibly from the clearing. "Allow me to walk you back to your home."

A sheet of lightning illuminated the sky, and, in the momentary flash, Arabella saw the man who held her as though he had aged twenty years, his black hair and beard peppered with grey. Then the sound of distant voices broke the spell, and the man, his face as young as it had been before, returned both hands to his gun, once again placing himself between Arabella and whatever danger he imagined was lurking behind the trees.

Arabella grabbed her slippers, threw her cloak over her shoulders, and ran as fast as she could. The man shouted at her, his words eclipsed by a peal of thunder. She ran over loose rocks and roots. She ran past low swinging branches. She ran until she found the wide expanse of the Mystic River, following its muddy bank back to the house on Gravel Street. She refused to stop until she was breathless in her sister's old nursery. She collapsed on the floor, her back pressed against the closed door. The swollen skies had opened as she darted across the Staffords' back lawn, and her dress had been drenched by heavy summer rain, but the heat and pressure of the scarred man's rough touch still burned beneath her wet sleeve. She lifted her fingers to her thistle pendant, twirling it round and round to calm herself as she tried to catch her breath.

Another streak of lightning split the sky, and she shook her head against her foolishness. She had come to America to find her father, not to look for trouble. She had only performed the solstice ceremony to feel close to the home she had left behind, confident that no stranger on Mystic's proper shores would venture into the forest, pluck her wreath from the water, and unknowingly ignite the ritual's power. Her healer's cloak may have helped her fade from the scarred man's sight, but if the magic of her solstice ceremony worked here in America, she was sure to encounter him again.

She tied her damp hair in a knot on top of her head and peeled off her wet clothes. She crawled beneath the frayed blankets on the nursery bed, muttering the half-forgotten words of a counterspell. She wanted to forget what had happened, but that night, in her dreams, the scarred man chased her through the woods and into the river, his animal heat bearing down on her half-naked body and drowning her in an endless swirl of blue light.

When William Stafford had received the letter from his daughter Anne informing him of her half-sister's arrival in Mystic, he had rolled his eyes in disdain. He had already lost a good deal of his fortune when James Alden returned from sea and took back control of his late father's shipyard, preventing all trade with the sugar cane companies of the West Indies and threatening William's business partnerships. Then severe weather had sunk several of the ships William had invested in, and he had been forced to travel south to broker important trade deals, instructing his daughter to quietly sell what she could and maintain the household on credit in his absence. He could not afford the dowry he had promised the Newbury family, and the last thing he needed was another daughter to support. Still, he remembered Catherine Porter fondly despite all the trouble she had caused him.

Now he stood on the brick pathway in front of his home and looked at his two daughters sewing in the front sitting room, their faces illuminated by the gas lamp on the table in front of the window. The girls were as different as night and day. Anne had his golden coloring, but she was small and mousy like his wife. Arabella had her mother's auburn hair and porcelain skin. If he played his cards right, he could command a decent price for her instead of having to pay someone to take her off his hands.

He ran his tongue over his swollen lip and reached up to wipe away the blood. At least the cuts and bruises on his face would paint a sympathetic picture. He stumbled up the path and opened the front door, letting the evening air waft into the sitting room. Anne rose from her chair, a look of horror upon her face.

"Father! Are you all right? What happened?" Blood dripped from a gash on his cheek. "Bessie!" she called frantically, "you must bring bandages!"

William ignored her and let his swollen eyes focus on Arabella. Anne's letter may have saved him the shock of meeting the girl unexpectedly, but it would not save him the shame of having to publicly confront his past once word got out she had arrived in Mystic. *Christ*, he thought to himself, *she looks exactly like Catherine*.

He gripped the high back of the parlor chair to steady himself. The hair on his neck bristled as the girl stood to greet him. If Anne hadn't written to warn him, he would have believed he was looking at a ghost.

He swallowed the mucus and saliva pooled at the back of his throat. "Arabella," he said, her name tentative on his tongue. The moment he had read the name in Anne's letter, he had known the girl was truly his. Catherine had shared the name before he had sailed away from Skye, so certain she was that she was carrying their daughter. He had wanted no part of the child then, and he resented the girl's presence in his home now, but there would be no use denying her, despite the troublesome gossip it would fuel among the families in his social circle. He had faced difficult situations before, and he trusted he would find a way to twist the unfortunate circumstance of her arrival to his advantage. He tried to smile, his split lip twisting into a grotesque grin.

"You're as beautiful as your mother," he said. The words sounded humble and kind.

Arabella opened her mouth, but it was Anne who spoke. "So, it's true then?" She could not keep the emotion from her voice. It was one thing to learn her father had cheated on her mother and another thing to hear him compliment his mistress's beauty. "She's your daughter? You don't even have the decency to deny it?"

William's face twitched in irritation as his dark eyes darted toward Anne. "She is," he admitted, all traces of his humility disappearing, "which makes her your sister, so you will amend your tone when you speak of her to me."

He winced as he reached into his jacket pocket and pulled out a few branches he had broken from a wild rose bush. The heady perfume of the pink blooms mingled with the iron scent of blood still smeared across his fingers. He held the branches out to Arabella. "It's not every day an old man meets his daughter for the first time," he said. "I can't welcome you to my home without offering you a gift."

She accepted the branches, holding their silky blossoms to her face. They smelled of the rich soil and salty breezes that had coaxed them to life. When Bessie entered the parlor with bandages, Arabella set her roses down on the table and dipped a cloth into a bowl of warm, soapy water. She held the cloth to her father's face, gently tending his wounds.

Anne, whose face had turned red with embarrassment at her father's harsh reprimand, stared at the flowers in disbelief.

"Those are Alden roses," she said, tears welling up in her dark eyes. "You took those roses from the Aldens' garden? For *her*? Father, how could you?"

"You think your father unfit to pluck an Alden rose, girl?"

"You *know* how James feels about his roses—"

"His feelings are written across my face."

Anne gasped, one hand flying up to catch the sound before it escaped. "*James* is the one who hit you?" Her eyes grew wide as she began to piece together the events of the evening. "If you stole his roses—"

"They aren't *his* roses—"

"Father, you already owe James a great deal of money! He's been threatening to take away our home for months! Why would you provoke him by stealing his roses? For *her*!"

"Hold your tongue, Anne—"

."At least tell me your trip has secured the money to pay back your debt!" She stamped her foot against the floor like a child used to getting her way. "At least tell me you have the money to pay my dowry as you promised!"

William tightened his grip on the back of the chair to stop himself from shutting his daughter's mouth with the back of his hand. He had promised his wife on her death bed that he would see Anne married to a wealthy gentleman, and he had done his best to fulfill that promise, but he would not tolerate her disrespectful tone much longer. He spoke through clenched teeth.

"Your wedding can be delayed until next year."

"Father, I am almost twenty-five years old!"

"Old enough to work if you can't secure a marriage without my money!"

"What work do you expect *me* to do?"

William sighed audibly. His wife had always coddled Anne, and the result had been an entitled young woman fit for nothing but marriage. "As I told you before I left town," he explained with growing impatience, "Elinor Alden is at death's door. James is going to need someone to look after his grandmother so he can run his precious shipyard. Pledge yourself in service to her on my behalf—"

"Father—"

"You know Ellie and I are old friends. If you make your proposal when James is not home to influence her, she will not turn you away. Your earnings will take care of the debt I owe James, and I'll find a way to raise the funds for your dowry by next year."

"You expect *me* to work as a nurse for Elinor Alden? The Newburys will not have me if they think our family has fallen so low as to pledge ourselves in service!"

"She's not long for this world, Anne, and your presence at Alden House will help me deliver the comeuppance James deserves. Mark my words, it won't be long before the high and mighty James Alden is the one indebted to me, and then the Newburys, and every other family in this town, will be lining up to pay *us* their respects."

Arabella rinsed the bloodied cloth she had used to dab her father's face. Water sloshed over the sides of the ceramic bowl. If Anne was almost twenty-five years old, then she had already been born when William had traveled to Scotland. When Arabella had shown up at Stafford House with Catherine's letter, Anne must have realized that her father had been unfaithful to her own mother, but she had still offered Arabella shelter and companionship while they waited for William's return. Arabella tried to imagine her father's beaten, broken face when it was smooth and young, tried to picture his grey hair shining like sheaves of golden wheat beneath the Scottish sun. Whatever mistakes William had made, and however bitter Anne felt about her father's infidelity, the two of them were the only family Arabella had left in the world.

"If Mrs. Alden will accept my services on your behalf, I'll work as her nurse. I have some experience in the healing arts, and I'm sure I can help her." They were the first words Arabella had spoken since her father had walked through the door. William flinched at their lilting sound. If he closed his eyes, he would swear the voice belonged to Catherine.

He turned away from Anne to look at Arabella, his quick mind considering the advantages her offer might present. His younger daughter would have grown up in poverty on the Isle of Skye, making her better suited to domestic work than Anne. She had crossed an ocean to find him, so odds were she would be more than willing to do as he asked once she established herself inside Alden House. Then there was the added bonus of her beauty. If she was anything like Catherine, James Alden would not stand a chance against her feminine allure. If William couldn't tear the boy down from his self-righteous perch, he would take great pleasure in entrapping him. There was more than one way for him to regain control of the Alden purse strings and restore the Stafford reputation James had tarnished.

He smiled and pulled Arabella into his arms. The embrace of a father felt strange to her, but she leaned against his chest, letting the warmth of his parental affection wash over her. It made her feel protected and safe. She wondered how she had survived for so many years without it.

"We're lucky you found us when you did," he said, believing it must have been fate which had brought her to his door so he could right the injustices James Alden had done to him. He reached into his jacket pocket and pulled out a silver flask. The sweet scent of spiced rum filled the room as he lifted it to his lips and swallowed its contents.

"I've had a long journey," he said, patting her shoulder before limping up the stairs to rest. It was best to keep his plans quiet, his options open. He looked over his shoulder, issuing strict instructions for Bessie to accompany Arabella to Alden House the next day. "You'll find Old Ellie alone first thing in the morning," he told his daughter. "Make sure she accepts your offer of employment before her grandson returns home from the shipyard."

Arabella wanted her father to linger so she could talk with him, so she could ask him about her mother, so she could learn more about the tragic love story her parents had shared, but he faded into the shadows of the second floor. Bessie carried the bowl of soapy water and bloodstained rags back to the kitchen. Anne picked up the roses William had stolen, twisting the blossoms with the tips of her fingers, her sharp, uneven breath the only sound in the room. A pink petal fell to the floor.

"Anne," Arabella said softly, "I didn't know your father had a family before—"

"*Our* father," Anne interrupted. "There's no use denying it any longer. *Our* father had a *legitimate* family before he met your mother. Why couldn't you have stayed in Scotland where you belong?"

"Anne—"

"*Our* father's infidelity will be the talk of the town before the week is through, and with another year's delay of my dowry, the Newburys will be well within their rights to tell Alan he cannot marry me."

"Why would they do that?"

"You know *nothing* about society!" Anne cried, and when she realized the volume of her voice had risen she glanced behind her, afraid she might find her father coming back down the stairs to silence her. When she turned around to face Arabella, she had regained her quiet composure.

"Elinor Alden is a kind woman and a highly respected member of Mystic society," Anne said, her tone formal, distant. "Since you are a *healer*, and an *independent woman*, you should do all you can to help her." She thrust the roses into Arabella's hand. "But stay away from her brute of a grandson. And his roses."

"I'm sorry, Anne," Arabella said, trying to soothe her. "I never meant to hurt you."

Anne straightened her shoulders, responding only because she could not bear to let her younger sister have the final word. "*Our* father is correct about one thing. We are lucky you found us when you did, because if you had disgraced our family while my mother was still alive, I would never have found it in my heart to forgive you."

Alden House stood on Greenman Avenue on the eastern bank of the Mystic River. It was taller and grander than the houses on Gravel Street, surrounded by gated gardens and large oak trees that divided it from the adjacent shipyard that shared its name. The clapboard siding was painted the color of a calm, green sea so that the house blended into the leaves and sky. A porch with stately columns and gabled trim wrapped around the front wing, providing welcome shade from the morning sun.

Although Alden House was a local landmark, known by everyone from New London to Stonington, the structure paled in comparison to the rosebushes which grew in abundance around the perimeter of the yard. Alden roses were not the cultivated blooms usually found in formal gardens; they were wild and free, their heart-shaped pink petals releasing an inviting perfume over long tendrils, sharp with thorns.

Elinor Alden sat in a rocking chair on the front porch, surveying the action on Greenman Avenue. Her grey hair was piled high on her head, and she wore a full black skirt and a black blouse covered by a black beaded shawl. An enameled walking cane, encrusted with jewels, rested by her side. Arabella could see the veil between the worlds stretched thin around her, a tear being kept at bay by the sheer strength of the old woman's life force.

Elinor watched with great interest as Arabella opened the cast iron gate and walked up the front path. It was not every morning a young lady came to visit, and Elinor was intrigued by this young lady who looked oddly familiar. The girl wore no hat or bonnet. She had not even taken care to pin her wild curls up off her neck.

"So," Elinor said after she had carefully considered Arabella's proposal, "you are William Stafford's illegitimate daughter." It was more observation than judgement. "I've known your father since he was a boy. He worked with my son, George, and both of my grandsons, Thomas and James, grew up with your half-sister Anne. I hear her engagement to the Newbury boy is all but settled." For a woman William had described as being at death's door, Elinor had a surprising amount of energy for town gossip.

"You grew up in Scotland?" she asked, trying to place Arabella's accent.

"The Isle of Skye," Arabella answered. "My grandmother and aunts were healers. They trained me in their craft, so I'm sure I can be of service to you."

"You're trained as a healer," Elinor mused. "Can you heal me?"

Arabella studied the translucent halo of light hovering above the elderly woman, its edges rippling like the waters of a tide pool. She knew the veil would likely tear itself open before the year was through.

"I can make sure your final months are not plagued by pain and suffering," Arabella said gently, looking directly into Elinor's dark eyes.

It was the right answer, for Elinor Alden, who had lived through the passing of her own beloved son and oldest grandson, and who detested nothing more than deceit, knew she was dying. She was not interested in physicians who would trade the quality of her days for quantity. She wanted to live while she was able, and she would not tolerate the presence of a nurse who would patronize her with falsehoods, but she was a God-fearing woman, suspicious of the old ways, and she had little patience for the healing arts.

"You say your grandmother and aunts trained you in their *craft*. What, exactly, do you mean by that?"

Arabella hesitated, wondering how much she should say. "My grandmother taught me the language of flowers and herbs," she explained cautiously. "She showed me how to brew healing elixirs and teas. She taught me to work with the elements to cultivate health and establish harmony—"

"Did your grandmother ever seek to harm others with her practices or her knowledge?"

"No." It was true, but a smile tugged at the corners of Arabella's lips as she recalled her grandmother's reputation on the Isle of Skye. "My grandmother's rede was to harm none, though she did keep her benevolence a secret from many of the men on our island."

Elinor laughed for the first time in many months. The sound rang out, decisive and clear. "Well, your grandmother sounds like an intelligent woman." She lifted her cane and pushed herself to a standing position. "Let's go inside and keep talking. I'll give you my decision by the day's end."

Although Elinor's body was failing her, her mind was as lively and as curious as it had ever been, and soon she had Arabella telling her all about the landscape of Skye, its magical fairy glens and its thundering waterfalls which poured over sandstone cliffs pleated like the folds of soldiers' kilts. At noon, Arabella made a pot of tea and a tray of sandwiches, carrying the refreshments to the front parlor where an ornate mantle was flanked by large mahogany bookcases which ran from the floor to the ceiling. A collection of Shakespeare's works lined the shelves, nestled among model ships and seashells the size of dinner plates. Above the mantle was an oil portrait of a beautiful woman with long black hair and piercing blue eyes. She held a bouquet of pink roses identical to the ones which grew wild along the side of the house.

By early evening, Elinor had grown tired and announced she would be heading upstairs to get some rest. "I find you delightful, my dear, and I'm happy to formally accept the terms of your proposal to work for me on your father's behalf, but, before you return home to William, I must insist you speak to my grandson James. You'll have to explain our business arrangement to him. He is little more than a boy in my eyes, but he has been the man of this house for several years now."

Arabella tried to protest, saying she would much prefer Elinor speak with her grandson herself, but the old woman held up her hand for silence. "If James gives you any trouble," she said, "any trouble at all, tell him I have need of your help. He will not deny me this."

Elinor's cane tapped steadily against the wood floors as she headed toward the sweeping staircase in the center hall. "There is food and drink in the kitchen if you get hungry while you wait for James. I've lost track of his comings and goings, and I have no idea when to expect him home." She mounted the steps, smiling to herself as new plans for the future unspooled in her mind. "William Stafford's illegitimate daughter. Yes, you will do just fine."

The kitchen, located in the back of the house, was less formal than the front rooms, but it was just as extravagant, filled with stores of dried food and fresh ingredients. Copper pots and expensive flatware lined the counters, and on the windowsill was a pile of wampum beads, their periwinkle surfaces smooth against the grain of the wood. A hook on the wall held a ring of elaborate iron keys, and a bowl of pink roses sat in the center of the large oak table.

Arabella gazed out the back window. Beyond the large garden and the Aldens' stables, the Mystic River wended its way through the evening air, its blue water blending with the pink and purple beams thrown down by the setting sun. She picked up a book that had been discarded on the table, running her fingers over the raised edges of the leather binding. It was a volume of Keats' poetry. She opened it and lost herself in the whispers of its pages. Poems danced through her mind like old friends.

It was more than two hours before she heard the sound of heavy footsteps on the pathway leading to the back door. She stood up as a large workman appeared in the kitchen doorframe, his clothes torn and dusty from long hours of physical toil. Her heartbeat quickened when she noticed the faded scar which slashed over the left side of his brow, ending just below his cheekbone.

His ocean blue eyes moved slowly over the shape of her dress, coming to rest on the curve of hair framing her face. She hadn't expected to see the scarred man again so soon, and certainly not in the kitchen of her new employer. She wondered if he recognized her, wondered if he had seen more in the woods than she realized. Her hand rose to her chest, finding her thistle pendant and twirling it round and round.

"Can I help you?" she asked to break the stifling tension of his silence. He had barged through the door as hastily as he had barged into the clearing in the forest. Even if the backdoor was a workman's entrance, the least he could do was knock.

He stared at her curiously, out of the corner of his eye, as he had by the bank of the Whitford Brook, and a strange mingling of fear and desire welled up in the core of her body. Her father's warning to secure employment before James Alden came home from work coupled with her sister's admonitions against Elinor's grandson already had her worried about meeting her new employer. She didn't think it would bode well if he arrived home to find her entertaining a workman in his kitchen.

"Can I help you?" she asked again. He didn't answer. After a few moments of silence, she continued talking, saying whatever came to her mind to fill the quiet chasm between them. "I've been employed by Mrs. Elinor Alden and I'm waiting here to explain my situation to her grandson who is expected home any minute." She wanted the workman to know they would not be alone for long. "If you would like me to deliver a message to Mr. Alden for you—"

"*You* have been employed by Mrs. Elinor Alden?" A shadow of disbelief passed over his face. He reached past her and picked up the book she had left on the table, letting it fall open to the page she had marked with a silk ribbon. "*La Belle Dam sans Merci.*" He read the title of the poem and looked back up at her. "The Beautiful Lady Without Mercy. Are you a fan of Keats?"

It was a simple question, but the tone of his voice and the intensity of his gaze were unsettling. "I'm waiting for Mr. Alden," she repeated, "who is expected home any minute—"

"So you can explain your situation to him—"

"Yes. That's what I said." An unnatural heat was rising from his body, and she took a step back toward the cool air wafting in from the window.

He calmly returned the book to the table. He removed his tattered jacket and folded it over the back of a kitchen chair, resting his hand on top of it. His knuckles were swollen and bruised.

"Then perhaps it would be best," he said, his eyes never leaving hers, "if you explain your situation to me."

The Alden family was one of the oldest and richest families in New England. Their ancestors had settled Mystic, claiming hundreds of acres of rich farmland along both sides of its river. It was George Alden, Elinor's ambitious son, who had built the Alden Shipyard on the eastern bank. Each new boat he had launched added gold to his family's coffers, and each merchant shipping contract he funded or facilitated elevated the Alden name among America's elite.

George Alden, a proud member of The Seventh Day Baptist Congregation, had been an active member of his spiritual and political communities, serving on the Stonington Town Council, managing farmlands, financing textile mills, and building boarding houses for shipyard workers and itinerant sailors. He had championed temperance, organized missionary work, and spoken out for the gradual abolition of slavery because he fervently believed that all men had been created in the image of God. He considered liberty of thought a central tenet of his faith, but had offered few personal liberties to his own sons, Thomas and James, as they were growing up. Instead, he had raised them with a velvet fist, grooming them to take their prestigious place in a world he had shaped to benefit them.

His sons had been well past their early childhoods when his wife Mary announced she was expecting for the third time. George believed the new baby would be a blessing, a reward for the hard work of his youth, but both Mary and the baby had died in childbirth, and only two years later his youngest son James, still distraught over the loss of his mother and eager to prove his budding manhood with a harpoon, had run away to sea, convincing a whaling captain sailing out of New London that he was a full four years older than fourteen. George, knowing the harsh realities and dangers of life at sea, had never wanted his sons to labor under the tyranny of a ship's captain, but James had come back from his first four-year voyage to the Pacific hunting grounds taller, broader, and wilder than he had ever been. No amount of arguing would keep James from forging his own life on the seas, and he had only returned to his land-bound responsibilities when his father and older brother died in a devastating carriage accident that had left his grief-stricken grandmother alone in their home on Greenman Avenue.

Managing the Alden Shipyard was a legacy James had never wanted. He detested spending his days at a desk, his eyes glazed over by endless documents and ledgers. At the same time, he loved taking part in the construction of the ships, his hands bending timber into vessels fit to soar across the oceans. His time on whaling and merchant ships had taught him how waves caress the curves of a bow, how winds whisper into billowing sails, how currents and eddies coax virgin vessels through the moaning deep. He designed and built ships which were lighter and faster than his competitors' ships, earning profitable deals for the shipyard that bore his family name. And, because his new responsibilities prevented him from escaping on the seas, at the end of his work day, he often changed his hat and dress coat for a shirt and cap, roaming the thick forests north of the Mystic River, searching for his beloved freedom in the shadows of the trees.

It was just a few nights ago on his trek through the north woods that he had come upon a wreath of white flowers floating in the Whitford Brook. Curious, he had plucked it from the water and traced the trail back to a strange woman, her hair still wet from the river, her sheer white dress unbuttoned at her chest. James, who had been raised on his mother's stories from the Old Country and who had spent his young adulthood in the company of superstitious sailors, half believed the woman was a fairy mistress, a *leannan sidhe*, who would feed on his life force if he looked for too long into her emerald eyes.

James had far too many plans for his future to allow himself to be trapped by a supernatural temptress, but when he had heard her speak, her lilting voice ringing through the woods like a silver bell, he could not stop himself from thinking that wasting away in this woman's arms might not be the most terrible way to die.

"You," James said, clenching his jaw against the litany of information the fairy woman from the woods had just shared with him, "are William Stafford's daughter?"

"And *you,*" Arabella responded, momentarily forgetting that the scarred man held her family's financial fate in his hands, "are the man who beat my father for plucking a few of your precious roses."

"Is that what William told you?" He shook his head, laughing cynically. "Was that before or after he asked a woman to pay his debts for him?"

"Do you think a woman incapable of taking on work to help her father?"

"I think a man should pay the price for his own actions."

James picked up his jacket with one hand and wrapped the other around the upper part of Arabella's arm. "There has been a grave misunderstanding, Miss Stafford. My grandmother and I will not be needing your services. Allow me to walk you back to your home."

It was the same command he had given her in the woods, and Arabella had no intention of following it.

"Let go of me," she said. He released her arm, but continued to glare at her, his broad body blocking her route to the back door. "Your grandmother told me you might have some reservations about my employment, but she has nevertheless agreed to accept my services on my father's behalf. If you have an issue with it, you'll have to take it up with her."

"Miss Stafford—"

Arabella turned away from him, moving down the long center hallway of the house.

"Miss Stafford!" he thundered, catching up to her as she emerged in the grand entryway. She pulled open the heavy oak door that led to the front porch. James reached over the top of her head and slammed it shut.

She spun around to look up at him, her body brushing against his chest, her wild hair releasing a perfume as crisp as the air of the nighttime forest. The scent of wildflowers and oakmoss wafted over him and he cleared his throat, trying to free his mind of the image of her naked body half-obscured by the mists rising up from the Whitford Brook. He noted the look of alarm on her face and shifted away from her, placing his hands in his pockets to make his massive frame look smaller and less threatening.

"There must be some mistake," he said, trying, but failing, to keep the frustration from his voice. "My grandmother would never hire someone to work in my home without consulting me."

"This is her home too, is it not?"

The corners of his eyes crinkled in surprise as they had in the woods, and Arabella wondered if he were more shocked by the thought that his grandmother might have needs that conflicted with his own or by the thought that any woman would dare to question his authority.

James rubbed his fingers over the stubble of his beard, trying to make sense of the situation. Elinor Alden was a proud woman who rarely asked anyone for help. Still, her deteriorating health was hardly a secret. The last thing he wanted was to make himself a pawn in one of William Stafford's twisted games, but he loved his grandmother, and he would deny her nothing.

"Did my grandmother truly tell you she needs your help?"

His question was sincere, and Arabella answered it honestly.

"She did."

He nodded his head, considering his options, and when he spoke again, the flat, commanding tone of his voice had reappeared. "If you're going to act as my grandmother's nurse in order to pay your father's debts, then your stay in my home will have to be permanent. I won't have you going back and forth between your father's house and mine."

Arabella's eyes narrowed in anger and confusion. "I can perform all the services your grandmother needs during the daytime hours."

"My terms are not negotiable."

"What need have you to keep me here?"

"Reason not the need, Miss Stafford." He regarded her with cool suspicion. "Your father may have fooled my grandmother, but he will not fool me. I will honor my grandmother's offer to employ you on your father's behalf, but you'll have no contact with William or Anne while you live under my roof."

"You'll hold me prisoner?" she asked in disbelief. "You'll keep me from my family? To take revenge on an old man for picking a few of your precious flowers?"

He shook his head again as though he was the one being unfairly accused. He moved closer to her, each step casting waves of prickly heat across her skin. He reached around her and pulled open the front door, resting his scraped and swollen hand on the frame above her head.

"You're free to leave if that is what you choose."

Frogs croaked in the river bed. Night insects buzzed, searching for companionship in the marsh grasses. A brown spotted moth fluttered across the threshold, drawn to the light of the candle burning on the entryway table. It circled too close, dipping one of its wings into the pool of melted wax in the silver dish below. It flapped helplessly before falling against the flame, igniting itself in a spark of immolation.

"And if I leave," Arabella's voice was shaking, "you'll collect my father's debt? You'll have his daughters thrown out on the street and sent to debtors' prison?"

Anne had told her heart-wrenching stories about the Stonington Town Farm, the area's poor house, a horrid place where paupers were forced to submit themselves to brutal working conditions until their debts could be repaid.

James set his shoulders against Arabella's desperation, his eyes blazing with stubborn intensity.

"I'll collect what is owed to me," he said.

Panic rose in her chest as her hopes for her new life in America began to collapse. Every muscle in her body tensed at the thought of willingly submitting to this man's arrogant commands, but if she chose to leave of her own free will, her father might be sent to debtors' prison, and it would be her fault. The only way she could help her family was if she agreed to stay with James Alden and follow his rules.

"Then I'll begin my service to your grandmother tomorrow morning," she said, hoping he would at least grant her the chance to say goodbye. "My father is expecting me to return home to him tonight."

"Of course he is," James said, taking her words as proof of William's conspiracy against him. He stepped onto the front porch, snarling against the bruised light of the evening. "But I'll be happy to temper your father's expectations."

He stormed down the walkway and mounted the black horse tied to the post in front of his house. Before Arabella could say anything to stop him, he was galloping down Greenman Avenue, heading toward the bridge that would carry him over the river to Gravel Street.

VII

Arabella paced as she waited for James to return. She had met men like James Alden on Skye, men who used their size and strength to intimidate others. Their battered wives had come to the Porter cottage for treatment, claiming they were clumsy, saying they had provoked their husbands, explaining away their broken bones and bruises as accidental injuries, but, in the end, Caitriona had always learned the truth. She had brewed the women rich, black teas steeped with marigold flowers and licorice roots. She had whispered words of comfort and encouragement in their ears. If her honeyed tongue failed to convince the women to leave their abusers, Catriona had paid visits to the men.

She had never allowed Arabella to accompany her.

Arabella walked over to the foyer table. The burned husk of the moth's thorax still floated in the melted candle wax, its wings dissolved by the heat of the flame. She fished out its body and carried it to the kitchen where she found a small wooden box and placed the moth inside. Tomorrow she would bury it, returning it to the earth. She looked across the river, watching as candles and lanterns began to glow in the windows on Gravel Street, their flames reflected in the moving water. Her father was only a few miles away, but he felt even further from her now than when she had first whispered his name into the moorland mists that curled around her cottage on the Isle of Skye.

If James Alden really was the monster Anne had described, then perhaps her father would refuse his unreasonable demand that she stay with the Aldens permanently. Surely a life together, even a life of poverty at the Stonington Town Farm, would be preferable to putting his daughter's safety in the hands of a selfish, violent man.

After a while, Arabella wandered back to the parlor where she had spent the afternoon with Elinor. Darkness had fallen in earnest, and she lit an oil lantern, lifting it up so she could study the portrait of the dark-haired woman holding the bouquet of wild, pink roses. It had been crafted with fine oil paints, mounted in silk, and hung in a gilded frame. The portrait, which was far from the most expensive thing she had seen in the Aldens' home, was proof enough that James was not collecting William's debt for financial reasons. The man had plenty of money to spare. He was persecuting her father for spite.

"I've brought you your things, Miss Stafford."

He spoke softly, his words tumbling across the quiet room. She turned to see him leaning against the wooden doorframe of the parlor's threshold, his broad shoulders filling the open space, his pose so still and so casual she wondered how long he had been standing there, watching her.

"Are my father and sister all right?" she asked.

He pushed himself off the door frame, stretching his limbs to their full length. "They're fine," he said, irritated by her implication he had resorted to violence though he could hardly blame her for it. "We merely discussed the terms of our arrangement."

"And my father agreed to let you keep me here against my will?"

"How long have you known your father?"

"What business is that of yours?"

The lantern flames, which flickered over the chiseled lines of his jaw, made his eyes sparkle like sapphires. "Anyone who knows your father wouldn't need to ask me if he agreed to my terms. Willam owes me a great deal of money and he would agree to any terms that benefit him."

"And I suppose you want me to thank you? For letting me work off a debt you clearly don't need repaid?"

He swallowed an angry retort and picked up her traveling case which rested at his feet. There was no point in continuing to argue since her father had already filled her mind with lies.

"Your sister didn't pack you many things," he said, eager to change the subject. "If you would like some new dresses, or if you require any items at all," he had no idea what things a woman might need, "you can sign my name at any of the shops in town. I assure you, Miss Stafford, *my* credit is good."

It was an unnecessary dig at her father, and it enraged her.

"I prefer all my wages be applied directly to my family's debt."

"I would never count your personal expenses against your wages—"

"And my name is not Miss Stafford," she said, taking pleasure in the look of surprise that crossed his face. "My name is Miss Porter."

He opened his mouth, closed it, and opened it again.

"But, you're William Stafford's daughter," he said, knitting his brow in confusion.

"It's the custom for women in my family to take their mother's name."

He squinted at her in the dim light, silence stretching between them.

"It's an odd custom," he finally said, "to deny a child the protection of her father's name."

"Is it so odd, when it's the mother's body and not the father's that births and provides for the child?"

It was a fact he could not counter, so he said nothing. She looked visibly upset by the night's turn of events, and he longed to offer her some comfort.

"I'm sure this arrangement can't be easy for you, Miss Porter," he said, letting her name linger in his mouth before continuing. "But rest assured, while you reside in my home, I'll provide you with everything you need."

"I need nothing from you, Mr. Alden," she countered, "except for your assurance that you will keep your fists away from my father's face."

He shook his head, his cynical smile returning. "It's late," he said. "Let me show you to your room." He held his breath as she moved past him, trying not to inhale the scent of wildflowers clinging to her unbound hair.

"You've seen the kitchen at the back of the house and the stables and garden beyond it. You've seen the front parlor. Between them is a formal dining room, and on the opposite side of the hall," he gestured across the wide space illuminated by a string of ornate oil chandeliers, "you'll find another sitting room, a library, a sewing room, and a music room where my mother used to play her harp and pianoforte. You will, of course, have free use of everything in this part of the house."

Arabella looked down the shadowy corridors which branched out from the grand entryway. Alden House was three times the size of her father's home, but it murmured with a cozy, comfortable sound, like the whispered conversations of loving grownups trying not to wake a sleeping child in the next room.

"I keep a private office in the west wing," James continued, his voice once again taking on the tone of command. "The door remains closed. No one enters without my permission."

"Why?"

"Don't open the door, Miss Porter," he said, the scar over his eye a white ribbon in the lamplight. "There'll be no end to my anger if you do." He gripped the handle of her traveling case and pointed her up the winding stairs. "After you."

He took her to a spacious guest room on the third floor of the house where a large canopy bed was piled high with white satin pillows. A dressing table was covered with a collection of colored glass bottles that reminded Arabella of her apothecary cabinet at home in Scotland. The walls were painted a soft blue and hung with patterned canvases depicting scenes from far-off places; the beaded eyes of jungle animals peered through green embroidered palm leaves and the waves of a tropical storm swirled in ribbons of silk thread. A desk, covered with papers, leaned against the far wall, and a cushioned chair waited by the open window where white curtains billowed in the soft, rose-tinted breeze. Next to the window was a tall shelf filled with books, their leather covers flooding the room with a musky, masculine scent.

"I hope your quarters are to your liking, Miss Porter."

"The preferences of a servant hardly matter, Mr. Alden."

He placed her traveling case at the foot of the bed. "Unlike your father," he said, "I don't employ servants in my home, nor am I interested in doing so. You'll be living under my roof. You'll be taking care of my grandmother. But don't ever forget, it is your father who has indentured you."

He stepped into the hall, intending to bid her good night but circling back, wanting to see her face one last time before he left. "And while you're a guest in my home," he said, because he could think of nothing else to say, "you will call me James."

"Very well, James." His name slid off her tongue, rustling like leaves drifting over a stone path. His heart constricted at the sound of it. "And you will call me Arabella."

He nodded once and bowed low to her, as though she were a high born lady and not a peasant from the Isle of Skye.

"Good night, Arabella," he said, closing the door.

She listened to his footfall on the stairs before moving to the window and parting the curtains. She was tired and angry, and a strange sensation in the center of her chest made it difficult to breathe. She leaned out into the night air, closed her eyes, and let the soft fingers of evening caress her tear-stained cheeks. She wondered what Caitriona would think if she could see her now. She was living in a house so grand it would rival the homes of Scotland's lairds, but it was a prison all the same. And yet, she knew she wasn't really a prisoner. *You're free to leave if that is what you choose,* James had said, his voice deep, firm, unyielding. She could have run away from him, she could run away from him still, but she had made a promise to her father, and in keeping that promise, she would strengthen her family. She would no longer have to face the world alone.

She heard a far-off cry and opened her eyes to see flames burning on the western horizon. She was about to call out for help when she realized the fire was nothing more than a memory trapped beneath a gaping hole that had been scorched into the veil more than two hundred years ago. She blinked, and the phantom flames disappeared.

She dropped into the chair by the window, tears slipping from her eyes as she looked out over the back garden. She had left the only home she had ever known. She had found and lost her family. Now, she was going to have to come to terms with the choices she had made.

She rested her head on the windowsill, finding comfort in the soft whinny of horses calling from the stables behind the house, in the quiet hum of mosquitos buzzing through the rose bushes, and in the throaty songs of nightbirds, their feathered wings flapping long and low, as they flew south over the darkened waters of the Mystic River, heading toward the freedom of the sea.

Part Three

Alden House

"That which we call a rose
By any other name would smell as sweet"
(Romeo and Juliet)

"I understand you made your acquaintance with my grandson, last night."

Elinor and Arabella were sitting in the Aldens' rose garden, seeking relief from the early afternoon heat. The sun shone hot and bright, and Arabella had carried Elinor's lunch outside to a table beneath the shade of a towering oak tree. She had discovered rows of neatly planted herbs behind the kitchen and harvested sprigs of lavender to brew a strong tea that would aid Elinor's inflammation. It was Elinor who had suggested she chill the tea, so Arabella had chipped away at the great blocks of ice packed tightly into the Aldens' private ice house and filled two tall crystal glasses with the shavings. The ice had melted quickly, leaving beads of condensation behind.

Arabella nodded in response to Elinor's statement. She watched a goldfinch dart about the yard, building a late season nest for its young.

"James tells me you'll be staying here with us," Elinor continued, scanning Arabella's face for signs of emotion. Arabella nodded again, but turned her attention to the rose bushes which bloomed in abundance along the garden gate. She didn't want to think about James.

"My daughter-in-law, Mary, planted the rose bushes," Elinor said when she noticed Arabella admiring the pink blossoms. "She carried the cuttings with her across the Atlantic and rooted them in pots when she reached America. When she and my son George married, she planted them in the stony soil of our garden. Everyone said the roses would never survive such trials, but they did not know Mary's determination." Elinor took a sip of her tea and smiled. "She used to sing to her roses each night, so they would bloom brighter the next day."

Caitriona had taught Arabella all about roses, their history and lore, how to cultivate them, how to harvest them for tinctures and syrups to lift spirits and soothe grief. Since roses were linked to Aphrodite, the Greek goddess of love, they were most often associated with romantic passion and fidelity, but Arabella knew they carried other meanings as well. In ancient societies, *sub rosa* confessions, those held beneath ornate plaster roses carved into ceilings, had been kept confidential on pain of death, so the Jacobite rebels in Scotland and Ireland, secretly plotting to restore an exiled Catholic king to the British throne, had pinned rose-shaped ribbons onto their hats and jackets as a coded way of identifying themselves to fellow supporters of their clandestine cause. Caitriona had taught Arabella that roses were the only flowers capable of storing memories, and that those who drink tea steeped from their hips ingest all the joy and beauty the plants have ever known.

"Where was your daughter-in-law born?" Arabella was surprised to learn the Alden family had recent immigrants among them.

"Mary came from Ireland," Elinor said, adjusting her shawl. She seemed as oblivious to the heat as the rose bushes did. "She was Catholic, and I am ashamed to say I objected to her marrying my son. My George had a strong faith, and the Alden name was well-established. He could have had his choice of brides." Elinor smoothed the fringe of her shawl with her wrinkled fingers. "But then, I suppose he did have his choice. His choice was Mary."

"Is it Mary's portrait that hangs above the mantle in the front parlor? The dark haired woman holding the roses?" Arabella had been comforted by the woman's kind expression as she had waited for James to return.

"Yes. My son had the portrait commissioned. Mary was a beautiful woman, I always admitted that, even when I tried in vain to stop the wedding." Elinor studied Arabella's face again. "In time, Mary and I came to an understanding. She was a sweet and loving mother to her boys." The old woman's voice trailed off. "My George loved her so."

Elinor told Arabella she had been away visiting her sister in Westerly, Rhode Island when Mary, pregnant with her third child, went into labor far earlier than anyone had expected. George was in Massachusetts with their oldest son, Thomas, who was beginning his studies at Harvard, and James, just twelve years old, had been the only one at home to run for the midwife. By the time help arrived, it was already too late. Mary died from blood loss, and the languishing baby ebbed away in James' arms.

Arabella had been in difficult birthing rooms and knew the pain such tragedies caused. She tried to imagine James as a frightened child, but her mind kept conjuring his broad shoulders, his brooding eyes, the chiseled lines of his jaw. Whatever had happened in the past, Elinor's grandson was no longer a little boy. He was a grown man. He had grabbed her arm in the woods. He had beaten her father for picking his roses. He was keeping her here, away from her family, with no explanation as to why. Arabella's hands clenched in her lap, her fingernails leaving crescent shaped marks on her palms.

"James seemed angry when I told him William Stafford is my father," she said, returning to the earlier thread of their conversation. She hoped Elinor might provide her with some information to help her make sense of her situation.

Elinor sighed. "There is a long and complicated history between the Aldens and the Staffords," she said, observing the wilting leaves of an overheated maple tree with feigned interest. Lines of grief gathered on her face. "Anne's mother was a member of our congregation before she married, and William worked in our shipyard offices for many years. When George and Thomas were killed in a carriage accident two years ago, it was your father who held our shipyard *and* our household finances together. I would have been lost without him."

"Where was James?"

"Aboard some God-forsaken ship." Elinor shook her head as though the memory alone caused her physical pain. It had been well over six months before her message about the death of George and Thomas had found James. He had left home after a bitter argument with his father, not telling anyone where he was going or if he ever planned to return. George had scoured the muster-rolls and crew lists of every ship that had disembarked from ports up and down the eastern seaboard, all to no avail. James had disappeared without a trace, and after the carriage accident, Elinor had wandered the docks placing tear-stained letters into the hands of every captain departing from Mystic, Stonington, and New London, begging them to inquire after her grandson when they sojourned with other ships at sea, praying he was still alive, hoping her words would somehow reach him.

"If my father helped you in your time of need, why does James hold him in such low esteem?"

"As I said, the history is complicated." Elinor lifted her crystal glass to her lips and swallowed a mouthful of tea before continuing. "When James finally returned home, I expected he and William would work together to run the shipyard, but for reasons I don't fully understand, they became bitter rivals." She smiled at Arabella, a glint of hope in her eyes. "Their estrangement never sat well with me, but your presence in our home is exactly what's needed to heal the rift between the two of them once and for all."

"Elinor," Arabella said, wondering how much her grandson had told her about the rules of her employment, "do you know James has forbidden me from seeing my family?" She couldn't keep the resentment from her voice as she spoke. "I don't think he's interested in healing anything."

"James has no right to keep you from your family, Arabella. I've told him that."

"But he has every right to collect the debt my father owes if I don't do as he commands. He made that abundantly clear."

Elinor sighed again, a sound of long-festering irritation laced with sadness. "James takes after his mother," she said, "and not just the dark hair and blue eyes. Mary was full of passion, and she had a temper. She was wild, headstrong, and secretive. But, when she loved something, a man, a child, or a rose, she loved it completely."

Elinor put her glass down on the table to signal she was done with her tea and their conversation. "Give James a chance to come to terms with our new arrangement. I'm sure, in time, he'll do the right thing."

As the afternoon wore on, Arabella considered what she knew about roses. They were difficult to nurture, but once they settled in rich soil, they would bloom throughout the summer and into the fall, their tight buds unfurling like spools of silk. Their powdery scent attracted pollinators, even as their sharp thorns repelled spiders and aphids. Their bark hardened, death-like, each winter, but when spring returned, fresh, new shoots of life burst forth from the old, a symbol of the beauty that blossoms from grief.

Roses had meant so much to Mary that she had carried them with her across the sea, a reminder of Ireland, the home she might never see again. Arabella reached up to touch her thistle pendant, tracing the swirls embossed in the silver. It was one of the few things she had carried across the Atlantic, but it seemed flat and lifeless next to Mary's winking roses. She wondered if Mary had ever brewed rosehip tea, letting its magic remind her of Irish pastures, lush and green beneath soft, spring rains. She wondered if William had known the intimate history of the roses he had so carelessly picked for her on the night he had returned to Mystic. And, because Caitriona had taught her that roses hide secrets as easily as they perfume the air with love, Arabella wondered exactly what roses meant to James Alden.

James, who had worked at the shipyard all day and taken his supper at The Whaler's Inn, did not come home until almost midnight. He had tried to lose himself in the boredom of ledgers and shipping contracts, but the numbers did little to expunge the lingering odor of oakmoss and wildflowers from his memory, so he had abandoned the day's paperwork in favor of sealing the hull of a newly commissioned ship. It was difficult, dirty work, but it had filled his head with the bitter, oily scent of tar, leaving him too tired to think about William Stafford's daughter.

He entered the house through the front door, extinguishing the lamps Elinor always left burning for him when he was out late. He made his way through the darkened hallway toward the west wing of the house where he kept his office, but the sound of water bubbling on the cast iron stove made him turn toward the kitchen. Three white candles, carved with strange sigils, flickered in the warm breeze blowing in through the open window, their bases arranged in a semi-circle around a stone bowl filled with crushed herbs. A ceramic pestle and a small, sharp knife, both stained the same violet color as the herbs, rested on the table next to a large, open book. James picked up the book and flipped through the yellowed pages, studying the faded pictures. It was written in a language he did not recognize.

He heard a gentle song, like the ringing of a bell, coming from the backyard, and he looked out the window. She was there, the woman he had been trying to forget, moving through the kitchen garden collecting leaves and flowers, her skin shining like pearls in the moonlight. He watched her until, suddenly aware of his presence, she stiffened and glanced over her shoulder, finding his face in the light of the window. She stilled, but only for a moment. Then she rose and floated toward the workman's entrance at the back of the kitchen. James turned his back to the window and leaned against the wooden counter, his eyes watching the door, patiently waiting for her to walk through.

"Hello, Arabella," he said when she crossed the threshold, his words calm, slow, controlled. He regretted losing his temper with her the night before, and he had promised himself he would not let it happen again.

He ran his thumb along the spine of her grimoire. Her body tingled as he stroked the leather binding, the steady motion stirring something deep inside her, as though he held her body, and not the book, in his strong, calloused hands.

She didn't return his greeting, so he spoke again, his deep voice low against the whining thrum of insects outside the window. "Shouldn't you be asleep at this hour?"

"You're not asleep."

Her challenge brought a half smile to his lips.

"No," he said. "But I'm not lurking in the garden."

She lifted her basket and gestured toward the mortar and pestle on the table, a defiant expression on her face. "I'm not lurking in the garden, James. I'm harvesting herbs to help your grandmother."

He surveyed the mortar, the pestle, the cauldron simmering with sweet-smelling herbs. "And this book?" he asked, opening the mysterious volume as he locked his eyes on hers.

"It's my family's grimoire—a book of medicinal remedies passed down from my ancestors," she added when his expression darkened at the strange word. "It's of no use to you. I'm sure you can't read it, unless you speak the Old Tongue."

He closed the book and set it back down on the table. It landed with a loud thump.

"What were you doing in the woods a few nights ago, Arabella?"

So, he had recognized her from the woods after all. Her heart fluttered as she remembered how vulnerable she had felt, standing in front of him in the moonlight, her white dress clinging to her wet skin. If he were truly the gentleman he was pretending to be, he would have let the awkward encounter fade into obscurity instead of bringing it up to humiliate her.

"What were *you* doing in the woods a few nights ago, James?"

Her words, as quiet and as heavy as his, brought back his half smile.

"It's common for a man to go hunting in the woods."

"It's common for a woman to go walking in the woods."

"No," he said. "It isn't. And you were doing more than walking."

Arabella looked away from him, trying to step around him to put her basket on the table so he would not see the color rise on her cheeks as she wondered exactly how much he had seen that night. Why hadn't she heeded Elizabeth's warning to be careful? Why couldn't her solstice wreath have drifted down the river and out to sea as she had intended? Why couldn't anyone other than James Alden have retrieved it? Her fingers closed around the handle of her basket.

He stood solidly in front of her, stopping her forward progress, waiting for her to look up at him before he spoke again. "What were you doing in the woods, Arabella?"

"I don't see how my going for a walk in the woods, however uncommon that may be here in America, is any of your business, James."

"Then let me explain why it's my business," he said, his slow, steady drawl making her stomach coil. "You're living in *my* house. You're caring for *my* grandmother. You're under *my* protection." His smile disappeared, and his blue eyes glinted, cold and sharp, like shards of ice. "Everything you do is my business."

She stared at him for a moment before shrugging her shoulders flippantly. "I was not living in your house or caring for your grandmother when you saw me in the woods."

The grandfather clock in the front hall began its midnight song. James waited for it to finish, the throbbing white scar on his forehead the only sign his temper was not as controlled as it seemed.

"Do you have any more herbs to harvest tonight?" he asked.

"Do I need your permission to complete my work?"

He forced himself to step back from her, straightening to his full height and taking a deep breath. "It may have been acceptable for you to roam unchaperoned through woods and gardens at night when you lived in your father's house, but your circumstances have changed, and you would do well to remember that." He gestured toward the back yard. "If you have more harvesting to do tonight, I'll stand guard to ensure your safety until you've finished."

"Then I'm finished," she said, placing her basket on the table.

He squinted at her, saying nothing, his jawline sharp and tight. He removed the cauldron from the stovetop and extinguished two of the candles, handing her the third to light her way back to her bedroom. Then he picked up the Porter Family Grimoire and held it out to her, his fingers brushing against hers as she accepted the heavy volume from his hands.

He watched her as she left the kitchen, and when he saw the flickering light of her candle flame disappear, he walked down the hallway and entered his office, closing the heavy oak door behind him.

Arabella's first few days as the newest resident of Alden House found her consulting her grimoire often. She mixed herbal teas and salves to store for future use, but was delighted to learn that, for the time being, she was most needed as a companion for Elinor, staving off the loneliness that often accompanies old age. Elinor's frail body, which had been draped in mourning colors since the untimely deaths of her son and grandson, was bent and doubled, her condition incurable, but she possessed a strength and vitality that reminded Arabella of Caitriona. Even Alden House itself respected Elinor's authority, standing prim and proper in her presence, relaxing only when the old woman retreated to her bedroom to rest, its exhalation soft, like a puff of smoke rising from an extinguished taper.

Since Elinor spent a good deal of time in bed and James spent most of his time at the shipyard, Arabella often found herself alone. It was during those private moments that she allowed herself to dwell on how much she missed her father and sister. She hadn't had the opportunity to ask her father anything about her mother, and her unanswered questions were wounds that desperately needed bandaging. Elinor had taken great pains to make her feel at home in her new situation, but she remained tightlipped about the tension between the Stafford and Alden families, and James' overbearing constraints on Arabella's freedom to come and go as she pleased prevented her from accessing important information about the past. She spent many long and lonely afternoons exploring Alden House, hoping one of the grand rooms might hold a clue to help her understand the Aldens so she could better navigate her complicated situation.

Unlike her father's house, which had yielded its true personality as soon as she had ventured beyond its public facing rooms, Alden House exuded a calm reserve that extended into its most private spaces. Still, an air of mystery clung to its walls. The house held secrets, as all houses do. "I'm here to help Mrs. Alden," Arabella whispered to the empty rooms, hoping her formal pledge would loosen the home's reticence. Caitriona had taught her to speak to their little stone cottage as though it was a living entity, so she had always bid it farewell when she headed out across the island and greeted it kindly upon her return, thanking it for its steadfast protection from the wild moorland winds. Perhaps beginning a conversation with Alden House might be the first step to getting the answers she needed.

"What stories can you tell me?" she asked, placing her hand on the mantle in the parlor and looking up at Mary's portrait. A summer breeze rustled the curtains, filling the room with the damp, salty scent of the Mystic River, but the house remained silent.

Arabella wondered how her home on the Isle of Skye would react if a stranger from a strange land stood inside and tried to unlock its secrets. Would it yield the stories of the Porter Clan to anyone who asked? It had taken her a lifetime to learn the peculiarities of her own family home, to know when a creak of the floorboards or a rattle of the windows was a call for attention and when it was an expression of comfort, a settling in. Although Arabella desperately wanted answers to her questions about the past, she realized she would have to earn the trust of Alden House before it shared its blood and stories with her. She would have plenty of time for that, she thought with a sigh, since she was stuck here for the foreseeable future.

She crossed the foyer to the music room where she discovered a wall of tall windows facing the north garden. Thick hedges of pink roses relaxed in the shade. Buttery sunlight bounced off the white keys of Mary's piano forte, painting harp-string shaped shadows across the papered walls. An exposed beam of wood running along the farthest window had been carved with the initials *T* and *J*, and beneath each letter, dates and marks recorded the growing height of the two boys over the course of their childhood. Arabella traced the letters with her finger, trying to imagine the large, empty house loud with the laughter of children. She studied the dates, observing how quickly James had passed his older brother in height, and noting how the marks stopped, abruptly, when he turned twelve, two years before he had first run away to sea.

Arabella continued down the hall, pausing when she reached the threshold of the sewing room, a small alcove tucked away at the end of the eastern corridor. She found wide chairs with tapestried pillows, perfect for lounging. A sewing kit lay half-opened on a low table, its contents strewn about as though patiently waiting for someone to return with a new item of clothing to mend. Arabella crossed the room to inspect the titles that lined the shelves of yet another bookcase. She selected a copy of *Northanger Abbey*, an expensive volume with a stamped gold design on its maroon-colored cover. She opened it, and a stalk of flattened fennel fluttered to floor, its aged yellow flowers, pressed and dried, crumbling on the rose-patterned carpet beneath her feet.

She had seen fennel growing in the far corner of the kitchen garden, the only plant in the yard, besides Mary's roses, which stretched itself wild and free. Arabella had explored the small garden thoroughly, looking for herbs to use in her medicinal remedies, drawing triskelion symbols in the soil to encourage new growth, wondering who tended its orderly rows. The Aldens did not employ any live-in servants, but their elaborate house and extensive grounds wanted for nothing. *While you reside in my home, I'll provide you with everything you need*, James had told her. Was this what wealth was capable of doing? Making sure every need was met like a wish? The thought of James made Arabella's insides twist with resentment, but beneath that feeling was another one, warm, sharp, and insistent, a feeling she didn't want to acknowledge.

She wondered when she would see him again.

She picked up the crumbled petals of fennel and closed them back inside the book before going to the kitchen to prepare an afternoon pot of tea. Tea had become an important part of her daily ritual with Elinor. Black current, raspberry leaf, and green hyson imported from overseas helped to loosen conversations as the women forged a friendship that quickly surpassed their working relationship. They shared tea in the garden, in the parlor, on the front porch, and in the yard, watching the bustle of horse-drawn carriages moving up and down Greenman Avenue and listening to the shipyard noises ring out with the regularity of a ticking clock.

"We mustn't dawdle," Elinor said, when she had finished her tea. She placed her cup firmly in its saucer. Tiny leaves clung to the painted porcelain. "You'll need time to get ready."

"Get ready for what?" Arabella asked. Elinor sometimes asked Arabella to accompany her to the shops or call on the ladies of her congregation, but she usually liked to stay close to home as the day began to ebb.

"I'm sure I told you." Elinor's lips curled into a sly smile. "James is coming home for dinner."

Dinner. Elinor had most certainly *not* told her about dinner.

She looked at the three dresses hanging in her bedroom armoire. None of them was suitable for a formal dinner in the Aldens' dining room. She remembered the disapproval on her sister's face when she had dressed for Alan's visit. At least Anne had given her a shawl to cover her threadbare garment. Arabella sighed and chose her moss-colored cotton dress with pintucks sewn beneath the curved neckline. It would hardly matter what she wore if she and James could not find a way to remain civil with each other in his grandmother's presence.

The women were already seated at the large mahogany table, plates of salted cod, root vegetables, and fresh bread placed before them, when James strode into the dining room. He crossed to the far side of the table, bending down to give his grandmother a kiss on her cheek.

"You're late," she admonished, her voice somewhere between teasing and scolding as she gestured toward the hallway where the clock had just finished its seventh strike.

He half smiled in response, glancing at Arabella as he plucked a crystal glass from the sideboard and opened a decanter of whiskey. Elinor had pinned

Arabella's hair up at the top of her head, leaving nothing between the green of her dress and the green of her eyes but her creamy white skin. A few stray tendrils had loosened themselves, curling around her face and along the curve of her neck. James pulled his eyes away from them and carried the glass and decanter to the head of the table, hesitating slightly before sitting down at the place Elinor had set for him.

He was freshly shaven, wearing a formal waistcoat and jacket that made him look younger and far less threatening than he had in the woods. His jacket hid the tattoos Arabella had seen on his arms, but a patch of ink spilled out from beneath the cuff of his left sleeve, covering the back of his hand with sharp, thorn-like marks, dark and sinister. Elinor scowled at the markings, and he shifted, placing his left hand under the table, away from her view.

Elinor took a sip of cider to rally herself and then smiled brightly. "How was your day at the office, James?"

He filled his glass, a generous pour, and swallowed a mouthful of the amber liquid, regarding her with suspicion. "It was fine, grandmother," he said cautiously.

Family dinners had been a staple of his childhood. His father had insisted he and his brother master the etiquette and decorum of their social station, but after George and Thomas had died, the tradition of sharing formal dinners in the dining room had fallen by the wayside. The sound of silverware scraping against porcelain was a somber reminder of all they had lost, and James had been surprised when his grandmother requested he come home for dinner that evening.

She was up to something. Of that much he was sure.

Elinor turned her attention to Arabella. "I thought it high time we officially welcome you to Alden House," she said. "You've been here nearly a week, and with James so busy at the shipyard, this is the first chance the three of us have had to break bread together."

A week. It felt more like a lifetime to Arabella. In the first few days of her confinement, she had hoped her family would contact her, but there had been no secret letters, no chance meetings, no signals from across the river. Her father and sister had been stripped away from her as quickly as they had been found, and although Alden House sat in the center of downtown Mystic, she was more isolated than ever. She blamed James, of course, imagining the violent threats he must have made the night he visited Stafford House to negotiate the terms of their financial arrangement. She wondered how such a cruel man could be related to the warm and welcoming Elinor.

Arabella could feel the weight of James' stare bringing the color to her cheeks, so she looked around the cavernous dining room to avoid making eye contact with him. There were two long cabinets filled with place settings and crystal glasses. Painted landscapes lined the walls. A sculpted hearth stood ready to host a cheery fire when the air turned cold. The entire living area of her family's stone cottage could fit inside the Aldens' dining room with plenty of space to spare. She suddenly missed the howl of moor winds blowing through the cracks of its crumbling foundation.

"Did you share family dinners in Scotland?" Elinor asked, attempting to stir conversation.

There had been many hungry years on the Isle of Skye, years when they had scoured their garden, using its bounty to stretch what little fish and meat they could afford, but even when food was plentiful, Arabella and her aunts had rarely gathered together around one table. Their work as healers and midwives kept them busy at all hours. "My grandmother often let soups and stews simmer over the fire," she explained, recalling the scent of nutmeg and coriander that welcomed her home at the end of a long day. "Our home was quite small, so the entire cottage smelled of her cooking."

"Mary sometimes made a shepherd's stew for dinner," Elinor said. "It was one of her family recipes and it was quite fragrant with herbs and spices." She turned toward her grandson, trying her best to engage him in the discussion. "Do you remember, James?"

"Yes."

The last thing he wanted to talk about was his mother. He looked at Arabella, her upswept hair luminous in the candlelight, strands of brown and red twisting into a rich auburn glow. Her silver thistle pendant, resting on the swell of her chest, gleamed in the gas light of the dining room chandelier. He tapped his fingers against the crystal pattern of his glass, determined not to fall into the trap of forced familial discourse his grandmother was laying for him. It was one thing if she needed William Stafford's daughter to be her nurse; it was another thing entirely if she expected him to enjoy it.

"Tell me Arabella," he said, his voice low and steady, "did your grandmother lurk in gardens and harvest her cooking herbs by moonlight?"

Her eyes narrowed, tiny emeralds in the dim light. He was goading her, trying to make her angry so she would argue with him and ruin the dinner Elinor had planned. She snapped her head toward him, a stray curl falling across the curve of her cheek.

"Elinor tells me you spent a good deal of your life aboard ships," she said. Her words, polite but clipped, took James by surprise. He hadn't expected her to change the topic of conversation.

"That's right," he said, glancing at his grandmother and then back at Arabella. The thought of the two of them talking about his past made him suddenly uncomfortable.

"And did the captains you served under pay attention to the phases of the moon? Did they chart its effects on the tides?"

His fingers stilled their tapping, curving around the glass in his hand, the cut crystal pattern cool against his skin. The moon was an essential element in celestial navigation, its gravitational pull affecting tidal currents at sea and dictating safe passage through shallow harbors. When he had hunted whales aboard the *Shepherd*, each full moon had provided enough light for the crew to gather on the top deck, toiling or celebrating through the night according to the captain's whim. He raised his brow, a movement so small it would have been imperceptible if not for the tightening of the scar that slashed over his left eye.

"They did," he said after a beat of silence.

"The moon affects the water beneath the surface of the soil much like it affects the water in the sea, pushing it and pulling it, providing plants with differing rates of hydration throughout its twenty-eight day cycle. Choosing to harvest beneath waxing, waning, full, or new moons helps me to best direct the potency of an herb's medicinal properties."

James said nothing, but his fingers began to tap the glass again, his rhythm steady and thoughtful.

"My own grandmother was not afraid of the dark," Arabella continued, her brisk tone gaining more passion as she spoke, "and there was no man on the Isle of Skye who would have dared stop her from working outside at night if that is what she chose to do, so, to answer your question, James, yes, sometimes my grandmother did lurk in gardens and harvest her cooking herbs by moonlight."

The air in the room swelled with tension, and Elinor frowned at James. "Arabella's herbs have been a tremendous benefit to me already," she said, hoping to clear the strained atmosphere that had been ignited by an argument she didn't fully understand. She slanted her chin mischievously. "Of course, you need not take my word for it, James. Why don't you join me for worship on Saturday? The elders of our congregation will be delighted to speak with you about how improved my health has been since Arabella's arrival."

His half smile returned, but he shook his head, raising his hand to concede her point. He had been waiting for it, the topic he knew was coming, the topic that always came. Whenever his father or brother had insisted he join his family for worship it had escalated into a brutal confrontation, but he didn't have the heart to quarrel with his grandmother. He knew her gentle chiding of him was her way of making Arabella feel comfortable in their home, of letting her bear witness to what was usually a private family squabble. It was her way of telling him her nurse had already become more than an employee; she had become a trusted friend who would keep their family secrets.

"I'll take your word for it," he said, before lifting his eyes to meet Arabella's. "My grandmother must be feeling better if she once again has the strength to chastise me for missing Saturday services." His words, laced with humor, held a hidden strain of sorrow. He raised his glass to offer a toast. "Your own grandmother must have taught you well, Arabella. You have my gratitude for a job well done."

Elinor, pleased with the slow but steady progress of her plan, smiled, reaching her wrinkled hand toward James. "My darling boy," she said, her dark eyes twinkling as she began to eat, "the three of us must all get together for dinner again soon."

June melted into July, and the Alden roses reached their fullest bloom, tinting the air with a hazy pink glow. Armfuls of blossoms had to be cut and brought into the house to make room for new buds to open. Bowls of roses graced the tables in the kitchen, dining room, sitting room, and entryway, and Elinor placed a vase of them atop the pianoforte in the glass-walled conservatory. The fresh fragrance of the roses floated through the home, mixing with the rich leather scent of the books lining the walls of the parlor and library.

As the Fourth of July dawned, Mystic bloomed with a spirit of celebration as thick and as lush as the Alden roses. The houses along Holmes Street, which stood so close to each other they could reach out and hold hands, were decorated with red, white, and blue bunting. Many businesses, including the Alden Shipyard, closed on Independence Day, setting their workers free to enjoy speeches, parades, and downtown festivities.

"Just wait until tonight," Elinor said to Arabella. "James will escort us down to the wharf which will be hung with thousands of whale oil lanterns." She looked off in the direction of the town center as though she could see her memories of years past floating through the humid air. "All the young men will be out well past dark, lighting their rockets and torpedoes, and families will gather together to picnic on the green so they can watch the fireworks launch over the mouth of the river." She smiled. "Everyone comes out to celebrate the Fourth of July."

"Everyone?" Arabella hoped Elinor would not notice the note of hope trembling on her tongue. She had never seen fireworks and was excited to watch them rip through the dark canopy of night, but the prospect of running into her father or sister at a town-wide celebration made her tingle with anticipation. If Independence Day was such an important event, surely Anne and William would be present, and in the bustle of the crowds, she might be able to slip away to speak with them. Arabella hummed an old Scottish tune as she packed a picnic basket with fruit, cheese, and bread, imagining the possibilities the night might bring, but by the time the afternoon had tipped toward evening, her plans were beginning to unravel.

"I'm afraid I'm too tired to go downtown tonight," Elinor said, airing herself with a painted silk Japanese fan her grandson had brought back from his travels. The heat of the day had taken its toll upon her frail body.

"Do you need something to drink?" Arabella asked. "Are you feeling unwell?"

'I feel like a woman of advanced age, and I doubt a drink will cure me of my years." Elinor sighed. "What I need is for you to walk down to the shipyard and collect James. He's the only one working today, so you need not worry about encountering any strangers on your way. The two of you should head downtown and secure a good spot on the green so you can have the best view of the fireworks. You'll have a splendid time together, and you can tell me all about it when you return."

Arabella stiffened at the idea of spending an evening alone with James. "If you'll be all right on your own, I'd prefer to walk downtown myself," she said. "I'm sure James is busy with his work. I don't want to disturb him."

"Nonsense." Elinor's reply carried an undertone of command that rivaled her grandson's. "James spends far too much time laboring like a commoner in that shipyard, and a social event will do him some good."

"Elinor—"

"An unmarried woman cannot attend the festivities alone, Arabella. You need a chaperone, and I'm not up to the task."

"But—"

"James always loved watching the fireworks when he was a little boy." Elinor held up her hand as Arabella continued to protest. "The two of you will attend the celebration together. That's my final word."

The purple shades of twilight had begun to bruise the summer sky by the time Arabella found James in the abandoned shipyard. The buildings were dark and quiet, so she had followed a lone flickering light to an open storage shed that smelled of tar and turpentine. James was there, honing his tools, the muscles of his back flexing beneath his work shirt as he slid a large knife across a leather strop, five long strokes on one side of the blade followed by five long strokes on the other. Arabella stood in the doorway watching him, not wanting to disturb the steady rhythm of his work. When he noticed her, so clean and beautiful in her crisp, white dress, a flash of concern crossed his face.

"What are you doing here?" he asked. "Is something wrong?"

"Everything's fine. Your grandmother sent me to remind you about the fireworks."

A swarm of mosquitoes buzzed in the shed, attracted to the lantern light. James looked at her curiously as he adjusted the strop in his hand and slowly pushed his knife across it three times. He flipped the angle of his blade, pulling it across the rough surface of the leather three more times to sharpen the opposite side.

"My grandmother hasn't watched the fireworks in years," he said when he had finished. "Does she really want me to escort her downtown?"

"She did," Arabella said, confused because Elinor had implied James knew of their plans, "but the heat has tired her, so she suggested you and I walk down to the green together."

James gripped his knife and moved each edge across the strop a final time, the motion of his wrist as he pulled the blade away from the leather making the freshly honed metal sing.

"My grandmother didn't mention anything about the fireworks to me."

"Well, if you're busy, I'm happy go on my own." It was more than she could have hoped for. An evening to do as she pleased.

James sheathed his newly-sharpened knife and turned away from her to hang his strop on an iron hook fastened to the wall. "My grandmother knows I would never allow you to go downtown on your own," he said.

"I didn't come here to ask for your permission, James."

"Then why did you come here, Arabella?"

"I already told you. Your grandmother sent me."

Her thin muslin dress clung to the curves of her body. He pulled his eyes away from it, unable to stop them from roaming over the long strand of hair that had loosened from her braid and spilled into the hollow above her collarbone. He wondered how a woman as smart and as beautiful as Arabella could be fooled by his grandmother's obvious meddling. He exhaled deeply and crossed the shed, reluctantly offering her his hand.

She looked at his palm, rough with callouses from years of manual labor.

She made no move to take it.

"You're not going downtown alone," he said, "so if you want to see the fireworks, you'll have to come with me."

The far-off sound of joyful music from the brass bands on the green floated through the shadows of the evening. Arabella imagined the wharf decorated with swinging lanterns. After more than a week of isolation in Alden House, she longed to attend the celebration, even if it meant she had to spend the evening in James' company.

She slipped her palm into his, her breath hitching as he tightened his grip. Then she let him lead her into the growing darkness of the midsummer night.

They passed the cooper, the chandler, and the long, dark ropewalk which stretched through a cluster of barn-like buildings where braided strands of hemp one hundred fathom long were rendered sea-worthy by craftsmen twisting thick threads in opposite directions. Arabella soon realized they were heading deeper into the empty shipyard, turning off the cobblestone pathways and moving down the trails of dry-packed earth that led toward the bank of the river.

"This isn't the way to the green," she said, slowing down midstride.

James tightened his grip and continued his rapid pace. His long legs kicked clouds of dust around the hem of Arabella's dress.

"We're not going to the green," he said.

He turned down a long wooden dock that jutted into the water. Small waves slapped against the pilings beneath them. He stopped in front of a tall shed and slid open a large barn door. Inside the shed was a boat, twenty-five feet in length, its sails rolled and tied to a single front mast. The boat bobbed gently in its slip, and James let go of Arabella, hopping into the stern before turning back and offering his hand to her once more.

She hesitated. She had not been on a boat since she had disembarked from *Martha's Destiny* and her memory of the fierce hurricane they had traveled through still haunted her. Even if she could find the courage to board the craft, she would miss the chance to see her family if she didn't venture downtown on foot.

"There's nothing to fear," James said when he saw the uncertainty in her eyes. "We're only sailing down the river and into Fishers Island Sound. Trust me, it's the best way to see the fireworks."

She didn't move.

"She's a safe vessel, Arabella." His voice softened, flowing from the shadows of the shed. "I designed her myself."

The hushed strain of a patriotic tune wafted over the river. She took a deep breath and lifted her foot over the bouncing gunwale. James' arm closed around her waist, pulling her up and into the boat. Before her feet could touch the deck, he had lowered her into a comfortable seat carved into the stern. He loosened the ropes and pushed the boat through the open passageway toward the downstream flow of the river. When he felt the current surround the hull, drawing the boat south toward the Sound, he loosened the sail and sat down next to Arabella, a carved mahogany and brass tiller jutting out between them.

The boat sat low in the water, and Arabella reached down to trail her fingers in the waves, sighing as cool breezes curled up to whisk away the sticky heat of the summer afternoon. She untwisted her braid and let the winds blow through her hair. James looked away from her, pretending to concentrate on navigating a river that was as familiar to him as it was to the birds of prey who hunted its shoals and shallows.

The village of Mystic was beautiful from this vantage point. Lanterns twinkled along both sides of the river like stars. They glided past houses and shops. The wood of the boat had been varnished to a shine, and the tiller, which James held fast in his right hand, had been chiseled to look like a rope, each side turned and etched with fine divots and lines. Arabella had seen small fishing boats resting along the shores of Skye and she had watched the great sailing ships and steamers moving in and out of the New London Harbor, their sailors rowing skiffs between their moorings and the land, but she had never seen a one-masted sailboat as beautiful as this one.

"Did you really design this boat?" she asked.

"I designed her, and I built her," James said. He spoke with pride. "Her hull is carved from white cedar and her rigging is arranged for speed. I use the same techniques to build the large merchant vessels that sail out of our shipyard. One of them made it to Hong Kong in just over one hundred days. That's a new record."

He slid his hand further down the tiller to make room for hers. "Would you like to steer our course?"

She placed her hand on the column of wood. The tiller jumped and shuddered against the rush of water running beneath the keel. When she pushed it to the left, the boat swung violently to the right. She gasped in fear, but James only smiled and cupped his hand over hers. He coaxed the tiller back into place, and the rudder returned the boat to the current.

"No harm done," he said, trying not to swallow the heady scent of the forest rising from her skin. Even on the river, surrounded by salt marsh and sea grass, he smelled oakmoss and wildflowers wafting from her body. Her hand was small and soft beneath his, and he squeezed it, helping her guide the tiller back and forth as she learned to control the movement of the rudder beneath the waves. She looked up at him, smiling, her freckled skin kissed pink by the winds.

"Curl your fingers around the tiller, like this," he said, arching her wrist. "If you keep your grip steady, you'll keep control of the boat. Every movement you make on deck affects what happens beneath the water."

As above, so below. She wondered if Caitriona knew their family mantra applied to sailing.

They drifted downstream, past ale houses bustling with holiday activity. A group of men in the crowded Spouter Tavern raised their voices in song. The wharf had been decorated with thousands of lanterns, as Elinor had promised. Their burning whale oil filled the air with the faint smell of fish. Families gathered on blankets spread over the grassy fields just past the center of town, positioning themselves toward the southern skies as they waited for the military ship anchored off shore to launch its rockets into the air.

The river meandered past marshes filled with night hunting birds, widening as it opened into the Sound, its current slowing and spreading beneath them. James stood up, locked the tiller, and, eyeing the ribbons that hung from the rigging to indicate the direction of the wind, fully unfurled the fore and aft sails, letting them grow big-bellied with the warm evening breeze. He adjusted the canvas, tilting and tacking until the boat moved in the direction he desired. Arabella felt the resistance of the incoming tide as the salty Sound collided with the river, and though James sailed the boat smoothly, she gripped the edges of the gunwale, frightened by the sudden depth of the dark blue ocean water.

They sailed close to the military ship, its rigging and decks decorated with patriotic bunting and nautical flags. James tacked against the wind and maneuvered around the tall ship, heading toward the center of Fishers Island Sound. Arabella glanced back to look at the gaping mouth of the Mystic River, remembering how Elizabeth had pointed it out to her as *Martha's Destiny* had sailed toward New London. She wondered if the far-off pinpoint of light in the darkening the east was the beacon from the Stonington Harbor Light, or perhaps the Watch Hill Lighthouse further down the coast, both structures standing tall and bright to guide wandering ships safely home.

When James decided they were in a good position, he trimmed the sails and dropped the anchor. The far-off music of revelers in the Spouter's Tavern had been replaced with the quiet breath of the wind and the steady suck of the waves. The boat bobbed and swirled in the choppy waters as the summer day rendered itself into a dusky haze of twilight.

"What happens now?" Arabella asked. She watched the ocean lick and caress the sides of the boat, thankful her seasickness had never returned after *Martha's Destiny* escaped the hurricane. She shivered, imagining the source of the shadows darting beneath the waves.

"Now," James said, casually perching himself on the gunwale as though he had no fear of the bouncing sea or the mysteries that lurked beneath it. "We wait."

The stars began to sparkle like beaded crystals caught in the net of night. The sun threw its last rays over the western horizon. The waning moon ignited in the east, casting a path of silver flames across the water. James, still and quiet now that the boat was anchored, rested his feet on a coil of ropes, his arms leaning against his bent knees. Arabella followed the lines of a large tattoo twisting around his forearm and under the folds of his rolled up shirt sleeve. The elaborate design looked like a thorny branch of roses drawn in faded ink.

"Do my tattoos offend you as much as they offend my grandmother?" James asked.

She blushed in the dusky light. She had been studying his skin as though it were a page in a book.

"Why doesn't your grandmother like your tattoos?" she asked, remembering how he had taken pains to hide them from her view at dinner. The inked roses on his hand and arm were the same size and shape as the roses in his garden, and Arabella assumed James wore them as a tribute to his mother.

Waves sloshed against the side of the boat for a few moments before he answered.

"A tattoo is hardly the mark of a well-bred gentleman," he said. "And then, of course, there is Leviticus 19:28." His voice took on the formal, dramatic tone of a pastor reciting a biblical passage to his flock: 'Ye shall not make any cuttings in your flesh for the dead, nor print any marks upon you.'"

"Does it go against your faith to get a tattoo?" she asked.

He shrugged his shoulders. "It's complicated. Some Christians think it's a sin to put graven images on the body." He flashed a smile that didn't reach his eyes. "My grandmother says she worries about the fate of my eternal soul, but I think she's more worried about what the elders of our congregation think."

Arabella had learned all about the Picts, the "painted people" who had ruled Scotland in the Iron Age and who had decorated their bodies with colorful symbols, and she had met several members of Clan MacLeod on Skye who had marked themselves with Viking emblems to commemorate their Norse ancestry. She did not believe this kind of body art would keep souls from entering the afterlife, but she wondered why James would so boldly reject his own family's faith.

"Don't you believe in the words of the Bible?" she asked.

"Words are tricky things," he said, surprised by her forthright question. "My father was a devout man. He believed the Bible was the inspired Word of God, but I spent almost eight years of my life aboard whaling ships. I sailed on merchant ships and expedition vessels for a few years after that. I served with men from all around the world. Some were Christian, some worshipped gods and goddesses, some even worshipped the ocean itself." He searched his mind for the right words, struggling to find them. "I'm not sure there's only one way to believe."

Arabella watched him as he spoke, marveling at how different he seemed on the water than he did on land. He was kinder and more contemplative, as though the turbulence of the winds and waves calmed him, giving him focus. She arched her eyebrows and smiled.

"Did any of the men you sailed with harvest herbs by moonlight?" she teased.

He laughed then, a bright, clear sound that echoed across the water.

"There are not many herbs to be harvested in the middle of the ocean," he said, "so you are the first to school me in that particular practice." He watched the moonlight dance on the water and became serious again. "You can't blame me for questioning you, Arabella. Respecting other people's spiritual practices and allowing them into my home are two different things."

"I don't blame you, James," she said quietly. She suspected his suspicions of her had more to do with his hate for her father than with a desire to persecute her faith. It was clear he cared deeply for his grandmother, and it was only natural for him to want to protect her from anything that he perceived as harmful.

"Did you get your tattoos while you were serving on whaling ships?" she asked, steering the subject back to his time at sea because she had liked the nostalgic tone of his voice when he had spoken about it. It had sounded unencumbered and full of light, as though it was free of the weight that comes from living on land.

"Most of them. There are long stretches of time," he said, "between the kills." He surveyed her expression, not wanting to frighten her, only continuing to talk because she seemed genuinely interested in what he had to say. "We used to carve designs into the spare bones and teeth of the whales we hunted, too." He leaned toward her as though he was telling her a secret. "If you ever run out of dinner conversation, just ask my grandmother what she thinks of the scrimshaw I brought home from my voyages. She'll go on about its ungodliness for hours. I think she hates it even more than my tattoos."

Arabella laughed. "Does it hurt to get a tattoo?"

"Sometimes. But pain is part of the process. It makes you choose your designs carefully because you don't want to endure the pain unless the change it causes is worth it." His smile deepened, crinkling the corners of his eyes. "The most painful tattoo I ever got came from a Tahitian sailor who pounded boar's teeth into my flesh. Another man tattooed me with sharpened turtle shells, but most of us just used needles."

"How did you choose your designs?" She looked down at the roses blooming on his forearm, wondering if their creation had caused him pain, wondering if he would say anything about Mary.

"Some designs have cultural meaning," he said. "And some tell the story of your time at sea. An anchor means you've crossed the Atlantic. A fully rigged ship means you've survived the trip around Cape Horn. I knew a man who had crosses tattooed on every knuckle to protect him from sharks, and another who inked a rooster and a pig on the top of his feet because he thought the marks would keep him afloat if the ship went down." He laughed at the memory. "He didn't even know how to swim."

He didn't mention his rose tattoo, but he stretched out his right arm, turning his palm up to the sky to show her another design, eight sharp points, alternately shaded in light and dark, etched into the large muscle between his elbow and his wrist. The points were looped with an intricate circle of Celtic knots. The design reminded her of the Wheel of the Year, a symbol that Caitriona had stitched onto cloth to help Arabella learn about the turning of the seasons when she was a child.

"It's called a compass rose," he said, "or, sometimes, a wind rose. It marks the cardinal directions, north, south, east, and west," he touched each of the four points on his skin, "and the ordinal directions in between. They say a sailor who wears this tattoo will always find his way home."

Arabella reached out to brush her fingers against the symbol. A breeze sighed off the water, and he stilled as his flesh tightened beneath her touch. She looked up at him, green eyes verdant in the moonlight.

"It looks like a star," she said.

He nodded, taking a moment to steady his breath before responding. "Stars are the keys to navigating the seas." Darkness was settling around them, and Arabella imagined she was listening to the voice of night as he spoke. "In the Northern Hemisphere, the North Star is a constant. All the other stars rotate around it, and if you pay attention to the patterns, you can orient yourself and your place in the world."

Follow your heart, her mother's letter had said, *let it guide you like the North Star guides sailors at sea, and you will not lose your way.*

Arabella looked up at the dizzying crowd of stars in the sky overhead. "Which one is the North Star?" she asked, her eyes scanning the vast reaches of heaven.

"I'll show you." He stood and pulled her up to her feet. The boat wobbled as their weight shifted, and she stumbled against him, grabbing his chest in fear, his body a warm and solid mass in the middle of the rocking sea.

"It's all right," he said, pulling her close to steady her until she settled. "You just need a minute to get your sea legs." His touch was gentle, nothing like it had been in the woods, and Arabella's heart beat deep inside her chest.

When she stopped trembling, he turned her, slowly, letting her lean her head and back against his body for support. He anchored one hand on her waist. She felt the heat of it, as though the inked roses on his arms might sear themselves into her skin through the thin muslin layer of her dress.

"There's a large bear, called *Ursa Major*, who walks the sky each night, wandering the kingdoms that lie east of the setting sun and west of the rising moon," he said, pointing toward the sky and tracing the outline of the constellation with his index finger. His voice took on the practiced cadence of a storyteller who had spent long stretches at sea. "The Greeks say Zeus transformed his paramour Callisto into a bear and placed her in the stars to hide her from his wife, but many tribes native to the Americas tell tales of a great bear that roams the sky as well. The Wampanoag call the bear *Maske*, and the Micmac of Nova Scotia speak of a white bear who was killed by seven hunters before being memorialized in the stars."

His words painted a great white bear in the sky above. Arabella rested her head on his shoulder, picturing the bear lumbering through the inky darkness, its breath soft against the lapping waves.

"In the center of *Ursa Major* are seven bright stars," James continued, reaching toward each one, "these four forming a cup, and these three forming a handle." He picked up her right hand and gently stretched it above her head, guiding her fingers to trace the patterns in the constellation. "It's known as the *Big Dipper* or the *Drinking Gourd* because it looks like a ladle scooping water from the sky."

She imagined filling a glass with liquid night and drinking the light of the stars.

"Now, if you follow these two stars in the cup," James said, "which are named *Merak* and *Dubhe* after the Arabic words for bear, you'll find *Polaris*, the North Star." He swept their entwined fingers through the sky and paused on a dimly lit orb hovering just above the horizon. "Do you see it?"

"Yes," she whispered, her body tingling with strange magic. A moment ago, the North Star had been eclipsed by a thousand blinking lights in the Milky Way, but now it sparkled, sharp and clear, and Arabella wondered how she had failed to notice it before.

When James spoke again, his breath was warm against her cheek.

"Once you find your true north, you'll never lose your way."

The night sky above them opened itself to Arabella like a book of wonder and mystery. As a child, she had been fascinated by the heavens, but Caitriona, whose soul was tied to the moors and mountains of Skye, had never taught her to read the stars. She glanced at James' arm, which still held hers aloft toward the horizon. His compass rose tattoo glowed on his skin, a pattern of light and dark, and she tried to envision him, huddled below the deck of a ship as a shadowy sailor hammered the design into his flesh, his sharp tools drawing forth red blood, his needles leaving black ink behind. Elinor had described her grandson as a rebellious young man who had run away to sea to escape the life his father had so lovingly crafted for him, but the compass rose on his skin, a talisman meant to help sailors find their way back home, implied otherwise. Maybe there was more to James Alden than what appeared on the surface.

"James," she began, wanting to ask him for more stories, but a loud wail cut through the air, eclipsing the sound of her voice. He lowered her gently into the seat at the stern of the boat just as the first Independence Day rocket exploded over their heads.

A bright flash was followed by another loud explosion, and then showers of light fell around the boat like enchanted rain. The cheers of the soldiers who had launched the rockets echoed over the water. They lit more fuses, sending shrieking missiles into the night, each one bursting in vibrant halos of color. Fireworks climbed through the sky and shimmered in the water as James' sailboat rolled and bobbed over gleaming trails of crystal light.

The missiles came faster and faster until the night erupted in a crescendo of blasts, and Arabella wondered if this was what it was like to live inside the Milky Way, swaddled by heat and light and sound. When the final rocket ripped through the sky, dissolving into soft lines of smoke that floated over the sea like ghosts, she sat, still and speechless, watching the last of the ashes plummet into the waves.

After a few minutes of silence, she realized her hand was resting on James' thigh. She pulled it away, embarrassed. Cool air curled into the empty space between them.

"Arabella?"

His voice was soft and concerned.

"Thank you for taking me here," she whispered. "It was a beautiful evening."

She could feel the magic spell of it slipping away, disappearing like the trails of smoke that were already blending with the wavering sea mists. She wished she could grasp the evening in her fingers and hold it close to her heart awhile longer. Here, with James, suspended between the sea and stars, her soul had swollen with joy for the first time since she had arrived in America, but she knew when they returned to the shore, the tension between them, born of a family conflict she did not understand, would only begin to grow again.

James opened his mouth as though he wanted to say something, but instead of speaking, he stood up and silently hauled in the anchor, his muscles flexing with each pull on the heavy iron chain. He adjusted the sails, directing them so the wind would propel them around the military ship and toward the mouth of the river, chasing the North Star upstream against the southward push of the current.

Arabella watched him work, his movements effortless, the boat an extension of his body. They passed the river's salt marshes. They passed the town wharf with its twinkling lanterns. They passed a few straggling revelers celebrating in the alleyways behind the Spouter Tavern. It was a long and quiet journey, but all too soon they entered the unsettled eddies that stretched between the Stafford and Alden houses.

James' smile began to fade away, replaced by the hard, familiar set of his jawline. By the time he had moored the boat and walked Arabella back to the house, the full weight of the troubled past had returned, twisting around them like an impenetrable hedge of thorns.

It had been a few days before the Fourth of July that William had received his invitation from Old Ellie. He had been waiting for it, banking on the maternal affection she had carried for him since the death of her own beloved son. The old woman had a soft heart, and William had known, even when James had outlined the ridiculous rules of their financial arrangement, that she would never allow her grandson to keep him away from his daughter indefinitely.

He had paused awhile before answering the invitation, letting early July ripen into the full, oppressive heat of summer, giving the forced loneliness his daughter was no doubt suffering time to fester. When he saw Jonathan Burrows' ship, the coastal clipper *Polaris*, cruise down the river and moor in the waters just beyond the Alden Shipyard, he sent word to Elinor to expect him for tea. If there was anyone he hated more than James Alden, it was Jonathan Burrows. His skin crawled whenever he thought of that young upstart sailing for the very company he used to control. "It's *unnatural*," he thought to himself as he climbed up the steps to the Aldens' front door, "for a man like that to prosper while I struggle to make ends meet."

He twisted his lips in contempt, thinking of all the money he had lost since James had returned from the Antarctic to claim his family inheritance. William had been spying on the prodigal grandson ever since, and though he did not yet have enough proof to bring about the boy's downfall, he was getting close. Anne had balked at his suggestion she ingratiate herself to Elinor, worried about the effect a position of service would have on her social standing, but the arrival of his younger daughter, a peasant from the Isle of Skye, had turned out to be just the luck William needed. All he had to do now was handle the girl correctly, make her his eyes and ears inside Alden House. He had no doubt she would be loyal to her father when the time came. Of course, Old Ellie would be crushed when he revealed her grandson's illegal activities to the world, but that was no matter. That arrogant boy had cost him his fortune, and he was resolved to see justice done no matter who got hurt along the way.

Arabella opened the door, a look of shock on her face. William removed his hat to greet her. He clutched the brim in his hands, reminding himself that although the girl looked just like Catherine, she knew nothing about him. He was a blank slate to her, and he would happily write himself into the role of paternal hero.

Her lips parted slightly, followed by a sharp intake of breath. The bright light of the summer afternoon made the green of her eyes shimmer like foliage in a sun-dappled forest. She unthinkingly grasped her silver pendant. It was identical to the one Catherine used to wear.

"Are you going to leave your father standing on the doorstep like a stranger?" he asked, growing annoyed at the awkward silence unfolding between them.

The percussive tap of a cane echoed against the wood floor of the foyer and Elinor appeared in the doorway. "Mr. Stafford," she said formally, before letting her voice drop into a warm and familiar tone. "It's lovely to see you, William."

"It's been far too long, Ellie," William said, bowing his head with a charming smile. "You look as ravishing as always."

"It seems the heat has affected your vision." Elinor laughed and turned to Arabella. "Show your father into the parlor, dear. I've closed the curtains against the sun so we can enjoy a proper visit."

Carriages were moving up and down Greenman Avenue, and although James had left for the shipyard early that morning and rarely returned home until well after dark, Arabella glanced nervously up and down the street. During the first week of her service, she had prayed her father would cross the river and rescue her from her captivity, but she had never dreamed he would be bold enough to call on her in broad daylight at Alden House.

"Elinor," she whispered, her heartbeat in her throat, "James said—"

"James is not here." Elinor winked at William who responded with a sly grin. "What my grandson doesn't know, won't hurt him."

"But—"

"We've waited long enough for James to come to his senses," Elinor explained. "I sent your father an open invitation to visit Alden House whenever he likes, and he has been wise enough to call while the two of us are home alone. What harm can come from a simple family reunion?"

William hardly needed a formal escort into the parlor. As soon as the front door closed behind him he hung his hat and jacket on a tall rack tucked into the corner of the entryway, strolling across the grand foyer as though he was its rightful owner. He made himself at home on a comfortable couch, entertaining the women with talk of the weather, the tides, and the tall-masted ships which sailed up and down the river between their homes. It was well over an hour before Elinor finally excused herself, as William knew she would, so he might enjoy a private moment with his daughter.

"Arabella, perhaps you can help me upstairs and then make some tea and sandwiches to enjoy with your father before he takes his leave," she said, pushing herself up with her cane. "Your visit has brought me much joy, William, and I do hope you'll call on us again."

He listened to the sound of Elinor's cane tapping up the stairs. He waited patiently until he heard his daughter return to the first floor and begin arranging plates in the kitchen. Then he rose and wandered around the parlor, searching the bookcases and end tables for clues, though he doubted James was stupid enough to hide the evidence of his thievery in plain sight. He sighed in frustration, half-comforted by the knowledge that he had charmed the women so easily he would have plenty of chances to explore the house more thoroughly in the future. Patience was the key. A warm breeze rustled the silk curtains, and he scowled at the casual opulence of the room. Not long ago, all of this had been as good as his, but that was before James Alden had slithered home from sea.

William touched a handkerchief to his brow, wiping away beads of sweat. There hadn't been any rain since the solstice, and the air had grown thick and oppressive. The windows of the parlor had been thrown open, and he inhaled the soft, sweet perfume of the Alden roses clustered along the south side of the house.

He hated them.

He knew what was going to happen when he heard heavy footsteps on the front path. He rolled his eyes. He had hoped to question his daughter alone, to direct her actions to suit his plans, but that couldn't be helped now. He was going to have to craft another sort of victory to make his tedious visit with the women worthwhile. He folded his handkerchief and tucked it into his pocket, turning just in time to see James Alden's massive frame appear in the parlor doorway.

"Hello, boy," he said.

When James walked into his house, the last person he expected to find standing in his parlor was William Stafford. He had been going through financial files and preparing reports in his shipyard office, work that always made his head hurt, when he had received a note from Jonathan Burrows, the captain of the coastal schooner *Polaris*, alerting him that their scheduled delivery had been unexpectedly doubled. James had happily abandoned the shipyard's monthly ledgers to prepare for Jonathan's shipment. His records regarding *Polaris* were stored in his home office, and he half hoped he might run into Arabella on his way to retrieve them. He had commanded himself to stay away from her, avoiding the house as much as possible since the Fourth of July, doing his best not to let himself look at her auburn hair gleaming in the candlelight each time his grandmother insisted he come home for dinner. But even with his self-imposed distance, he could not stop himself from thinking about her. He fell asleep dreaming of her body pressed against his, and he woke up remembering the soft curve of her fingers grasping his tiller beneath his guiding hand.

"What are you doing in my house?" he demanded as soon as the shock of seeing William had worn off enough to let him speak.

William raised an eyebrow. "Were you expecting someone else?" he asked. "Jonathan Burrows, perhaps?"

James crossed the room, stopping just in front of William. Although the old man's frame was much slighter than his, they were matched in height, and James looked directly into his dark eyes.

"What are you doing in my house, William?"

"I'm more than thirty years your senior and I've never given you leave to use my Christian name." William spoke as though he was reprimanding a child. "The least you can do is give me the courtesy of addressing me as Mr. Stafford." He plucked an enameled music box from the corner of the fireplace mantle and opened it, watching the metal cylinder turn, its pins and notches tinkling a stilted tune. The music slowed, and he snapped the lid shut.

"Did you really think you could keep me away from my daughter?" he asked.

"Your *daughter*?" James clenched his fists. The thought of this man claiming paternity over a woman he treated like an indentured servant made him sick. "Do you mean the *bastard* you fathered while you were married to Anne's mother?"

"I hear you like the bastard well enough," William snarled. "I hear you've taken her sailing, just the two of you, not a chaperone in sight."

James shook his head in disgust. "Arabella lives with me, William. I *am* her chaperone."

The older man cocked his head at the sound of his daughter's name on James' tongue. He had heard it, clear as day, the passion beneath the boy's fury. He flashed a cruel smile, thinking of the possibilities this new knowledge opened to him.

"If you've soiled my daughter's honor, you'll answer for it by marrying her."

"Her *honor*? What honor can she possess, being your *bastard*?" The scar on James' temple throbbed, angry and white. "And I've already told you, the blood of the Aldens and the Staffords will *never* mix!"

A creak of the floorboards. A rattling of porcelain cups. James swung around to see Arabella, holding a tray piled high with cucumber sandwiches and slices of iced lemon cake. The sight sent an unadulterated rage coursing through his veins. William hadn't stopped by unannounced. He hadn't come to Alden House to threaten him and provoke him as he had on the day they had argued in the rose garden. *She* had invited him, willfully breaking a rule she had promised to follow.

"What do you think you're doing?" he shouted, forgetting his pledge not to lose his temper with her. He had believed they had shared a moment of connection on the river, but she had tricked him, making him lower his defenses so she could invite her father into his home as soon as his back was turned. "Was I unclear when I laid out the conditions of your employment, Miss Porter? Do you think you can disobey my orders without repercussions?"

William grabbed James by the collar, and James shoved him backward with such force that the old man staggered across the room, knocking his jaw against the corner of a bookshelf and falling to his knees. The enamel music box he had been holding smashed against the stone hearth, its hinge broken, its chime calling out its final notes.

"James! Stop!" Arabella let the tea tray crash to the floor. The dainty cups and plates shattered to pieces as she rushed toward the men, but James closed in on William, who pushed himself to his feet, smiling as he wiped a stream of blood from the corner of his mouth.

"Touch me again, old man," James said, his voice and body now dangerously still. "Touch me again, and the injuries you suffered in my rose garden last month will be a gentle memory compared to the ones you'll suffer in my parlor today."

"James!" Arabella cried, "please stop!"

"I'm not afraid of you, boy" William sneered, ignoring his daughter. "You're nothing but a common thief hiding behind your father's noble reputation."

James grabbed William's arm, knocking him off balance as he dragged him toward the door. Elinor, brought downstairs by the sounds of the commotion, appeared behind Arabella, her mouth hanging open at the scene of destruction taking place in her parlor.

"You've missed a visit from Mr. Stafford, grandmother," James said. "He's just leaving, and he's taking his daughter with him, so if you still have need of a nurse, I suggest you post an advertisement for one who knows how to follow the rules of our home."

"Let go of him!" Elinor cried.

"I told you this would happen when you insisted on hiring—"

"James Patrick Murphy Alden—"

"Don't talk to me like I'm a child—"

"You're acting like a child!" Elinor's voice shook with embarrassment and anger. "Let go of Mr. Stafford's arm this instant!"

James released his grip, letting William fall to the floor. "Get out of my house!" he shouted, all pretense of polite conversation dissolved by his growing fury. "And take your scheming daughter with you!"

"James!" Elinor rapped her cane against the floorboards, commanding everyone's attention. "Mr. Stafford is *my* guest. He is here at *my* invitation, not Arabella's, and I will *not* have you treat him like a criminal!"

James turned to look at his grandmother, studying the proud lines of her face. He squinted his eyes, trying to wrap his mind around what she was saying.

"*Your* guest?" he asked after a moment of silence. "*You* invited him here?"

"Perhaps you'd like to see the letter?" William interjected, standing and pulling a piece of paper from his pocket, trying to draw James back into their ugly confrontation.

"I told her," James said, looking at his grandmother but pointing toward Arabella, "that she would have no contact with her father while she worked for me. You *know* that."

"And she has done exactly as you asked even though you have no right to demand such a horrid thing! As I said, William is *my* guest, so if you insist on being angry with someone, you can be angry with me."

He shook his head, seething as he processed the haughty tone of her confession. His grandmother had lived in Alden House since before he was born. She had helped his parents raise him. She had cared for him when his mother died. She was the only family he had left, and he did not want to argue with her, but she had betrayed him by inviting William into their home after he had expressly forbidden it. When he spoke, his words were harsh and slow.

"Tell *your* guest to get out of *my* house before I throw him into the street."

Elinor's face blanched white, and William grabbed James by the collar once more. "Do you know what your father would do to you if he heard you speak to your grandmother like that, boy?"

"William, please," Elinor pleaded as the two men began to grapple again.

"I'll teach him to have some respect for his elders, Ellie—"

"William!" Elinor cried again, on the verge of tears. In a moment she had remembered herself, regaining her composure and returning to her practiced tone of grace and propriety. "Mr. Stafford, I think it best if you take your leave. I didn't realize my invitation would cause such turmoil, and I withdraw it, with my deepest apologies, until such time as my grandson, who is, of course, the rightful owner of our home, chooses to relax the rules regarding your daughter's employment." William untangled himself from James, giving Elinor a pointed look. "Perhaps your daughter can see you home," she said, trying to offer her old friend some level of concession. "I'll send our carriage to retrieve her later this evening, and I'm sure, in time, the four of us can forge a new agreement of mutual respect that works for everyone."

An amicable separation from his daughter enforced by Mystic's most respected matriarch was not the outcome William had desired from the day. He had foolishly hoped Elinor would take *his* side, that she would see what a brute her grandson was, but she had always carried a soft spot for James, making excuses for him instead of holding him accountable for his behavior. His eyebrow twitched and then settled as he came to terms with her edict. It wouldn't help his cause to push Old Ellie further than she was willing to go. He would have to recalibrate and find another way to gain access to the secrets James was hiding inside Alden House.

"Very well," he said, inclining his head to Elinor's will. He offered his daughter his arm. At least he would have the chance to talk to her as they journeyed over the bridge. That would give him plenty of time to instruct her future actions and to make sure that she, at least, remained firmly on his side.

"The terms of our arrangement have not changed, William," James said. His voice, now devoid of fervor, still teemed with threat. He jutted his chin in Arabella's direction. "If she leaves this house with you, she never returns, and all financial agreements between us are null and void."

William clucked his tongue in resentment and disgust, but gave a sarcastic nod of acquiescence before his daughter had the chance to protest. He would rather suffer the indignity of being thrown out of Alden House than lose the financial arrangement he had brokered with James, and the last thing he wanted was for Arabella to be evicted alongside him.

"Oh, James," Elinor said, her voice full of shame, her dark eyes blinking away a film of tears. "How can you be so cruel?"

James said nothing.

William bowed low to Elinor in gratitude for her invitation before moving swiftly toward the entryway to retrieve his hat and coat.

"This isn't over, boy," he hissed, lowering his voice to a whisper so the women would not hear him. "Sooner or later, your sins are going to catch up to you, and I look forward to watching you fall when they do."

James stood at the parlor window, trying to forget the expression of anguish he had seen on Arabella's face as her father exited the house. Elinor had immediately demanded to speak with him privately, and Arabella had retreated upstairs without even looking at him.

James watched far-off storm clouds gather on the darkening horizon. His grandmother was trying to reason with him, justifying her invitation to William. It was her way of mending fences, her way of upholding societal expectations, and she was horrified he had contradicted her domestic authority in front of her guest. William was Arabella's father, and James had no right to come between the two of them, no matter what had happened in the past. Her rebuke droned on and on, and James, still wounded by her betrayal, saw no point in contradicting her. He studied the skies, wishing he were departing the brackish coastal waters of Fishers Island Sound and sailing toward points unknown, avoiding the dangerous side of the impending storm by trimming his jibs to windward.

"James, are you listening to me?"

He did not need to listen. He had heard her lectures about his barbaric behavior toward the Staffords a thousand times before. He turned away from the window and picked up the music box William had dropped on the hearth. It had belonged to James' mother. The corner had been badly dented in its fall, and the lid would no longer close. James placed it gently back on the mantle.

"Why today, grandmother?" he asked. "If you issued William an open invitation to visit our home two weeks ago, then why did he come *today*?"

"His timing hardly matters, James," she retorted. "If you could have seen how happy his visit made Arabella—"

"He waited two weeks before he visited the long-lost daughter he claims to love. He waited until the day Jonathan's ship sailed into the river. That's not a coincidence."

"Have you ever considered that William's interest in your business ventures with Jonathan might stem from his genuine concern for you and for our family's wellbeing?"

"No."

Elinor let out an exasperated sigh. "William has known you since you were a boy. He worked with your father and your brother for many years. He was practically family, James. I know he has his faults, but he's not the monster you and Jonathan believe him to be—"

"You don't know him as well as you think you do—"

"I *know* he's Arabella's father! I *know* that when George and Thomas died, he—"

Her voice trailed off, and an uneasy silence, far more uncomfortable than her lectures about upholding the sanctity of the Alden name, filled the sweltering room. It reminded him of the terrible quiet that had permeated Alden House when he had first returned home after his father's death. His grandmother had been afraid to speak to him, afraid to touch him, thinking he was nothing more than an apparition cast by her grieving mind.

James had been sailing under Jonathan Burrows' command on the *Nymph*, a small sloop commissioned to hunt seals and chart maps of the wild Antarctic terrain, when Elinor's letter about the accident had finally reached him. It was Jonathan, the only one aboard who knew James by his true name rather than by the name on his stolen identification papers, who had received the correspondence during a parlay with another ship. He had broken the news to James, one of the hardest things he had ever had to do, and then promptly relinquished his position as captain to accompany his friend home on the first boat they crossed that was bound for New England.

Now James sat down on the couch next to his grandmother, shifting uncomfortably, his frame too large for the petite cut of the formal furniture. His rage had faded into a deep film of regret that pooled at the back of his throat. He knew William had comforted his grandmother in the darkest months of her grief, but he also knew William had exploited that grief, siphoning their family's money into his own accounts and using the Alden Shipyard to make unethical deals that would line his own pockets. James, wanting to protect his grandmother from William's treachery, had never told her the truth.

He took a deep breath to steady himself. He hated talking about his father's death, but he could not let his grandmother's tearful mention of George and Thomas go unanswered.

"If it could have been me, instead of them—"

"James, please don't—"

He took her small hands in his and looked into her eyes, willing her to let him finish. "If it could have been me, instead of them, if I could have died in their place, I would gladly have done it." He had wished it so often he could envision his father and brother walking into the parlor after a long day of work. He could imagine the look of relief that would cross his grandmother's face knowing she and the Alden name were safe in their virtuous hands.

A tear dropped from Elinor's eye and James reached up to softly brush it away. "I know that if *they* were here, instead of *me*, things would be easier for you." He swallowed again, his words thick with emotion. He had tempted death every day he had sailed upon the wild seas, and he would never understand why the death that should have been his had come for his father and his brother in the relative safety of their hometown. "But I'm the only one left to carry the Alden name now," he continued, "and, right or wrong, I'll carry it as I see fit."

"James—"

"I *am* grateful for whatever comfort William provided you when I wasn't here to shoulder your grief, but I won't abide his presence in my home or his inquiries into my business." He lifted her hand to kiss it before rising. "Don't go behind my back and invite him into this house again, grandmother. I'm far too old to be handled like a child."

"Where are you going?" she asked sadly.

"Out."

He picked up a few large shards of porcelain that littered the parlor floor, placing them neatly on Arabella's discarded serving tray. "There's no need for you to wait up."

"You owe Arabella an apology, James."

His only answer was half a smile as he crossed to the foyer and opened the front door.

Elinor stood up and peered out the front window, watching his tall shadow move down Greenman Avenue and toward the line of storm clouds rolling in from the sea.

Part Four

Spouter Tavern

"There is a tide in the affairs of men,
Which, taken at the flood, leads on to fortune;
Omitted, all the voyage of their life
Is bound in shallows and in miseries"
(Julius Caesar)

There are few professions which create a brotherhood among men more than service at sea. Surrounded by endless swells of water which can slake no man's thirst, a ship is its own community bound by its own set of unwritten rules. The sailors eat, sleep, work, and fight in close, cramped quarters. When the sun is high and the waters run smooth, they create, leaving marks of their individuality on discarded shells or skeletons stripped clean of flesh, but, when the skies turn black and Neptune's trident stirs the seas, they toil together as one, their lives and deaths determined by a common destiny, for not even their captain, who is regarded as a god, can control the undulations of the tides.

James Alden and Jonathan Burrows had both grown up in the same small Connecticut town, but it was aboard a New London whaling ship named the *Shepherd* that they became brothers. As the son of a prestigious businessman, James had often been sent to collect paperwork and supplies from the Burrows Cooperage where Jonathan, half James' size but four years his senior, worked long days, splitting staves and hammering metal hoops to create the barrels and casks that stored the shipyard's goods, gun powder, and liquids. Whaling ran through Jonathan's blood; his Wampanoag and Pequot ancestors on his father's side were among the first people to hunt North Atlantic right whales in the waters stretching from Long Island to Nantucket, and, in the evenings, after his work at the cooperage was done, he taught James to wield a harpoon in return for lessons in reading, writing, and arithmetic. The two boys had plotted their escape from a world that sought to mold them for months before they were brave enough to act upon their desires, and it was not until their first four-year voyage to the Pacific hunting grounds aboard the *Shepherd* was well underway that they had finally found freedom from the parental and civic authorities that had tried to define their futures.

Of course, just as the boys were breathing a sigh of relief at having escaped their childhood miseries, they were simultaneously learning about the miseries of being men. Life aboard a whaling ship was far from the adventure they had imagined. Each day was filled with dirty, monotonous work, and any respite they were granted came in the form of long, tedious watches spent perched one-hundred feet above the bucking deck, their eyes peeled for any sign of a whale. Their captain, a devout Quaker, was a kind man who taught them all he knew about navigating the oceans, but he was also a vicious task master, and he saw every circumstance, the presence or absence of whales, the churning of a storm, the inevitable bickering among his men, as a test of his own faithful resolve, fiercely punishing and rewarding his crew as he believed it would best please heaven.

"'And God created great whales, and every living creature that moveth,'" the captain had said, gently quoting the scriptures to reassure his men early on in the voyage, "keep your eyes and hearts open, boys, and God will provide for us."

After months without any whale sightings, the captain's sermons grew less gentle. "'And God said, Let us make man in our image, after our likeness; and let *them* have dominion over the fish of the sea,'" he would roar, cracking his whip as his men searched the waves for whales, not caring if the animals came from God or the devil, so long as they came to relieve the crew from the captain's persecutions. "We're doing God's work, boys," the captain would thunder. "Put your backs into it!"

When the first call of "Thar She Blows!" finally rang out through the air, the men had scrambled across the decks to lower the whale boats and give chase. Jonathan, who had joined the crew as both the cooper's assistant and an oarsman, took his place in the middle of the lead vessel with James nervously gripping his heavy harpoon in the bow and the captain barking orders from the stern. Over a thousand feet of whale line had been carefully coiled, looped around the loggerhead, and connected to the iron. The line would be long enough to keep the whale tethered to the boat if she dove when she felt the bite of the harpoon.

It had been a frantic chase through unfriendly currents, and when James stood up and launched his weapon deep into the flesh of the sixty-foot beast that swam beneath the water's surface, his heart pounded with the elation of a warrior. The whale had thrashed in pain, almost stoving the small boat and flinging its men into the briny sea, but James knew he had hit his mark. The toggle at the end of his iron would hold. After the whale had tired herself with pulling the boat through the water, her frantic flails covering the men in salt and foam, the captain had come forward and plunged his shanked lance into the wounded animal, piercing her lungs and breaking her heart to pieces.

The great whale had gasped and choked, struggling to breath, blood sputtering up from her blowhole with each painful exhalation. Without air, her violent movements slowed, and she swam in ever smaller circles, a mournful spiral that would only end with the sweet release of death. When her flurry was over, she beat the water with her tail one last time as if to bid the ocean farewell. Then she turned fin out, rolling over on her side, and James, his own heart now pierced with the steely realization of what he had done, knew she would breathe no more.

The exhausted men had hauled her fifty-ton carcass back to the ship. They attached her to the starboard side with iron chains. They began the cutting in, stripping her flesh from her bones and slicing her blubber into pieces as thin as bible pages. The *Shepherd* carried its own tryworks, so fires were set on the blood-slicked decks. The cauldrons flickered through the night, rendering the once majestic creature into casks of oil that would fuel the soft, twinkling light of countless lanterns on shore. The spermaceti they scooped from the whale's dismembered head, a rose-tinted fluid that hardened into a violet-scented wax as soon as it touched the air, was worth so much money it was known as liquid gold.

"'And God said, Let there be light: and there was light,'" the captain had bellowed as the ship fires burned like the flames of hell. "And God saw the light, that it was good: and God divided the light from the darkness.'" The captain had roamed through his flock of men, clapping them on their backs as they worked, congratulating them on a job well done.

And then the *Shepherd* had sailed on for three more years, searching for leviathan to haul up from the peaceful depths, so the men could reap their oil and illuminate the world.

"So, William Stafford's illegitimate daughter is living in your house? Working as a nurse for Elinor?"

James nodded. He downed a shot of whiskey. He was seated in a shadowy corner of the Spouter Tavern with Jonathan Burrows, who reached for the bottle that rested on the table between them. The crowded room was filled with sailors on shore leave. Laughter and bickering filled the air as drunken men played cards and rolled dice. A few raised their glasses in song or flirted with painted women perched on their laps before inviting them out to the alleys behind Water Street. No one paid any attention to James and Jonathan huddled in the dark by the large stone mantle.

"Christ, Jimmy. I've only been away for a month. Is your grandmother all right?"

"I don't know," James said. "She seems better."

"And this girl, William's daughter, she was in the woods the last time you delivered my cargo?"

James nodded again.

"And then today, *after* I sailed into port, William showed up at your house?"

James nodded a third time.

"That can't be a coincidence, Jimmy." Jonathan, whose dark eyes often danced with laughter, grew serious. He filled their glasses and pulled at the gold hoop in his ear. "If things have been compromised—"

"I think we should off load your cargo tonight instead of waiting until tomorrow when we move the timber to the storehouse," James said before Jonathan could finish his thought. The wide bottomed hull of *Polaris* was stacked tight with Carolina pine and live oak from Georgia, hard, dense wood James used to construct the frames of his ships.

Jonathan leaned forward, tilting his head slightly to the left the way he always did when he wanted to listen carefully. "And the delivery date?" he asked.

"We'll keep it the same as scheduled."

Jonathan studied his friend's expression. "You're sure? You know the delivery is twice as complicated because of the unexpected size." Extra cargo always meant extra risk.

"I'm sure, Jonathan," James said. "William won't be coming back to my house anytime soon. It's the safest place to store the cargo until delivery."

A brawl between two sailors broke out on the far side of the barroom, sending tables and chairs toppling over and igniting the ire of Mrs. O' Shaughnessy, the barkeep's portly wife. She grabbed the shillelagh that hung in a place of honor behind the bar and swung it over her head, swearing at the offenders and shooing them outside to settle their differences without damaging her tavern's property.

"God, I love that woman." Jonathan laughed, downing his whiskey as the two drunken sailors spilled into the alley where their argument was swallowed by distant rolls of thunder.

James, still replaying the events of the afternoon in his mind, ignored the entertaining scene. "My grandmother told me she was the one who invited William into our house," he said, trying to put the pieces of the last few weeks together, "but I found her in my garden in the middle of the night."

"Your grandmother?"

"No. Arabella. William's daughter," James added when Jonathan did not recognize the name.

"What was William's daughter doing in your garden in the middle of the night?"

"At first I thought she was meeting her father, giving him information, and then I thought she was—I don't know—she said she was harvesting herbs."

"Harvesting herbs? In the middle of the night?"

"Do you remember, when we were kids, and everyone used to talk about how William was unfaithful to his marriage vows?" James asked, dismissing his friend's questions. "They said it was because a woman had bewitched him. They must have been talking about Arabella's mother."

Jonathan's loud chuckle cut through the noise of the tavern. "If it's witchcraft that made William stray from his marriage bed than there must have been covens in every port he ever visited. You and I both know the reputation he earned from his days at sea, and I trust a sailor's yarn more than I trust society gossip that's been filtered through the voices of children."

"But you do remember the stories they used to tell when we were kids. They were talking about her mother, Jonathan."

Jonathan leaned back in his chair, crossing his arms over his chest and releasing a patient sigh. "I remember the stories they used to tell about *my* mother, Jimmy."

Jonathan's mother, a Black woman of West African descent, had been born in servitude to the Burrows family. Legally enslaved until the age of twenty-five by Connecticut's Gradual Abolition Act of 1784, she had tended to the Burrows' house and children, as her own mother had before her, milking their cows, cooking their food, and sewing their clothes. She had died at the tender age of twenty-four while giving birth to Jonathan, who had in turn been deemed the property of the Burrows family until he came of age. Jonathan had never known his mother, but he carried her dark skin and warm brown eyes, and he had grown up working grueling hours in the Burrows' Cooperage, listening to ignorant customers claim his mother had come from a long line of Vodou practitioners who could cast spells and charms to both heal and harm.

"There's something strange about her, Jonathan," James said.

"My mother?" Jonathan asked, his voice coiling like a snake about to strike.

"No. Arabella."

"William's daughter?"

"Yes." James swirled the dregs of whiskey in his glass. "She showed up on my doorstep and convinced my grandmother to hire her without even consulting me. She knows about healing and science and poetry. She doesn't seem to care what anyone thinks about her, especially me. She's *nothing* like William or Anne. And she's far more loyal to them than they deserve."

Jonathan looked at his friend curiously. "Are we going to talk about her all night, Jimmy?" he teased. He poured two more shots in an attempt to change the subject. "If you want to move my cargo into your house in the dead of night, we have a good six hours to kill, and the Spouter Tavern has whiskey and women at the ready." He gestured around the smoky room, giving James a good-natured shove. "We can always start a row. Nothing clears the mind like being chased down the street by Mrs. O' Shaughnessy and her shillelagh."

James finally smiled. He and Jonathan had been on the receiving end of Mrs. O' Shaughnessy's shillelagh more than once, and it definitely had a way of clearing the mind.

"As tempting as a night of courting trouble sounds, I need to take care of a few things before we make the transfer."

"Suit yourself," Jonathan said casually, trying to mask his concern about everything James had told him. Their business was a dangerous one, and if William or the local authorities caught them transporting illegal cargo, they would face serious repercussions. Jonathan's strategic mind was already plotting alternate scenarios in case James' plan ran aground, but he trusted his friend's instincts, and he would never cloud it with his own worries unless necessity required it. He stood up, clapping James on the back.

"I'll meet you halfway through the middle watch," he said with a grin that looked more reassuring than it felt. He gave a quick salute and pointed to the half-finished bottle on the table. "It's your turn to settle up." He made his way through the noisy tavern, stopping only to plant a kiss on a surprised Mrs. O'Shaughnessy's ruddy cheek.

By the time James settled the bill and left the tavern, the skies had opened, pouring a steady stream of rain down from the clouds. He had walked into town, needing to move the large muscles in his legs to release the tension of the afternoon, so there was nothing he could do but endure a soaking on his way back home. He arrived at Alden House damp with sweat and precipitation. He hung his wet jacket on the coat rack by the front door to let it dry. He ran his hands through his hair, shaking the water off like a dog.

He glanced into the quiet parlor as he made his way down the hall. The tray Arabella had dropped when he had shoved William against the wall had been cleaned up, the porcelain shards of the cups and plates swept away. It was not yet nine o'clock, but James hoped Arabella had already retired for the evening. He had work to do in his office before meeting Jonathan again, and he didn't want another confrontation.

He felt it as he walked past the music room on his way to the back of the house, the same heightened sensation that had made him pluck her white-flowered wreath from the river, the same clenching in his chest that had drawn him toward the clearing in the woods on the night he had first seen her. He paused mid-stride, leaning against the wide frame of the music room doorway, peering into the shadows of the candlelit room. She was sitting in an upholstered arm chair by the large windows, her feet tucked up beneath her, a copy of *Paradise Lost* closed on her lap. Her head rested against the chair's tall wing.

He shifted, and the floorboards squeaked beneath his weight. She did not turn to look at him. She did not say anything. She only sat still, watching the rain create patterns of loveliness against the glass.

"It's the best place to watch a storm," he said softly, not wanting to disturb her but unable to stop himself from speaking, "unless you're frightened by thunder and lightning." When he was a boy, he and his brother had piled pillows and draped blankets across the furniture by the music room windows on rainy days, pretending they were sailing pirate ships through dangerous seas.

She tilted her head toward him, a hard look in her eyes. "I'm not frightened of bad weather when there's land beneath my feet." Her voice was dismissive, as though she had responded to defend her bravery rather than to extend a conversation.

He remembered countless gales that had felled the rigging during his years at sea, recalled the unsettling feeling of being hurtled into turbulent swells of white water. The squalls that had caught his captains unawares had been the most dangerous of all, and on several occasions, he had been ordered to climb the masts and secure the open sails while the ship, a helpless plaything of the winds, rolled precariously over the waves. James, gripping the swinging ropes and water-logged timbers, had been plunged beneath the ocean, lifted up to the clouds, and plunged back beneath the waves again and again in such dizzying succession that he had barely been able to distinguish the sea from the sky.

"A storm does feel more threatening on the ocean," he agreed.

"Did you really come in here to talk about the weather?"

The candles threw a flickering light across her face, and the sight, coupled with the pattering sounds of rain against the window, gave James the distinct impression he was looking at a fresh water *merrow*, an oceanic mermaid, or an ancient siren so fierce and beautiful men willingly drowned themselves for the chance to touch her. He was possessed by the sudden urge to lift the folds of her skirts and see for himself whether they covered a fish tail or a pair of human legs made of soft, creamy skin that might yield to his touch.

He moved into the room, wanting to be closer to her. The candlelight shone against the damp linen of his shirt, revealing the dark shadows of the tattoos on his chest.

"My grandmother thinks I owe you an apology," he said.

"And what do *you* think?"

He gripped the back of his neck and let out a long breath. He knew he deserved her ire after his outburst in the parlor that afternoon, but he was trying his best to make amends, and her attitude certainly wasn't helping.

"I'm sorry, Arabella." He looked directly at her and spoke with sincerity. "I shouldn't have blamed you for your father's visit, and I shouldn't have lost my temper with you without giving you the chance to explain."

She placed the copy of *Paradise Lost* on a side table and stood up, her legs unfolding beneath the volume of her dress. She was a human woman after all, he thought, shifting his broad body to the left, subtly positioning himself between her and the doorway to the hall so she would have to linger in the room a while longer. She stared at him, no sign of forgiveness on her face.

"If you owe anyone an apology, it's my father."

"I owe William nothing," he said.

She rolled her eyes and tried to move around him but he widened his stance, anchoring his feet to the floor, making it harder for her to reach the door.

"Please move aside, James." Her words were gravelly, as though she had been crying. "I'm tired, and I want to go to bed."

"I haven't given you permission to leave yet."

He knew it was a ludicrous thing to say even before he saw her mouth round with indignation. When he had returned home from the Spouter Tavern, he had wanted nothing more than to avoid seeing her, but now that she was standing in front of him, he could not bear to let her go. "We're not done with this conversation," he added, trying to give context to his statement.

Bright green flames of anger ignited in her eyes. "We *are* done with this conversation," she said, "and I don't need your permission to leave a room."

He didn't know how to explain the turmoil of his feelings toward her, how he ached to pull her body against his and push her away at the same time, how he wanted to kiss her until she was breathless even though he would never be able to trust her because of the circumstances that had brought her into his life. His own anger rose in reaction to hers.

"Do you know how often a sailor swabs the decks, Arabella? Coils the ropes? Scrapes the rust from the anchor chains?" The muscles in his jaw grew tighter with each question.

"What does that have to do with anything?"

"Every day," he said sharply. "And not because the deck needs swabbing or the ropes need coiling or the anchor needs scraping. He does it, every day, because the captain orders it. And he does it, every day, until the captain orders him to stop." It was the way men built trust at sea, the way they learned to depend on each other. Rules and regulations were important boundaries for dictating behavior, and they should only be broken by those willing to face the consequences. Why couldn't she understand that?

"You are not my captain." She drew each word out to emphasize her point. "And this house is not a ship."

He wanted to tell her that her impertinence was a perfect example of why women were banned from serving at sea, but he thought the better of it. He looked around the room, trying to find some reason, any reason, to keep her from leaving. His mother's pianoforte and harp rested in their places of honor by the far wall. "Do you play?" he asked, nodding toward the instruments.

"No." Her exasperation at yet another change in the direction of his conversation was palpable. "Do you think I had a music room with a piano and a harp in my cottage on the moors of Skye? My family barely had enough food to survive."

James kept his eyes on hers, but lowered his chin as he let out another long breath. "I didn't mean to offend you," he said. A streak of lightning flashed outside the window, momentarily illuminating the room. "I've heard you singing while you work in the garden. You have a beautiful voice, so I thought perhaps you had studied music."

She looked annoyed, but the flames in her eyes softened at his unexpected compliment, and he took it as a sign to continue talking. "My mother loved music," he said. "She used to sing to me when I was little, songs in what you call the Old Tongue. I never knew what the words meant."

He walked over to the far wall of instruments, giving Arabella a clear path to the hall.

"My father gave my mother this piano as a wedding gift." He trailed his fingers along the ivory keys. "And for their first anniversary, he had this harp specially built for her and shipped over from Ireland." He touched its soundbox, carved from a single piece of hollowed willow and painted with intricate Celtic designs. "She called it her *cláirseach*. I haven't played it since she died."

"*You* play the harp?" Arabella raised an eyebrow, clearly surprised by the thought of an ill-mannered, tattooed sailor playing such an ethereal instrument.

"You wound me, Miss Porter," he joked, feigning great offense. He plucked the strings, turning a series of small levers located at the top to tune them. "It takes great patience to learn the harp, so, whenever I got into trouble for losing my patience as a boy, my father forced me to sit inside and take music lessons from my mother." He smiled. "I assure you, I had more than enough practice to become quite accomplished."

Arabella knew the harp was an important symbol of Celtic culture. Depictions of the instrument had even been carved into eighth century Pictish stones on the Isle of Skye. In the Middle Ages, when harp strings were crafted of gold and silver wire instead of animal gut, its players had been regarded as the counselors of kings, leading troops into battle with the ringing sound of their notes.

James sat down on a small wooden stool and tipped the harp toward him, letting it rest lightly on his shoulder. He dropped his left hand to pluck a low rhythm and raised his right hand to play a melody, filling the room with a vibrating tune that moved across Arabella's skin like a wave of water. He smiled at her, a twinkle in his eye. Then he suddenly dampened the strings, ceasing their cry, leaving her with an aching desire to hear more.

"I suppose you know all about *Dagda*, the chieftain of the *Tuatha Dé Dannan*, and *Uaithne*, his jewel encrusted harp?" James asked. Arabella had heard stories of the *Tuatha Dé Dannan* from Caitriona, but she was too distracted by the placement of James' hands to remember the details. He was holding the harp exactly as he had held her body on the night they sailed beneath the stars; her head had rested against his shoulder, and his left hand had cradled the curve of her waist while his right pointed upward toward the sky.

"Tell me," she said, her fury with him momentarily quelled by the hope he would play more music as he spoke.

He moved his fingers across the strings again and Arabella shivered, imagining his fingers floating across her skin.

"Well, *Dagda* had a cauldron of plenty that never ran out of food, and a mighty club that could take and restore life with a single blow, but his most powerful weapon was his harp, *Uaithne*, which could summon the four seasons at *Dagda's* will." His deep voice fell back into its storytelling cadence, and Arabella wondered if he had ever held his crewmates rapt at sea with the stories he had learned from his Irish mother.

"*Dagda* played three noble strains of music to defeat his enemies," James continued. "The first was *Goiltai*, the sorrow strain. It made his adversaries weep so they could no longer see the battlefield through their tears." James struck a few deep, resonant chords that penetrated Arabella's chest, pulling hidden regrets from the innermost chambers of her heart.

"The second was *Geantrai*, the joy strain. It made the soldiers laugh and drop their weapons." He moved his hands upward and plucked a long run of trilling notes so lively she giggled.

"The third was *Suantrai*, the sleep strain. It lulled *Dagda's* enemies into an enchanted slumber," James said, composing a soft, slow tune that melted into the air like morning mist. Each string trembled against the tension of the forepillar as James plucked and pulled with relentless concentration. Arabella closed her eyes and listened to his song, her breath growing shallow, a corresponding quiver thrumming deep inside her body, the high notes curling around the base of her throat, the low notes purring beneath her abdomen.

James dampened the strings again, flooding the air with another painful silence. She sighed and opened her eyes.

"*Goiltai*, *Geantrai*, and *Suantrai*," he whispered, not wanting to shatter the sacred quiet that had settled over them. "Laments, celebrations, and lullabies. All the songs in the universe are composed from these three strains."

Arabella sat down on the bench in front of the piano to stop her legs from shaking. The silence that had followed James' song was deafening, and Arabella spoke to fill the empty space created by the stillness of his hands.

"Did your mother ever tell you about *Cana Cludhmor*?" she asked.

He furrowed his brow, searching his memory. "Celtic goddess of—sleep?" he guessed.

She smiled. "Some say she was a goddess of dreams and inspiration, but others say she was a human poet of great skill and renown. She's often credited with the invention of the harp."

James nodded as though the story sounded vaguely familiar. Then he shrugged his shoulders. "I liked my mother's stories about warriors best," he confessed.

"Of course you did." She shook her head in admonishment. "Well, one evening, after a terrible argument with her husband, *Cana Cludhmor* took a midnight stroll to clear her head—"

"A woman walking alone? After dark?" James interrupted playfully. "My mother would never have told me such a sordid story."

Arabella rolled her eyes again, but smiled and continued her tale. "She heard music, and she followed its sounds to the shore where she found the rotting carcass of a beached whale. The wind was blowing through the sinews still attached to its skeleton, and the melody was so beautiful that *Cana Cludhmor* lay down on the sand and fell asleep beneath the stars. Her husband found her the next morning and, to make up for all the anguish he had caused her, he carved a frame, using wood he had gathered from a nearby forest, and strung it with cords made from the animal's tendons so his wife could always carry the song of the winds and the whale with her."

James watched her lips move as she spoke, her words an incantation in his ears. He had taken part in the dismemberment of dozens of whales. He had tasted their blood in the back of his throat as he hacked and boiled and rendered their bodies into currency. He had listened to sea breezes rattle the chains which held their rotting flesh fast against the side of the ship. It had never been anything but ugly, but somehow, with her story, Arabella had colored his recollections of that destruction with a poignant beauty. Now, in his memories, he could hear the song of it, the tortured lament of the murdered whale, the boisterous merriment of the crew, the somber strains of one last lullaby as the animal's unused remains were finally released to find eternal rest on the bed of the sea.

"Did you ever play the harp for your shipmates?" Arabella asked when she noticed James had grown thoughtful at her story.

"No." James laughed, trying to imagine the rough sailors he had served with gathered in his mother's elegant music room. "But my friend, Jonathan, had a flute carved from the tooth of a sperm whale. It was given to him by one of the Māori of New Zealand. The first time he blew into it, the notes sounded like water flowing over jagged rocks. Our captain thought we had sprung a leak." He laughed again. "My mother should have taught me to play the flute and the fiddle instead of the piano and the harp. It would have made me far more popular with my shipmates. But then, I suppose my mother would have hated it if she had known I would grow up to become a sailor."

"Why?" Arabella asked.

His brow wrinkled in surprise at her question. His grandmother, his father, and even his older brother, Thomas, had often told James that his choice to run away to sea had been a selfish one, that his name and fortune came with responsibilities he had no right to forgo. He had assumed Arabella would share his family's social prejudices against career seamen.

"It can be a dangerous profession," was all he said, gesturing away the heavy topic of conversation.

"The men on the merchant ship that brought me to America didn't play instruments, but they did sing while they worked. Sea shanties mostly, and hymns when they worshipped together."

James nodded. "Work songs ease the burdens of labor." The endless calls and responses he had used to raise sails and haul ropes had lightened his tasks and helped him bond with the other members of his crew. "And, they're a way of filling an ocean landscape with something human," he explained. "I suppose the same ideas apply to spiritual music."

Arabella's grandmother and aunts had often hummed tunes while they worked in their garden or boiled their potions. Perhaps it had been their way of combatting the tedious nature of their own labor, their way of filling the earth and air with their human presence, their way of reminding the goddesses they were there.

"I liked the way the sailors' voices echoed over the water," she said, trying to picture a dark and brooding James taking part in a rowdy refrain. "But I thought the ocean made her own music as well."

He stilled for a moment, studying her, watching the candlelight shimmer on her skin.

"My mother always told me there were songs in the sea and stars," he said quietly, as though he wasn't quite sure whether he wanted her to hear him. "She came from seafaring people along the western coast of Ireland, and she said the winds and waves of her homeland created melodies so primal they stirred the soul with memories of heaven. She said that was why people composed music, to remind them of the celestial place from which they had come and to which they would one day return."

"It sounds like your mother had a beautiful way with words."

"She did." He touched the gilded designs painted on the frame of the harp. "She was always telling us stories and singing us songs." James rarely spoke of his mother to anyone, and it felt both strange and sacred, sharing his childhood secrets with a woman he had met only a few weeks ago. "She said the river behind our house repeated her melodies, like a mockingbird, carrying the strains of her music down to Fishers Island Sound and out into the Atlantic. She said her songs were her gifts to all the young sailors, lonely and far from home, who needed a mother to lull them to sleep."

His throat tightened and he swallowed before continuing. "She died a couple of years before I first shipped out to sea, and, since all ocean waters eventually mix together, I figured her songs must have circumnavigated the globe by then. Whenever I was posted on watch, with nothing to do but keep a weather eye on the horizon, I used to listen for them."

"Did you ever hear them?" she asked gently.

He nodded his head, slow and thoughtful. "Yes. I think so. Though whether I heard her songs or heard my memories of her songs, I don't really know." He looked at Arabella. The hazel streaks in her eyes rippled like tidal currents.

"There's a stillness before a storm at sea," he said, strangely compelled to continue sharing things he had never shared with anyone before. "When you're sailing headlong into dark clouds, before you reach the line of high wind and water that looms in the distance, everything grows eerily quiet." He smiled sadly, as though his recollections brought him equal parts pleasure and pain. "Somewhere between that silence and the following rush of winds and waves, that was when I heard my mother's songs."

She surveyed the lines of his profile, usually so hard and tight, now smooth and soft in the dim light. "Did you encounter many storms at sea?" she asked, wondering how often he had listened for Mary's music.

He laughed then, her innocent question releasing his melancholy. "You don't sail for over ten years without encountering storms, Arabella."

"Were you ever afraid?" she asked, remembering the harsh edge of panic in Robert's voice as he had commanded his men through the hurricane that had almost sunk *Martha's Destiny*.

"You'd be a fool not to fear a storm at sea," he said. "I've seen walls of water eighty feet high, men swept overboard by rogue waves, masts snapped in half by the force of winds so strong you can do nothing but bend yourself to their will, but sailing into that power, that danger, it makes you feel alive, like you can slip the bonds of earth and fly straight up to the stars."

Her eyes widened in fear at his descriptions of the ocean's might, and he laughed again, trying to explain his odd affection for what sounded like a death wish. "On my very first voyage, we were stuck in the doldrums for almost three weeks. It's an area near the equator where the wind circulates in an upward direction so it can't be harnessed to push against the sails," he explained. "There was nothing around us but still water and stagnant light. It was horrible. I'd take my chances against a raging tempest any day."

James still remembered what it felt like to be caught in that windless swath of ocean. He had been too green to realize the dangers of it, the potential for running out of food and fresh water, the delirium that could set in among the men, the scurvy and sickness that could spread in the stifling heat. He had known only that he stood aboard a ship made for movement, unable to move. It was the same way he had felt when he had returned home after his father's death and found himself faced with a lifetime of running the Alden Shipyard.

"I never asked for this, Jonathan," he had confessed to his friend as he sat uncomfortably at his father's former desk, missing the push and pull of the tides, wishing his older brother had lived to inherit his family's money and legacy instead of him.

"And I never asked to be born a slave, Jimmy," Jonathan had replied.

James never complained about his lot in life again.

Now he studied Arabella as the candlelight illuminated the curves of her impossibly beautiful face. "Would you like to learn how to play?" he asked, calling her attention back to the harp.

He tilted the instrument off of his shoulder, returning it to its standing position. Then he opened his legs, creating a space for her between his body and the harp, beckoning her over with a tap on his thigh and a nod of his chin.

She rose and glided over to him, hesitantly lowering herself onto his lap. The muscles of his leg tensed beneath her. The sweet, smoky scent of tobacco clung to his rain-dampened hair. He put his hands on her hips, shifting her so she faced the harp, letting his fingers linger a moment longer than was necessary. Then he found her hand, taking it in his and stretching it toward the top of the harp.

"Arch your fingers, and use them to pull the strings toward you," he said, coaxing them into the proper position. "Your thumb turns upward and plucks the strings away."

"But I don't know the notes," she protested, nervously pulling her hand from the strings. His breath was warm on the back of her neck, and she couldn't concentrate on what he was saying.

He moved her hand, gently but firmly, back toward the instrument. "The harp already holds all the notes you need. All you have to do is release them into the air."

He adjusted his fingers against her hip, and a warm, tingling sensation coursed through her body. "*Goiltai*, *Geantrai*, and *Suantrai*," he reminded her. "Laments, celebrations, and lullabies. All the songs in the universe are composed from these three melodies, but *you* are the only one who can play your tune. The notes you choose, the softness of your touch, the rhythm of your movement, the intention of your soul, these things make a song your own, even if its score has already been played a thousand times before."

"But—"

"Arabella," he said, elongating the syllables her name in mild frustration, "Just let the tune flow from your heart to the harp. You can't make a mistake."

As within, so without. Could it really be so simple? She pushed her thumb against a string and then pulled each finger toward her in succession, smiling at the tremble of the chords, delighted she had managed to make the harp sing, until one of the sharp strings pierced her index finger, and she cried out in pain. A dot of blood, hot and red, welled up from the scrape.

James stood them up, keeping one arm around her as he reached into his trouser pocket for his handkerchief. He turned her toward him and wrapped the silk cloth around her finger. "Are you all right?" he asked.

She nodded. The cut was small. It throbbed at the end of her finger.

"I should have warned you," he said with a comforting smile. "My fingers developed callouses long ago, but I remember how the strings used to bite." He lifted her chin, looking into her eyes. They were clear, no trace of fresh tears. The cut was uncomfortable, but it would cause no permanent damage.

He stroked the side of her face with one hand, squeezing the tip of her finger with the other to stem the bleeding. "Isn't it strange that a sound so beautiful must be pulled into the world through pain?" he whispered, his thumb hovering dangerously close to the edge of her full, pink lips.

She looked down at her finger, wrapped in his handkerchief, cradled in his hand. Her blood seeped through the fabric, staining the white silk, bringing the sordid events of the afternoon back to the center of her mind.

She pulled her hand away from him.

His handkerchief fluttered to the floor.

"What's wrong?" he asked, confused by the sudden, harsh glint in her eyes.

"You should be careful, James," she said, her voice as hard as stone. "You don't want my blood to mix with yours."

"What?"

"My *blood*," she repeated, angry with herself for being swept away by his stories, angry with her body for responding to his touch, angry that the solstice ritual which had brought them together was more powerful than her own better judgement. "You don't want my *bastard* blood to mix with yours," she said, taking a step backward from him.

The room began to spin around him, careening like a ship caught in a treacherous squall, and the color drained from his face as he realized she had overheard his conversation with William. There was nothing he could say to defend himself. He had no excuse for the callous things he had said about her. He had only wielded the words to hurt her father, and he had been too furious to realize the words might hurt her too.

"Arabella, I didn't mean—"

"You didn't mean to call me a *bastard*?" she asked, uninterested in hearing his half-hearted justification for his behavior. "Or you didn't mean for me to hear you call me a *bastard*?"

He recoiled at the sound of the offensive word in her mouth.

"Arabella—"

She turned toward the doorway, and he reached for her wrist, trying to pull her back to him.

"Let go of me!" He slackened his grip, but kept his hand circled around her arm until she pulled it away from him.

"Arabella, please," he said. "Don't judge me by words I only said in anger."

"Words are powerful things, James." A sheen of moisture coated her eyes, making them shimmer like shards of sea glass buried on a sandy shore. She wasn't sure why his insult had stung her so. "If a man's own words can't be used to take his measure, then what can?"

"A man's actions mean more than his words."

"His *actions*?" she asked, tilting her head in disbelief at his answer. "Like blocking a woman from leaving the room after she tells you she's tired and wants to go to bed? Like beating a helpless old man because he dares to visit his daughter without your permission?"

The night was spiraling out of his control. Why couldn't she understand? He regretted hurting her, but he could not, he would not, apologize for what he had said and done to William. Her father was far from a helpless old man, and she would be better off once she realized that.

"I didn't mean what I said about you." His voice was both thick with regret and laced with anger because she was refusing to let him explain. "And my words weren't meant for your ears." He lowered his chin, but kept his eyes locked on hers. "If you're tired and you want to go to bed, then you should go."

She glared at him.

She did not move.

"Now," he said, placing his hands in his pockets and stepping away from her. He should have known better than to let himself think of her as anything more than William Stafford's daughter. He should have left well enough alone and walked past the music room without talking to her. He wanted her to leave the room before his feelings for her grew any deeper than they already had. "You should go to bed. Now. I won't stop you."

She narrowed her eyes, angrier with his incomplete apology than she would have been had he offered no apology at all. She curtsied in mock submission to his will.

"With thy permission, then," she said, nodding to the book she had discarded on the end table.

She turned away from him before he could reply, withdrawing from the room like a wood-nymph, leaving his handkerchief, which had been stained crimson by her bastard blood, on the floor at his feet.

The rain continued through the long, sleepless night and into the next day, tattooing the roof of Alden House with marks the sky alone could see. James had left in the early hours of the morning to work in the shipyard, and Elinor, embarrassed by the scene her grandson had caused the day before, continued to offer her apologies to Arabella.

"If I had known there would be a row, I would never have placed you or your father in such an uncomfortable situation," she explained, rolling the edge of her shawl with nervous fingers. "I've spoken to James about it, and I believe, in time, I can make him see reason." The old woman sighed. "His animosity for William cannot last forever, and even if it does, he cannot allow it to come between a father and his daughter."

Arabella didn't blame Elinor for what had happened. If anything, she was even angrier with James for causing his grandmother so much pain. It would not be long before Elinor's illness progressed. She needed care and attention, not a senseless family feud. James was too selfish, too stubborn, and too egotistical to realize how little time his grandmother had left.

The rain lasted for three days. It fell from the hazy, grey skies, bouncing up from the cobblestones and flooding the garden paths with rivers of thick, wet mud. One evening, after Elinor had retired to her bedroom, Arabella sat alone by the open parlor window, watching the last of the storm clouds dissolve into heavy bands of mist. A lamplighter made his way down Greenman Avenue, touching his flame to the whale-oil soaked wicks of each street lamp, creating streams of glowing light beneath the somber sky.

The grandfather clock in the hall chimed. In the silence that followed, Arabella heard a ghostly tune, sad and slow. She thought James must have returned home and slipped into the music room to play a lament on his mother's harp, and she stood up, searching the darkness that had fallen around her. She peered into the cavernous hallway.

"James?" she whispered.

Hearing no response, she called out again.

"Elinor? Is anyone there?"

The house fell silent. Arabella listened to the ticking of the clock, trying to distinguish its rhythm from the quickened pace of her own heart. She had just sighed in relief, thinking she must have imagined the song, when it began again, soft as a lullaby, its notes halfway between moaning and humming.

She turned back toward the open window, wondering if the lamplighter was whistling while he worked, but he was already far past the house, heading toward the shipyard offices.

Her eyes fell to the rose bushes lining the front gate. The pink blossoms, heavy with rain, tipped themselves toward the ground, a congregation of dewy flowers bowed in solemn prayer. Mary used to sing to her roses, and James believed the river had carried his mother's lullabies out to sea. Was Arabella hearing a spectral melody that had been imprinted in the garden? Or had Mary's song circumnavigated the globe and been returned to its point of origin by the tides pushing in from Fishers Island Sound?

She glanced at the oil portrait over the mantle, trying not to think about James' piercing blue eyes, which were the exact shade of his mother's. She knew art sometimes captured a human's essence, allowing a spirit to forge pathways between the worlds, and she wondered if the cherished painting commissioned by George Alden was acting as some sort of ghostly portal. She reached up and slid her fingers over the thick brushstrokes of Mary's dark, luminous hair. A soft, feminine presence settled over the room, but the veil remained solid.

It was not Mary's song she was hearing.

It was something else.

She stepped into the empty hallway, a shiver running down her spine. Elinor, who always worried about James returning home to a dark house, had left several candles burning on the entryway table. Their flames flickered, throwing wild streaks of light up the long, curving staircase. Arabella lifted one of the silver candelabras, grasping its heavy base with both hands. She spun slowly around the cavernous space, directing the warm light toward the sewing room, the music room, the dining room, the library.

"James?" she whispered again. "Elinor?"

A haunting tune was the only answer. It unfolded in fits and starts, its notes high and then low, sorrowful and then soothing. She held her breath and listened.

It was coming from the west wing.

She glanced over her shoulder, remembering James' edict that no one was to enter his office without his permission. She kicked off her slippers and crept down the center hall. The floorboards creaked, but the Persian carpets, soft and thick beneath her bare feet, swallowed the sounds of her footsteps.

She entered the kitchen, pausing in front of the hook which held a ring of iron keys. James and Elinor had never mentioned the keys to her, and she had never seen anyone use them, but she assumed one of them must open the office door. She balanced the heavy candelabra in one hand while she lifted the keys in the other. They were cool to the touch, with elaborate, rounded bows and long, smooth barrels. One key tingled, ever so slightly, on the tips of her fingers, and she grasped it tightly as she continued down the west wing hall.

"Is anyone there?" she asked when she had made her way to the end of the long, dark corridor. James' deep baritone echoed in her mind. *Don't open the door, Miss Porter. There'll be no end to my anger if you do.*

She placed her hand on the raised panels of the door, her heart throbbing in fearful anticipation. She fancied she could feel the wood breathing beneath her fingers. What would she find if she opened it? Would James be there, waiting to accuse her of trespassing, threatening to throw her out of his house for violating his interdiction?

She watched the candelabra's light cast ominous shadows over the wood's swirling grain. Perhaps she should retreat upstairs and lose herself in the pages of a novel or a fairy tale. Perhaps she should pretend she had never heard the ghostly tune. But, what if her father was right? What if James *was* a thief, keeping a hoard of smuggled goods in his office? What if someone was trapped behind the door, calling out for help?

She slid the key she had chosen into the iron keyhole, feeling its teeth click into place against the lock's open grooves. She paused, listening.

Then she turned the key and pushed open the door.

A gust of damp night air blew her cotton nightgown against her body, raising gooseflesh along her spine. The office window was open. White curtains billowed into the room like ghosts. A thick hedge of rosebushes clustered innocently beneath the casement, their heady blossoms fat and dewy in the humid evening breeze. The hum of night insects mingled with the endless babble of the Mystic River, but the room itself was strangely quiet, the haunting song replaced with silence.

James' office smelled of tobacco and sandalwood, a warm, earthy scent. Jade figures, ivory statues, and primitive ornaments lined the shelves on the wall, souvenirs from his travels around the globe. A pair of deep leather sofas flanked a table littered with nautical charts and forest maps. A mahogany mantle graced the far wall. Above it was an oil portrait of a fully-rigged ship sailing through stormy seas. A painted moon cast its silver light onto the crests of the waves below.

Arabella tiptoed cautiously around the perimeter of the room, thrusting her candelabra into each dark corner. She found a pile of scrimshaw on a small table and picked up an egg-shaped piece, a tooth, she realized with a shiver. She ran her thumb across its smooth surface, tracing an elaborately carved mermaid. She wondered if James had crafted the intricate design. She wondered if he had killed the whale whose tooth she held in her hand.

She put the scrimshaw down on the table and moved toward a large desk set beneath the open window. A blue leather book with a gilded ship on its cover rested on top of more maps and charts. She traced the golden letters of the title with the tip of her finger. *The Odyssey.* She opened it to a page marked by a satin ribbon that had been sewn into the binding. She leaned closer, trying to read the words.

Without warning, the wind buffeted, sucking the white curtains out toward the lawn. The window rattled as the heavy front door of Alden House slammed shut. The candelabra slipped from Arabella's hands. Hot wax splattered, almost igniting the piles of papers on the desk, and she frantically blew on the wicks, extinguishing their beads of light and plunging herself into pitch-black darkness.

There was nowhere for her to hide. If James came down the west wing corridor instead of heading straight up the stairs, he would find her trespassing in his private space, wearing nothing but her nightgown. She wasn't sorry for what she had done. The strange sounds she had heard coupled with her father's accusations about James' thievery were more than enough to justify her intrusion, but she would rather defend herself by the light of day, fully clothed, with Elinor by her side.

She darted toward the place where she thought the door was located, banging her leg against the sharp corner of the table, scattering the maps and charts. There was no time to cry out in pain, no chance to put everything back in its proper place; there was only the staccato beat of her heart pressing her forward in terror.

She found the door and stumbled down the hallway, ducking into the large pantry at the far end of the kitchen. She sank against the wall, hiding among sacks of flour and sugar, willing her heartbeat to settle.

Heavy footsteps echoed down the center hall. They came to a halt at the kitchen entrance.

She could feel him there, lingering on the threshold; she could see the light from his lantern glowing in the crack between the floor and the pantry door. She held her breath, trying not to move, wishing she had her healer's cloak to protect her from his sight.

After what felt like an excruciatingly long time, the footsteps continued down the west wing corridor. Arabella listened until she heard the office door open and close. Then she flew out of the pantry, ran through the kitchen, down the hall, and up the stairs to her bedroom where she crawled beneath the safety of her covers.

When she awoke the next morning, the slippers she had discarded in the entryway were in their usual place at the foot of her bed, and the blue leather book she had found in James' office was open on her night table, its pages stained with three large drops of hard, crusty wax.

"You went into her *bedroom*?"

"*She* went into my office."

"Jimmy," Jonathan's voice was deadly serious amid the din of the crowded Spouter Tavern, "tell me you understand that her going into your office when you're not home and you going into her bedroom while she's sleeping are two *entirely* different things."

James looked away from him and Jonathan reached across the table, shoving him hard enough to knock the whiskey glass out of his hand. It fell to the floor and smashed into pieces.

"Oi!" Mrs. O'Shaughnessy thumped her shillelagh on the top of the bar.

Jonathan raised both hands in quick apology but kept his eyes locked on the scowling James. "Sorry, Mrs. O'Shaughnessy," he sang out cordially to the old woman without turning around to look at her. "We'll pay for the glass, and it won't happen again."

Mrs. O'Shaughnessy shook her head indulgently. James and Jonathan were two of her best customers, but it wouldn't help the Spouter Tavern's reputation if she allowed them to act like beasts.

James scowled at Jonathan, grabbing the glass from his hand and downing what was left before refilling it and placing it in the middle of the table where they could both reach it. "I told her the night she began her service that she was *not* allowed in my office," he said. "You know what could have happened if she found something."

"Yes," Jonathan said with more than an edge of sarcastic annoyance, "I know what could have happened if she found something. And I also know you and I are going to have a long talk about how we remedy this situation before I bring any more cargo into your shipyard."

"Your cargo was delivered without issue, Jonathan," James countered.

"Yes, but then after the delivery *you* decided to play some kind of cat and mouse game with William Stafford's daughter."

"I'm not playing a game," James said, his voice rising, his fists clenching. He hated being treated like a child. "I put the book in her bedroom so she would know what it feels like to have *her* private space violated."

"And you think that little lesson is going to stop her from sticking her nose in our business?" He wanted to pin James against the wall and squeeze the breath from his throat. "You're not thinking clearly."

"Your cargo was delivered without issue, Jonathan," James repeated, louder than before. He took another swig of whiskey from the glass and slammed it back down on the table. "I know having her in my house complicates things, but I told you, I'll handle it. You have no right to question my commitment to our business."

Jonathan leaned back in his chair, angrily pulling a coin from his pocket. He rolled it over his knuckles, a practice he had mastered during long, uneventful watches on board the *Shepherd*. It helped him think, and with James' mind so clouded by thoughts of Arabella, Jonathan needed to think for both of them. His friend was walking a dangerous line, one that could threaten their entire operation.

"All right, Jimmy," he half conceded, "but I've listened to you talk about this girl long enough. I want to meet her before you and I set the terms for our next delivery."

He tossed the coin and a handful of bank notes on the table to pay for the whiskey and the broken glass.

"Tell your grandmother to expect me for dinner."

The next evening, Elinor sat at her dressing table, preparing herself for Captain Burrows' visit. There had been a time when Alden House had been host to New England's most coveted social gatherings. Elinor and her husband had planned elaborate dinners and parties for statesmen and politicians, and when George and Mary had taken their turn at the helm, high society guests had been known to sing and dance among the roses until daybreak. But now, after all the loss the family had suffered, even their recent use of the dining room for occasional dinners seemed stilted and new.

Elinor clasped a golden chain hung with charms of gleaming jet at the back of her neck. She surveyed her appearance in the looking glass. She sighed, wondering exactly when she had become so old. It had been more than a year since she had seen Captain Burrows, and she knew his alert mind would notice the changes to her appearance that her own grandson failed to see.

It was certainly strange each time Jonathan, a Black man and a former slave, joined them for dinner. Everyone in Mystic knew of the childhood friendship between James and Jonathan, but a formal dinner always raised eyebrows. Her son George had been a staunch supporter of abolition, but Elinor had lived a sheltered life, and her entire social circle had been confined to well-to-do families with skin as white as her own. There had been a time she had thought it distasteful that her son allowed James to spend so much time with the Burrows' boy, a decision he must have regretted when the two of them ran off to sea to join a whaling crew. They were halfway around the world when George had finally discovered the name of their ship, and Elinor had begged her son to pursue the *Shepherd* with the full force of the law, hauling the fourteen-year old James back home and returning his conspirator to the Burrows family where he belonged. George had refused, saying Jonathan had already endured eighteen years of slavery, and the Aldens would not be responsible for condemning him to the harsh punishment doled out for desertion. As for James, he had made a man's choice, and he would have to live with the consequences of it.

Elinor had blamed the Burrows' boy for James' rebellion against his father, a rebellion which had continued, in some form or another, each time James returned home on furlough from sea, but, after George and Thomas had died, It had been the Burrows' boy, by then a captain commanding the *Nymph*, who had received Elinor's desperate letter and escorted her grandson back home to her. In the terrible weeks of pain and grief that followed, Captain Burrows had been a voice of comfort and reason, guiding James like an older brother. He had helped him to sort out the shipyard's complicated finances and convinced him to stay home in Mystic. More than that, he had tenderly lifted the Aldens from the depths of their sorrow with his kindness, compassion, and good humor.

There had been an uproar when James had hired Jonathan to sail his shipments of lumber and supplies up and down the eastern seaboard. It was one thing for the elite of Mystic to support abolition and another thing to treat a Black man, free or not, as an equal, but James, by far the most radical of the Alden men, didn't care what anyone said. Elinor supposed it had been William's objection to Jonathan's prominent new position that had forced James to dismiss him from the company and their home, and though she had lamented the loss of William's companionship, there was nothing more important to her than keeping James at home.

She would never be anything but grateful to Captain Jonathan Burrows.

She unfolded the invitation she had received by messenger earlier that day, holding it up to the gas lamp on her dressing table. The thick, white parchment was inscribed with gilded ink.

Mr. William Stafford requests the pleasure of
Mr. James Alden's, Mrs. Elinor Alden's and Miss Arabella Porter's company
at the marriage of his daughter
Friday, August 1st at 6 o'clock
271 Spring Hill Lane

The invitation couldn't have come at a more opportune time. She would approach the topic, which was sure to cause a stir, during their formal dinner tonight. Jonathan exerted a calming influence on her grandson, and James was less likely to act out in his former captain's presence, no matter how upset he might be by William's invitation.

Of course, as far as Elinor was concerned, there was no room for discussion. There had not been a fashionable wedding in Mystic without the Alden Family on the guest list for decades, and, as the current guardians of the bride's younger sister, both she and James would be expected to attend. The Aldens' support of Arabella would go a long way toward settling the illegitimate girl's tenuous position in the social order, and publicly welcoming Anne's half-sister at the wedding was a smart move for everyone involved. Even William knew that, judging by the invitation. All Elinor had to do was convince her grandson to be reasonable.

She took a final glance at her visage in the mirror, pinching her cheeks one last time to add a flush of color to her sallow skin. It seemed only yesterday she had been the blooming bride, her older sister pinning her veil into her upswept hair. She sighed again, pushing herself up with the jeweled knob of her cane before heading downstairs to greet her guest.

V

"Mrs. Alden," Jonathan sang out, removing his hat and bowing low to his hostess as he entered the house, "it's been far too long."

Elinor offered her hand, and Jonathan brought it to his lips, winking as he delivered a courteous kiss. He tilted his chin toward James, tossing his hat and jacket to him in greeting.

"May I introduce Captain Jonathan Burrows," Elinor said, guiding her nurse forward. "Jonathan, this is Miss Arabella Porter."

"Miss Porter." Jonathan bowed his head. "I'm delighted to make your acquaintance. I've heard much about you. May I call you Arabella? It's a beautiful name for a beautiful woman."

She smiled and nodded, wondering exactly what Jonathan had heard. She had been worried about meeting the man Elinor had described as James' oldest childhood friend, and she was taken aback by his quick wit and gracious manners. She had expected him to be surly and taciturn like James.

"And, of course, you must call me Jonathan," the captain added, sweeping Arabella down the hallway and into the dining room, showing an easy familiarity with each passageway and corridor.

"I'm told you're a healer," he said as they sat down to steaming bowls of Windsor soup. He picked up the spoon that had been set before him, an inked turtle shell visible on the back of his hand. "I trust Mrs. Alden is doing well under your care?"

"I've never felt better, Jonathan," Elinor interjected, taking the opportunity to place her newly-delivered wedding invitation in the center of the table. "And just in time, too. In two short weeks our family will be celebrating the nuptials of Miss Anne Stafford and Mr. Alan Newbury."

An awkward hush fell over the room.

James looked down at the invitation. Jonathan looked at James. Arabella looked at Elinor, surprised she had decided to broach the topic before the main course had been served. She had been present when the messenger had delivered the invitation into Elinor's hands, but she had little hope James would allow her to attend.

"Why would my father invite James to Anne's wedding?" she had asked Elinor shortly after the messenger departed. "They hate each other." On the Isle of Skye, weddings were intimate affairs, and invitations were reserved for family and friends who wished the young couple well.

"Social etiquette dictates it," Elinor had replied with pride, "just as it dictates our attendance, no matter what my grandson says." She had treated Arabella to a cautiously optimistic smile. "Anne is your sister," she added as though that fact settled everything. 'Let *me* handle James."

Arabella had returned Elinor's smile with a doubtful shake of her head. The last time Elinor had tried to *handle* James it had ended with a brawl in the parlor, and that was *before* Arabella had entered his office without permission. She wondered how her father had managed to raise the money for Anne's dowry and wedding so quickly. When she had agreed to work for the Aldens to pay down William's debt, he had seemed on the brink of economic disaster. If he had reestablished his financial security, why hadn't he offered to settle his debt with James when he had visited Alden House only a few days ago? Arabella had developed a keen affection for Elinor and wouldn't dream of abandoning her post, but she wished she could carry out her duties from a place of financial and social independence.

Now Elinor gestured to the invitation, breaking the stilted silence of the dining room.

"Anne has waited a long time to become a bride," she said, "and her reception will be the event of the summer."

James surveyed his grandmother, raising his glass and taking a long, slow drink.

"You grew up with both Anne and Alan," Elinor prodded. "I'm sure you'll want to offer them your best wishes on their new life together."

"And I'm sure you can offer my best wishes for me, grandmother," he said, "since you're clearly so determined to attend the ceremony."

"Arabella and I are *both* determined to attend."

Another awkward hush. James reddened under the weight of everyone's gaze. They were all looking at him, all expecting him to cause a scene, as though he was the one who was unreasonable, but he wasn't as ignorant of social etiquette as the three of them liked to believe.

James had known the invitation would arrive eventually. He knew, even now, that he could not forbid Arabella from attending her own sister's wedding. Whispers about William Stafford's illegitimate daughter had already begun to stir, and keeping Arabella away from the public celebration would only fan the flames. It would be best for her to make her society debut on his grandmother's arm. The Alden name wielded enormous influence among the wealthy of Mystic, and Elinor's choice to attend a high-profile event with William Stafford's illegitimate daughter in tow would stop the tongues of many who might otherwise disparage Arabella's character. Still, William was the host of the wedding, and he would no doubt use the opportunity to interrogate his youngest daughter, which might make things difficult for Jonathan and James.

James finished the whiskey in his glass. Then, seeing no other way to acknowledge his grandmother's announcement than with his acquiescence to her will, he spoke.

"Very well."

"Very well?" Elinor echoed. "I would think you'd have more to say than that, James."

He ran his finger around the top of his glass, making it sing, a childhood habit that had always annoyed his proper grandmother. If he had contradicted her and forbidden them from attending, she would have admonished him for being contrary, but now, having readily agreed to what she wished, she challenged him for not being amenable enough. He let out a frustrated sigh.

"What is it you require me to say, grandmother?"

"I require you to say, no, I require you to *promise*, that you will do nothing to prevent Arabella from attending her sister's wedding, and, if you choose to attend, as you *should*, you will do nothing to irritate Mr. Stafford or to cause a scene like the one that recently took place in our parlor."

"William is the one who caused the scene in our parlor."

"James—"

"I have no objection to Arabella attending her sister's wedding under your supervision," he interrupted, not wanting to listen to another of his grandmother's lectures, "and I'll do nothing to disrupt the celebrations, so long as she agrees to have no contact with her family once the reception ends."

He turned to Arabella, inviting her to respond, but she only stared at him. She certainly wasn't going to thank him for one evening of supervised freedom.

Unsatisfied with her silence, he provoked her with a question.

"Tell me, Arabella, how are you enjoying *The Odyssey*?"

Her hand froze in midair, her spoon hanging above the soup in her bowl.

She had been livid when she had found his book on her night table, furious when she realized he had entered her room while she slept. She couldn't tell Elinor what he had done without admitting to her own transgression, which, she realized, was exactly what he wanted, so she had said nothing, taking care to slide a heavy dressing table in front of her door before she went to sleep each night. She had hoped he would at least have the decency not to begin an argument about what had happened in front of his grandmother and a dinner guest.

The captain shot him a warning look across the table, but James ignored it. Jonathan was the one who had insisted on coming to dinner. Let him see for himself how headstrong and unmanageable William Stafford's daughter could be.

"My favorite part of *The Odyssey*," James said after his question had hung in the air unanswered for an uncomfortable amount of time, "is when Aeolis, the god of the winds, ties the wayward breezes in a bag and gifts them to Odysseus so he can guide his ship directly home to Ithaca. I'm afraid that passage may have been difficult for you to read. Someone spilled wax on the page."

He stifled a grunt, and Arabella had the fleeting impression that Jonathan had kicked him under the table.

She had been too upset with James to read the book he had left in her room, but she was familiar enough with the tale to know he was trying to provoke her. Odysseus had ordered his men not to open Aeolis' bag, and, fearing their captain was keeping a secret hoard of riches for himself, they had disobeyed his order, releasing hurricane force winds which blew them back out to sea. She was not going to give James the satisfaction of rising to or shrinking from his veiled accusation about her entry into his forbidden office. She may have violated his private space, but he had done the same to her, and he was in no position to pass judgement.

"I read *The Odyssey* when I was a child, James," she said, meeting his gaze directly and telling him about the wealthy laird who had allowed her to borrow books from his library in return for access to the Porter women's healing elixirs. "The scene you speak of is a tragic one. The trouble could have been easily avoided if Odysseus had trusted his men enough to tell them what was inside the bag."

"So, you blame *Odysseus* for his men's transgressions?" He leaned forward in his seat, shaking his head. "Their captain gave them a direct order and *they* failed to follow it."

"Why should they follow his orders?" She let her spoon fall into her bowl to emphasize her point. "He was hiding valuable information from them. He was *always* hiding valuable information from them, like the time he forced his crew to plug their ears with wax so he alone could hear the sirens' song."

Arabella had seen a painting of Odysseus, lashed to the mast, driven mad by the heart-wrenching song of the sirens as it mixed with the rush and flow of the churning seas.

"Odysseus had his men plug their ears with wax to *protect* them from the sirens' song," James countered angrily. "If the crew had heard the music, they would have run the ship aground in rough seas. They all would have died."

"All but Odysseus died before reaching Ithaca, anyway," she pointed out, "and if the sirens' song was so dangerous, why didn't he plug his own ears with wax? Why would he risk his own life, and the lives of his entire crew, just so he could listen to a song?"

James' mouth was open, ready to continue the argument, but her last question stopped him mid-breath. On the night he had first seen Arabella in the woods, her dress clinging to her wet skin, her wild hair feathered around her face, he had believed she might be a siren, a temptress, a deadly *leannan sidhe* lying in wait to steal his soul. He could have walked away from her. He could have turned her out of his house and insisted his grandmother find a new nurse. But even now, even knowing the threat her presence caused to the work he and Jonathan were doing, he did not regret plucking her wreath from the river. He did not regret letting her into his home and into his life.

When he spoke, his voice was as soft as it had been the night they sailed down the river.

"Some songs are worth hearing, no matter the cost."

Jonathan watched the two of them, his dark eyes darting back and forth as they volleyed, his nimble fingers rolling a coin over the knuckles of his hand. It had been more than a decade since James and Jonathan had boarded the *Shepherd*, and Jonathan prided himself on knowing his friend, his brother, better than anyone else. He had taught James how to throw a harpoon and how to seduce a woman. He had sailed by his side and later commanded him at sea. He had protected him during barroom brawls and sheltered him as he mourned the loss of his entire family. He had even saved James' life on more than one occasion, but he had never seen his friend in as perilous a position as he was tonight, stripped of all reason by his desire for a beautiful woman.

"And if Penelope wanted to hear the sirens' song?" Arabella asked James, refusing to let the argument go even though James had pulled back from his pursuit. "Would you have the same admiration for her as you do for Odysseus?"

James had read *The Odyssey* countless times and had never once considered how Penelope, Odysseus' wife, might react if she had been afforded the same opportunities as her husband. Penelope had never been anything more than a background character to him, a reward for the struggles Odysseus had endured. He tapped his fingers on the table thoughtfully.

"I would have great admiration for Penelope if she wanted to hear the sirens' song."

It was Elinor who answered, her voice pulling James and Arabella from a conversation that had become so intimate they had forgotten two other people were in the room. "But, life cannot be sustained by siren songs alone." The old woman raised her glass, bidding the others to do the same. "Let's enjoy our soup before it gets cold."

She turned her attention to Jonathan, entertaining him with a story about an extravagant wedding she had attended in her youth. He responded with a raucous tale of an island celebration that had resulted in seven marital unions before the night was over.

"Will you attend my sister's wedding ceremony?" Arabella asked Jonathan. She knew he was James' oldest friend, so she assumed he had grown up with Anne and Alan as well.

Jonathan squinted at her as though she was a puzzle that needed solving.

"No," he said.

When the meal was finished, Elinor announced her intention to retire, apologizing for her weakened state and assuring Jonathan she would be all the better tomorrow morning because of the joy he had brought her tonight. Both men stood in polite deference as the old woman took her leave, but when Arabella tried to follow in her wake, Jonathan, still wanting to know more about the girl who had whipped his friend into such an emotional frenzy, gently stopped her.

"The night is young, Arabella." He took her by the hand. "Let's continue our visit in the parlor.

"So," Jonathan said with a charming smile, "you hail from Scotland?"

The oil sconces on the parlor walls had been turned up to flood the room with light. Jonathan relaxed in a chair by the open window opposite the couch where James and Arabella sat. He puffed on a pipe that released the sweet, cherry scent of tobacco into the room. The storms that had been ravaging Mystic for days had finally cleared, and the damp night air buzzed with mosquitoes. Midsummer fireflies winked in the bushes.

"I was born on the Isle of Skye, a small island off the north-west coast of Scotland."

Jonathan's dark eyes twinkled. "Well, that must be why you get on so well with Jimmy," he said. "I hear the Scots are half as drunk and twice as stubborn as the Irish."

James threw him a menacing look, but Arabella could not help laughing at the off-color quip, which Jonathan had delivered with a light, humorous tone. The air in Alden House seemed less oppressive with Jonathan in it, and she suspected the captain often used jokes to keep his friend in check.

"I wasn't born in Ireland," James reminded Jonathan, trying not to stare at the upward curl of Arabella's lip when she smiled. "My mother was."

"And yet, you have inherited her Irish temper, Jimmy." Jonathan laughed, unable to resist teasing his friend. "Look, Arabella. His jaw already begins to clench."

"Jimmy?" Arabella turned to James. "Do your friends call you Jimmy?" she asked.

"No."

"I'm afraid I'm the only one allowed to call him Jimmy on account of a very poor wager he made while we were sailing the Indian Ocean," Jonathan explained, laughing heartily.

"And we're *not* discussing the terms of that wager tonight," James growled. Jonathan laughed louder, but leaned back in his chair, blowing a ring of smoke out the window.

"I won't say another word about it," he said, winking at Arabella. "I know exactly how far I can push my limits with him before he gets truly angry."

"What kind of name is Burrows?" Arabella asked innocently, wondering what country Jonathan's ancestors had come from.

The light in Jonathan's eyes dimmed for a moment. "Burrows is the name of the man who owned me," he said. "My dark skin does not come from the sun and sea alone. I am of mixed race, though the details of my genealogy are difficult to trace."

Arabella bit her lower lip, worried she might have said something to offend him. "I didn't think slavery was legal in this part of the country."

Jonathan brought his pipe back to his mouth, so James took it upon himself to explain. "When the State of Connecticut outlawed slavery, it provided for gradual emancipation," he said. "The law was amended in 1797 to grant children born to enslaved women full freedom at the age of twenty-one."

"My mother was born into transitional bondage to the Burrows family," Jonathan added, "and, since she gave birth to me while still under that contract, I was born into transitional bondage as well. I was eighteen when Jimmy and I ran off to sea, and there are some who say we should be grateful the law didn't pursue us, since being an escaped slave and harboring an escaped slave, even in a free state or on the open ocean, are serious crimes, but I extend no gratitude to men who turn a blind eye to the evils of slavery, however fair or reasonable those men believe themselves to be."

He puffed his pipe. Its bowl glowed dark red.

"In fact," he continued, "there are some who say I owe Mr. Burrows three years of labor to make up for my desertion, but they're wrong." All traces of mirth disappeared from his voice. "I owe Mr. Burrows nothing."

His phrasing sounded oddly familiar, though Arabella couldn't place where she had heard the words before. "Why do you keep the Burrows' name?" she asked. She did not understand why a free man would continue to use the name of a family that had enslaved him.

Jonathan shrugged his shoulders. "It's only a name," he said, his smile returning. "After four years trapped onboard the *Shepherd*, listening to our captain address me as *Mr. Burrows*," he bellowed in a practiced imitation of the captain that made James laugh, "I couldn't imagine being called anything else."

"You sailed for *four* years before returning to Connecticut?" Arabella's journey across the Atlantic had taken almost two months, and she would not have wanted to be adrift for even one day more.

"Our first trip aboard the *Shepherd* lasted four years," Jonathan said. "And, by the time we returned to New London, Jimmy and I owed so much money to the ship we had no choice but to go back out on another three-and-a-half year voyage a few weeks later." He paused, looking thoughtful. "Well, I had no choice. Mr. Alden would have happily paid any price to keep his youngest son safe and dry on land."

It had been one of many tumultuous battles between father and son, one that had lasted the entirety of James' first shore leave. George had offered to cover the costs his son had accrued on the voyage in return for the *Shepherd* releasing him from all future duties, and the captain of the ship, a reasonable man who had children of his own, and who had not realized when he had first departed that the boy who was to become his best harpooner was a fourteen-year-old run away from a well-to-do family, had readily agreed, advising James to take full advantage of the opportunities his family's wealth and affection afforded him. James had stubbornly refused to listen, rejecting his father's money and returning to sea.

"Why wouldn't you let your father help you?" Arabella asked. She had grown up in a family of women who worked together, each taking on extra duties or submitting themselves to assistance without question and according to need.

He looked at her for a long moment. The lines of his jaw grew tight.

"It was my debt," he said. "It wasn't my father's responsibility to pay it."

"At least Jimmy and I boarded the ship willingly," Jonathan said, deftly steering the conversation toward an entertaining story about crimping tavern owners who drugged unsuspecting patrons and dumped them, beaten and blindfolded, onto whaling ships setting out on voyages. "Imagine the poor fools who had to come to terms with the fact that, through no choice of their own, they'd see nothing but salt water and whale blood for the next four years." He laughed as though drugging a man and shipping him out to sea was part of a long-standing joke.

"It all sounds so lawless," she said, trying to imagine a world of kidnapping and killing on the open ocean.

Jonathan shrugged. "The ocean is a lawless place, but when the laws of the land have been written to hold a man back, lawlessness has its appeal." His sly smile returned. "Now, why our Jimmy, who stood to inherit a fortune on land, chose a life of toil and danger on the high seas is another conversation entirely."

He puffed on his pipe again, pointing at James as he continued.

"I've seen this man stare down a tempest without shaking, and I've never met anyone, not even the Native Wampanoag, who can hurl a harpoon like he can. He was just under sixteen years old when he hit his first mark in choppy seas, but instead of reveling in the accolades like any respectable harpooner would, he felt guilty about killing the whale."

"That's enough, Jonathan," James said, the color rising on his cheeks.

But Jonathan was just getting started.

"It was almost six months before we spotted another whale, and we dropped our long boats to give chase. We had pulled up right alongside a monstrous beast, she had to be forty feet long, floating on eerily calm waters. It was an easy shot, but Jimmy stood up and threw his iron into the ocean on the opposite side of our boat." He shook his head, chuckling at the memory, curious to see exactly how much his friend was willing to reveal to William Stafford's daughter. "If you want to hear a good sea yarn, Arabella, ask him what happened after that."

"What happened after that?" she asked, looking expectantly at James.

James had never shared the story of that day with anyone. The sea had been clear and blue, a humpback whale lolling in gentle swells as the open boat pulled alongside. She did not try to flee or turn and attack as the sperm whale he had killed had done, and when James had stood, poised to strike her with his iron, he had seen her calf, still young enough to nurse, swimming in the deep, still waters beneath her.

Even now, after so many years had passed, he did not regret his decision to spare her life, but he had been wholly unprepared for the fury of his captain, who had lunged at James, wrestling him backward to the bottom of the small boat, tying his hands with ropes and hauling him back to the ship where he had been strung up, mercilessly flogged for insubordination, and left hanging shirtless on the deck through the night, an object of scorn and derision. The veteran sailors, who had never seen their God-fearing captain so angry before that day, had closed their eyes as the thwack of the whip wrote angry red stripes onto James' back and shoulders. Jonathan alone had watched each lash fall, flinching as the knotted leather raised welts across his friend's tender flesh, refusing to look away even when the sight of blood had turned his stomach. He had stayed with James through the long, painful night, defending him against retribution from a few surly crew members who blamed him for turning the captain's mood so foul. It had not been until weeks later, after another whale had been spotted and James, under the stern direction of his captain, had obediently felled her with his iron, that his crime against the *Shepherd* had been fully forgiven.

Arabella's green eyes stared up at him, waiting for him to tell his story, but he only shook his head. "Let's just say I never missed my mark again."

A scuffle on the front porch drew their attention and James threw himself in front of Arabella, covering her with his body as shards of glass flew across the parlor. A large stone, bound with blood-stained paper, had been hurled through the window. It rolled to a stop in the middle of the room.

"Is anyone hurt?" James asked, his arm still thrown protectively over Arabella.

"I'm fine." Jonathan had ducked to the floor a half-second before the glass shattered, narrowly avoiding a direct hit from the stone. He stood, his hand reaching for the pistol at his waist. James grabbed a pistol from the side table drawer.

"Stay here," he commanded as he ran outside into the dark heat of the night. Jonathan moved toward Arabella, ushering her toward the interior of the house.

"Shouldn't you follow him?" she asked, resisting his gentle direction. "What if James needs your help?"

"He told us to stay here, and that's what we're going to do." Jonathan's voice was calm. "Jimmy knows how to take care of himself."

He tucked his pistol into the waist of his trousers and steered Arabella into the hallway. "Let's move away from the window."

VII

Jonathan guided Arabella all the way to the library, a room with tall shelves lining the walls and only two small windows hung in deep alcoves above cushioned seats. He cracked them open, listening intently before pulling the velvet curtains shut so no one could look in from outside. The thick fabric muffled the sounds of distant shouting and commotion.

"What happened?" Arabella asked, still stunned by the loud scream of breaking glass. "Did someone throw a stone through the window?"

"It appears so."

"But why?"

"That remains to be seen."

The room was dark, but Jonathan made no move to ignite the gas lamps, and it took a few minutes before Arabella's eyes adjusted to the dim light. Jonathan perched casually on the arm of a tufted sofa, angled so he could see both windows and the door to the hallway, his weight centered at his feet like a large jungle cat ready to pounce at a moment's notice. His expression was placid, his demeanor relaxed, but the lines of his body were tense, his senses heightened. The perfume of the roses outside the windows mingled with the musky scent of wet, burning wood.

"So," Jonathan said after a prolonged period of silence in which he had been regarding Arabella closely, "you're William Stafford's daughter."

"I am."

"Jimmy tells me your father recently stopped by for a visit."

He was watching her with his practiced concentration, his head tilted slightly to the left. His tone was polite, but it had lost all its warmth. She had the distinct feeling he was doing more than making casual conversation.

"Do you hate my father as much as James does?" she asked. She was tired of playing polite games.

"There's a long and complicated history between the Aldens and the Staffords," he said.

"So I've been told."

He smiled, an attempt to convey he meant no harm, but the frivolity that had permeated the earlier part of the evening had vanished. She supposed Jonathan's uncanny ability to provoke fear with nothing but a tilt of his head served him well when he commanded ships full of men at sea, but she found his mercurial temper disconcerting.

He leaned closer to her, flashing a small smile. "Did you and your father get to spend much time alone together before James came home and interrupted your visit?"

James and Jonathan had clearly discussed the details of what had happened that afternoon, which meant the captain knew more about the Stafford-Alden feud than he was letting on.

"Elinor was with us," she answered defensively. "She invited my father for tea."

"Mrs. Alden is a kind and generous woman. What did the three of you talk about?"

"Nothing of note. The weather, the tides, the boats sailing on the river. I think he mentioned your ship, *Polaris*."

"Did he now?" Jonathan stilled, his voice growing deadly quiet. "And have you seen your father since then? Have you spoken with him today?"

"Why are you asking me these questions, Jonathan?"

He held her gaze, unblinking. "Just trying to pass the time. It's not often I converse with beautiful women. In fact, I'm shipping out again soon, and I won't be back with new cargo until the end of September. The thirtieth, to be exact. An easy date to remember."

The front door creaked open. Jonathan jumped to his feet, his hand only moving away from the pistol at his waist when he saw his friend enter the library. James was disheveled, his dinner jacket discarded, his white shirt torn and scorched. He held the paper-wrapped stone that had been hurled through the parlor window in his hand.

"Did you see anyone?" Jonathan asked, gripping his friend by the shoulders and scanning his body for injuries.

"I didn't see any faces." His eyes were red rimmed and he coughed uncontrollably for a minute before settling his lungs with a deep breath. "The window was a distraction. They set fire to the storehouse that holds your timber. It was sheer luck I circled back that way." He coughed again, trying to clear his throat of smoke and ash.

"Is the blaze contained?"

"I wouldn't be here if the blaze wasn't contained, Jonathan." A shipyard fire was a threat to the lives and livelihoods of all the men who worked there. The flames could leap between the close-packed buildings, igniting the kegs of flammable whale oil stored in the sheds. "I rang the alarm and the boys in the boarding house brought buckets and pumps. It was the storm that saved us. Everything was still damp from the rain, so the structure didn't burn, but your entire shipment is charred beyond repair." He swallowed painfully. "I posted guards to keep watch through the night."

His report concluded, he handed the stone to Jonathan and turned toward Arabella, running his blackened hands up the exposed flesh of her arms, neck, and face, making sure she had no cuts from the broken window. His skin was so smudged with sweat and soot she could not see his scar. Jonathan watched the two of them for a moment before speaking.

"How did the fire start, Jimmy?"

James stiffened, his back and shoulders tensing. They both knew how the fire had started. Jonathan only wanted him to say it aloud, in front of Arabella, to prove a point, and James had no choice but to answer him.

"The fire was deliberately set in the north corner of the storehouse." The words, sharp as glass, scraped the sides of his throat.

"We need to talk," Jonathan said, his eyes flicking from James to Arabella and back to James again. "Alone."

James nodded and followed him into the hallway. They turned toward the west wing corridor.

"James," Arabella said, stepping into the hallway behind the men, "you're hurt. You need tending."

"I'm fine," he said, his words at odds with the look of discomfort on his face.

She pursed her lips, annoyed with their disregard. When James had run out into the night in pursuit of the assailants, Jonathan had readily obeyed his command to stay inside, and when James had returned from the fire, he had seamlessly passed his authority back to Jonathan, following him down the hall at his first request. She was the only one of them with any healing knowledge, but now they were both ignoring her, denying her even a shred of their respect. Smoke inhalation could have dangerous side effects. She should brew a pot of slippery elm tea and marshmallow root to relieve the pain in James' throat. She should hold his head over a bowl of boiling water steeped with thyme to calm his ragged breath.

"James, please," she said again, "You're hurt, and you need looking after."

Jonathan pushed open the office door. James turned back to her.

"I'm fine," he repeated. "Get some sleep, Arabella. Jonathan and I will make sure no harm comes to you or Elinor tonight."

"But James—"

"Now, Jimmy." Jonathan placed a heavy hand on his friend's shoulder, and James crossed the threshold to the office, shutting the door behind him.

The click of the cast iron lock echoed down the west wing hall.

Part Five

Newbury House

"You have witchcraft in your lips"
(Henry V)

Early the next morning, Alden House was quiet. The furniture that had been toppled by the flying stone had been returned to its usual position, and the broken window glass had been removed from the pane. A warm breeze flitted through the open space left behind, filling the curtains as though they were sails pointed into the wind.

Arabella walked down the center hallway of the house, pausing to glance into the empty library where Jonathan had taken her after the assault on the front window. The faint scent of tobacco from Jonathan's pipe still hung in the air, and behind it was a lingering odor of smoke and charred wood that made her stomach clench.

She entered the kitchen pantry, taking her Porter Family Grimoire down from the high shelf where she stored it. Its binding creaked as she opened it. She flipped through the pages until she located a section labeled *Saining*. She ran her finger over the slope of the *S*, tracing the elegant swirl of her grandmother's script.

The saining rites recorded in her grimoire were a compilation of practices for blessing, protecting, and purifying both people and places. Seasonal rituals had been inscribed alongside the everyday blessings her family spoke over newborn babies, sick children, laboring mothers, and elders setting out on their final journeys across the veil. She flipped to a series of weathered pages littered with spells for protecting a home. In the old days, the Porter women had sometimes been called upon to bless the home of a newly married couple or rid an old home of negative energies. One of Arabella's great-aunts had been born with the gift of communicating with the dead, and she used it to listen to spirits' needs, negotiating their peaceful coexistence with the living.

On the Isle of Skye, Arabella's family had performed rites of protection on their lonely stone cottage each Hogmanay, first traveling together to collect water from a ford routinely crossed by both the living and the dead, and then ceremoniously pouring the sacred liquid over the thresholds of their windows and doorways. The veil was always thin at the turning of the year, and Arabella, whose fairy gift allowed her to feel the open spaces between the realms, was particularly sensitive during liminal times. As a little girl, she had been frightened of the ghosts who gathered in the shallow water of the sacred ford, their spectral essences rising from the currents like fog. She did not have the ability to speak with the spirits as her great aunt did, and she could not hear their demands, so she had clung to Caitriona's skirts, refusing to let go for fear the wandering souls would drag her back through the veil with them. Her grandmother had dipped a wrinkled finger directly into the ford, tracing a swirling symbol of protection on Arabella's forehead, the back of her hands, and just above her heart, softly whispering the same incantation they used to bless their home each year.

"What are you doing?" Arabella had asked as the icy water reddened her skin.

"Our bodies are houses for our souls," her grandmother had explained, kissing each of her tear-stained cheeks. "I offer you this blessing, my child, so your body, like our cottage, may be a safe haven to you throughout the year, protecting your spirit from all harm."

Arabella had felt the enchantment of it, had seen the remnants of the protective symbols long after the water marks had dried. When she had looked up at the ghosts gathered beneath the footbridge, she no longer felt afraid, so Caitriona had deemed the blessing a tradition worth repeating, anointing her granddaughter's body with sacred water as each new year approached. This had been the first year Arabella had celebrated Hogmanay without her grandmother's blessing. Now, only six months later, she was living in a new home, in the New World, surrounded by threats she did not understand. She needed to do something to make herself feel safe.

She had not been given many opportunities to familiarize herself with the local landscape, but she knew water from the Mystic River would work for her saining ritual because it was regularly crossed by both the living and the dead; townspeople traveled over the wooden bridge to get from one side of the village to the other, and Indigenous spirits gathered in the shallows on the river's western bank, driven eastward by the phantom flames of a massive fire. She slipped out the kitchen door and through the back gardens, hurrying across the pathway behind the house until she reached the river's grassy shore. White-breasted seagulls soared in the sky above her, bathing themselves in dawn's early light, as she patiently waited for the meandering current to fill her glass jars.

She brought the water back into the morning hush of the house, pouring it into her cauldron and bringing it to a boil. She added crushed sage, rosemary, and rue, letting the potion deepen into a rich amber color. When it cooled, she poured it into a shallow bowl and carried it throughout Alden House, sprinkling drops of the consecrated liquid onto each doorway and windowsill.

When she reached the broken window in the parlor, she paused and glanced over her shoulder, suddenly nervous. The Porter Rede required consent before engaging in spell work of any kind, and Arabella had not asked the Aldens for their permission before beginning the home protection ritual. But, she reasoned, why would they object to a simple charm that would fortify their home in the wake of last night's attack? Besides, she had already set the ritual into motion, and her actions would cause no harm.

She dipped her finger into the bowl of water and, using a fluid motion, drew a Dara Knot on the oak window frame, each line and curve interlocking seamlessly, no beginning and no end. When she had traced the design three times, she closed her eyes and whispered a rhyme.

Spirits of North, South, East, and West,
I call upon you to heed my request,
Shield us with earth, air, fire, and sea,
As I will it, so mote it be.

She said it three times in the old language, three times in the new, and three times in the old again. The breeze from the open window caressed her as she spoke, and she watched the water-drawn symbol rise in the air like mist, its vapors wrapping itself around Alden House in a shield of magical protection.

"Whatever are you doing?"

"Elinor—I was just—I thought you were asleep."

The old woman's eyes moved from Arabella to the broken window. The strange marking Arabella had drawn on the casement was already beginning to fade, the water seeping into the knots of the wood.

"It's a rite of protection," Arabella explained, her cheeks coloring beneath Elinor's curious gaze. "I thought—well, especially after what happened last night—"

"What happened last night?" Elinor interrupted sharply. She had slept through the excitement, and as Arabella relayed the details about the unseen assailant who had thrown a stone through the parlor window and set the shipyard on fire, the old woman's face grew pale.

She dropped into a nearby chair.

"Where is James now?" she asked.

"I haven't seen him this morning. I don't think he's home."

"And Captain Burrows?"

"*Polaris* is no longer docked in the river. Jonathan told me he would be out of town for a while, but he plans to return with more cargo on September thirtieth."

Elinor nodded, her eyes scanning the broken window. "Arabella, what, exactly, were you doing when I walked into the room?"

Arabella placed her bowl on the table and she sat down next to Elinor, doing her best to explain the tradition of saining, describing how, on the Isle of Skye, her family followed each new year's ritual cleansing by carrying burning juniper branches through the house, letting their thick smoke settle into each nook and cranny.

"You gathered this water from the river behind our house," lines of concern crossed Elinor's forehead as she spoke, "because you believe it is a place regularly crossed by both the living and the dead?"

"No one saw me." The color that had risen on her cheeks deepened from pink to scarlet. "In Scotland, many Christians keep the old traditions."

"Oh, Arabella," Elinor said, twisting her hands in her lap. "We're not in Scotland."

"I'm sorry, Elinor. I should have asked your permission before performing the ritual."

The old woman shook her head, gesturing away the apology. "This is your home, at least for now, and I want you to feel safe in it. I only ask you to use discretion. There are many who might find your ritual—" she searched her mind for the right word "—strange." She offered a reassuring smile. "I'll talk to James, but I'm sure the broken window and the shipyard fire were nothing more than childish pranks. He'll find the culprits and put a stop to their nonsense. We have nothing to worry about."

She stood up, a clear sign she considered the conversation finished. "Now, if your ritual is done, perhaps you can accompany me to town. We have a wedding to prepare for, and we both need new dresses."

"Of course I'll to accompany you to town," Arabella replied, "but I don't need a new dress. I made it clear to James that all my earnings were to go toward my father's debt." She asked Elinor if she might use some silk thread she had found in Mary's sewing room to embellish one of her cotton gowns.

"Arabella," Elinor said with a patient sigh, "you do not have a dress appropriate for the grandeur of your sister's wedding, and no amount of embellishment will make anything you own suitable." She held her hand up to stop Arabella's protest before it began. "You are the illegitimate sister of the bride. I don't say it to be unkind; I say it because it's true. Everyone in Mystic will be attending Anne's wedding, and they will all be looking at you. The least we can do is give them something to look at, something that makes them see you as more than the unfortunate circumstance of your birth."

Arabella's shoulders stiffened in defense. She had had no choice or control over the conditions of her making, and she cared little for what Mystic's social elite thought about her. Her dresses might be simple in their material and construction, but she wasn't ashamed of them.

"I don't have the money to purchase a new dress."

"But I do. I have money *of my own*, and I'm determined to use it while I'm still living."

"Elinor—"

"Dressing is an art form, Arabella. It's a way of telling a story about yourself, and, it's one of the only ways a woman in our society is granted free reign to speak her mind. There are rules, of course, which is why your peasant clothes are unsatisfactory for the occasion at hand, but you'll find that if you play within the rules, you can do quite a lot to shape public perception."

Arabella looked down at her skirt, its faded blue and green pattern the mark of the Porter Clan. Did it advertise she was poor? An immigrant? Illegitimate? It was all true, but the sting of the labels seemed greater now that she had arrived on America's shores. She remembered how Anne had dismissed her tattered skirts and implied she was unfit to sit at the table when Alan had visited for dinner.

"Think of a new dress as a form of protection," Elinor said, "a type of saining. There's nothing harmful or ill-intentioned in my desire to purchase it for you, and it will help people to see the kind and beautiful young woman you are." She patted the back of Arabella's hand. "Your grandmother taught you to work magic with potions and spells. Let me to teach you how to work magic with silk and ribbons."

Arabella smiled, thinking Caitriona would have enjoyed Elinor's analogy.

"I don't know how I'll repay you," she said, wondering exactly how much money a suitable wedding ensemble was going to cost.

"My darling girl," Elinor returned with a smile of her own, "the joy you've brought to my life is payment enough."

II

Elinor directed Arabella to the most expensive dress shop in town, breezing past the gowns hung on the racks at the front of the store and proceeding directly to the large rolls of silks and satins lining the back wall. She had worn nothing but black since the death of her son and grandson, but she chose several fabrics in shades of pearl-grey and lavender, half-mourning colors appropriate to the joyous occasion. She held a swatch of teal silk up to Arabella's face. Its threads were a blend of turquoise, sapphire, and aquamarine, and its sheen was the shimmering blue-green of the sea on a summer evening.

"This color suits you," she said.

Arabella was reminded of the water in the fairy pools on Skye and the glint in James' eyes when the sunlight hit them. She rubbed the swatch between her fingers. It was as soft as a cloud. She had never owned anything so extravagant.

It was then that she heard the laughter. She turned her head to see two young women rummaging through the sample gowns hung on the rack by the front window. They were whispering to each other. She couldn't hear what they were saying, but she had the distinct impression they were talking about her.

"Pay them no mind," Elinor said, offering the young women a glare that immediately quieted them. They exited the shop, and the bell above the door rang its merry tune.

Arabella was used to being the object of whispers and strange looks. She had been receiving them since she had first arrived in Mystic, long before anyone could have guessed she was William's illegitimate daughter. Was the entire town really so suspicious of anyone who came from outside its borders?

The seamstress directed Arabella into a curtained dressing room and twisted a measuring tape around her bust, waist, hips, and arms. She jotted down numbers and sketched rough designs as Elinor offered advice.

By the time they exited the shop, they had received solemn assurances that two new dresses would be delivered to Alden House in time for the Newbury wedding, and Arabella had begun to believe that silks and ribbons just might carry their own form of magic.

Although James refused to employ live-in servants in his home, he allowed Elinor to hire a day maid to help her and Arabella dress on the afternoon of the wedding. He had given the women no indication of his intentions to attend or excuse himself from the nuptials, but before he left the house to spend the day working in the shipyard, he had procured a coachman to brush and ready his best horses and prepare his private carriage to bring Elinor and Arabella to the ceremony at Newbury House. He did not want them to make the journey in one of the crowded stagecoaches which had been hired to shuttle guests back and forth.

After fastening the buttons on Elinor's lavender brocade jacket, the maid turned her attention Arabella who had not had anyone offer to help her get dressed since she was a small child.

"I'll need you to grab hold of the bed post, miss," the maid said after she had pulled a new corset over Arabella's linen shift. The corset, lined with whalebone and baleen extracted from the jaws of North Atlantic right whales, had been sewn with a row of metal eyelets.

Arabella did as she was told, and the maid pulled forcefully on the corset's stays.

"Oh!" A sharp pain seized Arabella's ribs.

"Begging your pardon, miss," the maid apologized in a voice much gentler than her vice-like grip. "The dress will sit better if the corset is laced tight." She braced Arabella's back with a raised knee and yanked again, squeezing her waist and rounding the curves of her bosoms and hips. When the maid was satisfied with the hourglass shape the corset had wrought, she helped a breathless Arabella step into a crinoline and then the blue silk gown which had been crafted in the latest French style with a tight, V-shaped bodice and full skirts that billowed toward the floor.

Arabella felt dizzy when she saw herself in the looking glass. She placed her hand on the dressing table to steady herself, unsure if it was the tight squeeze of the corset or the beautiful drape of the gown that had taken her breath away. Iridescent roses had been stitched across the bodice, along the hem of the dress, and around the cuffs of the long, fitted sleeves. A delicate white lace peeked up from the sloping neckline and from beneath the long sweep of the skirt, surrounding the gown with an ethereal glow. Arabella felt as though she had been wrapped in the silk swells of an enchanted ocean, seafoam cresting across her sculpted figure in swirls of sparkling silver roses.

The maid pulled Arabella's curls up onto the top of her head so that the alluring back panel of the dress was on full display. She wove an aqua blue ribbon, the same shimmering shade as the dress, into the intricate design of her hair. Threads of silver roses spilled down the ribbon's length, fluttering over the exposed flesh of Arabella's long, graceful neck.

"Now for the finishing touch." Elinor handed Arabella a small velvet box. Inside was a pair of rose-shaped silver earrings and a matching bracelet with rose petal charms. Diamonds winked from the center of each blossom.

"These belonged to Mary," Elinor said looping the bracelet around Arabella's wrist.

"I can't wear these." Arabella's heartbeat quickened at the thought of donning Mary's bracelet and earrings. "James will be angry if he finds out I've worn his mother's jewelry without his permission."

"If James had bothered to be in this house long enough for me to request his permission, I would have done so, but seeing that he has not, he certainly can't blame us for doing as we please." Elinor clasped the long drop earrings in place. The diamond petals twinkled in the afternoon light.

"James has no use for his mother's jewelry, and he has no reason to object to me loaning it to you for such a grand occasion," Elinor reassured her. She adjusted Arabella's silver thistle pendant so it dangled just above the lace at her chest. Then she stepped back to view the full effect of the ensemble. "Your necklace is *rustic*," Elinor chose the word carefully, "but every American wedding needs a dash of Old World charm."

Arabella glanced in the mirror, watching the petals of Mary's earrings dance each time she turned her head. The effect was striking; the silver of the jewelry blended with the iridescent threads of the dress, and even her thistle pendant gleamed. Perhaps Elinor was right. James had not bothered to spend any time at home since the night of Jonathan's visit, ignoring his grandmother's requests for family dinners for the last two weeks. Maybe, given the circumstances, Mary's jewelry might act as a talisman of protection, tricking casual onlookers into thinking she couldn't possibly be the illegitimate daughter they were so curious to meet.

"Excuse me, Ma'am." The coachman, an old friend of the Alden family, appeared in the doorway of the bedroom. "The horses and carriage are ready."

"Well, then, we've no more time to argue," Elinor said with a satisfied smile of approval as she followed the coachman into the hall.

Arabella sat uncomfortably on the velvet covered bench of the enclosed carriage, her body held straight and still by the stiff corset beneath her garments. The practiced trot of the horses swayed the cab from side to side, and the tight cut of the gown trapped Arabella's breath somewhere between inhalation and exhalation. The sun, low on the horizon, still burned with stifling heat, but the air held the promise of a cool evening, perfect for the sunset ceremony which was to be held in the gardens of Anne and Alan's newly constructed home.

Arabella wondered if her sister knew the first of August was an auspicious day to be married. Halfway between the summer solstice and the autumn equinox, *Lughnasadh* was the beginning of the harvest season in Scotland, a time to commemorate the death of *Lugh's* foster mother who had collapsed of exhaustion after clearing the fields, a time to give thanks for all the earth mother provides. On Skye, there had been athletic games in the villages and communal bonfires on the mountain tops. The Porter women had always risen early to celebrate the first harvest, walking among the foothills of the Cuillin Mountains, gathering black feathers for the souls who had passed away and decorating their hearth with gold-tipped plumes of bracken to cultivate wealth and happiness. They used to spend the long afternoon and evening moving between their garden and their tiny cottage kitchen, preparing a feast of peas, potatoes, and fresh baked breads spread with homemade blackberry and elderberry jams.

"Let us pause, together, to give thanks for all we have, to draw down abundance for our harvest, our health, and our home," Caitriona used to say as Arabella and her aunts held hands around a candle made from the wax of honeybees that had nested in their garden for generations.

"As above, so below. As within, so without. As the universe, so the soul."

The family had repeated their mantra in unison, their voices ringing like a choir of bells.

The Alden carriage slowed as the horses approached their destination. Newbury House was a large white home, constructed in the Greek Revival style, with a low-pitched roof and tall Corinthian columns framing the front entrance. Streams of wedding guests were being led through the house and into the back gardens, where the rock wall which separated the Newburys' property from their neighbors' had been decorated with hundreds of glass shaded candles. The minister of the ceremony, one of the elders from the Seventh Day Baptist congregation, greeted guests in the entryway, and he waved the women over to him. Elinor pointed Arabella toward the winding staircase in the empty front hall.

"You must go and greet the bride."

Arabella's lips parted in surprise. "Anne and I hardly know one another," she said, suddenly afraid to part ways with her companion. She could feel the eyes of the other guests surveying her and she wished she could hide beneath the folds of Elinor's pearl grey skirts.

"You're the bride's sister," Elinor said with a tone that brooked no argument. "That's all that matters today." She asked one of the attendants to lead Arabella upstairs to Anne's dressing room.

"You must trust me on this," Elinor said, her voice softening when she saw the panic in Arabella's eyes. "I'll save you a seat in the garden."

Arabella followed the attendant up the staircase and down a long empty hall. The walls were white and vacant, a blank canvas on which the soon-to-be newlyweds would begin writing their lives.

Anne stood in a large room at the end of the hall surrounded by three day maids cloaked in black aprons. One smoothed the bride's white satin dress while the other two pinned her lace veil into place. Her fine, golden hair had been parted in the middle, plaited into a low bun, and graced with a crown of orange blossoms. The room held a canopied bed and a dressing table laden with brushes and combs. A brilliant bouquet of pink roses lay on the corner of the dresser, releasing a heady fragrance into the air.

"Arabella!" Anne turned, her lips parted in shock as the attendant knocked on the open door.

Arabella twisted her thistle pendant. "Elinor—Mrs. Alden," she said, amending her speech to include the formal honorific, "said I should come to see you before the ceremony." The last time the sisters had spoken to one another Anne had accused her of disgracing their family and ruining her life. "You look beautiful, Anne," Arabella added because it was true. The bride was glowing.

Anne floated across the room, her dark eyes moving up and down Arabella's elaborately clad figure. "Where did you get this dress?"

Arabella forced a smile as Anne inspected the silver roses stitched into the bodice. "Elinor had it made for me. She said I had nothing appropriate to wear for your wedding."

"Well, she were right about that," Anne said. "I'm just glad you didn't wear your tartan."

Arabella rolled her eyes, relaxing slightly. This was the sister she remembered from her first few weeks in America, haughty, sarcastic, and judgmental, but much kinder than she seemed on the surface. Anne turned back to the mirror mounted above her dressing table. She picked up her bridal bouquet, holding the posy in front of her and twisting back and forth, viewing her appearance from each angle.

"I should go, and let you get ready for the ceremony," Arabella said after watching her for a few moments. "I only wanted to tell you how happy I am for you and for Alan."

"Wait," Anne said, stopping Arabella just as she was about to exit the room. "I'd like you to stay."

The bride dismissed her maids, who curtsied and walked into the hallway. She waited for them to close the door. An awkward silence coated the room.

"I don't think I've ever thanked you, Arabella," Anne said, her words soft and sincere.

"Thanked me for what?"

Anne stroked the pink petals in her bouquet. There was no mistaking their distinctive shape.

"Anne, are those—"

"Alden roses?" Anne asked, anticipating her sister's question. "Yes. They're from James." She attempted to grimace as she said his name, but she could not sustain the mask.

"James?" Arabella must have misheard. "James Alden?"

"Yes. He brought them to me a few minutes before you arrived."

"James is here? He brought you flowers?" Incredulity, followed by a twinge of jealousy Arabella did not care to acknowledge, bubbled up in her chest.

"I don't think he'll stay for the ceremony," Anne said flippantly. "It's probably for the best he doesn't. But yes, he was here."

"I don't understand." Arabella's entire life had been upended by James' hate for her family. Why would he gift her sister a sentimental bouquet? "James attacked our father for picking his roses, Anne, and, apart from today, he's forbidden me from seeing you and William. You've never spoken a kind word about him. In fact, you warned me to stay away from him. Why would he bring you flowers?"

"There is a long and complicated history—"

"—between the Aldens and the Staffords." Arabella finished Anne's sentence with a frustrated sigh. "That doesn't answer my question." Why was everything in Mystic shrouded in such secrecy?

Anne adjusted her veil. The soapy scent of orange blossoms flooded the room.

"Arabella," Anne said, lowering her voice to a whisper and nervously glancing toward the door, "I think you should know something. James is the one who paid my dowry."

"What?"

"He paid for my wedding as well. Alan used all of his savings to build us this home because my father—*our* father," she corrected herself, "*promised* me he would pay for my wedding." A shadow of sadness passed over Anne's face. "The entire town believes our father is tonight's host, but, you and I both know he can't afford any of this. My dress, my veil, the candles in the garden, the food our guests will enjoy at the reception, James paid for all of it."

"Why would he do that?" Arabella asked. It didn't make any sense. She ran her hands down the curve of her waist, wishing her corset weren't so tight, wishing she could take a deep breath to calm her racing heart. "Why are you telling me this?"

Anne shrugged her shoulders nonchalantly, as if the answers were both outside her grasp and none of her concern. "I suppose he did it because he wants me to be happy. And I suppose I'm telling you because you volunteered to make yourself his prisoner to pay off our father's debt, and I think you should know." She reached for Arabella's hand. "James would never have agreed to help me if you hadn't convinced his grandmother to hire you." She was on the verge of tears. "That's why I wanted to thank you. This day wouldn't be happening without you, and I don't think you understand how much this marriage means to me."

"Of course I do," Arabella said, still confused by the course of events but wanting to offer her sister some comfort. "I know how much this day means to you and to Alan."

"But, how could you? You once told me the women in your family never marry."

"Well, that's true, but we were often called upon to bestow the old blessings before official marriage ceremonies on our island."

"The old blessings?" Anne blinked away her tears, regarding Arabella in the same curious way Elinor had when she first learned about the Porter family craft.

Arabella bit her lower lip, wishing she could pull back the phrase. She shouldn't have mentioned the old blessings. She was already an object of curiosity to everyone on the guest list, and the last thing she wanted to do was call attention to the things that made her different. "They're simply meant to bring luck and love to a newly married couple," she explained.

Anne raised a skeptical brow, but then hope and excitement flashed in her dark eyes.

"Can you bestow one of your old blessings on me?"

Arabella quickly shook her head. "I don't think they're an accepted part of a Christian wedding ceremony here in America."

"Well, no, of course not, but, there must be an old blessing you can bestow on me now, in secret, while it's just the two of us?" Anne's voice dropped to a conspiratorial whisper. "Alan doesn't need to know."

"The old blessings are not party tricks, Anne. They're sacred wishes offered with the consent of *both* the bride and the groom."

"Arabella!" Anne stamped her foot upon the floor and sighed dramatically. "How can you be so selfish? If one of your old blessings can bring my marriage luck and love, why wouldn't you want to share that with me?"

"You and Alan are about to declare your love for one another in front of your friends and family. Surely that means more to both of you than a blessing from the Old Country."

"Alan and I are about to *marry* each other in front of our friends and family. Marriage and love are not always the same thing."

"Don't you love Alan?"

"Of course I love Alan," she cried, "and I think Alan loves me, but there was a time I thought my parents loved each other, and *you* are proof they didn't." Anne's emphasis stung Arabella more than she wanted to admit. It was uncomfortable being reduced to the living embodiment of her father's sins against Anne's mother. "Alan is a good man and I know he'll honor me as his wife, but I don't want to end up being unloved," Anne's breath hitched slightly as she spoke, "like my mother."

The tears clinging to the end of Anne's long lashes wrenched Arabella's heart. She took her sister's hand. "Love is something you choose, Anne. If you and Alan continue to choose each other, as you're choosing each other today, then your marriage will have all the luck and love it needs, but, if you truly think an old blessing will bring you comfort and happiness, I'll offer you one."

Anne's smile returned, and she rushed to the door, throwing it open and dispatching one of her maids to gather the ingredients Arabella said she needed for the blessing. Fifteen minutes later, the two sisters were holding hands over a small white candle that had been anointed with oil, rolled in crushed sage, and sprinkled with rose petals from Anne's bouquet. They had drawn the curtains closed for privacy, but a breeze parted them slightly, and Anne shivered in the slant of golden light that filtered through the shadows of the room.

Arabella took Anne's hand in hers, spreading the fingers wide. She brought a sharp needle to the tip of her third finger, piercing the skin and squeezing a small drop of blood onto the hot wax pooled on top of the candle.

May you be each other's light in the darkest of storms.
May the union you forge never be torn.
By earth, air, fire, and sea,
As true love wills it, so mote it be.

Arabella repeated the blessing, in the old language and the new, until Anne's fears and worries were lifted from her shoulders and carried away by the wavering smoke.

"When the flame burns out the spell will be complete," Arabella whispered. "You and Alan will have a beautiful life together."

Anne nodded gratefully, watching as the candle melted, its wax oozing over the salt that held the taper upright in the shallow bowl. The sound of footsteps in the hallway made her jump.

"Father will be here to escort me to the garden soon," she said, smoothing her dress and picking up her bouquet. "You should go and find a seat before the ceremony begins."

Arabella glanced back at her sister as she left the room. A sheen of magic had draped itself over Anne's shoulders like a beaded shawl. Evening sunlight wafted through the narrow opening of the curtains, bathing her in an ethereal glow. She looked like a fairy bride from the old country, awaiting her beloved's arrival.

Arabella smiled as she realized Elinor was right; every American wedding needs a dash of Old World charm.

Newbury House was perched on the side of a small hill, so although the summer sun still teetered above the horizon as the wedding hour neared, the sunken garden behind the kitchens, where the ceremony was to take place, was already dusky and cool. Spring Hill Lane was located a few miles from the river that wended its way through the center of town, a new road carved out of native forests and surrounded by tall, thick trees. Long tables with refreshments had been set up along the rock wall in the Newburys' yard, and several rows of beribboned chairs had been positioned toward the thick woods which winked with the lights of a thousand whale oil lanterns.

Arabella emerged from the house to find finely dressed guests lining the yard, gathered in pockets of lively conversation. She scanned the crowds, searching for James' tall frame among the multitudes of black-jacketed men. Not finding him, she made her way over to Elinor, who was relaxing in the shade, her cane resting on the chair next to her to save a seat for Arabella as she had promised. It was not until Arabella drew closer that she realized Elinor was talking with William. He rose from his seat when he saw Arabella. His grey hair, still flecked with strands of gold, shone against the dark color of his formal attire.

He offered her a stiff smile, painfully aware that everyone in the vicinity was watching them. William's indiscretions had never been a secret, and he doubted any man who had known Anne's mother would have faulted him for finding comfort outside his marriage bed, but publicly acknowledging his illegitimate child at the marriage of his only legitimate offspring remained an uncomfortable reality for him. He had steeled himself against the ripples of social backlash he would suffer because of it. He had taken comfort in knowing the gossip would fade quickly, as it always did. He had even relished the protection that Elinor's approval of Arabella would no doubt provide, but that was before his daughter had draped herself in a gown so elaborate the entire town would be talking of her beauty for months to come.

"May I introduce you to Miss Arabella Porter, the bride's sister," Elinor said to a group of guests who were gathered nearby and who were watching the awkward scene between Arabella and her father unfold. William bowed his head cordially in their direction before excusing himself to prepare for the ceremony.

"You can't expect him to shower you with his attention tonight, the circumstances being what they are," Elinor said gently when she noticed Arabella's disappointment at her father's retreat. "Things will work themselves out in time. You must be patient."

Arabella was relieved when Anne finally made her entrance into the garden, sending an expectant hush over the crowd as everyone shuffled to take their seats. William escorted the bride across the lawn, shaking Alan's hand as they reached the head of the meeting space. A gust of warm wind lifted the bride's veil and ruffled the petals of her bouquet.

There were sweet and somber speeches from the minister and church elders, followed by the couple's vows and a silent contemplation of God's enduring presence, punctuated only by the quiet mumbles of voices in prayer. After the ceremony, guests were directed back inside Newbury House, which had been filled with borrowed chairs and tables, for the wedding feast. Hired chefs had prepared a variety of poached fishes, and a large, layered fruitcake, which had been frosted with rich, white icing, stood on display, ready to be boxed up and sent home with well-wishers. Arabella followed Elinor dutifully, attending to her needs as best she could amid endless introductions and questions from curious guests. The house was crowded with revelers and servants, and although

Elinor had prophesied things would settle quickly, Arabella could not help but notice the murmurs and glances thrown in her direction throughout dinner. She did her best to ignore them, just as her father had ignored her, but she was grateful when Elinor, preoccupied with a crowd of older women who had joined her table to discuss their plans for future charity events, consented to letting her slip away from the banquet for a short turn in the garden.

"Stay within ear's reach," the old woman cautioned.

It was much cooler in the garden. The purple shadows of twilight had deepened, and the flames from the candles and lanterns created an enchanting backdrop of flickering light. Small groups of guests, mostly men, lined the manicured lawn, and a few young couples had retreated toward the edge of the tree line for privacy. Silver platters of savory finger sandwiches and sweet breads had been placed next to large glass serving bowls filled with lemonade and cider.

A quiet corner of the garden beckoned to Arabella, and she moved toward it, the blue shades of her silk dress fading into the night like spilled ink. The endless chatter of the wedding guests dwindled to a low hum indistinguishable from the woodland sounds of the forest, and she breathed a sigh of relief, grateful she could no longer hear the half-whispered barbs and veiled references to her illegitimate status. She removed her gloves, placed them on the rock wall, and stretched her fingers in the evening air. She watched the late summer fireflies flit around the lantern flames, enjoying the warmth of the evening wind.

"I suppose this is the only way I can speak with my daughter, then, shrouded in darkness and in secret?"

William had sidled up behind her, and she turned, smiling brightly at him before the sarcastic tone of his words settled in her mind. She had hoped to see him. She had wanted to have a moment to speak with him alone, but he was regarding her with an air of annoyance, as though she had done something wrong, and a wave of nervousness rolled over her.

"It was a beautiful ceremony," she said politely. He cocked his head and glared at her, insulted, though she had intended no harm. She had momentarily forgotten it was James, and not William, who had paid for the wedding, and judging by his irritated reaction, any words that complemented James Alden or his clandestine contributions to the evening would be taken as an affront to William's pride.

He leaned close to her, his dark eyes angry and bloodshot, his breath stale with rum. There had been no alcohol served at the wedding, but several men had hidden flasks in their jacket pockets, emptying the spirits into punch bowls when they thought no one was looking. William had evidently imbibed in several cups of spiked punch, or perhaps he had a flask of his own hidden in his jacket. Either way, the effect was disconcerting. He had never been anything but kind and charming in Arabella's presence, but now he seemed combative and unsteady on his feet.

"You must be quite happy with the impression you've made." He placed his gloves in his pocket and pulled out a cigar, biting the end of it and lighting it with a candle from one of the lanterns. He puffed several times, the flame expanding and contracting wildly. Arabella watched as it settled into a bright red glow between his lips. He clutched the cigar with his teeth, and held the candle dangerously close to her, surveying the elaborate details of her dress, her jewelry, her upswept hair, before placing the taper back into its glass jar on the rock wall.

"How much of the money you claim you're earning on my behalf did you waste on dressing yourself tonight?" William asked.

"How much money did you waste on rum and tobacco?"

She had responded without thinking, forgetting he was her father and would expect her to answer him respectfully even though the tone of his own question had been rude. He flicked his newly lit cigar on the ground, mindlessly stamping it with his foot. He paused a moment before baring his teeth and backhanding her. Her fingers flew up to her cheek in surprise, and he pushed her deeper into the shadows, circling her arm with his fingers.

"Who do you think you are," he demanded, "talking to me like that?" He shook her violently, and she cried out in surprise and pain. He had not hit her hard enough to hurt her, but he had frightened her, and she wished she had listened to Elinor and not wandered so far from the house.

"I—ow—" she yelped as he pushed her against the rough bark of a large oak tree. "My dress was a gift from Elinor—from Mrs. Alden," she tried to explain, hoping he would cease his assault once he realized she hadn't spent any money on herself.

"A gift?" The end of his cigar still glowed in the patch of grass beneath their feet, and Arabella was afraid her long skirts would scrape against it and ignite. "I sent you to the Aldens to earn your keep, girl, not to accept gifts that bind you to them!"

His voice was rising in volume, and she searched the lawn, looking for someone to help her, but no one noticed them over the sounds of laughter and the rustle of leaves. "You allow James Alden to throw your own father out of the house you're living in, and then turn you around and let him dress you like his whore!"

"Good Evening, Mr. Stafford."

James emerged from the shadows, planting his feet slightly apart and clasping his hands behind his back in a posture of polite greeting. His eyes held William's in a level stare before glancing toward Arabella, and if it had not been for the familiar tightening of his jawline and the telltale throbbing of the scar above his left eye, she would have thought he was happy to see them.

"Are you enjoying yourself, Miss Porter?" he asked courteously, as though he had not just stumbled upon her father manhandling her in the garden. She opened her mouth to answer him, but didn't know what to say, so she simply nodded.

James turned back to William, his voice genial, his eyes as hard and as cold as ice.

"I've promised my grandmother, and both of your daughters, that I would cause no trouble tonight, but if you do not remove your hand from Arabella's arm and walk away from her in the next ten seconds, I will break that promise." He spoke slowly, his words a clear and decisive threat.

"Don't tell me how treat my own daughter, boy," William sneered.

"Your daughter resides in *my* household and is therefore under *my* protection, not yours." He removed his gloves and took a step closer. "How many times do I have to remind you of that, William?" He dropped his hands to his sides, his fists curling, his knuckles growing white with pressure. "Five seconds."

The two men stared at each other, each carefully weighing the consequence of their next move. A shout of laughter drifted over to the shadowy corner of the yard. A group of young men were engaged in some sport on the other side of the lawn. William ran his tongue over his dry lips. He would like nothing better than to teach James a lesson in front of the town's assembled guests, but if he tested the boy's temper now, after he had reprimanded his daughter for her transgressions, he risked casting himself as a villain, and that would never do. Still, more than half the guests at the wedding knew James for what he truly was, and they would certainly rush to William's defense if things got physical.

"Three seconds," James said, his cordial mask beginning to slip. "It was a beautiful wedding. It would be a shame to ruin it."

William turned toward Arabella, a cruel smile animating his weathered face. "You'll never be one them, no matter what you wear," he said, spitting on the ground at James' feet. "The promise of an Alden is worth less than dirt."

He released his grip just as James' ten second countdown had run its course, but not before grasping the silver bracelet dangling from his daughter's wrist and yanking it toward him. The chain snapped in two, and William viciously slapped the pieces of it into James' hand in a gesture that would have looked like a friendly, if somewhat vigorous, handshake to anyone who happened to glance their way.

"The next time you want to bedeck *my* daughter in your mother's jewelry, boy," he said, his voice a low, curling snarl, "you will ask me for my permission first."

He strode across the lawn and back toward the house, stumbling over the uneven ground. James bent down to pick up his discarded cigar, disposing of it in a puddle of rain water that had collected in a divot of the rock wall. Its embers fizzed when they touched the water, and a wisp of foul smoke rose into the air.

"I'm so sorry, James," Arabella whispered once her father was gone. Tears flowed over the reddened mark on her cheek. "Your mother's bracelet—Elinor wanted me to—and now it's—I shouldn't have—"

"I don't care about the bracelet," he said gently. He placed the remnants of it into his pocket. "Did he hurt you?"

Bruises were blooming on her arm, and a sharp red stripe was rising on the inside of her wrist where the clasp of the bracelet had cut her skin, but she was more humiliated than hurt. She shook her head.

"He's drunk, Arabella." James' voice was calm and steady in the dark. "He's not in his right mind. Whatever he said to hurt you, I'm sure he didn't mean it."

"Why are *you* defending my father?" she demanded, directing her anger with William toward James because he was the one still standing in front of her. "He's only upset with me because of *you*! Because you're keeping me from him to settle some ancient score between our families!"

He nodded, and let out a deep breath, choosing not to remind her she had willingly agreed to the terms of her service. "I'm not defending your father," he said calmly, trying to absorb her emotions rather than amplify them. "I just want you to know you're more than his daughter, Arabella. You're more than the bride's sister or my grandmother's nurse, and if he, and the other guests at this wedding can't see that, the fault lies with them and not with you. Don't let the words of an old fool hurt you." He half smiled and tilted his head. "Don't let the words of a young fool hurt you either."

It was his way of apologizing for calling her a bastard weeks ago, comparing himself to the man he hated most in the world, the man who had just called her a whore, but she didn't want his apology. She was tired of being in the middle of a feud she knew nothing about.

"I don't need you to save me from my own father."

He lifted his hands in a conciliatory gesture. His deep, baritone voice slid across the night, soft and patient. "What do you need, Arabella?" He brought his hand to her shoulder in a gesture of comfort. "What can I do to help?"

She was possessed by a desire to lean into him, to forget everything that had happened, to let him wrap her in his strong arms. "I'd like to go home," she whispered. "Can you please just take me home?"

A warmth settled over him as he realized she was talking about Alden House. However upset she was with him for coming between her and her father, his house was no longer her prison; it had become her sanctuary. An errant breeze stroked the candle flames, and James reached up, lifting a lantern down from the nearest tree.

"I'll have to leave the carriage for my grandmother," he said, pausing to make an apologetic gesture because they both knew Elinor was having the time of her life. "But if we cut through the woods at the end of the main road and then follow the river, it's only a few miles back to town. Do you think you can manage?"

On the Isle of Skye, Arabella had walked from her stone cottage at the edge of the sea, through the moors, and around the island daily, sometimes traversing close to ten miles when she had important deliveries. At that moment, she would have happily walked twenty miles to escape the tension of the evening.

"Yes, James," she said, too relieved by the thought of slipping away from the crowds to take issue with his underestimation of her physical abilities. "I think I can manage."

James immediately flagged down an attendant to send word of their departure to his grandmother and to offer their farewells to the bride and groom. Then he lifted Arabella over the stone wall that marked the edge of the Newburys' property, guiding her through a vacant field and around to the main street so they did not have to pass through the crowded house where they might run into William.

Spring Hill Lane was dark and quiet, but Arabella, who had never traversed the moors of Scotland in a heavy silk gown with her waist cinched tight by the stays of a whalebone corset, had difficulty with the uneven terrain. James shortened his gait to match hers, pleasantly surprised by how slowly she was moving. Now that they had left Newbury House, he was in no rush to end the evening.

The air smelled of jasmine and dahlias and the first hint of autumn's coming harvest and inevitable decay. The bouncing flame of their lantern flickered across the road. When they heard the crunch of horse hooves on the gravel behind them, James guided Arabella to the shadows of the tree line to let the stagecoach, which was busy shuttling groups of wedding guests back home, pass.

"Your grandmother wasn't sure you'd attend the wedding," Arabella said after the stagecoach had retreated and they had walked in silence for some time.

"My grandmother often thinks the worst of me." He shrugged his shoulders. "Alan and I were in the same class in school, so I thought I should congratulate him. I even told the bride how beautiful she looked." He dropped his voice, letting his eyes follow the line of silver roses that trailed down Arabella's bodice. "Though, to be fair, that was before I saw you in this dress."

"This dress was a gift from Elinor," she explained quickly. She felt raw from her father's accusations about wearing such finery and she had taken James' compliment as yet another criticism. "I haven't charged any personal items to your credit."

He turned away from her so she would not see his pained expression. He would give her a thousand dresses if only she would allow it.

At the end of the lane, James lifted his lantern toward the tree line. A footpath had been worn into the thick woods, invisible to all but those who knew where to look for it.

"This shortcut will lead us to the river walkway," he said, placing his hand on the small of her back. The path ran between two tall trees which curved inward toward the gaping mouth of the forest. "Once we get through the woods, the moon will light our way. I've used this path many times, Arabella. There's nothing to fear."

He was so earnest in his reassurance, she could not resist teasing him. "But James," she protested with mock terror, "what if we come across the Mystic *Dullahan*?"

He laughed, and the bright sound bounced off the tree bark. He much preferred her teasing to her tears. "Where did you hear about the Mystic *Dullahan*?"

"My sister, of course," Arabella answered, lowering her voice as though she was telling a ghost story. "Anne told me all about the headless rider who haunts the streets of your hometown after dark, flicking his horses with whips crafted from human spines. Like you, she thought it unseemly I dared to venture outside at night without a chaperone, and she wanted to scare me into compliance."

"Are you telling me Anne Stafford and I are on the same side of an argument?"

"She's Anne Newbury now," Arabella said, correcting him with glee, "and yes, my sister and you are far more alike than either one of you realizes." He winced, and Arabella laughed at the rise she had initiated with her comparison. She stepped onto the dark footpath, but he reached out to stop her, entwining his fingers in hers.

"The ground will even out when we reach the river," he said when he felt her hand tense beneath his. "Until then, I'll need to keep hold of you. I don't want you to fall." He moved in front of her, his lantern illuminating the gnarly roots which crossed the ground beneath their feet.

They traversed a series of large boulders before reaching a fairly clear part of the trail. "The legend of the *Dullahan* comes from Celtic lore," Arabella said, allowing her hand to relax into the warmth of his grip. "Did your mother ever tell you about *Coiste Gan Cheann*, the *Dullahan's* soundless coach, pulled by six headless horses?"

"My mother was a fan of cautionary tales," James admitted. "She told me many stories to scare me into behaving."

"Did they work?"

"Sometimes," he said, laughing.

Night animals scavenged in the undergrowth. An owl called out in the distance.

"Legends like the *Dullahan* are useful for keeping people from venturing out into the dark," he mused. "And they're useful for keeping the authorities from investigating those who do."

It was a curious thing to say, and Arabella wondered what he meant by it. When she had first seen James in the woods, she had been so preoccupied with escaping that she had not given much thought to *his* reason for being there. He had told her he was hunting, but he had carried no pelts, no evidence of a recent kill, and in all the time she had been living with the Aldens, she had never seen him bring home any hunting spoils. He and Jonathan had not pulled out their pistols to hunt *animals* after the stone had been hurled through the parlor window. There was so much about James she didn't know.

"You said you went to school with Alan," she said, trying to picture the two men as boyhood friends. "Do you think he and Anne will be happy together?"

"Why wouldn't they be happy?"

"Anne seemed nervous when I spoke to her before the ceremony," Arabella said.

"All brides are nervous."

"Maybe, but I think learning she has a half-sister made her question the sanctity of marriage." She grew quiet for a moment. "I didn't know, when I came to look for my father, that he had a wife and daughter before he met my mother."

"If you had known, would you still have made the journey?"

"I'm not sure," she said.

They were nearing the river, and the gurgle and rush of the current filled the silence before he responded.

"Then I'm glad you didn't know."

They had emerged from the wooded area onto a moonlit path, and she looked up at him, surprised by the softness in his eyes. Realizing they had reached steady ground, she let go of his hand. He stretched his fingers as the cool night air purled over the warm places where their flesh had been pressed together.

"Is it true you paid for Anne's wedding?" she asked.

James stopped walking. "Who told you that?"

"Anne told me just before the ceremony. She said you paid her dowry as well. Is it true, James?

He turned toward the river, embarrassed, and the tense lines of his profile answered the question he didn't.

"I don't understand," she said. "After everything that's happened between you and William, after everything you've done to keep me from my family, why would you do something so kind for Anne? And why would you keep it a secret?"

"It was part of the agreement William and I reached when you came to work for my grandmother." He spoke nonchalantly, as though the cost of an extravagant wedding was no more than a business expense.

"The work I do for Elinor would never earn me enough to pay for a wedding like the one we attended tonight, let alone a dowry, on top of my father's debt. If that is the bargain you struck, you can't be a very skilled negotiator."

He started walking again, and Arabella followed at his side, counting twenty paces before he spoke again. "I've known Anne since I was a child," he finally said. "And," he hesitated, letting out a long breath, "she was once betrothed to Thomas."

"Your *brother*, Thomas?"

"Yes."

"*My* sister and *your* brother were once engaged to be married?"

He nodded. "It wasn't a love match," he explained, "at least, I don't think it was. Thomas was four years older than me, and I'm almost two years older than Anne, so they didn't know each other very well."

"Then why were they engaged to be married?"

"Our fathers made the arrangement." His voice stretched taut across the space between them. "Your father ran several merchant companies and investments through the Alden Shipyard, and he thought the marriage would strengthen our families' business ties. My father thought it was time for Thomas to settle down and beget the next generation of Aldens, so he agreed. I did everything I could to convince my brother to call off the engagement, but Thomas refused to go against our father's wishes."

"Is that why you and William don't get along?"

"That is one of *many* reasons we don't get along," he said caustically. "Though, when I first returned to Mystic after my brother's death, William expected me to make good on my father's promise to unite our families in holy matrimony. He didn't care which Alden man Anne married, so long as the union granted him the money and power he desired."

"My father wanted Anne to marry *you*?"

James stilled and stared down at her, amusement dancing in the deep blue circles of his eyes. "Would I make so hideous a bridegroom?" he asked with a roguish smile that brought a bright flush of color to her cheeks.

"I didn't mean—"

"Answer the question, Miss Porter," he demanded, affecting seriousness. "Am I so repulsive you can't imagine any woman wanting to marry me?"

Her eyes fluttered upward and she smiled. He had to know how attractive he was. He had a confident way of moving through the world, and even his scar, which slashed from his forehead past the chiseled ledge of his cheekbone, was an oddly attractive imperfection. On a different face, the scar might have been repelling, but on James' strong countenance, it added an intriguing layer of vulnerability. He looked like a man who understood the consequences of his actions, and still chose to act in spite of them.

"You're not hideous, Mr. Alden," she admitted, addressing him with the same teasing tone he had used for his inquiry. "I just can't imagine you being married to my sister."

He laughed then, and Arabella knew she had not truly offended him. "Anne wouldn't have been happy spending her life with me, and I don't regret rejecting William's proposal, though I suppose I could have been more polite while doing so."

"Another one of the many reasons you and my father don't get along?"

"Yes."

The grassy pathway had given way to gravel as they neared the shipyard, and James' shoes crunched against the stones as they walked.

"Do you think your father and brother would have wanted you to marry Anne?" Arabella asked. James rarely spoke of his family, and she wondered if he would try to change the subject.

"My father and brother wouldn't have expected me to marry Anne, not after all the terrible things I said about William." There was a slight trace of regret in his voice. "When my second whaling voyage aboard the *Shepherd* ended, my father convinced me to return home and sail aboard the merchant ships that imported goods through his businesses. William had investments in many of those companies, and he ran all the arrivals and departures at the shipyard. He and I had several volatile disagreements about the types of people we should partner with and the types of goods we should import, and my father often had to step in and settle them. When I learned about the engagement, I told my father William was using his daughter as a pawn to bolster his own influence at the shipyard."

"Did your father believe you?"

"No, he did not." He slowed his speech, drawing out the words to convey the strength of George's anger at James' accusation. "And, somehow, our argument about William escalated into an argument about the future of the shipyard and my lack of religious faith and what my father deemed my complete disrespect for his paternal authority."

Elinor had told Arabella that James' last words to his father had been angry ones, but she had never revealed that James and his father had been fighting about William.

"We were arguing in the shipyard offices," James continued, the old story, dormant for so long, unspooling from his lips like fishing line, "and Thomas and William both barged in when they heard us yelling, which, as you can imagine, only made things worse." He watched the river as he spoke, squinting as if he could see the painful memory in the water's rippling surface. "My father was so furious he struck me. He hadn't done that since I was a child. And I almost hit him back. I probably would have hit him back if my brother hadn't stepped between us." Thomas had placed his hands on James' shoulders, begging him to calm down, convincing him that nothing good would come of trading blows with their father.

"My father demanded I apologize to William, and I refused, so he told me to get out of his office and get out of his sight. Within a week, I was halfway around the world, sailing under Jonathan's command." He kicked at the gravel beneath his feet. "I never saw my father or my brother again."

It had been an early April evening when James had stormed away from the shipyard offices, the lyrical peeping of frogs in the river marsh doing little to assuage his frustrations. He had walked all the way to New London where he had stolen a set of Identification Papers from a drunk sailor in a tavern alleyway. Even Jonathan had not realized James had joined his crew until he spotted him working on deck shortly after their departure. He had waited to approach him until the day after the ship had reached open waters, taking a position on James' left side during an early morning watch.

"Right whale, two hundred yards to the east," he had said jovially, scanning the wide expanse of the Atlantic where the rising sun was dappling the sea with blinding light. "Should we drop the boats and give chase, Jimmy?"

The *Nymph*, a seal hunting ship belonging to the same fleet as the *Shepherd*, had been commissioned to map the uncharted waters of the Antarctic. It was far too small a vessel for whaling, but the thought of a chase made James smile for the first time since he had boarded.

"We'll never catch it." James pointed to the spray curving up from the animal's spout. "It's a fin whale." Long hours aboard the *Shepherd* had taught them to identify the species of their prey from telltale shapes of flukes and watery arcs of exhalation. Fin whales were fast, sperm whales aggressive, and humpback whales often traveled in pods. Each required unique hunting strategies.

Jonathan laughed at the correction. He kept his eyes on the water. "Do you want to tell me what happened?" he asked. He had noticed the bruises on his friend's face and knew the only reason he would have joined the *Nymph's* crew under a false identity was to escape some kind of trouble on land.

"It's nothing," James said. "Just another argument with my father."

"What was this one about?"

"The same thing they're all about." The ship rolled over a long swell. A sea bird dipped close to the waves, searching for its morning meal. "But now, my brother is engaged to Anne Stafford."

"William's daughter?"

James nodded in response.

"Jesus Christ."

Jonathan knew all about the tumultuous rivalry between James and William, but he also knew that George Alden, an honest and intelligent man deeply moved by the strength of his youngest son's convictions, had been taking slow and steady steps to relinquish his shipyard's contracts with West Indes plantations for years, and he reminded James of that fact.

"He should have severed all ties with the West Indes long ago," James said. He had little patience for his father's measured approach to social change. "William's going to make a fool of him, and he and Thomas are both too stupid to see it."

"Did you say that to your father?"

James nodded again.

"Christ, Jimmy. No wonder he hit you."

James waved the comment off as though his father's violence was of no consequence, so Jonathan asked a question that underscored the obvious flaw in James' decision to abandon his shipyard position. "So, how do you plan to fix things with your father and keep moving your family's business in the right direction from the deck of my ship?"

It was a question James couldn't answer, so they had sailed in silence, listening to the slap of the waves against the hull. "You should at least write to your family and let them know where you are," Jonathan finally said. He still harbored guilt for bringing the fourteen-year-old James along with him when he had run off to sea, but at least then, they had sailed under their true names, which meant the Aldens would have received word if James or the *Shepherd* had met with peril.

James shook his head at the suggestion, as stubborn as he had ever been. He didn't want to think about anything but the wind, the waves, and the back-breaking work that awaited him in Antarctica. He was tired of being an Alden.

"Well, I'm always happy to have you aboard," Jonathan said, knowing it was useless trying to convince his friend to do something he had already decided against, "but you need to understand that sailing under my command is a different thing than sailing by my side."

"Aye aye, Captain." James smiled as he wielded the title with pride; Jonathan had worked hard to rise to the prestigious position, and James knew the safety and well-being of his ship and crew would come before their friendship. "Don't worry, Jonathan. I know how to follow orders."

"Your father would beg to differ."

James had finally laughed, and the captain took his spyglass out of his coat pocket and tossed it to him. "Two-hundred yards to the east," he repeated, before crossing the deck and heading toward the stern of the ship to meet with his officers. James lifted the spyglass to his eye just in time to see the distinctive black flukes of a right whale rise from the surface of the water.

Now James scanned the Mystic River as the whale of the past breached in his memory. Arabella watched him, wondering if he had told her about his violent argument with his own father to make her feel better about her argument with William. The pain of losing his father before getting the chance to resolve their differences was written in the tense lines of his face.

"I'm so sorry James," she said.

"Don't be." He didn't want her pity. "I loved my father, Arabella. He was a great man, and I was lucky to be his son, however difficult it may have been sometimes. Besides," he shrugged his shoulders, "I probably was acting like a child who deserved to be reprimanded, though I was far too angry to realize it at the time."

"Well, I *can* confirm you are quite childlike when you argue," she said with a sly smile.

"Oh, you can?"

"Yes, you are stubborn, pig-headed, unyielding, insufferable—"

"*Insufferable*?" His bright, clear laugh echoed over the water. "My father would have loved you," he said sincerely. "And you would have loved my brother, Thomas."

"He does sound more agreeable than you."

James smiled sadly. "He was."

"But, none of this explains why you paid for Anne's wedding."

James huffed deeply, running his hands through his hair. "When I came back to Mystic and fired your father from the shipyard, the Stafford family fell on hard times. William lost his livelihood, and then, through a string of poor choices and bad investments, he ended up owing me a great deal of money. I never thought about how any of that might affect Anne, but then you agreed to help my grandmother, which makes me responsible for your welfare, and Anne is your sister, so I feel responsible for her welfare, too." He let his lips curve into a relieved smile. "Well, I *felt* responsible for her welfare. She's Alan's responsibility now."

"And the roses?"

His smile did not disappear, but it faded into something wistful. His voice grew quiet.

"My brother's death couldn't have been easy for Anne," he said. "I wanted her to know—I wanted everyone to know—that Thomas would have been happy to see her moving on with her life."

Elinor had told her that dressing was an art form, a way of telling a story. By gifting Anne a bouquet of his mother's roses, James had been telling a story of his own. He had been saining her sister, offering her his family's protection as she entered into a new marital union. Anne's bouquet of Alden roses had let the entire town know that Thomas' brother supported her relationship with Alan Newbury. Arabella looked down at the silver roses on her dress. Was that why her father had taken such issue with her appearance? Had he seen the floral embroidery and Mary's rose petal jewelry as James' claim upon her loyalty, a loyalty he believed belonged to him?

They had neared the shipyard, and James pulled open the north gate. Without the clang of hammers and nails that rang through the daylight hours, everything was still. The wind rustled in the river grasses and the air smelled of damp pine and salt. Arabella knew they were behind Alden House when the powdery scent of the roses welcomed them home.

"What did you think of your first American wedding?" James asked, stopping between the riverbank and the back gate of his garden. He was not yet ready for their walk to be over, though they had traveled at such a slow pace he wondered if his grandmother had already returned home with the carriage.

"Tonight's wedding was," Arabella searched her mind for the right word, "measured."

"Measured?"

She giggled. "Yes, it was—quiet."

"Well, the Newburys are a conservative lot," he laughed. "But do tell me, what are weddings like in Scotland?"

"Oh, I'm not sure you could handle a Scottish wedding, James." She reached for his arm as if to brace him for a great shock, and his muscles flexed beneath the soft touch of her fingers. "There's music," she whispered playfully, "and dancing."

James tilted his chin. "You think I can't handle dancing?" His parents had forced him to take years of lessons in his youth, preparing him to escort wealthy young women to cotillions and quadrilles when he came of age. He slipped his arm around her waist, pressing the small of her back with his hand, and her chest flattened against the long, hard length of his body. She blushed with surprise at his tight embrace, struggling to steady her breath as her corset squeezed the air from her lungs.

"James—"

"I'm sorry, Arabella," he said, pretending he was filled with deep regret for what he was about to do. He lifted one of her arms into the air to ready them for a waltz. "You've questioned the dancing prowess of America's sons, so now, I have to teach you a lesson." He flashed a wolflike grin. "On behalf of my country."

"James—wait—" They were the last words she managed to utter before their bodies began swaying in unison, his deep voice humming a romantic tune. Soon her breathless laughter was curling into the night air as he twirled her up and down the river's edge, his feet moving in practiced precision, the swish of her silks eclipsing the murmur of the winds and the waves. She clung to his broad shoulders as they danced beneath the night, and she tipped her head back to watch the stars snake across the inky sky, the entire cosmos swirling around them long after he slowed to let her catch her breath. When he stilled, she rested her head against him, panting wildly, her cheeks flushed from their strenuous movements.

He loosened his grip, ever so slightly, glancing down at her with eyes that had softened into blue-grey clouds. The smooth plane of her chest rose rapidly up and down. He caressed a stray curl that spilled over her forehead like a curling vine.

"Don't tell me you're going to swoon," he teased.

"I am most certainly *not* going to swoon."

"I think I know a well-planned swoon when I see one, Arabella."

"James!" She spoke with as much incredulity as her oxygen-deprived body allowed.

"I have made *many* women swoon."

"Well, I am *not* going to swoon." Her eyes flashed like emeralds in the moonlight, but she smiled at his teasing.

"It would be terribly predictable if you did swoon, Arabella," he said with a wink.

"I am *not* going to swoon!" she insisted again, though she felt so lightheaded from laughing she worried she might. He chuckled, allowing his eyes to roam over her exposed skin. From this angle, he could see just beneath the lace trim of her low, sloped neckline. He touched the edge of her décolletage and trailed his fingers up to her collarbone.

"Relax," he said, his voice deep and soft. His hand curled around the back of her neck, his thumb resting on the vein where her pulse fluttered. "You just need to breathe. In and out, like the tides."

"I know how to breathe," she said, willing her inhalations to slow, a task made more difficult by the placement of his fingers.

"Have you learned your lesson Miss Porter?" He watched her chest rise and fall as he spoke. "Or do I still need to demonstrate my dancing abilities to you?"

She pressed her lips together, refusing to dignify his questions with answers, but her protest ended as soon as he pulled her back into a dancing embrace.

"Wait!" She laughed. She had just caught her breath, and she didn't want to lose it again. "I've learned my lesson, Mr. Alden," she admitted contritely. "My apologies to America."

He released her with an expression of disappointment. He didn't want their evening to end.

"What about the wedding ceremony itself?" he asked, hoping she would stay with him by the river and talk to him all night. "The vows? Are they different in Scotland too?"

"The vows depend on the church, much like here, I imagine," she said. "But many Scottish ceremonies feature a traditional vow during the handfasting."

"Handfasting?"

"It's an old custom performed at weddings, or sometimes at betrothals which are binding for a year and a day," she explained. "The woman places her hand on top of her beloved's hand—"

"Show me," he interrupted, slowly turning his right palm up to the sky and extending it toward her. The sleeve of his formal jacket covered the compass rose tattoo on his forearm, and his eyes, now piercing blue in the moonlight, held hers, waiting.

She hesitated a moment, her lips parting slightly, but she placed her right hand face down over his. She curled her fingers lightly around his wrist. He did the same, his callouses rough against the soft silk sleeve of her dress.

"What happens next?" he asked, his voice as low as the rumbling of the river.

"The couple's hands are tied together," she said, arching an eyebrow at the innuendo in his amused expression. "It symbolizes the knotting of their families, their lives, and their souls."

His lifted his left hand and pulled at the aqua blue ribbon holding the intricate twists of her hair in place. Her loose curls tumbled around her shoulders as the ribbon, its silver embroidered roses shining like stars, fluttered free. He twisted it around their joined hands.

"What are you doing?" she whispered.

"I'm a sailor, Arabella." He knotted the ribbon, wrapping it around her wrist, binding his arm to hers. "Never underestimate a sailor's ability to tie a knot." He tugged in demonstration, and the ribbon held fast.

"Now," he said levelly, "the vows."

She looked up at him, trying to read his expression, her body feeling the same strange pull toward him that it always did, her mind still warning her to be cautious. She bit her lower lip, unsure if she wanted to speak, but somehow unable to stop herself.

"*I give ye my Body, that we Two might be One.*" Her voice was soft, timid, a whisper.

"*I give ye my Body, that we Two might be One,*" he repeated, waiting for her to continue.

"*I give ye my Spirit, 'til our Life shall be Done.*"

"*I give ye my Spirit, 'til our Life shall be Done.*"

His free hand brushed her thick hair away from her neck. Her silver thistle pendant sparkled against her chest, which had begun to move in its pronounced rhythm once more.

"And, after the vows?" he asked, his question rising through the layers of the night, his words falling over her like a shower of soft, spring rain.

"After the vows," she said slowly, "it's customary for the couple—to kiss."

He cupped her chin, tilting it upward so he could study the curve of her lips. He had always been far too distracted by the green of her eyes to notice her lips, but now he believed he could lose himself in the shape of them. They were pink and plump, parted ever so slightly to allow air into the chamber of her mouth, and James felt every muscle in his body tighten in jealousy of the very air she was breathing. He wanted to pass through those lips and into that soft opening. He wanted to taste her, pleasure her, possess her. He lowered his face to hers, his own lips barely brushing against her skin, an unspoken plea for permission.

She shivered in the starlight, a moan escaping from her throat, so soft it sounded like a sigh. He gripped the nape of her neck, pressing against her until she melted into his embrace. He twisted his fingers through her hair, gently opening her lips with his tongue. Then he kissed her, and kissed her, and kissed her, his movements silky and strong, tender and powerful, tentative and unrelenting. He kissed her until the world was nothing but the beating of their hearts and the rushing of their breath and the swirling of the river pounding against the shore.

A far-off call from somewhere across the water pulled him from his bliss, and he opened his eyes to look at her, suddenly, painfully aware that the clench in his chest was far more than animal lust or passion. He had been with other women before, but he had never felt anything close to the yearning that had wrapped itself around his heart when he had kissed Arabella.

"James?" His name was a summons rolling off her tongue, a wanting that beckoned him closer, the sweet sound of it on her lips almost stopping his breath. He let his free hand slide from her face, skimming her waist as it came to rest at his side.

"James?" she repeated, opening her emerald eyes to show him the ache his departure had wrought in her.

"I'm sorry, Arabella," he said, forcing the words from the back of his throat. "I can't."

"You can't what?" she asked, wanting him to kiss her again instead of talking.

He took a step back from her to stop himself from covering her with his lips again. He had been playing a dangerous game, taking her sailing, teaching her to play the harp, finding a thousand reasons to brush against her in the privacy of his home so he could inhale the wildflower scent of her skin. But none of that had changed the fact she was William Stafford's daughter. He would never be able to marry her, not after everything that had happened, everything that was still happening, between their families. And if he couldn't marry her, he had to let her go.

"I shouldn't have—I'm sorry—this will never work."

"*This*?" Her desire for him was rapidly dissolving into indignation.

"It's too complicated." His voice was hoarse, hollow, apologetic. He had treated her poorly. He had taken advantage of her vulnerability, and now he needed to be a gentleman and remove himself from all temptation before things between them went any further. He could not kiss her openly, deeply, along the walkway of the Mystic River where anyone might see them and declare her reputation ruined. "I'm sorry, Arabella," he said again, steeling himself against her infuriatingly beautiful expression of anger.

"You're *sorry*?" Her breath pushed her chest against the bodice of her dress making the embroidered roses glimmer in the moonlight. She yanked her arm away from his, but her movements only tightened the ribbon that held them fast.

"Stop," he commanded as she tried to writhe away from him, twisting her wrist against the tight binding. "You'll hurt yourself."

"Untie me!"

"I will," he promised, "but you need to hold still."

She stopped moving so he could loosen the knot, turning her hand upward and away from his fingers as soon as the ribbon began to release. He paused his unraveling, trying to caress the red stripe on the inside of her wrist in apology.

"Arabella—"

She yanked her arm away from him again, and this time the ribbon that had joined them fluttered to the ground. She turned and moved, as quickly as her corset and gown would allow, toward the iron gate of the Aldens' garden. She opened it, letting it clang behind her. He listened to the rustle of her skirts in the grass, wincing when he heard the kitchen door slam shut.

He stood alone between the garden and the river, his blood pounding through his body with unflagging force as he cursed the circumstances that had forced him to release her. He bent down and picked up her discarded ribbon, squeezing it in his fist. Then he turned and hurled it with every ounce of his strength, hurled it as he had once hurled his heavy harpoons into the hides of leviathan, but, having no weight, the ribbon only drifted through the night air, floating calmly down to the water, refusing to give his anger the satisfaction of hitting a mark.

The ribbon circled helplessly in an eddy, a blue and silver snake. James stood, silently watching, as the current coaxed it toward Fishers Island Sound and the cold, unforgiving waters of the Atlantic Ocean beyond.

Part Six

The Cottage by the Sea

"O, no! it is an ever-fixed mark,
That looks on tempests and is never shaken"
(Sonnet 116)

A stifling heat spread across the month of August as the dog star, *Sirius*, rose in the late summer skies. July had been a wet, humid month, its warmth tempered by cooling rains that bathed the soil and bounced up from the cobblestones in thick columns of hazy mist, but August's heat was dry and thick, the kind of heat that scorched the earth, turning everything but the Alden roses into a dusty shade of brown.

If a fire had started in the Alden Shipyard during those dog days of August, it would have been impossible to contain. One small spark would have exploded into flames that roared and roamed like living beings, burning through the barrels of oil stacked in the storehouses, igniting the dry timber of the close-packed buildings, reducing the massive shipyard to mounds of cinder and ash.

Fire was not the only threat to Mystic during the month of August, for the burning weather that withered the crops and wilted the flowers took its toll on the minds and bodies of the village residents as well. Forced to stay still in the shade and shadows, women had little to do but talk, and the slightest strain of gossip was a nectar that sweetened the boredom of their long, parched days. Rumors flickered like flames, jumping from the mouths of wives to the ears of husbands who, tired from their labor in the sweltering heat, gathered at local taverns, pouring hearsay as freely as they poured glasses of whiskey and pitchers of ale.

It was in this dangerous atmosphere that the juiciest gossip to hit Mystic in more than twenty years spread like raging wildfire. It began with the words of a day maid who had been employed to dress the bride at the Newbury wedding, and who had witnessed Anne Stafford and her illegitimate sister performing a strange ritual before the Christian ceremony. The maid had described the eerie details of the dancing flame and the drops of blood to her cousin, a spinner in the textile mills, who had relayed the story to her co-workers, adding that the skies had darkened when Arabella had taken Anne's hands and started speaking in a foreign tongue. The spinner's co-workers had shared the information with their husbands, and the husbands had repeated sordid versions of the tale to their colleagues and friends. By the end of August, the story of Arabella Porter's mysterious behavior had reached a group of men who regularly gathered to gamble at the Spouter Tavern, and one sultry night, a naïve, young dockhand, emboldened by hours of drinking, made the mistake of approaching James Alden to ask him about the witch who was living in his home.

James, who had been drowning three weeks of his own frustrations in a bottle of whiskey, lunged at the dockhand as soon as he heard Arabella's name cross his lips, pushing him into a darkened corner of the tavern where he pummeled him with his fists, hitting him again and again, refusing to stop even after the man's skin had been split open and blood had begun to pour down the front of his shirt.

When the angry thump of Mrs. O' Shaughnessy's shillelagh failed to slow James' assault, the dockhand's friends tried to intervene, one of them desperately swinging a knife through the air and slicing James' bicep. James roared in pain, shoving the half-conscious dockhand across the room and wrestling the knife-wielding attacker to the ground. He held him in a headlock while three more men from the dockyard pulled at James' arms and kicked at his ribs, pleading with him to let the man go free.

In the end, James was lucky the young man who had confronted him had been surrounded by loyal friends who had come to his aid before James could kill him. He was lucky Mrs. O' Shaughnessy had rung the alarm for help. He was lucky the local authorities who answered her call had been able to pry him from his assailant before any permanent damage had been done. And, he was lucky to be George Alden's son, because the Head Watchman, an old friend of his family, had sent him home with nothing more than a stern talking to and a warning not to darken the door of the Spouter Tavern until he sobered up and learned how to behave like a gentleman.

James stumbled down Greenman Avenue, hoping to find his house quiet. He had been avoiding Arabella since their tragic kiss by the river, afraid that too much time in her presence would rid him of his resolve to treat her as nothing more than his grandmother's nurse. He entered the house through the back door, leaned against the kitchen counter, and pulled his shirt over his head to survey the bloody gash on his arm. The wound throbbed in unison with the bruises on his face and ribs, and he held a cloth up to the cut to stem the flow of his blood. He closed his eyes against the pain, and when he opened them, he saw Arabella standing in the silvery moonlight pouring in from the window, an expression of shock and horror on her face.

She was wearing a thin, white nightgown.

The fabric clung to the curves of her body, and his heart jumped at the sight.

That was moment his luck ran out.

"What happened?" she demanded.

James steadied himself against the counter, pulling his gaze up to meet her eyes. He studied the flecks of sapphire and brown winking beneath the green hue of her irises. They shimmered like pebbles in a bed of shallow sea water, and he shook his head to rid himself of the illusion.

"A small misunderstanding," he said, his tongue slurring over each syllable.

The bruises on his face and chest were already beginning to darken. He smelled of smoke, sweat, whiskey, and blood.

"Does this have anything to do with my father?"

He looked away from her. It was a fair question. He and William had come to blows twice since Arabella's arrival in Connecticut, but William's last interaction with his daughter had been a volatile one, and he could not understand why she was still so concerned about her father's wellbeing.

"This has nothing to do with your father." His voice was rough and gravelly because one of the men he had tussled with had wrapped a rope around his neck while trying to drag him off the young dockhand. Red scratches circled the skin beneath his jaw. "I'm perfectly capable of fighting with men other than William."

It was a stupid thing to say, but his head was pounding, whether from the whiskey he had ingested or the blows he had sustained, he did not know.

His right hand grasped the wet, darkened cloth beneath his left shoulder. Blood flowed steadily over the muscles of his forearm, seeping through his fingers, trickling down the thorny vine of his tattooed roses. The ink markings on his chest, usually covered by his shirt, were on full display as he swayed against the counter, and Arabella tried not to stare at the hard muscles beneath the designs.

"You're drunk," she said when he staggered to adjust his grip on the cloth.

"And you're—" he paused, searching his cloudy mind for an appropriate insult. He wanted to say something to provoke her because he was in pain and because she was staring at him with such disdain, but a moonbeam fell on the creamy skin above the neckline of her nightgown, rendering him almost speechless.

"Beautiful," he said, before he could stop himself. "You're beautiful."

She narrowed her eyes at his drunken compliment, and, suddenly conscious of her own state of undress, plucked a woolen shawl off the chair, pulling it around herself. She went into the pantry and returned with a tray piled high with matches, candles, needles, spools of silk thread, clean strips of cloth, and small, glass bottles filled with various herbs and ointments. She removed the dirty cloth he held against his arm and wrapped his wound with fresh linen. "Hold this," she instructed, guiding his hand into place.

"I didn't ask you for your help." It was a half-hearted protest. The only thing he wanted, and the last thing he needed, was to be aroused by the soft touch of her fingers on his skin.

"Your wound has to be cleaned and stitched, and I doubt you can manage it on your own given your current state of inebriation."

She lit several candles, flooding the dim room with bright, bouncing beads of lights that hurt his head. She set a kettle of fresh water to boil on the stove, adding basil, bay, cinnamon, comfrey, and rosemary to the liquid. By the time the pot began to fuss and simmer, the kitchen was filled with a warm, earthy scent.

He watched her as she worked. She mixed her potions with ease, measuring the herbs by touch, laying her cleaned instruments on a fresh cloth to dry. She unwound the blood-soaked linen from his arm and wiped his skin with the scented water. His tight muscles relaxed beneath her hands.

He marveled at the gentleness of her touch, offering her one of his half smiles. She raised an eyebrow and poured a vial of alcohol over his wound.

He cursed in pain, pulling his arm away from her.

"Don't be such a baby." She threaded her needle, passed it through the flame of a candle, and, ignoring his pronounced and vulgar expressions of discomfort, began the slow, painful process of stitching James' flesh back together.

He need not have worried about his romantic reaction to Arabella's tending. She gripped his elbow with little sympathy, fiercely plunging the sharp edge of her needle into his skin and pulling the thread tighter with every stitch.

"Is this really necessary?" he asked after a particularly aggressive stab. He winced and pulled his arm away once more.

"I can cauterize the wound with hot iron if you prefer."

He didn't reply, but, preferring a needle to a flame, he gave her his arm again, and the room fell silent. The cut was long and deep, and she had to stop stitching every so often to rinse his skin clean of fresh blood. By the time she had closed the wound and mixed a thick poultice to spread over the line of stitches, the numbing effects of the whiskey had worn off. James felt a throbbing soreness in his arm, in his head, and in every spot a fist or a foot had connected with his body.

"Are you going to tell me what happened?" Arabella asked, tying a fresh cloth around his bicep to hold the poultice in place.

"It's not important." He closed his eyes, wishing he could disappear. When he was a child, he used to close his eyes whenever he got himself into trouble, hoping that if he couldn't see his father, his father wouldn't be able to punish him. It had never worked, of course, and it didn't work now. When he opened his eyes, Arabella was still standing in front of him, her arms folded over her chest. The fabric of her summer nightgown was so thin, he thought he might be able to see through it if only he could stop the room from spinning.

"If I need to tend to the consequences of your *small misunderstandings*," she hissed, "then I think I have the right to know what happened."

Frustration flooded his aching body. Why did she always appear before him at the worst possible moments in his life, tempting him with her intoxicating scent of oakmoss and wildflowers? If she had been asleep, as she should have been at this late hour, he could have passed out with another bottle of whiskey so he wouldn't have to think about the curve of her lips and the black web of lashes hovering over her impossibly green eyes. If he had never discovered her sneaking through the woods, her body wet and glistening from the river, her face hypnotizing in the midsummer moonlight, then his delivery of Jonathan's cargo would not have been interrupted. It was *her* fault he had argued with Jonathan about their business dealings, and it was *her* fault he had broken Mrs. O' Shaughnessy's rule about fighting in the Spouter Tavern. If she wanted to know what had happened, if she wanted to know just how much she had complicated his life, he might as well tell her and be done with it.

"This small misunderstanding was about defending *your* honor, Arabella."

"You said this had nothing to do with my father."

"It doesn't," he spat. "Not everything is about William."

"Who else would take issue with my honor?"

"Only the entire town!"

"What are you talking about?"

He pushed himself up from the counter, looming over her with his full height. He wanted to chastise her for what she had done, but a small voice in the back of his pounding head stopped him. He knew he should give her the chance to explain herself before he took the drunken words of a dockhand as absolute truth.

"Are you a witch?" he asked viciously, half-curious, half-embarrassed to be posing the question aloud. He was a grown man who thought himself above believing in stories meant to scare children, but the question of whether Arabella was a witch had gnawed at him the entire time he had known her.

She took a step back from him, flinching at the angry sound of the word in his mouth.

"Why would you ask me that?"

"Why won't you answer me?"

"Because you're a fool!"

"Because *I'm* a fool?" he shouted, forgetting it was the middle of the night and his elderly grandmother was asleep upstairs. "I'm not the one calling you a witch, Arabella. Everyone in Mystic is calling you a witch. They're saying you performed witchcraft with your sister. At her *Christian* wedding!"

"Then everyone in Mystic is a fool!"

He wanted to smash her glass vials on the ground and throw her cauldron through the window so she would take his revelation about the rumors seriously. He clenched his fists at his sides to keep himself from hurling her tray of instruments across the room

"I almost killed a man tonight because he said you were using dark magic in *my* house, so the least you can do is answer my question!" He moved closer to her. "Are you a witch?"

"And what if I am?" she cried. "There's *nothing* ugly about the word witch until it comes from the mouth of an *ignorant* man!"

She turned to storm out of the kitchen, but he grabbed her wrist and pulled her back to face him.

"Did you and Anne perform witchcraft before her wedding?"

"What I do with my sister is none of your business!"

"Of course it's my business, Arabella! I've already told you, *everything* you do is my business!"

They were the same words he had said to her the night he had discovered her gathering herbs by moonlight, and she realized that despite everything that had passed between them since then, he still thought of her as his to command, he still believed his position as her employer gave him the authority to direct her actions.

"Anne asked me to offer her a blessing before her wedding ceremony," she said, not because she owed him an explanation but because she wanted to prove him wrong. "It's not my concern if someone saw our ritual, labeled it as witchcraft, and started a rumor about me." She held her head high, but her voice broke as she spoke. "I don't need or want *you* to rise to my defense when others accuse me of being a witch because you have all but accused me yourself, and not one person who has wielded the word, including *you*, knows anything about what it means!"

A tear slipped from her eye, and James exhaled loudly, rubbing the knot on the back of his neck where Mrs. O' Shaughnessy's shillelagh had landed a glancing blow.

When he spoke again, his voice was controlled, his expression gentle.

"What kind of blessing did you offer her, Arabella?"

Arabella described the oil infused candle, the crushed sage and orange blossoms, the drop of blood she had taken from the third finger on Anne's hand where her heart's blood flowed. She repeated the blessing for him, letting James hear the beauty of it in the old language and the new.

"I did nothing wrong," she said.

He nodded his head, though he understood how her actions had been misconstrued. He would defend her honor with his dying breath. He would suffer a hundred beatings to keep her name out of the mouths of those who wished her harm, but he might not always be there to stop such treacherous accusations.

"I know your faith is important to you," he said, "but you need to be careful."

"We're not living in the 1600's. America is supposed to be a land of religious freedom."

"What America is supposed to be and what America is are two different things," he said.

His jaw settled back into its tight position. The blackening bruises on his face made his scar more prominent. She regarded him with a stubborn look, and he reached out to take her hand. A wave of heat from her fingers traveled through his sore muscles, spiraling deep into his chest, his abdomen, his groin.

"You need to be careful, Arabella," he repeated firmly. He needed her to know how dangerous a small rumor could be when it was given room to grow. "It's bad enough the entire town is still talking about your mother. You shouldn't give them a reason to talk about you as well."

Her eyes reduced themselves to gleaming slits. The atmosphere in the room grew cold.

"Why is the town talking about my mother?" she asked, tension ringing in her voice. She realized her arrival had altered William's public perception among the social elite, but not even the people of Mystic could blame a woman they had never met for her father's indiscretions.

James closed his eyes again, wishing he hadn't said anything. He was tired, and every muscle in his body was sore. When he opened his eyes, she was still there, refusing to move until he answered her.

"Everyone used to say your mother was a witch who cast a dark spell on William to make him break his marriage vow." He spoke softly, wishing he could kiss away the shadow of pain that crossed her face.

"Why would people say something so cruel about a woman they had never even met?"

James opened his mouth to respond, and then closed it again in confusion. He squinted his eyes, studying her. "Catherine Porter," he said after a few beats of strained silence, "she's your mother?" He didn't wait for her response before continuing. "She must be your mother. You share her name. You look just like her."

"How do you know what my mother looked like?" Arabella's heart lodged in her throat. "My mother died in a shipwreck when I was a baby."

"Catherine Porter? William's mistress?" He swallowed uncomfortably. "She used to live here in Mystic."

"Catherine Porter? Lived *here*? In Mystic? My *mother* lived in Mystic? She's alive?" Her questions flowed, one after the other, sweeping toward him like a rising tide.

"Yes—No—I'm sorry—Arabella, I thought you knew." James took a deep breath, trying to explain his jumbled thoughts. "Your mother lived here in Mystic when I was a boy, but she died several years ago, sometime after I went to sea."

"Catherine Porter, *my mother*, Catherine Porter, lived here in Mystic when you were a boy?" Her voice echoed with disbelief. "With William?"

He shook his head. "Anne's mother was William's wife. But everyone knew he kept a mistress in a broken down cottage by the sea." His lip curled in disgust. "He told everyone Catherine had bewitched him. He said she had evil powers. He said he couldn't be held accountable for his actions in her presence."

"Why would he say something like that?" James was lying to her. He had to be lying to her. He was saying terrible things to turn her against her father. "My father loved my mother! I have her letter to prove it!"

James shook his head again. "I don't know what your mother's letter says, but William turned her into an outcast to save his own reputation. That's not love, Arabella."

"You're lying!"

Her eyes were wet with tears, but he had already said too much to take everything back. "I'm not lying. William labeled her the Mystic Witch. People in town blamed her for everything—fires, ships lost at sea, bad weather, damaged crops. Women used to cross the street to avoid her when they saw her walking in town. Boys tested their courage by throwing rocks through her windows, all because of a rumor your father started." He hated telling her these things, but he needed her to listen. "This is why you have to be careful, Arabella. People fear what they don't understand. And fear is a dangerous thing."

All her life, Arabella had believed her mother had perished in a storm at sea, hopelessly pursuing her one true love, and in the course of one evening, James had destroyed that belief and, along with it, the foundation of everything she had believed herself to be. She thought of the whispers that had followed her since she came to Connecticut, the strangers who had looked at her as if they were seeing a ghost. Even Elinor and Anne had pointedly asked her about her faith, questioning whether her spells and incantations carried ill intent. She knew, deep in her heart, James wasn't saying these things to hurt her. He was telling her the truth.

"You said my mother lived in a broken down cottage by the sea," she said. "Do you remember where it is? Can you take me there?"

"It was in a cove somewhere between here and New London. It was in ruins even then. I don't know if it's still standing."

"But you know where it is? You know where it was?" She was crying openly now, tears streaming down her cheeks. "Please, James! Can you take me there? Now?"

He was exhausted, but he pulled his soiled shirt over his head and led Arabella to the stables behind his house.

Arabella had never ridden a horse, so James chose his largest steed, a chestnut-colored Narragansett Pacer that could carry the weight of two riders for the length of the journey. He fitted the horse with a bridle, mounted its bare back, and helped Arabella climb up behind him. He held his horse to a slow trot as they rode through the center of town and over the drawbridge, giving Arabella a chance to become accustomed to the animal's movements. As they reached the deserted pathways to the southwest where the murmur of the river became a memory, he stirred the horse into a gallop to cover ground as quickly as possible.

"Don't let go of me," he said over his shoulder.

He held the reins in his right hand, looped around a small traveling lantern that provided them with dancing light. His left hand reached back to steady Arabella's leg. She clung to his waist as they thundered down the dirt roads that led toward the coves lining the western end of Fishers Island Sound. She bounced on the animal's hindquarters which lunged forward with increasing speed, and it was not until James dismounted the horse, walking ahead to guide it through the stones and briars of an isolated trail, that she found a comfortable balance on the Pacer's back.

The trail opened into a clearing that held a dilapidated, clapboard cottage, its broken shutters creaking in the breeze. Behind the tiny house was an overgrown garden surrounded by a chipped picket fence, and behind the fence was a grass covered mound with a sandy pathway worn down its center, the lone barrier between the house and the sea.

James tied his horse to a tree and helped Arabella dismount.

"I haven't been to this area in a very long time," he said. They had ridden for almost an hour through the murky dark air of the shoreline before finding the path. "I think this was your mother's house, but I can't be sure."

The moon was rolling in the midnight clouds overhead, and a beam of light from James' lantern swept across the low lying brush. Purple spikes of Scottish thistle poked up among the weeds.

"This was her house," Arabella said, as she moved through the thistles and toward the decaying door.

When Arabella was a little girl, she had walked with Caitriona across Scotland's wild moors, listening to her grandmother recite the sacred names and magical properties of the native vegetation, but it was the holy thistle, *Carduus Benedictus,* that had been the first flower to take root in Arabella's heart. Thistles were more than an amethyst hue rolling across grassy hills, more than a sweet, musky scent saturating the air. Thistles were a part of her homeland's history. Thistles were a part of the Porter family legacy.

Scotland's love for the thistle began in the thirteenth century when Norsemen dragged their long ships onto rocky Highland shores to launch barefoot attacks against sleeping Scottish clansmen. The invaders howled in pain at the thistles' sharp bite, awakening the Scots who soundly defeated their enemy in the Battle of Largs. By 1470, the humble thistle was so revered that Scotland's King James III had its image minted onto the country's coins, and less than one hundred years later, *The Most Ancient and Most Noble Order of the Thistle* had been established, its chivalric motto, *nemo me impune lacesset,* declaring no one provokes a Scot with impunity. The Porter women, whose history on the Isle of Skye was renowned, had adopted the thistle as their family symbol, burning it into the leather covers of their grimoires, stamping it onto silver pieces of jewelry, and pressing it into wax seals for their letters and paperwork, its spikes and swirls protecting their bloodline's mysterious secrets.

Caitriona had taught Arabella how to identify the varied species of the plant, spear thistle, meadow thistle, creeping thistle, marsh thistle. She had taught her how to harvest the white and silver seeds beneath the periwinkle down, separating and drying them for use in teas, tinctures, and talismans. Arabella remembered the first time she had tried to pick a thistle bouquet. The prickles had cut her hands, and her grandmother had to place bandages on the pads of her fingers to stop them from bleeding.

Arabella had not seen fields of wild thistle in her travels through Connecticut, and she did not know if the flowers were native to the Americas. She did not know if her mother had carried thistles with her across the Atlantic as James' mother had carried roses. She did not know if Catherine had found a way to restore life to the dried thistle seeds which would have lined her own healer's cloak, the soft grey uniform that had been spun for all the women in the Porter line. What she did know was that the thistles beneath her feet had been deliberately planted in a sacred swirl of protection around the run down cottage, and she hoped the home at the center of the hallowed space, a home born of her absent mother's blood and story, would reveal its secrets to her.

It was James who pushed open the cracked, wooden door of the cottage. One of the hinges snapped from his effort, and the heavy door dangled precariously in its frame. He lifted it and propped it against the wall so the threshold gaped open. He entered the abandoned cottage, surveying the rotting beams on the ceiling and the faded paper tacked on the walls. Peeling strips of newsprint, which had been used as insulation against a long-past winter's frigid temperatures, rustled in the warm wind. Mice skittered in the corners.

"Be careful, Arabella," he said, helping her through the doorway.

The one-room cottage was small and cramped. A large stone hearth occupied the center wall, a dented pot still hanging from its rusted iron crane.

A bed stood in the far corner, and a small wooden chair rocked, as if stirred by ghostly motion, back and forth in front of a broken window.

Arabella scanned the veil, searching for a gap that might allow her to see her mother's spirit, but the separation between the worlds was solid.

This lonely little cottage, built of rotting wood, shattered glass, and howling despair, had been her mother's home. Arabella wondered how much blood had been spilled on its floors. She wondered what somber stories the walls would tell if she stayed long enough to listen. She closed her eyes, but all she could hear was the chirping of the crickets, singing their mournful tune of summer's end.

"Arabella?"

She had momentarily forgotten James was standing next to her, and she turned to face him in the dim light of his lantern's flame.

"How did you know where my mother lived?" she asked, an edge of accusation creeping into her voice. "Were you one of the boys who tested their courage by throwing rocks through her window to frighten her?" A wave of nausea rose within her as she imagined a young James taking part in such a heartless game.

Shame clouded his eyes but he kept them locked on hers. "Yes," he admitted. "I was only ten or eleven years old, but I was old enough to know better. When my father found out what I'd done, he dragged me back here to fix the window and apologize to your mother. He was not a man who would allow his sons to persecute a woman, any woman, even those he didn't agree with or understand."

Arabella had never seen a portrait of James' father. She knew James had his mother's dark hair and her Irish blue eyes, but in that moment, irrationally angry with him for playing a childhood prank on the woman who had abandoned her, she hoped James had inherited his size and strength from his father, and she hoped his father had punished him for what he had done to Catherine.

He half-smiled, reading the train of her thoughts. "Your mother was sweeter and far more forgiving than my father was, though she did threaten to turn me into a frog if I ever bothered her again."

Arabella laughed then, in spite of her anger. A tear slipped down her cheek. It was the kind of thing Caitriona would have said.

"It would've served you right."

He nodded. "Your mother winked at me when she said it, so I *thought* she was joking, but now, having been on the wrong side of her daughter's temper a few too many times, I realize I should have taken her warning more seriously." He was teasing her, trying to soften her anger and make her smile, and it was working.

"Well, if *you* had the fairy gift of transfiguring people, I would have been turned into a frog ten times over by now."

There was nothing he could say to defend his fiery disposition, so he threw his shoulders up in acquiescence. He looked toward the threshold of the open door, as if he could see his father and his ten-year-old self still standing in the sea mists.

"My mother learned she was pregnant the next year," he continued, "and she insisted on hiring your mother as her midwife. I sometimes wondered if it was her way of making up for what I had done."

"My mother worked as a healer?"

"She did, though mostly for poor women and immigrants who lived on the outskirts of New London. There were not many in Mystic who would have put their health in her hands, not after the things William said about her."

"It didn't bother your mother that everyone thought Catherine was a witch? It didn't bother your father?"

"My father wasn't thrilled about my mother's choice, but he would never deny her anything." He sighed, not knowing what to say. "My mother was an immigrant. She was all alone when she came here from Ireland, and things were difficult for her before she met my father. Your mother didn't have a man to protect her, and I think my mother wanted to help her."

"Catherine was a Porter woman, James. She would not have needed a man to protect her, no matter how difficult her life was, and, even if she did need a man, she had my father."

James shook his head. "I already told you, William had a wife, Anne's mother."

"William may not have been able to *marry* my mother, but that doesn't mean he didn't *love* her. It doesn't mean he wouldn't have done everything he could to protect her. Even if it's true you heard vicious rumors about Catherine being a witch, you can't know it was William who started them. You said yourself, you were only a child."

"This is where William forced her to live, Arabella." He gestured around the broken room as though the cottage itself was evidence of her father's lack of devotion.

"You said this cottage has been abandoned for years! I'm sure there was a time when it was a lovely home." She doubted her words even as she said them; she could feel sorrow and anguish stamped into the walls. Still, James had no right to pass judgement on her parents' relationship, especially after admitting to taking part in Catherine's persecution.

"Your father was *friends* with William, James. Would he have been friends with a man who mistreated a woman?"

James shook his head again. "William worked for my father, and my father respected his experience and social standing. That doesn't mean they were friends."

Her eyes flashed with anger at his clarification, and he let out another long sigh. He wanted to say something to offer her some comfort. "I think our mothers would have been friends if their circumstances had been different. Your mother called on us regularly at Alden House when my mother was with child. They talked in the Old Tongue for hours. I always liked the sound of it, though I never knew what they were saying."

Of course Catherine would have made regular visits to Alden House if she was Mary's midwife. It was the way Porter women had been taught to practice their craft. "You must minister to more than the illness or the condition," Caitriona used to say. "You must minister to the soul as well." On the Isle of Skye, Caitriona and Arabella had spent long hours in the homes of pregnant women, assessing the progress of both the mothers' bodies and their spirits. Arabella's heart filled with a childlike jealousy as she realized James had spent more time in her mother's presence than she had. The uncomfortable feeling only ebbed away when she remembered Mary's pregnancy had ended in tragedy.

"James, was my mother there when your mother—"

She couldn't finish asking her question. An agonizing silence settled between them. James nodded his head, closing his eyes against the memory of his mother's tortured sobs as she held her dying infant, trying to forget the terrible stillness that had followed her final breath.

He had never spoken about the details of that night to anyone, not even Jonathan. He didn't want to speak of them now, but he needed Arabella to know that her mother's life, however difficult it may have been, had been valuable.

"When it was all over—your mother—she stayed with me. The rest of my family was away, more than a day's ride from town. No one thought the baby would come so soon." He swallowed the sudden thickness that arose in his throat. "I don't know what I would've done if your mother hadn't stayed with me."

The shrouders, a group of professional mourners paid to prepare the deceased for laying out, had come to the house as soon as word of Mary's death had spread, but James had lashed out at them, not wanting them to touch his mother or her baby. It had been Catherine who had calmed him down, who had promised him she would clean their bodies and arrange them peacefully in their bed. She had helped James light a candle, and she had whispered a strange prayer, using the old language his mother had loved. She had watched over James as he sat by his mother's side through the long, dark night.

"My father had told me to look after my mother while he was away with Thomas." A little boy's grief curled somewhere in the deep baritone of James' voice. "I thought it was my fault she died. I thought my father was going to blame me for what happened."

"I'm sure he didn't blame you, James."

"No, he didn't." George Alden had rushed home, making it back to Connecticut in half the anticipated time, and he had wrapped his bear-like arms around his son.

"My father told me it was all part of God's plan. He said the Lord works in mysterious ways, and we had to be grateful for the time we had with her." The events of the night and weight of his memories had filled James with exhaustion. He sank into the rocking chair by the window. The weathered wood creaked beneath his legs. "He was trying to make me feel better, but I couldn't comprehend how anything so terrible could be a part of God's plan. I never willingly attended Saturday worship again."

Outside the window, a whip-poor-will called out, marking the hour with its warbling. Arabella wanted to be angry with James for not telling her about Catherine sooner, but how could she blame him for remaining silent when the only memories he had of her mother were wrapped up in the loss of his own?

"Your mother was more than her death, James. The pain and fear she must have felt, they were only a small part of her life story."

The softness of her words slipped beneath his skin, comforting him from within.

"Why did you want to come here tonight?" he asked.

"I never knew my mother," she said, looking around the dilapidated cottage. The pain of perpetual absence was less sharp, less intense than the pain of traumatic death, but it had been a part of her life, a dull ache in the well of her heart, for as long as she could remember. "I thought I might find a piece of Catherine here."

She walked over to the bedside table where an oil lamp, long extinguished, was covered with grime and dust. She found a moth eaten book, *Ivanhoe* by Sir Walter Scott, resting on the corner of the table. She picked it up and opened it to a page that had been marked by an aged stalk of flattened yellow fennel. The ink had faded with time, but it still relayed the loyal majesty of the chivalrous knight, Sir Wilfred of Ivanhoe, as he championed Rebecca, the woman he would always love, but never marry.

She found an apothecary cabinet along the back wall, its shelves lined with jars of murky liquids and moldy herbs. She picked up each vial, trying to identify its contents, wondering how her mother had used them. She opened boxes and drawers, moving slowly about the room, searching for something, anything, to help her understand, to help her heal. After a while, she heard the sound of gentle breathing and turned to find James, still awkwardly slumped in the chair by the window, sleeping. A line of pale, red blood oozed through the sleeve of his shirt just above his fresh wound. She would need to clean and change his bandage for him when they returned to Alden House. She would need to launder the blood from his shirt so it did not leave a stain.

She continued to search the moonlit cottage while he slept, and on the table under a stack of mildewed papers, she found a heavy book, stamped with the Porter Family seal, spikes and swirls of Scottish thistle burned into the leather cover. She knew the book was a grimoire; she could feel the magic rising from its pages. The stiff spine opened with an ominous creak. The handwriting inside matched the script of the letter Hamish McPherson had given her. Stranded in America, without access to her family's shared knowledge and ancient tools, Catherine had created her own scriptures, connecting with her ancestors by recording remembered recipes and spells. Arabella turned the pages, noting traditional remedies and familiar incantations mingled with the names and likenesses of American herbs and wildflowers. Catherine had drawn pictures of the New World blooms next to lists of their medicinal usages; bright orange calendula to ease the pain of sunburns, yellow chrysanthemum to cure a common cold.

Tucked into a silk pocket sewn in the grimoire's back cover, she found a folded letter inscribed with her name. *Arabella.* The desolate air in the cottage stirred when she touched it.

She lifted it from its resting place and held it to her face. It smelled of decay, and the edges of the paper were brittle and dry. Arabella had thought the letter Hamish had given her would be the only communication she ever had from her mother, and, afraid she might lose the pages in her travels, she had committed it memory. *I loved you the moment I first felt you flutter inside my womb*, the letter had said. *Follow your heart, and you will not lose your way.* She had followed her heart all the way to America, and, somehow, it had led her to this broken-down cottage where a second letter, tucked into her mother's grimoire, called out to her across space and time.

She had hesitated before opening Catherine's first letter, afraid that reading it was a betrayal of the grandmother who had raised her.

She was not going to hesitate again.

She picked up James' lantern from its resting place on the cottage floor and carried her mother's letter into the night.

She walked past the garden and down the worn path to a secluded stretch of sand lapped by the salty, rolling waters of the Sound. The beach tilted toward the east, toward the Atlantic Ocean, toward Scotland, and she wondered if her mother had ever come here to gaze into the morning mists that rose off the waters, thinking about the daughter she had left behind.

When Arabella had made her crossing, she had whispered the names *William* and *Catherine* into the sea, hoping they were a magic spell that would carry her to shore. Had Catherine ever whispered *Arabella* into the waves? Would Arabella have heard her voice, whisked to Skye by the ocean winds, if only she had known her mother was alive, and if only she had tried her hardest to listen?

She unfolded the letter and let her mother's words mingle with the churning sounds of the rising tide.

My Dearest Arabella,

How strange it is for me to write your name across my paper after all these years. My pen travels up the slope of the "A" before plunging down the other side, reminding me of the white-tailed eagles that used to soar up the peaks of the Cuillin Mountains before gliding back down toward the sea. Arabella, a name that means "beauty," a name that means "prayer." Your name is all I have ever given you, and your name is all I will ever know of you, fitting punishment for a woman who left her daughter motherless in the shadows of our island moors.

The last time I wrote to you, you were an infant, your auburn hair and green eyes binding you to the Isle of Skye, the only home the women of our clan have known for centuries. By now you must be almost grown, and I imagine you following at the heels of my mother, wearing a healer's cloak of your own as you learn our family's craft. I wonder if my aunts have taught you to sing beneath the moon as they taught me so long ago. It seems I was a different person then, living a different life, before my mind and heart were clouded by romantic fantasies. Now, as my life on earth draws to its close, I am compelled to write to you one last time, sharing my story with you in the hopes that it may one day help you write your own.

When I left Scotland to find your father, I was not just running toward something. I was also running away from something. On the Isle of Skye, I was one invisible woman in a long line of healers. In your father's arms, I thought I would be something more. He told me he loved me, and, not knowing anything of romantic love, I believed him. It took me a lifetime to understand that love does not force you to change who you are. Love is not a lie.

My journey to find your father was fraught with challenges. My ship encountered a fierce storm in the Atlantic, and a few of us drifted for hours upon the wreckage before being rescued. The boat that plucked us from the water was bound for the Americas, but far south of my intended destination. I was forced to seek mercy where I could find it. I endured unspeakable trials. Alone and unprotected, I suffered what I had to suffer, believing that when I finally found your father in the imagined kingdom East of the Sun and West of the Moon, he would remove the iron shoes of my persecution and carry me to my happily-ever-after. I should have known, even then, that a woman who abandons her only child deserves no fairy tale ending.

I did not know your father was married to another woman until I reached Connecticut, but even after I learned the truth, I did not leave him. There has always been a connection between us. We are inexplicably drawn to each other, and, flattered I had left my home and family to find him, your father housed me in a rotting cottage on the edge of the sea, making false promises about the future. He told me he had never loved his wife. He told me she was a sickly woman. He told me once she passed, we would no longer have to remain in hiding. We would sail home to Scotland to make our peace with Caitriona and meet our daughter. Foolishly, I agreed to remain his secret. I lived half a life, going nowhere, seeing no one but your father, waiting for a happiness that would never come.

Years of solitude passed before I could stand it no longer. Winters were particularly rough; sleet and snow pounded the coastline, and frigid winds prevented your father from visiting me. One year, he did not come to me even after the landscape had thawed and bloomed, so I walked into town, asking strangers I met along the way where I could find William Stafford. They directed me to his palatial home on Gravel Street. A woman, small but healthy, sat by the front picture window, playing with a golden haired child a few years older than you would have been at the time. William had never told me he and his wife had a daughter, just as he had never told his wife and daughter about the mistress he kept in his broken down cottage by the sea.

I stormed into the parlor, frightening the woman and her child, demanding an explanation. When your father learned what I had done, a terrible confrontation followed. He beat me and threatened me. He told me I meant nothing to him, but, the next night, as I cried out for all I had left behind in Scotland, he came to me, kissing my bruises, tending to my wounds. He said I had pushed him beyond reason, and that if I took more care not to anger him, he would never harm me again. Wracked with guilt for all I had done to both my family and to his, I forgave him, but, of course, his vow not to hurt me again was only another one of his lies. I have forgiven him dozens of times between that night and this one, believing I had no choice but to accept his false apologies because my own actions had rendered me unlovable.

In my misery, I often dreamed of returning home to our island, but I believed you would be better off without me, so I stayed here in this strange new world, loving William, hating William, serving penance for my mistakes. I had left my home, my calling, my daughter, all because I had believed I needed a man to complete me. How I wish I had known that, despite my imperfections, I have always been complete. Perhaps then I would be telling you all this, instead of committing my final words to a piece of paper you will only find long after I am gone.

Despite William's protests, I eventually returned to my duties as a healer, cultivating a small garden, growing herbs and flowers to brew potions and poultices as my mother once taught me. I sought the favor of the fairies, leaving offerings in return for their blessings. In the boarding houses of New London, I found poor men and women in need of my healing knowledge, and helping them has given my broken life some small purpose. Each child I have delivered, each sickness I have cured, each elder I have helped across the veil, has been a balm for my pain and my sorrow.

There is nothing I can do to heal myself, now. No healer, not even one as powerful as Caitriona, can extend my mortal coil beyond the next few days. When I last saw your father, he was kind to me, and for that, I am grateful. I allowed him to comfort me, even though I know he is the one who first labeled me a witch, a label which has forced me to live in the shadows so I do not dim his light.

Your father will find my body when I pass, but he will not find this letter. I will leave it, tucked into my grimoire, enchanted with sigils that only the blood of my blood can break. One day, you will find it. Of this I am certain, for the fairy gifts which run through our blood tell me it will be so. When I close my eyes, I can see you reading my words in the shimmering light that shines between a far-off midnight and dawn. You are so beautiful, Arabella. I only hope you know that thoughts of you have filled my final days with joy. I only wish I could have offered you some of that same joy in return.

I have asked your father to bury me under the evening primroses in my Moon Garden, a patch of earth where I have managed to cultivate some light in the darkness that has been my life. Evening primrose is a night-blooming strain of the Scottish primrose that flourish along our streams and lakes at home, their roots spiraling deep into the soil, their white petals glowing like a field full of stars. I planted the primroses among datura and brugmansia, devil's and angel's trumpets, their cone-shaped blossoms pointing both downward to the soil and upward to the sky. There, I will rest, my body looking over the ocean waters toward the Isle of Skye, my spirit singing out my heartfelt laments for my mother, my daughter, and my home.

Although it is no excuse for my behavior, I was little more than a child myself when I birthed you and left you. I know Caitriona filled your life with love, teaching you how to work with the elements and forage the earth, but I also know my absence must have caused you great pain. I hope you can forgive me. I hope you can learn from the mistakes I've made. I hope life will be kind to you when you make mistakes of your own. I hope you know, in spite of everything I have done, in spite of everything I have failed to do, I have always loved you. I want you to know that loving you has saved my soul.

You may wonder what a woman like me, a woman who foolishly left her family for the false promises of a man, can know of love, but, in learning firsthand what love is not, I have also discovered what it is. Love is the tender intention behind imperfect words and actions. Love is the bright light that guides us through shadows, and the warm touch that anchors us in turbulent waters. Love is forgiveness. Love is truth. Love is beauty. Love is prayer. Love, for ourselves, our families, our partners, our friends, and for the miraculous world that unfurls around us, is our most humble and sacred calling.

I pray you will know the kind of love which grows rather than withers, which builds rather than destroys, which soothes rather than harms. As a Porter women, you have no doubt learned about the power of words, how to use them to speak your will into being. But, my child, when it comes to matters of the heart, you must do more than speak your own will. You must also learn to listen. Listen not only to what others say, for words can be wielded with wicked and false intent. Listen to what others do. Listen to what you feel.

I never should have left you, my sweet Arabella. My greatest wish, that we would meet again on this earth, will never come true, but, somewhere in the deep beyond, you will find me waiting, penitent, with Caitriona and Una and Aoife and the long line of Porter women whose prayers have protected you since the starlit night you were born. Love is the only thing we carry with us across the veil. I wish you a life so filled with love that, one day, far from now, when it is your turn to step through the threshold, you may slip from the painful bonds of this life in a cloud of peace and contentment.

Always remember, Arabella, even in death, love never ends.

Your Mam,

Catherine

Arabella's fingers trembled as she gripped the final page of her mother's letter. Had it really called her here, to this place so far from her home on the Isle of Skye? She looked up at the stars, wondering if her mother was watching her from somewhere beyond the veil.

When she had read Catherine's first letter, she had believed her parents' love for one another was true. She had hoped finding her father would fill the aching gap of loneliness in her life. She had defended her father, devoting her life in America to helping him, and now she had learned that James' horrible accusations against her father were true. William had hurt Catherine. He had made her feel unworthy of love. Arabella remembered her father's angry, red-rimmed eyes when he had confronted her at Anne's wedding. Would he have hurt her the way he had hurt her mother if James had not been there to stop him?

The thought of James stilled her heart. He was far from the perfect man. He was wild, headstrong, and secretive, but he was also protective and kind. He had only told her the truth about her father because she had needed to hear it. She knew, instinctively, that he would never harm her; he would never try to make her feel small or ashamed.

The stars overhead began to fade as the sky brightened on the eastern horizon. Arabella studied them, remembering how James had taught her to navigate the seas by their light. He had placed himself between her body and the dangers of the woods on the night they had met. He had shielded her from shards of glass when a stone was thrown through the parlor window. He had been wounded while protecting her reputation. He had taken her to an abandoned cottage in the middle of the night in the hopes she might learn something about her mother. She closed her eyes and listened. She heard the love in his heart. She felt the love in her own.

James had said he would never mix his family's blood with hers, but he had never told her he didn't love her. If love was the only thing that could be carried across the veil, shouldn't they allow their love to grow regardless of how complicated their family histories might be? Shouldn't they revel in their desires here, in this realm of flesh, so that one day their spirits might be comforted by the memory of each other's touch?

Arabella folded her mother's letter, placed it beneath a heavy rock, and walked down to the water's edge. A stripe of red light from the rising sun threw itself across the watery horizon like a river of blood. When she heard the sound of heavy footsteps thudding against the sand, she turned toward the pathway that led from the cottage to the beach.

James was striding toward her, a look of fury on his face.

"What in God's name are you doing out here alone?" he shouted as he closed in on her. "I woke up and you were gone—Arabella, do you know how worried I was? I had no idea what happened to you!"

"I just needed some air."

"You just needed some air?" His forward motion stopped when he reached the shoreline where she stood, her bare feet bathed in salt water. "If you needed air you should've woken me instead of leaving the cottage on your own! It's the middle of the night and we're in the middle of nowhere and—"

"And I'm perfectly fine—"

"You could've been attacked by a stranger!" His scar pulsed above his eye as he recounted the fears that had run through his mind when he awoke to find her missing. "You could've encountered a wild animal. You could've slipped on the rocks. You could've hit your head. You could've drowned in the water. You could've gotten lost—"

"None of those things happened, James." She smiled to calm his overreaction, but it only enraged him more.

"Those things could've happened, Arabella!" He placed his hands on her shoulders and pulled her closer so she would listen. "I didn't know where you were!"

"You're right," she said softly, her unexpected acquiescence wringing surprise from his brow. "I'm sorry I scared you." She hadn't meant to frighten him, and she knew he deserved an explanation. "I found a letter from my mother, and I needed to read it alone."

He released her, letting his hands trail down her body until they came to rest against her hips.

"You found a letter?"

She nodded but said nothing.

"You should've woken me." he repeated stubbornly.

She turned away from him, not wanting to continue their never-ending argument about her right to move through the world as she pleased. The brightening stripe of sky above the horizon faded from red to a rosy yellow. It shimmered like a golden thread, making the firmament above inkier by contrast. Stars still glowed in that darkness, each one a pearl stitched into the coal-black cloth of night.

"Arabella," he said, his tone contrasting with the soft music of the water frothing over the pebbled shore. "I'm trying to talk to you."

She turned back to face him. "I don't want you to *talk* to me, James."

"Then what do want?" he asked, his frustration mounting. He had taken her to her mother's cottage against his better judgement, and still she tested him at every turn.

'I want you to kiss me."

The tide stilled when she spoke. Then a wave curled over the sand, covering their ankles in seafoam, and James felt his blood begin to rush and pound through his body, warming him in spite of the early morning chill rising from the bubbling water. He took a step back, worried her words alone might spur him to action.

"I want you to kiss me, James," she said again. She had wanted it far longer than she was willing to admit. She had been drawn to him even before he had plucked her wreath from the river, when she had first seen him shaping a stubborn piece of wood into the bow of a ship as she walked through the deserted shipyard with her sister. There was something between them that was deeper than thought, deeper than choice, and she was tired of denying it.

"Arabella—"

"Don't you want to kiss me?"

She could hear his yearning for her in the way the syllables of her name slid over his tongue. He held himself completely still, moving only his hands, alternately gripping and stretching them to release the tension that was building like fire within him. His heat drew her closer, like the sun drawing forth the first buds of spring.

He backed further away from her, slowly shaking his head in response to her question. She deserved a man who would honor her, a man who would marry her, not a man who would ravage her on a deserted beach as he wanted to do.

She moved closer to him, looking up at him, her green eyes pale in the moonlight.

"Don't you want to kiss me, James?" she asked again, bold, bashful, coy.

"Yes." It was a confession tainted with ire. She was tempting him, and she had no idea how dangerous he could be. "I've wanted to kiss you since the moment I first I saw you, half-naked, by the river in the woods."

She blushed, her coquettish expression so alluring he could not stop himself from gripping her arms and pulling her toward him.

"Every time you look at me," he continued, aroused by her desire for him, "every time you smile at me, every time you challenge me, every time you anger me with your intractable, reckless behavior, I want to kiss you until you can no longer think straight."

His voice wrapped around her like sea mist, and she blinked, slowly, demurely, her long, black lashes alternately obscuring and revealing the beckoning green light of her eyes.

"Arabella," he said, letting her name unfurl like a warning from his lips, "I want to do so much *more* than kiss you—"

"Then why don't you?"

It was a simple question, but it provoked him, and his grip on her arms tightened. He watched her chest rise and fall beneath the loose folds of her nightgown.

"Why don't you, James?"

"Because I can't."

"Why can't you?" she demanded.

"Because I can't marry you, Arabella." He let go of her, his hands balling into fists. "I can't ask William for your hand in marriage. I won't. And even if

I could, if your father thought our marriage would make *me* happy, he'd never allow it. He'd fight me at every turn."

"I didn't ask you to marry me, James," she said. "I asked you to kiss me."

A breeze blew in from the east, making the flame of the lantern she had carried to the beach flicker. The sheer, white linen of her nightgown pressed against her thighs, her waist, her chest, and James hardened at the sight.

"You don't know what you're saying." He held out his hand in an effort to keep a respectable distance between them. "If I let myself kiss you, if I let myself be with you without planning to marry you, you'll be *ruined*." A lifetime of social indoctrination had anchored the rules of polite society into his mind. "It's not possible for us to be together without a marriage, and a marriage is not possible because William and I will never reach an agreement."

"You're the one who doesn't know what you're saying!" she said, unleashing her own irritation in response to his patronizing explanation. "You and William don't have the right to decide who *I* choose to be with! And you certainly don't have the right to declare me *ruined* no matter what I do!"

"You don't understand what will happen if we—"

"I *do* understand, James! I'm not an innocent child in need of your protection! I'm not an ignorant debutant looking for a husband! I'm a Porter woman from the Isle of Skye!" Pride flashed in her eyes as she repeated her family traditions. "The women in my clan have never married. The women in my clan do not adhere to the rules of men. The women in my clan raise their daughters to be strong, independent thinkers. Don't use your backward, patriarchal ideas to tell me what I'm allowed to do!"

"Arabella—"

"I hardly know my father, and from everything you have told me, from everything my mother's letter says, he's not the man I hoped he would be. But I *am* more than his daughter, and I'm tired of you using William as an excuse to stop yourself from being with me!"

"What if I'm not the man you hope I am either, Arabella?" It was a question that haunted him daily. His work with Jonathan had already threatened his home and his family's shipyard. He couldn't let it threaten her safety as well. "Even if we could find a way to marry without William's blessing, even if we could find a way to be together without William using our relationship for his own benefit, I can't offer you the protection of my name, not knowing that one day, my name might be a source of shame to you."

"I don't need a man to give me his name. I already have a name of my own."

She stepped toward him, drawn to him in spite of her anger, her lips brushing against the dark stubble of his face. She knew he kept secrets locked behind his office door, she knew her father believed him a criminal, but in that moment, suspended between the dark of the dying night and the light of the coming day, she did not care. Her body was alive, and it desperately, achingly called out for his touch.

"I want you to kiss me, James," she said for the third and last time, her voice dropping to a whisper. "I want you to do so much *more* than kiss me."

He stared at her as though she was an ethereal creature from another world. Then he reached out to caress her face, gently, afraid she might dissolve into smoke beneath his fingers. She sighed in pleasure, and he covered her lips with his, letting the tightly wound knot of his self-control unravel, letting each fraying strand of his civility snap with a frightening and exhilarating intensity.

The restraint he had shown when he had kissed her by the river was replaced by something primal and possessive. He loosened the ribbon that held her nightgown tight against the top of her chest, and the fabric fell from her body, pooling in the damp sand beneath her feet.

He dropped one hand, letting it glide slowly down her spine and over the swells of her backside, cupping her softness, pulling her closer. He wanted to take her, right there on the edge of the shore, where the ocean froth licked the rocky sand, but he forced himself to pull away, gulping the cool, night air to slow the fire burning within him.

"James?" she whispered, suddenly fearful. His pause had left a coil of torment deep inside her belly. If he walked away from her again, if he left her alone and wanting as he had on the bank of the river, she would never forgive him.

"My God, Arabella." His voice was deep and reverent, like a prayer. His eyes traveled with deliberate slowness over the curves of her hips and chest, coming to rest on the thistle pendant dangling between her breasts. It sparkled like a tiny moon, looped around her neck by a thread of silver starlight. "You're so beautiful."

She felt helpless, more naked now that she was no longer pressed against him. A chill rippled over her bared skin. She tried to lean closer to him, wanting the warmth of his hands against her body, but his fingers rested firmly on her shoulder, holding her at arm's length.

"James?"

"Let me look at you, Arabella" he said. "Please. Just let me look at you."

He traced the curve of her swollen lips with his thumb and then slowly, slowly trailed his fingers down the long column of her throat, across the plane of her chest, and over her breasts, swirling and circling around and around the tight, pink centers until she shivered in the moonlight. When she pressed herself into him again, he slid both hands around her and lifted her into his arms.

"Oh!" She gasped at the ease with which he had swept her off her feet. He smiled at the sound, cradling her against the pounding in his chest as he carried her up the beach.

He thought briefly of taking her back to the cottage, but he placed her down on a smooth mound of damp sand, and she burrowed into the earth. He lowered himself beside her, his lips barely touching hers, his eyes open, watching her. He brushed away the strands of auburn hair that had fallen across her chest, and a sound, deep and guttural, curled from the back of his throat as he revealed her naked body to the night once more. His hand swept, slowly, oh so slowly, over her abdomen, his palm moving steadily downward, leaving a molten trail of need in its wake.

"James—"

It was more breath than name, but it made him pause, his hand resting on the soft, warm curve where the tops of her thighs met.

"I want to do so much more than kiss you, Arabella," he repeated, his fingers twitching against the most private, most sensitive part of her body. "So. Much. More." Each word was a warning, thick and dark against her cheek. "But I need to know—I need to know you're sure."

She arched her back beneath him, willing his hands to move again, wondering how much longer he was going to make her wait. "I'm sure," she whispered, reaching up to stroke the damp curls at the base of his neck. She found his lips in the shadows above her and kissed them gently, looking into his eyes as she repeated his words. "So. Much. More."

He growled, letting his hand resume its sweet, slow, maddening progress. She felt him, hard and pulsating against the curve of her hip, and she looped her arms around him, clinging to the broad muscles of his back as his fingers parted her thighs. His tongue slid into the chamber of her mouth, echoing the movements of his fingers below, in and out, back and forth, round and round. He found a steady rhythm, playing her body like an instrument, pulling and plucking, groaning with his own pleasure as she twisted and sang beneath him.

"James," she cried. "James, I—"

"Do you want me to stop?" he asked, searching her eyes for signs of distress.

"I don't want you to stop." Her breath was hot and ragged in his ear. "I need you, James. Please, I need you now."

In a moment he was naked except for the bandage she had tied around his arm. His lean, tattooed chest pinned her to the ground. A mix of relief and gratitude coursed through his veins as he entered her, his body bearing down like a ship sinking into a storm-tossed sea. He was gentle at first, letting her respond to the growing tempo of his thrusts, reciting her name like a litany, its musical sound an invocation of his desire.

She gripped his shoulders, her nails sinking into his inked skin, her hips rising and falling with the increasing strength of his motion. She wrapped her legs around him, and he kissed her again, his lips hard, urgent, demanding as she crested upward in a spiral of pleasure. When her mouth finally rounded into a ringing cry, he released himself into her, a shower of stars splitting open the night sky.

He held her in his arms as waves of rapture washed over them. They were so close to each other, their hearts beat as one.

"Arabella," he said, trying to catch his breath, "that was—you are—"

But he had no words to describe what had happened between them or the enormity of what she was to him. He knew only that the timeline of his life would be forever divided by this moment. There was his life before Arabella, and there was his life now.

He had moored himself inside her, and he never wanted her to let him go.

By the time James awoke, a bright, warm sun had extinguished the stars. The sound of the surf, the far-off call of sea-birds, the sharp pain in his wounded arm, and the dull ache of his bruised ribs had all conspired to rouse him from his slumber, but he smiled contentedly at Arabella who still slept, her leg draped over his thigh, her head resting on his chest as though he were her pillow. His fingers absentmindedly stroked the curve of her hip until she began to stretch and stir next to him. She looked up at him, blinking in the mid-morning light.

"Good morning," she said, shy and blushing beneath his gaze.

His response was a kiss. He rolled her onto her back, wanting to take her in the broad light of day to prove last night had not been a dream.

"What time is it?" she asked, as his mouth began to follow the trail his hands had mapped the night before.

"What time is it?" He circled her wrists, pinning them to her sides and adopting a tone of affected severity that made her giggle. "If, after last night, you have the presence of mind to ask me about the passing of time, I haven't done my duty to you, Miss Porter, and I must beg your leave to try again." He had done his best to slow himself, he had wanted her to enjoy every stroke of his fingers, every brush of his lips, but now he was hard with wanting, and he let his tongue slide quickly down the center of her chest toward the cradle of her hips.

"James—please—"

"Please what?" he murmured, tightening his grip upon her wrists so she couldn't move.

"Please—stop."

He released her hands. He slid himself up until his eyes were level with hers.

"Arabella?" His expression darkened with concern. "Have I done something to—last night was—but I'm sorry if I—"

He felt tongue-tied, like a teenaged boy instead of a full grown man. He supposed that was what came of ravishing a woman on the beach instead of acting like a gentleman. He had lost himself in his pleasure, and now her hesitation brought the scandalous reality of their situation rushing back to him.

She sat up, drawing her arms around her knees and pulling them to her chest. He pushed himself up and sat behind her, brushing the sand from her damp skin. "Have you changed your mind? Do you regret what happened between us?' he asked hesitantly, bracing himself for her answers.

He traced the constellations of freckles on her back, lingering on a crescent shaped birth mark just below her shoulder. He wanted to chart her freckles like he used to chart the stars in the sky, using them to navigate every inch of her body, but her silence was deafening.

"Arabella—"

She glanced over her shoulder at him. "I don't regret what happened between us, James," she said, smiling. "In fact, I would very much like it to happen again, but, the sun has risen, and I think we should return home before Elinor notices we're gone."

Elinor. He stood up and pulled on his trousers, scanning the horizon to measure the angle of the light. He knew it was far too late in the morning for them to head home now. They would need to cross the drawbridge to reach Alden House, and the streets of downtown Mystic would already be busy with shoppers and merchants beginning their day.

He took her hand and brought her gently to her feet, pulling his shirt over her head to cover her nakedness. It was dirty and blood-stained from his fight at the Spouter Tavern, but he had left her nightgown by the water line, and the fabric had been soaked by the rising tide. What had he been thinking, bringing her to an abandoned cottage in the middle of the night? He shook his head at his own stupidity. He was going to have to find a way to return her to Alden House without anyone seeing her if he wanted to keep the illusion of her honor intact.

"We can't go home now, Arabella," he said. "Not until after nightfall."

"James—"

"I can't get us home without going through town, and I'm not bringing you through town dressed like that."

She arched her eyebrows. "You had no problem with the way I was dressed when we rode through town last night."

"We're not married, Arabella," he said, ignoring her challenge, "and we don't have plans to get married." He watched her face as he spoke, looking for signs of remorse regarding the agreement they had reached. "No one can know we've spent the night together."

"We spend every night together, James. We live under the same roof."

"It's not the same thing, and you know that." He realized it wasn't fair for him to be angry with her, not after he had allowed their union to happen, but she was acting as though the revelation of their intimacy would be something trivial, something people would forget about as soon as the next piece of gossip took hold.

"I've already told you I don't care what people say—"

"I care." His voice was as harsh and as unyielding as it had been before they kissed.

"Your grandmother will be worried when she wakes up and finds no one at home."

"Trust me when I tell you that my grandmother is the last person on earth who would want us to ride through town half-clothed in broad daylight."

He was not going to cede his position to her no matter what she said, but he didn't want to spend the morning arguing, so he walked down to the shoreline to retrieve her sodden nightgown. He wrung it out over the sand, the muscles of his back and chest flexing beneath his tattoos. Arabella had seen his markings in the candlelight as she had sewn his wound closed, and she had seen them under the starlight when they had come together on the beach, but this was the first time she had studied them beneath the bright light of the sun. In darkness, the designs blended into one large field of ink, but now she saw patterns that told the story of his time at sea. She saw an anchor and a fully rigged ship, tattoos that revealed he had crossed the Atlantic and rounded Cape Horn. She saw a series of long-tailed swallows in flight, each one indicating he had traveled five-thousand nautical miles. She saw ebony sailing ropes twisted into Celtic knots and crosses, and star-filled skies covering stormy seas. She saw a triskelion, its three dark lines spiraling outward from a solid center point just above his heart.

She watched him walk back up the beach and place her nightgown on a patch of sand to dry. She could tell by the stubborn set of his shoulders that he was not going to take her back to Alden House.

"Well," she sighed, "if you refuse to bring me home until nightfall, what, exactly, do you plan to do with me for the rest of the day?"

He half-smiled at her, letting the sight of his shirt clinging to the top of her hips push his real and present concerns about their social predicament from the forefront of his mind. Then, in the shallows of the water, against a tree in a nearby patch of forest, over the smooth, wet rocks that lined the eastern facing shore, he made her forget, again and again, about the passing of the time.

VII

It was past noon when James untangled himself from Arabella to find food and water for his horse. He gathered some early harvest apples from a nearby grove of trees and led the Pacer to a clover-filled field fed by a running stream. Then he went inside the cottage and began removing rotten floorboards and broken shingles, hoping to make it safer for Arabella's exploration. He was worried about the integrity of the decomposing roof, and he cautioned her to stay outside, so she wandered the circumference of the cottage, peering through the broken windows, admiring the glistening sheen of sweat that coated his muscles as he moved heavy pieces of debris. After a while, she rounded the side of the cottage, drawn toward the decaying garden gate that led to her mother's final resting place. She lifted the broken latch, hovering on the threshold, listening to the hinges creak as they swung back and forth in the breeze. She took a deep breath and stepped through.

She walked past broken beds once filled with herbs and flowers, and found secret spaces surrounded by hedges so tall they felt like private worlds. The remnants of asparagus, snap beans, radishes and potatoes, all long forgotten, rested among still robust flowers and gnarly weeds that had pushed their way upward through years of neglect. Worm-eaten leaves, still thriving in the harsh conditions, waved in the winds. Arabella ran her hands over the plants, whispering a greeting in the old tongue. They were her kindred spirits, after all. They, too, had been planted and abandoned by her mother. They, too, continued to grow, searching for their slant of warmth and light.

She found what she was looking for, the patch of evening primrose, in the western corner of the garden. It was surrounded by unkempt mounds of witch hazel, cowslip, and meadowsweet. A few bright petals, resilient in their growth, punctuated brown layers of mud and dirt. Rodents burrowed in a patch of wilted datura, their trumpet-shaped blooms, which last just twenty-four hours before shriveling, discarded like breadcrumbs among the vines.

She dropped to her knees in the cool, dark soil, studying the leaves of the evening primrose. They coiled around each stem, lance-shaped and serrated, red vines mapping their dark green background. In Scotland, primrose, which was said to sprout up from the untimely death of maidens whose lives had been reaped too soon, was used to grace marriage beds. It was believed to be the key that opened the door to *Faerie*, an enchanted realm just beyond human reach.

Arabella wondered if William had truly buried Catherine here, beneath the night-blooming flowers that had offered her mother some light and hope in the darkness of her life. It would have been a kindness, for even amid the rot and mold that had taken hold of the vegetation, Arabella could see the poignant beauty of her mother's garden. It was easy to imagine fairies had once gathered here to sing and dance, drawn by Catherine's humble offerings. Their magic still lingered, like fleeting shadows in the undergrowth. Were these fair folk native to American soil? Or had they followed her mother across the sea from Scotland, otherworldly immigrants forced to find a home in a hostile, foreign land?

She closed her eyes, watching patterns of gold and amber heat dance across her darkened lids. Behind the gentle suck of the tide and the quiet hush of the waning summer afternoon was a soft, half-imagined sound, like the ringing of bells. The trio of noises mysteriously combined, shaping themselves into the tune of an old Scottish ballad her grandmother had used to sing her to sleep.

O dig me a grave, and dig it down deep
And strew it all over with primrose so sweet
And lay me down easy, no more for to weep
Since love was the cause of my ruin.

The song was unmistakable. Arabella had hummed it to herself a thousand times over the course of her life, letting its familiar melody soothe her, but she had never stopped to think about the somber meaning of the words. Had Caitriona taught the same song to Catherine when she was a child? Was that why Catherine had asked William to bury her here, beneath the evening primroses, where their daughter might one day find her, drawn to her sacred resting place by an echo of their family's lullaby? She strained her ears, trying to determine the source of the music, but the ringing sound had faded away, and all that was left was the rush of wind and waves. She suddenly understood why James had circumnavigated the globe, searching for the elusive remnants of his own mother's song.

She wiped a tear from her eye as she stood up, resolved to read the rest of her mother's garden as if it were a book, its words written in a language of herbs and flowers. Among the witch hazel and meadowsweet, she found basil and garlic, lemon balm and rosemary, plants known for their healing properties. But she also found hemlock and nightshade, mandrake and monkshood, henbane and wormwood, plants with malevolent uses, plants known to cause harm.

At home in Scotland, Caitriona had gated off a small section of earth where she had cultivated poisonous vegetation, letting clusters of foxglove grow tall and beautiful, their purple and pink bell-shaped blossoms scraping the sky. Favored by fairies, foxglove featured in many Scottish folktales, and it was said red foxes wore the flowers on their feet to dampen the sounds of their footsteps when they were hunting. As a little girl, Arabella had loved the thought of wearing foxglove slippers, and, one day, hoping to outfit the feet of her dolls to ready them for a woodland ball, she had broken her grandmother's rule about entering the gated section of the garden alone. Caitriona was behind her in an instant.

"I told you not to touch them."

"But why?" Arabella had asked.

Catriona had pursed her lips before providing an answer. "The toxins in foxglove can make you sick," she said.

"Then why do we grow them?"

"Because even the most toxic plants can be helpful if they are wielded with good intentions." Caitriona had kissed her granddaughter's hand and sent her back into the house. "One day soon, I'll teach you how foxglove, like the holy thistle, can be used to heal the human heart, but, until then, you must follow my rules and remember it is dangerous to play with things you don't fully understand."

Now Arabella wondered if Catherine had used the toxic plants in her garden to heal or to harm, but the answer was lost to time.

Arabella worked in the garden for the rest of the afternoon, clearing debris from neglected vegetation still searching for the sun. The scent of something cooking reminded her she hadn't eaten anything all day. She followed the smell down to the beach where she found James roasting a long wooden skewer of fish over a small bonfire.

"How did you manage all this?" she asked, visibly impressed.

He offered her a thick filet wrapped in a leaf he had plucked from a nearby tree. "The *Shepherd* once careened in a small archipelago in the South Pacific," he said. "The Natives taught us to catch fish and start fires with nothing but sticks and kindling." He unsheathed his pocket knife and flaked off a steaming piece of white fish, holding it between her lips.

They feasted as a line of low clouds rolled in from the sea. James told her how he had waded into the water and stabbed at the darting, iridescent shapes beneath the waves until he had caught enough fish for their dinner. Arabella told him what she had learned from Catherine's letter and what she had found in her garden.

"Do you think my father really buried my mother beneath her evening primroses?" she asked quietly. The question had been swimming through her mind all day. "Do you think it's possible my father may have loved her enough to grant her final request?"

"I don't know," James said. His mood had darkened when she had described how William had beaten her mother, and, as much as he wanted to comfort her, he couldn't bring himself to say anything that would cast her father in a favorable light, so he slipped his arm around her and pulled her closer.

Clouds of insects rose in the swaying grasses near the tree line, and, after a few minutes of silence, Arabella knelt on the sand, taking his injured arm in her hands and unwinding the bandage she had tied the night before. Her stitches held tight, but she rinsed the area with water, cleaning the bloodied cloth in a stream and wrapping it back around his arm to keep the cut free from sand.

"I'll mix another poultice when we get home," she said, "but I'm not sure I can stop the wound from scarring."

He lifted his shoulders as though it was of no consequence to him. "Every scar tells a story," he said, winking at her. "This one tells the story of how much trouble you cause me."

Her eyes widened into bowls of dancing green light.

"How much trouble *I* cause *you*?"

He laughed, nodding his head toward the bandage. "You have to admit," he said flexing his muscle beneath her touch, "it makes me look fierce."

"We'll see how fierce you are when I remove your stiches."

He laughed again, and kissed her. It would not be long before darkness fell, before they had to return to reality, but right now, she was wearing his shirt, and her hair was blowing loose in the breeze, and her skin smelled like wildflowers. He wished the moment could last forever.

"The scar on your face," she said tentatively, glancing up at the white line seared over his left eye. "What story does it tell?"

"An old story." He rubbed his fingers over the mark as though he were trying to jar the memory loose. "A fire broke out in the shipyard when I was a boy. It was about a year before I ran away to sea. It was winter, and the air was dry, so the flames leapt between the buildings like they were alive."

Arabella knew fire was the most volatile of the elements, one that could rage out of control, casting reflections of itself far into the future. Elinor had told her about Captain Mason's fateful attack on *Siccanemos* in 1637, so it didn't surprise her to learn that Mystic, a place where the boundary between the worlds had been permanently scarred by the flames of war, was prone to fires.

"It was nighttime," James continued, his storytelling cadence giving shape to his words so that Arabella saw his memory in the air above him like a painting. "The sky had an eerie, orange glow. When my father heard the alarm, he ran outside to battle the flames. He told me to stay in the house with my grandmother. Obviously," he shrugged, "I didn't listen."

Arabella pictured a young James, his face still smooth and scarless, rushing headlong into danger after his father had commanded him to stay home.

"There were at least a dozen men trying to douse the flames with buckets of water. Another dozen were emptying a shed to create a firebreak that would stop the heat from reaching the barrels of whale oil stacked on the docks."

She remembered the look of alarm on Jonathan's face when he had asked James if the flames from last month's attack had been contained. "Were you worried about the whale oil igniting when Jonathan's timber was set on fire?" she asked.

He nodded. "That fire was much smaller than the fire of my childhood, but any uncontrolled fire in a shipyard is a dangerous thing," he said. "Almost everything in a shipyard is made of wood. Everything burns. And if you can't contain the flames before they ignite the fuel, you'll never stop them."

While fire was fleeting and volatile, wood was strong and sturdy. If the two elements mixed in perfect balance, they created life-sustaining heat and light, but without proper protections, their union often led to destruction. James poked the embers of his campfire with the sharpened end of his stick. They jumped and flickered in response.

"I've never seen anything like that fire," he continued. "It was an inferno. We were surrounded by moving pockets of flame. The roof of the shed ignited while I was still inside. The flames leapt toward a stack of whale oil barrels in the corner, and everything blazed, hot and white, like hellfire. I heard a sound in the rafters above my head and I looked up." He pointed to his scar. "Something hit me and everything went black. Luckily, Jonathan saw what happened. He dragged me into the street just before the roof collapsed." He smiled. "At least, that's the way he tells the story. Like I said, I was knocked out cold. I didn't wake up for three days."

"You could've lost your eye," Arabella said, imagining burning embers filling the winter air. "You could've been killed."

"Oh, my father would have killed me if my grandmother hadn't stopped him," James said. "It was the year after my mother died—and—well, I'd never seen him that angry with me." He absentmindedly rubbed his fingers over the bandage on his arm. "He was so mad I disobeyed him and left the house without telling anyone."

"Oh, really?" Arabella shot him a such a pointed look he had to laugh.

"If you're trying to draw a clever comparison between me and my father, you'll have to take it up with Elinor. She swears I'm my mother's son."

"Speaking of Elinor," Arabella said, and he immediately wished he hadn't. "We should get back to her, James. We've been away all day, and she must be sick with worry."

He looked up at the sky, its western horizon still streaked with ribbons of purple and pink. The late August light would fade quickly, but it would be another hour before they had the cover of darkness to hide them from sight.

"The moon needs to rise before we can head home, Arabella," he said. He would use it to light their way. It would be safer than lighting his lantern if he hoped to keep their journey a secret.

She sighed. "Well, I hope you have more stories to tell me."

He laughed again, the setting sun filling his eyes with aqua light. He pushed her, gently, until she lay stretched on the sand beneath him. "I did learn quite a few stories from the island women of the South Pacific," he said, kissing her as his hands moved toward her hips. "And I can tell them without using words."

"I think you're forgetting something, James," she murmured.

"What's that?"

She pushed against his chest, turning his back flat against the sand. Then she smiled innocently as she climbed on top of him, straddling him, letting the wide collar of his shirt fall over one of her shoulders as her fingers traced the patterns of ink on his chest.

"I was born on the Isle of Skye," she whispered, moving her hips back and forth in a series of slow, seductive circles, "which makes *me* an island woman. So, maybe *I* should tell *you* a story, without words, while we wait for the moon to rise."

He regarded her with awe, reaching beneath the folds of his shirt, guiding her until she settled over his already throbbing desire. Then he pressed his fingers into the soft flesh at the base of her spine.

And he prayed the moon would take her time.

Night arrived all too soon, dressed in black mourning clothes to mark the end of their joy. James guided Arabella and his horse down the stony pathway that led to the main road. When the ground evened and smoothed, he mounted the Pacer, keeping Arabella in front of him this time, holding her tight as they meandered slowly home.

The retail sections on either side of the drawbridge were quiet, and James kept their gait to a walk so as not to attract any attention with the frenzied sound of galloping hooves. He turned down several side streets to avoid the bustle of the taverns near the pier, steering his horse through the south gate of the empty shipyard and settling him into the stables behind Alden House. He threw a saddle blanket over Arabella's shoulders, trying to cover her nightgown and shawl as best he could to prepare for their meeting with his grandmother.

He knew she would be waiting.

She was sitting at the kitchen table, nursing a cup of milky tea. She had assumed the two of them must have set out early in the morning, before she had risen from bed, and although she quite liked the thought of James spending time with Arabella, she had grown impatient for their return. She had begun to worry they had been hurt or that rumors of an entire day spent in each other's company without a female chaperone might take a sordid turn. Still, nothing had prepared her for the moment they entered through the back door.

She stood up, taking in her grandson's disheveled appearance, his wrinkled clothes stained with blood and dirt. When Arabella emerged from behind him, her unbound curls tousled by wind, the white muslin of her nightgown trailing beneath nothing but a crude, wool blanket, Elinor's face went deathly pale.

"James Patrick Murphy Alden," she hissed. "What have you done?"

Part Seven

Polaris

"Hark, do you hear the sea?"

(King Lear)

"The two of you spent the *entire* night together?"

James pressed the palms of his hands into his forehead until a kaleidoscope of colors danced behind his eyelids. He had just spent the better part of an hour recounting what had happened at the Spouter Tavern and explaining how he had taken Arabella to Catherine Porter's abandoned cottage by the sea, but all his grandmother seemed to care about was their breech of social propriety.

"By the time I realized what we had had done, it was too late to return," he said.

They were still gathered in the kitchen, James and Elinor seated at the table while Arabella tended to a kettle on the stove, hoping a fresh pot of tea would calm the tension that had been created by their late return. Arabella's nightgown was stiff and scratchy with sand and salt water. The cuts and bruises on James' face had deepened in color, and the tattoos Elinor detested were visible beneath the loosened collar of his tattered shirt.

"When we left the house, I thought we would be home before first light," James explained, trying to justify his actions. "Once the sun rose, I knew we couldn't return without being seen, so we had no choice but to wait for darkness."

"You had no choice?" Elinor's face was drawn tight with disapproval. "You *chose* to leave this house with a half-clothed, unmarried woman!"

"I know." James ran his hands through his rumpled hair. "I wasn't thinking."

"Oh, it is painfully obvious you were not thinking!" Elinor leaned on her jeweled cane and used it to push herself up to a standing position. "Do you know what could have happened, what still might happen, if the two of you were seen?"

"We weren't seen."

"You were drunk and hurt and half out of your mind, traipsing through the night with Arabella on the back of your horse, and you expect me to take *your* word that you weren't seen?"

James tugged at the sleeves of his torn and bloodied shirt. Scratches crossed his swollen knuckles.

"We weren't seen," he repeated.

Elinor paced back and forth in front of James' chair, her feet and cane tapping out an awkward three-beat rhythm as she spoke. "It's bad enough you stay out all hours of the night, drinking and fighting like an animal! It's bad enough you and Jonathan have risked this family's reputation with your questionable business dealings! But now, you compromise a young woman who is supposed to be under your protection! Have you given any thought, any at all, to what William is going to say?"

Elinor pointed a shaking finger in Arabella's direction.

"*She* may have some excuse for behaving as the two of you have, being what she is, but, *you* were raised to be better than this, James!"

He stood up, knocking his chair to the floor with his sudden movement.

"Don't talk about her like that—"

"You have proven her a wanton—"

"Don't talk about her like that!"

James had never, in the history of his life, raised his voice to his grandmother, and the shock of it registered on the old woman's lined face. He exhaled loudly and bent down to pick up his overturned chair. He put it gently back in its place.

"I'm sorry," he said quietly, "I shouldn't have yelled at you, grandmother, but I need you to listen to me. None of this is Arabella's fault, and I won't let you disparage her just because you're angry with me. I promise you, we weren't seen."

The ticking of the grandfather clock in the hall echoed like a beating heart. The tea kettle that Arabella had set on the stove whistled, and she removed it from the heat.

"You'll have to marry her," Elinor said, her voice as resolute as his.

"Grandmother—"

"It's the only way to fix this. I'll speak with William. He won't be happy to learn that you've taken advantage of his daughter, but he's a reasonable man, and, given his own past, he may have some sympathy for your situation."

"You're not going to say anything to William."

"Oh, I know this business is usually conducted among men, but with the history between the two of you being what it is, I think it will be far safer for me to broach the subject. With any luck, William will see that the best thing for everyone is that the two of you marry quickly and get ahead of—"

"I'm not going to let my *grandmother* broker a marriage arrangement for me," he said, gripping the back of his chair in frustration. She had been speaking more to herself than to anyone in the room, and his interruption took her by surprise. "No one will be saying anything to William."

Elinor stopped her pacing and glared at him. "If you think you're going to marry William's daughter without asking for his permission first—"

"Arabella and I are not getting married."

Elinor opened her mouth to respond. No sound came out. James glanced at Arabella before bringing his eyes back to his grandmother.

"You *will* marry her, James," Elinor said when she was able to speak. "And you will do it directly."

"Arabella and I are not getting married," he repeated.

"William will not allow you to ruin his daughter without answering for it! When a man and a woman of your social standing act as the two of you have acted, a marriage *must* follow! You *know* this!"

"That's only true if their actions have been brought to light, and I've already told you, *three* times, we weren't seen."

"James—"

"No one is saying anything to William. No one knows what Arabella and I have done."

"*I* know what you have done!" Elinor cried. "*You* know what you have done! *God* knows what you have done!" She slammed her cane against the floor as she spoke, "You cannot run away from this and leave Arabella to pick up the pieces! You cannot go back to living your life as though it were yesterday—"

"I'm not running away," he said, struggling to keep his voice under control. He had run away from his troubles on multiple occasions in his youth, shipping out to sea after vicious arguments with his father, and he knew his grandmother would always hold that against him, but he wasn't a boy anymore. He was a man, and he had the right to make decisions about his own life. "Arabella and I have discussed our plans for the future, and they don't include marriage."

An expression of horror passed over Elinor's face. "Are you telling me that the two of you plan to continue—"

"Yes."

"Without getting married?"

"Yes."

"Oh, James,' she said, shaking her head and lifting her dark eyes to his. "How could you? In your *father's* house?"

"It is *my* house!" His voice rose in volume again, as though he were commanding a ship full of men instead of speaking to his elderly grandmother. "My father left this house to *me* when he and Thomas died, and *I* am the one who will determine what happens under its roof, not *you*!"

Elinor's chin shook, and she sank into her chair, covering her face with her hands. She choked back a sob, and James gritted his teeth against the sound of her grief. He would rather be flogged than listen to his grandmother cry. He wished he could pull back his angry reference to the passing of his father and brother, a sensitive topic that still caused her great pain.

"I'm sorry," he said again. "I didn't mean to—"

Elinor slapped her hand against the table, silencing him. "I don't need or want your apologies, young man," she said, speaking to him as though he were an errant child. "I *know* your father left *this* house, the house that *my* husband grew up in, the house that *I* raised your father in, the house that *I* have lived in since the day I was married, to *you*. You may own this house, but how dare you imply that your father would support your dismissal of my rightful concerns! George and Thomas would have both agreed with *me* regarding your dishonorable behavior! And neither one of them would *ever* have spoken to me as you have tonight!"

"Grandmother—"

"Do you expect Arabella to put her trust in a man who thinks so little of women that he stops his own grandmother from expressing her opinion because it contradicts with his? You have *ruined* Arabella's reputation for your own pleasure, and you offer her *nothing* in return, not even those few rights guaranteed to a women by a legal marriage! You *know* what will happen if the two of you are discovered!"

"I'm not going to let anything happen to Arabella—"

"You already have let something happen to her! And yet you refuse to do the right thing! You refuse to marry her! *She* is the one who will have to live with the shame of this transgression when your secret is inevitably discovered!"

Elinor shook her head, blinking away the tears that had welled up in her rheumy eyes.

"Oh, James," she sobbed. "What would your own mother say if she could see you right now?"

James closed his eyes. For a moment he was unable to move. Then he lowered himself into his chair. He placed his hand on top of Elinor's. Her skin was dry and cold, and he ran his fingers over the knobs of her knuckles as he had when he was a child. He did not know how to explain his relationship with Arabella to himself, let alone describe the details of it to his grandmother. He had spent half his life on the wild and lawless seas, but he had been raised to be a gentleman, and he knew what he and Arabella were planning to do went against the social and religious codes his family had instilled in him.

"I won't let any harm come to Arabella." He squeezed his grandmother's hands, bidding her to look at him. "I promise I'll protect her reputation. I promise we'll be discreet."

"You're resolved against marriage, then?" she asked, jutting her chin stubbornly. "The two of you are determined to continue your relationship in secret?"

"Yes."

Elinor pushed her chair back and stood up.

"I suppose I am to blame for all of this. I saw the spark between the two of you. I encouraged it, hoping you might respectfully court her and marry her, hoping your union would heal the rift between the Aldens and Staffords, hoping you would find comfort in Arabella when I died."

"What are you talking about?" The expression on his grandmother's face was beyond anger, beyond grief; it was a wary acceptance of fate that chilled him to the bone.

"I'm dying, James," she said, wielding the words like weapons, letting them sink into her grandson's flesh like an iron harpoon. "Don't look at me as though you don't believe me. Arabella can confirm it."

He glanced from Elinor to Arabella and back again, his eyes squinting, his scar growing tight.

"And now you want to fill the final months of my life with shame." Elinor's voice dripped with condemnation, and she turned to walk out of the kitchen, stopping only once to deliver her final blow. "If you wanted to disregard everything your parents and I have taught you, if you wanted to forsake everything the Alden name stands for, you could have at least waited until I was dead."

Her feet and cane tapped their rhythmic beat against the wooden floors as she exited the room. James listened as the sound faded down the hallway and up the sweeping staircase at the center of Alden House.

"James, are you all right?"

He had been staring out the window at the herb garden behind the kitchen since his grandmother's abrupt exit. A moth fluttered against the windowpane, drawn by the light of the kitchen candles.

"Is it true?" he asked without turning around. His arms were wrapped across his chest, his fingers unconsciously gripping the wound beneath his shoulder as though he could press his irrevocably cut flesh back together with the force of his will. "Is she dying?"

"Yes."

The news should not have been a shock to him. He knew his grandmother was advanced in years, he knew she had been growing weaker, but somehow, the cold, hard truth of it stunned him.

"Why didn't you tell me?" His words were laced with a strain of accusation Arabella had often heard when she had worked as a healer on the Isle of Skye.

"It's never been a secret." She wished there were something she could say to make him feel better. "Elinor knew she was dying when she hired me."

"Why would she do that? Why would she hire you, knowing who you are, if there was nothing you could do to heal her?" He turned around to face her. "I allowed you into our lives, I allowed *William* back into our lives on the premise that she needed you to *heal* her."

"No one can heal her, James."

He leaned back against the counter, his scar throbbing over his eye. His entire life had been turned upside down since Arabella's arrival. He had called her horrible names. He had accused her of unspeakable acts. And now he had shouted at his dying grandmother for doing the very same things he had done, even though he knew she was only trying to protect Arabella from the consequences of his own reckless actions.

"There must be something you can do, something I can do, to help her," he said, refusing to accept he had to lose yet another person he loved after yet another bitter argument.

She moved closer to him. She placed her hand on his arm, caressing him until his muscles relaxed.

"You can't stop her death, James, but there are a thousand moments of life between this day and the day she will die. You can care for her and comfort her while she still draws breath in this world, and you can hold her hand and let her know you love her when she's ready to leave it." The words fell from her tongue, sweet and golden, like honey, a balm to his pain. "She's angry now. She's upset because she thinks we've betrayed her, but if you *listen* to her concerns, if you hold your ground without losing your temper, the two of you will find a way to make peace. And I promise you, I'll be here to help her, and to help you, for as long as you need me."

She took his hand, and he watched as she intertwined their fingers together.

"What she said about what you are, about the way you were raised—"

His voice trailed off as though the weight of his guilt had finally become too heavy for him to carry. He cleared his throat. "I'll talk to her Arabella. Even if it's true she's dying, I won't let her say those things about you again."

Her eyebrows lifted into a pointed arc. "I believe you've said worse things yourself," she reminded him playfully.

He nodded his head in contrition before squeezing her hand. "You know none of it's true—the cruel things I've said, the cruel things she's said—you know whatever happens between us, I'll always protect you—"

She leaned into his chest. stopping his rambling thoughts with a gentle kiss.

"I know," she whispered, her breath skirting across the stubble of his beard. "You don't have to say it."

He slid his fingers down her waist, resting them on the curve of her hips and looking into her eyes. He stared at her for a few moments before speaking.

"Would you?" he asked, the question tentative on his tongue. He had no idea how he would handle William's interference in his life if he married Arabella, but his grandmother's words had cut him deeply. "Would you marry me if I asked you?"

Her eyebrows arched again. She shook her head, and her refusal felt like an arrow through his chest.

"You shouldn't ask a woman to marry you because your grandmother demands it, James."

He nodded, sighing inwardly at his pervasive inability to say or do the right thing. "I *will* talk to her," he said. "She's going to have to accept things as they are whether she approves of our relationship or not."

"You can't issue her an order and expect her to follow it. She's your grandmother, not a member of your crew. Give her some time."

"It sounds like you're the one issuing an order."

"It's the only way you'll listen."

He smiled, surprised by the surge of joy she had managed to stir in him. He knew he should regret what they had done, but when he held her in his arms and lost himself in the endless green fields of her eyes, the troubles of the world seemed to fall away. He tucked a stray curl behind her ear, pulling her into an embrace and resting his chin on the top of her head.

"I love you, Arabella," he said, a wave of relief washing over him as he finally let the words escape from his lips. They blinked, like fireflies darting through distant woods, and when she spoke, it seemed as though she had captured his words in the palms of her hands and returned their magic back to him threefold.

"I love you, too."

The following morning, Arabella woke to a quiet house. James had already left for work, and Elinor was sitting in the garden, fanning herself beneath the shade of the tall oak trees. Arabella entered the pantry, searching for the small jar of dried rose hips she had harvested from the garden. They had been among the first pieces of false fruit to appear, replacing the spent blooms of high summer, and she had just enough to prepare one pot of Memory Tea, a concoction that would slowly release all the beautiful recollections the rosebushes had ever known. She combined the rose hips with black tea leaves and lemon peel, scooped the dry mixture into a muslin sachet, and filled a large ceramic teapot with hot water. While the tea steeped, she whispered the words Caitriona had taught her, in the old language and the new, her breath mixing with the plumes of steam rising from the pink-tinged liquid. She carried the teapot into the garden with a tray of blueberry bread.

"I thought you might be hungry," she said, setting the tray on a table and pouring the tea into a painted cup.

Elinor did not look at her. She did not answer. But she did take a sip of her tea.

"I'm sorry about last night." Arabella sat down and took her hand. She had grown up in a family full of women, and she had learned the importance of addressing conflicts directly so hurt feelings did not fester. "Everything happened so quickly. I was the one who asked James to take me to my mother's cottage. He never meant to upset you."

Elinor sighed and took another sip of tea.

"The two of you have both defended the other's actions to me, but neither of you seems to understand the consequences that may come of what you've done."

Arabella spread some butter on a piece of bread and offered it to Elinor, telling her about the Porter Clan and their unconventional thoughts on marriage. Elinor listened with curiosity, and, at Arabella's prompting, she shared the story of how she had fallen in love with her husband, James' grandfather.

"Elinor," Arabella said after their conversation had loosened some of the old woman's anger and disappointment, "you must have known my mother when she lived in Mystic. Why didn't you ever tell me about her?"

Elinor rolled the edges of her shawl with her fingers. "Your mother spent a good deal of time in our home when Mary was pregnant, but the two of them often conversed in Gaelic. Beyond that, all I know of your mother's life is that it ended in tragedy because she refused to conform to societal rules. I don't want the same thing to happen to you."

Elinor finished her tea, and Arabella poured her a second cup. Slowly, the rose hips began to work their magic, passing on their memories of warm sunshine and river breezes with each tart, floral mouthful.

"I don't know how James grew into such a stubborn young man," Elinor mused. "He was the most beautiful little boy, so thoughtful, so much like Mary." The sun had reached its zenith in the sky, and the old woman stared at the far corner of the lawn where a large rosebush swayed, still blooming in the late-summer air. "He used to pick me bouquets of roses," she said, her voice laced with sweet sorrow. "I never realized how badly the thorns cut his fingers."

Arabella took a sip of tea from her own cup, letting the memory released by the rose hips unfold in her mind's eye; James, a little boy with big blue eyes, gathering armfuls of pink blooms in a bucket, his expression stoic against the bite of the thorns.

"He's still the same little boy inside, Elinor," she said, but the old woman, as stubborn as her grandson, shook her head, and Arabella knew it was going to take several weeks of patient conversation and endless pots of rosehip tea before the conflict between the two of them showed any signs of healing.

August ripened into September without any rumors surfacing of what had happened between James and Arabella at the cottage by the sea, which provided Elinor with a small measure of comfort. Nevertheless, she remained distant and judgmental. One evening in late-September, James came home and found her dozing in the front parlor. A side window had been cracked open and the rose bushes swayed beneath the casement, their pink petals deepening into rich autumnal shades of burgundy and brown.

He stood on the threshold of the room, watching her sleep. Arabella had told him his grandmother had several months left to live, but every time he looked at her, she seemed so small and so frail. He wondered if she would still be alive to see the roses bud in the spring.

More than ten minutes passed before she awoke with a start.

"How long have you been standing there?" she asked.

"I just walked in now."

The two of them had been treading softly in a space between love and anger for the better part of three weeks, carefully avoiding any topic that might lead to another confrontation. Elinor listened to the chimes of the clock on the mantle, noting the late hour.

"Where have you been?" she asked, shivering in the evening air. He lifted a knitted blanket from the back of the wing chair by the window and carried it over to her, spreading it across her lap.

"I was at Catherine Porter's cottage," he said. "The walls are rotting. The roof is ready to collapse. I want to make it a safe place for Arabella to visit in the spring, so she can tend to her mother's garden."

"That cottage, and the land it sits on, belongs to William, James."

He did not respond. William had abandoned the cottage when Catherine passed, and as far as James was concerned, no one but Arabella had any right to claim it.

Elinor pressed her lips into a straight line, knowing his silence was yet another dismissal of her valid concerns. "Arabella is in our garden if you're looking for her."

He glanced out the window. The moon would be rising over the horizon soon, providing Arabella with enough light to harvest the last of the season's herbs. He sat down on the couch next to his grandmother. He wanted to speak with her alone.

"I'm going to take Arabella sailing on Saturday," he said. Autumn and winter were fast approaching, and he would need to prepare his boat for storage in the river shed, scraping the bottom clear of barnacles, readying the lines and sails for next year.

"Another week of missing Saturday services," Elinor replied, her voice flat and hollow. "But it's hardly necessary for you to announce your absence anymore."

He let his grandmother's provocation hang in the air unanswered.

"I have a gift for Arabella, and I want to show it to you," he said.

He pulled a small jewelry box out of his pocket and passed it to Elinor. Inside was a silver ring crafted of two intertwining bands. Each band was fitted with a row of diamond chips which sparkled against the box's black velvet swaddling.

"Does this mean—"

"No," he answered quickly, before Elinor could begin planning their wedding ceremony in her imagination. "I've already told you we're not getting married, grandmother."

She closed the box and handed it back to him. "You can give Arabella any of my jewels, James, any of your mother's." The Alden women had amassed large collections worth far more than one simple ring. "You know everything under this roof is yours to do with as you see fit." He winced as she reiterated the sentiment he had hurled at her in the height of their argument. "Why have you gone to the trouble of buying her something new if you aren't even willing to ask for her hand in marriage?"

"I want her to have something special, something all her own."

"Why are you telling me this, James?"

He turned the box over in his hands for a moment before responding. "Because I want you to know that what you think of me, what you think of the way I would treat her, of the way I would treat any woman—it isn't true."

He placed the box back inside his jacket pocket and looked at his grandmother. "This ring is my promise to her. It's my promise to love her and care for her and protect her. I'm telling you this because I want you to know, that in spite of all my faults, I'm a man who's capable of keeping my promises."

"A promise made on the deck of your sailboat is not the same thing as a vow made before God."

His rubbed his hands along his thighs and turned his eyes away from her. The candles on the table flickered, their dancing light illuminating the portrait above the mantle. James looked at it for a few minutes before turning back to his grandmother.

"I don't need God's blessing on my relationship with Arabella," he said. "But I would like yours."

She turned her attention to the blanket in her lap, kneading the soft yarn between her fingers. "You'll give Arabella this ring, you'll carry on with this relationship, whether I give you my blessing or not, correct?"

He squinted his eyes in the dim light, distressed by the direction of her thoughts, but he answered her honestly. "Yes."

"Then why does my blessing matter?"

He got up and walked over to the window to stop himself from responding in anger. He counted the number of petals that lay beneath the rose bushes in the garden. He counted the steadfast blooms still clinging to the branches. He counted the stars just beginning to glow in the late September sky. He closed the windowpane and latched it shut. Then he turned to look at his grandmother.

"It's been more than three weeks," he said. "How much longer are you going to stay angry with me?"

"James Patrick Murphy Alden." She spoke quietly, singing the syllables of his name and shaking her head at him like she used to do when he was a child. "I've been angry with you since you were fourteen years old, and I don't plan to stop anytime soon."

He opened his mouth in surprise, but she continued speaking.

"You were just a boy, a *boy*, signing four years of your life away to a whaling ship," Elinor said, retreating into the stores of her memory. "You were long gone before we even knew where you were. It had only been two years since we lost your mother, and your father was terrified he had lost you too."

Her voice trailed off. James was acutely aware that his family disapproved of his choice to run away to sea, but they had never talked about what had transpired at home after he left. He had assumed his father had been furious. The thought of George Alden being terrified of anything seemed impossible.

"George was my only son," Elinor continued. "He was, he *is*, my pride and my joy, and I will *never* forgive you for hurting him the way you did, even if you were too young to know any better." Her voice wavered with emotion. "Each time we heard of a shipwreck or the death of a crewman at sea, he would drop to his knees and pray for your safe return. Each time word of a successful hunt reached our shores, his eyes glowed with pride. I think a part of him admired what you and Jonathan had done."

James shook his head. "I don't think I would call it admiration, grandmother," he said with a wry smile, remembering how fiercely his father had fought to keep him on shore when he had finally returned. The evening after the *Shepherd* had moored in New London Harbor to off-load its barrels of whale oil, the crew had gathered at a local tavern. James and Jonathan were in the middle of a spirited celebration when Thomas walked in, his fine clothes and polite manners at odds with the rag-tag uniforms and gruff actions of the sailors. James, who had already signed on to ship out again in three weeks' time, had not planned to visit his family until just before his next departure, hoping to minimize the arguments he knew would follow the announcement of his intentions, but Thomas had warned him that their father was waiting outside with a carriage to bring him home. If James did not come out of the tavern to talk to George, George was going to come in.

It had been a long, uncomfortable ride back to Mystic followed by three weeks of intense fighting about James' future. It wasn't until James had returned from his second whaling voyage, debt-free, that he agreed to sail aboard the merchant ships disembarking from his father's shipyard so he could remain closer to home.

"Now you want to know how long I am going to stay angry with you," Elinor said, her frail voice rising and falling like a candle flame that burns more brightly when the wick grows short. "I can hardly remember a time I was *not* angry with you, James. And yet, I have always loved you. Before you, I never knew such anger and such love could sit side by side in my heart."

She sighed, and James lowered his eyes to the floor.

"You came home to me in my darkest hour, after George and Thomas died. Oh, it took you far too long to get here, but you *did* come home to me, and now you are all I have left in this world. It *infuriates* me to think I am going to die before I see you married to the woman I know you love."

He crossed the room and sat down next to his grandmother. He looked around the parlor, remembering how full of life, how full of laughter it had been when he was a child.

"I can't imagine this house without you," he said before he could stop himself. His long legs stretched past the end of the couch, and Elinor rested her hand on his thigh.

"Houses live longer than people do, James. I've watched four generations of Aldens live and die in this house." A tear slipped out of her eye, pooling in the deep wrinkles at the corner of her cheeks. "It's a beautiful ring," she said, nodding toward the box in his pocket, "and I know, in my heart, you're a good man, but I will not give you my blessing to carry on against the laws of God. If you want my blessing, you need to make amends with William and ask Arabella to marry you."

"If you would just listen—"

"I don't want to listen. I don't want to spend the time I have left arguing with you. I'm not going to change my mind." She spoke with finality, but managed a smile for the first time since the night he had taken Arabella to her mother's cottage by the sea.

"Don't look so upset about it," she said. "We both know you'll do as you please whether you have my blessing or not. I only hope one day you'll come to your senses and marry Arabella. I want the two of you to fill this house with beautiful children, each one more trouble than the next. You deserve your fair share of trouble after all the trouble you've given me."

He nodded his head and lifted her hand to kiss it, an apology for all that had passed between them and for all he could not bring himself to do. When Arabella came in from the garden, her basket full of late season herbs, she heard their mingled laughter. The sound dissipated the tension that had been hanging in the house like morning fog, leaving a phantom mist of familial love and understanding behind.

By Saturday, the skies looked threatening, but James, who wanted to take Arabella to a place as beautiful as she was, promised the storm would stay out to sea until after nightfall. He had been careful not to show Arabella anything more than polite affection in his grandmother's presence, and he looked forward to Saturdays, when Elinor spent the majority of the day worshipping and dining with the elders of their congregation. It was then that he and Arabella would come together, desperate and hungry for each other, in the empty shipyard offices, in the stables behind the house, in the vacant work sheds among rolls of canvas sailcloth and lengths of thick, heavy rope. Now, he wanted to sail her to a deserted stretch of the Atlantic, just past the protected waters of Fishers Island Sound, where they could be completely alone.

Arabella had packed a basket filled with bread, cheese, and bright, red apples, the fruits sliced down the centers to reveal their hidden stars. She pulled her grey healer's cloak around her as James steered them down the river and toward the cool breezes of the Sound.

"One day I'll sail us to the Isle of Skye, and you can show me the Cuillin Mountains and The Old Man of Storr," he said after she told him of her island's rugged landscape and looming outcrops. Arabella, who still had nightmares about the terrible storm she had encountered while crossing the Atlantic, wasn't sure she would ever find the courage to sail back home to Scotland. As they rounded the tip of Fishers Island and entered the deep, rough ocean waters, she gripped the gunwale with both hands.

Dappled sunlight perched on the waves like a thousand white butterflies pausing to rest in their flight. Tomorrow would be the autumnal equinox, when the earth would once again balance itself between light and dark. Just six months ago, she was walking alone through the swaying grasses and swarming bees of Scotland's moors, and now she was sailing over ocean swells with the man she loved, seagulls and cormorants dipping and soaring above their heads.

The boat lurched over a large wave, and Arabella eyed a few dark clouds low on the horizon. "Maybe we should turn back," she said.

"There's no need to worry." James smiled and tacked the sail, filling the canvas with wind.

"But, you said a storm was rolling in, and this boat is so small." She remembered how *Martha's Destiny* had been eclipsed by the height of angry ocean waves, and she couldn't imagine traversing turbulent water in James' twenty-five foot sailboat, no matter how seaworthy it might be.

"This boat isn't small, Arbella." He laughed. "Our whale boats were about the same length, and they carried five rowing men plus the captain directing us from behind."

She tried to imagine pulling up alongside a great whale in the middle of the ocean. "Are there whales swimming beneath us right now?" she asked, a tone of alarm in her voice.

"Probably not. The Wampanoag used to hunt these waters long ago, but now men have to travel far distances to find whales." He stood up, rolling the sails and dropping the anchor so the boat stilled its course. A white crest swelled over the gunwale, spilling seafoam across the deck. He locked the tiller in place, and leaned against the top of the small berth sunk into the bow, pulling Arabella toward him. The sun was warm now that they had stopped moving, and he unclasped her cloak, folding it and placing it in a box on the deck.

"If there was a whale in the water below us, how would we know?"

"We wouldn't know unless it surfaced," he said. "On board the *Shepherd*, we posted watch from sunrise to sunset each day. The crow's nest sat eighty feet above the deck, so our lookouts could see for miles in every direction, and even then, we only spotted a few dozen whales each year."

"Were you ever posted on watch?"

"Of course. We all were, but Jonathan was our best lookout. He taught me to search for changes in the color of the water instead of searching for whales. He always says if you want to find something valuable, you have to catch it out of the corner of your eye, like a falling star."

Arabella scanned the water which stretched in every direction as far as she could see. "Where are we?" she asked.

"We're not that far from shore." He pointed toward a flat line of earth which she could barely discern from the rolling seas. "You can see the coast if you look for it. The Natives call it Turtle Island."

"Is that why Jonathan has a turtle shell tattoo on his hand?"

James nodded. "His father had Pequot and Wampanoag blood. Jonathan never really knew him, but we sailed with many Indigenous men who told us their tribal stories," he said. "We used to keep track of the passing days with Jonathan's tattoo. Every turtle shell has thirteen plates for the thirteen full moons of the year, and twenty-eight platelets for the number of days in each moon cycle."

On the Isle of Skye, the Porter Clan had celebrated each full moon of the year: *Quiet*, *Ice*, *Seed*, *Pink*, *Flower*, *Mead*, *Horse*, *Grain*, *Harvest*, *Hunter*, *Dark*, *Cold*, and *Blue*. They would dance beneath the moon's silver glow, drawing down its power for potions and remedies. Arabella smiled, thinking the moon had known both she and James long before they had known each other; the celestial orb that shone above the earthy moors of Scotland was the same one that floated over the rolling waters of the sea.

A wave splashed over the boat and Arabella gripped James' shoulder.

"You don't have to be afraid of the waves," he said, pulling her closer. He tilted her face up to his and kissed her until she felt dizzy. When he released her, she turned her head from the lapis blue of his eyes to the dark blue of the sea to the slate blue of the sky and back again. She was adrift in an endless swirl of blue.

He reached into his pocket and brought out a small box, holding it out to her like an offering.

"Open it," he said.

The silver and diamond bands of the ring twinkled in the sun, intertwining circles of sparkling light. She traced their paths with her finger.

"It didn't belong to my mother or my grandmother," he explained, remembering what had happened the last time she had donned Alden jewelry. "I had it made just for you. Look at the inscription on the inside."

She lifted the ring from its velvet pouch, squinting at the Gaelic words delicately carved into the inside loop of the silver. *Grá Mo Chroi. Cara M'anama.*

"Can you read it?" he asked.

"*Grá Mo Chroi.* The love of my heart," she whispered. "*Cara M'anama.* The friend of my soul." She looked up at him, a tear slipping from her eye. He reached up to brush it away.

"I may not be able to marry you," he said, "but I want you to know how I feel about you." He kissed her, a soft, tentative brush of his lips against hers. "I pledge my heart and my soul to you, Arabella, in this life and in the next. Always."

Another wave rocked the boat, throwing Arabella off balance. It had only been a month since she and James had come together on the beach behind her mother's cottage, their bodies melding into one another in a way she had never experienced before. Whenever she was close to him, she felt a tingling sensation, the deep pull of magic that had been ignited by her solstice ritual. She knew James felt it too, but pledging his heart and soul to her in the world beyond would prove a far more complicated task than loving her body in this one.

"Always is a long time," she said quietly, not wanting him to make a promise he couldn't keep. She placed the band in his hand. He closed his fist around the ring.

It was not the response he had expected.

"Arabella—"

"I can't change who my father is," she said. *You'll never be one them, no matter what you wear*, William had warned her. *The promise of an Alden is worth less than dirt.* "And I can't change my faith. Not even for you."

"This ring has nothing to do with your father or your faith," he said. He stared at her, waiting for her to respond, his scar white against the sun-darkened skin of his face.

"You've already told me my father is the reason you can't marry me. And I've already told you the women in my family have never married. The faith I practice is different from yours, so much so that you and Elinor have both asked me to hide it from public view. You can't brand me with a ring and magically transform me into the woman you and your grandmother want me to be."

He shook his head angrily. "I'm not trying to brand you, Arabella," he said. "And I'm not trying to transform you into something you're not. This ring is a gift, for *you*, from *me*."

"James—"

"Let me finish." His voice was harsh and tight. He opened his palm. The ring glistened on his callouses, an unbroken circle of light, a Celtic knot with no beginning and no end. "I know we come from different worlds, but for reasons I can't explain and don't fully understand, my heart and my soul are knotted with yours. Even when you frustrate me beyond reason, as you're doing right *now*, I don't want to be separated from you." The sea, sharing his vexation, roiled beneath them, and he closed his fist around the ring again, his fingers turning white with the pressure of his grip.

"I want you to have this ring, but if you don't want to wear it, if you think wearing it requires you to change the essence of who you are, you can throw it into the ocean. If you don't feel the same way I do, you can tell me. I'll to take you back to shore and I'll never lay my hands on you again, even if it kills me. But I need you to know, I *need* you to know, that no matter what you decide, no matter what happens between us, now or in the future, I love you, and there's nothing William or Elinor or even God himself can do to stop me."

He kissed her, a rough, pressing kiss that only ended when he placed his forehead against hers and exhaled deeply. When he spoke again, his voice was soft against the howling of the winds.

"*Grá Mo Chroi.* The love of my heart. *Cara M'anama.* The friend of my soul. That's who you already are, not who I'm trying to make you be."

He opened his palm again, lifting the ring to the level of his heart, steeling himself against his fear she might toss it off the side of the boat.

The wind moaned off the water, and Arabella watched James as the boat moved up and down on the waves. Here, alone with him, away from their families and their life on land, everything seemed so simple.

She held out her right hand, the one James had tied to his own when she had taught him about handfasting on the night her sister had been married. He smiled in relief, his expression as bright and as joyful as the sun itself. Then he kissed her, slipping the ring onto her third finger, and guiding her to the bench carved into the stern of his boat. He pulled her down onto his lap, losing himself in her lips.

Waves slapped the side of the boat with rhythmic intensity. Arabella looked up, glancing warily toward the dark clouds gathering on the horizon. "The storm is still a few hours off," he said, pulling her face back toward his.

"I promise you—

He kissed her cheek.

"I will sail us—"

He kissed the hollow at the base of her neck.

"Safely home."

He kissed her mouth, tugging at her full, pink lips.

His hands moved up to the top of her dress, a soft blue cotton she had brought with her from Skye. Its bodice was laced up the front with a long, black string. He untied the string, pulling it slowly through each of the grommets until her chest fell loose against the fabric.

"What are you doing?" she asked, glancing nervously at the vast open space around them. Despite the storm waves building beneath them, the sun overhead was still bright, the air above still clear. They weren't alone on a deserted beach in the shelter of a protected cove, and she was worried someone might see them even though there wasn't another boat in sight.

"Haven't you heard the stories sailors tell?" he asked with a mischievous grin. The slick sound of fabric sliding over metal carried across the water as he continued unlacing her bodice, and she blushed, remembering the bare-breasted figureheads on the front of the great merchant ships that sailed across the Atlantic. Even Robert, the captain of *Martha's Destiny*, had told her the sight of a naked woman could shame a turbulent sea into submission. James shifted his legs, spreading her knees beneath her skirts so she straddled him as he helped her slip her arms out of her sleeves.

"Hold onto my shoulders," he said, his thumbs caressing the sensitive flesh beneath her breasts as he spoke. A brisk sea breeze whipped through her hair, undoing her braids, reddening her exposed skin. He reached under her skirts, fingers whispering along calves and thighs, lifting her up, unbuttoning his trousers. The boat bucked beneath them, and she gasped aloud as the waves pushed him up and into her.

"I—oh—" She twisted the linen of his shirt as he pressed her hips down against him with each new swell of the ocean. She arched her back, pushing against the movement.

He laughed, watching expressions of pleasure dance in her eyes. "I told you not to be afraid of the waves."

"Oh—I—" Her breath was coming hard and fast. He swallowed a groan and smiled. One hand cupped her bottom and the other reached up to spread the ocean's mist into a glistening streak across her naked chest. He found her fingers, entwining them in his so the cool silver of her ring rubbed against his skin as they moved with the urgent, unforgiving flow of the water.

She titled her head toward the sky, lost in a sea of sensation, anchored only by the aching hardness between her legs. He watched her face grow flush. He watched her silver thistle pendant bounce between her breasts. He watched icy sea drops roll down the slopes of her warm, palpitating skin.

When it was over, she fell against his chest. He freed his hand from beneath her skirts, rubbing the length of her back until his own breath slowed. Then he brought her newly ringed finger, still entwined in his, to his lips.

"*Grá Mo Chroi.* The love of my heart. *Cara M'anama.* The friend of my soul," he said, his voice still rough with desire.

"Always," she whispered, believing, in that blissful moment, that the words he had inscribed on the ring were true.

James sailed Arabella safely home as he had promised, lashing his boat to the shipyard dock just as the storm clouds opened. He scooped her off the deck, laughing as he carried her over wet gravel and muddy puddles. He built a fire in the parlor as soon as they entered Alden House. Then he stacked a pile of pillows on the floor so they could sit beside the flames, warming themselves as the logs popped and hissed.

It was to be the first of many cozy fires, for the storm had ushered in the change of the season, and soon the warm, clear days of late summer were a distant memory. James redoubled his efforts to make Catherine Porter's cottage safe for Arabella, replacing rotting wood with fresh lumber and adding new slate shingles to the roof. By the end of September, he was so focused on finishing the project as a surprise for Arabella that he temporarily relegated the daily running of his shipyard to the lawyers and merchants who worked in his offices, electing to sleep at the cottage so he did not have to waste time traveling back and forth. He returned home after a few days' absence to find his house quiet. Arabella was in the back yard, reading a book of poetry. Elinor was sewing in the parlor. A note addressed to James rested on the entryway table. It was dated that afternoon, the third of October, and it was written in Jonathan's hand:

Starkweather and Shetley.

8:00.

Tonight.

A chill ran down his spine as he read the order. He had forgotten all about *Polaris*' scheduled shipment, the one he and Jonathan had agreed to in July.

Polaris had been due to pull into its home port on the thirtieth of September.

And Jonathan had expected James to be waiting.

P*olaris* was the first ship James had built when he returned home to Mystic after the death of his father. Inundated with legal papers and financial ledgers he did not understand, and surrounded by long, flat stretches of motionless land, James had found his only solace in the large work shed by the river. He had designed and directed the construction of a graceful coastal clipper that would transport cargo with maneuverability and speed. The rounded hull had been shaped from live oak frames that extended upward like the ribcage of a great whale, its deep, hidden spaces covered with oak planking and held together with black locust pegs. The masts and decks had been crafted of white pine, caulked with oakum, and spread with a thick, sweet-smelling resin. Named for the star that helped sailors of the Northern Hemisphere find their way, *Polaris* sat tall and proud in the water, its fore and aft sails scraping the skies.

A ship of *Polaris*' speed and caliber required a skilled and determined master to command her, and James had gifted her freely to Jonathan who had lost his captain's rank in New London's whale and seal hunting fleet when he had abandoned his post on the *Nymph* to accompany James back home from the Antarctic. James and Jonathan had christened *Polaris*' bow with a bottle of whiskey instead of champagne, raising their voices in sea shanties instead of prayer. *Polaris* was the only ship housed in the Alden Shipyard that did not belong to a group of wealthy investors, and her schedule was subject to the whims of James and Jonathan alone. She had sailed all the way to China, trading tea, opium, and spices between the far east and Europe, and she had carried whale oil and furs across the Atlantic, but most often, she sailed down the North American coast, delivering New England goods in exchange for the hard, dense lumber James used for the production and repair of ships in the yard. Each time James watched *Polaris* slip down the river to start a new journey, he wished he were aboard, raising the sails instead of pushing a pen across the papers that cluttered his father's and brother's old office desks.

When *Polaris* pulled into the river on the thirtieth of September, the date Jonathan had specifically given to Arabella so he and James could test whether she would share the information with her father, a mob of armed men waited on the dock. Jonathan had coordinated his arrival with the evening's flooding tide, lowering the anchor and letting it drag through the silt of the river bed so he could steer his large ship toward the wharf for unloading. A stout line had been tied to the pier and wound around the capstan to fit *Polaris* against the dock, and as soon as she was secure, Jonathan had instructed his men to lower the gangway so he could greet his waiting adversaries.

"Good evening, gentlemen," he had said, mentally taking their number, seven men, including William Stafford, plus two officers dressed in watchman uniform, only one of whom Jonathan recognized. The unknown officer stepped forward.

"Take out your papers," he said, one hand resting on the billy club at his waist. Jonathan looked over the watchman's shoulder at the small crowd of men gathered behind him. Most of them lived in Mystic and had worked in the shipping industry, frequenting the Burrows Cooperage where Jonathan had labored as a boy. They all recognized him, but they glared at him as though he was a stranger.

Jonathan calmly reached into his jacket pocket and took out the slim, tin container he used to carry his Seaman Protection Certificates, the papers which proved he was a free man and a member of the American marine workforce. Jonathan kept his papers on him at all times, especially when he had business in Southern ports where bounty hunters regularly conducted searches for enslaved men escaping on the high seas. He was rarely asked to produce his papers in his hometown, and he had never been asked to do so in New London, a city where large numbers of free Black sailors congregated in tenements and boarding houses, but he knew his failure to comply with the request of a watchman, however impertinent a request it was, would land him in irons.

The watchman wrenched open the lid of Jonathan's water-tight container and scrutinized the papers, noting their reference to the captain's pierced ear and turtle shell tattoo. There was no question Jonathan Burrows was the man he claimed to be, but then, one word from the silent members of the mob standing behind the watchman would have confirmed as much.

"We've been given a credible report that *Polaris* is transporting stolen goods," the watchman barked, returning Jonathan's papers and wiping his hand against the thick cloth of his jacket. "We'll need access to your logbooks and cargo lists, and we'll need to confirm the identity of every Black and Native man on your crew."

It was the twilight hour, and the fading autumn sun sent its weak rays through the tree line on the opposite side of the river, giving the watchman's skin a gilded sheen. Jonathan slid his tin of papers back into the pocket on the inside of his jacket. When he spoke, his words were soft and practiced, the antithesis of the stern authority with which he commanded his men at sea.

"You'll find the papers of every man on my crew in order, sir."

"Papers can easily be forged," William said, separating himself from the crowd.

"As to the ship's records," Jonathan continued, never taking his eyes from the watchman, "*Polaris* is registered under the name of Mr. James Alden, the owner of this shipyard. He'll confirm the identity of my entire crew, and grant you access to board the ship and review its logs."

William's lips curled into a smile. "What a pity he's not here," he said. He twitched with palpable joy, relishing his long-awaited moment of revenge. "Move aside, boy, and let us conduct our search unimpeded."

Jonathan had nothing illegal in the holds of his ship. He had known that if Arabella did feed her father information regarding his undocumented arrival, William would request an official search of his ship. When the search yielded nothing, William's future attempts to accuse *Polaris*' crew of smuggling would fall on deaf ears, providing them with a small measure of relative safety from any further interference in their business. But Jonathan had not anticipated the absence of James. *Polaris*' crew, a collection of highly skilled Black, Mulatto, and Indigenous men, all carried Seaman Protection Certificates to certify their free status, but the copies that authenticated the documents were locked in the safe in James' shipyard office. The watchmen had the right to detain Jonathan and his men in the county jail until the copies of the papers were produced or until respected community members swore affidavits on each man's behalf. Jonathan had seen free men in free states illegally sold back into slavery under the guise of the Fugitive Slave Act, and he did not want to give the small mob of justice seekers the chance to abuse their power.

"If Mr. Alden is not in the shipyard, send someone to get him," Jonathan said, his voice growing clipped. The peak of Alden House was visible from the docks, and every man in the crowd knew exactly where it was.

"Are you telling us how to do our job, boy?" the watchman asked, taking a step closer to the captain. "Mr. Stafford already told you, James Alden isn't here."

Jonathan's crew outnumbered the small mob, but both watchmen had pistols in their belts, and two of the men in the crowd held the leashes of large dogs that panted heavily against the strain of their collars. The evening air was wet with the river's chill, and the canines' whimpers echoed off the wood of the ship.

With a silent motion of his head, Jonathan commanded his crew to stand down.

The armed men boarded *Polaris*, ransacking its holds, confiscating its logbooks, and arresting the entire crew on suspicion of forged papers. The men were locked in the crowded county jail for almost forty-eight hours as authorities searched for citizens willing to offer sworn statements of their free status. Jonathan had forced himself to stay awake through the long, uncomfortable days, rolling a coin over his knuckles as he calmed the fears of his worried crew and dreamed about the pain he was going to inflict when he finally got his hands on James.

V

Starkweather and Shetley, located across the street from The Whaler's Inn, was in the heart of downtown Mystic. Known for its prestige and luxury, the restaurant had recently hired a French chef who cooked entrées to order, making it a popular spot for wealthy businessmen and prominent politicians to gather.

James sat at a small table covered in fine white linen, nursing a glass of whiskey. It was half past eight o'clock, and Jonathan still hadn't arrived. James stared at the fine china place setting in front of the empty chair across from him. The whiskey he had ordered Jonathan gleamed beneath the whale oil candelabra. James pulled at the chain tucked into his waistcoat and checked the time on his father's old pocket watch.

It was another twenty minutes before Jonathan arrived, his captain's uniform cleaned and pressed to perfection, the stale smell of the prison's holding cell washed away. He strode decisively over to James' table and sat down across from him, removing his hat and placing it on the peg at the back of the chair. He glared at James, waiting for him to speak.

"Jonathan—"

"The last of my crew was released from custody this afternoon."

When James had returned home from the cottage and found Jonathan's note, he had stormed to the shipyard, demanding explanations from the merchants he had left in charge. They had informed him of the confrontation between a group of watchmen and the crew of *Polaris*, and James had immediately journeyed to the county jail to inquire about the arrests. There, he learned William had filed a report against *Polaris* on suspicion of stolen goods. Although no contraband had been found in the search, the crew had been lawfully detained until verification of their free identities was secured.

"It was nasty business, but it had to be done," the head watchman, an old friend of George Alden's, had explained. "Forging papers is a serious crime, and without access to the documents in your safe, we needed credible citizens to confirm each man's free status." He had cast his red-rimmed eyes directly on James, issuing a stern warning. "Mr. Stafford's allegations of smuggling were unconfirmed by evidence, but his accusation alone is alarming, especially given the long history between your families. Your father would roll over in his grave if he thought you were using the company that bears his name to conduct *any* kind of illegal activity. I'd like your assurance this has all been a misunderstanding."

James had offered it, swallowing his pride to thank the elderly watchman for his help in freeing the crew. Then he had walked the streets of Mystic until eight o'clock, wondering how he was going to explain his unexpected absence to Jonathan.

"Where were you, Jimmy?" Jonathan demanded, his voice echoing through the quiet restaurant.

James glanced around the room, longing for the din and shouting of the Spouter Tavern where they would be free to argue without anyone noticing them. A group of businessmen to their left was engaged in a whispered conversation with a flustered waiter, and an out of town couple, who had walked over to Starkweather and Shetley from The Whaler's Inn, stared silently in James' direction.

"Do you remember Catherine Porter's cottage by the sea?" he asked, turning back to Jonathan whose eyes narrowed dangerously at what seemed like a purposeful evasion of his question.

"Where were you?" he repeated angrily.

"The cottage, Catherine Porter's cottage, is falling apart. I've been staying there to make some repairs." He took a sip of whiskey to calm his nerves.

"There's a garden behind the cottage, and I thought Arabella might like to bring it back to life next spring," he explained.

The out-of-town couple had not yet received their meals, but they rose to leave, a look of distaste on their faces. Jonathan tapped his fingers on the table and leaned toward James, waiting for the couple to cross behind him before he replied.

"You missed one of our scheduled deliveries because you were busy playing house?"

"I wasn't playing house, Jonathan. I was fixing the roof of the cottage."

"The roof of a cottage William Stafford owns," Jonathan pointed out, clenching his teeth together. He wanted to kick James across the ornately decorated room. "You and I agreed on the thirtieth of September when I was here in July," he said.

"I know." Jonathan had taken great pains to explain the details of his plan on the evening his cargo had been set on fire, but so much had happened since then that the date had slipped James' mind. "I should've been there."

The waiter, who had failed to placate the group of businessmen, hurried to another table at a desperate signal from a customer. Jonathan leaned closer to James, turning his chin to the left.

"They searched my ship—"

"You wanted them to search your ship—"

"I didn't want them to haul my men to the station like animals."

James ran his hand across the back of his neck. He knew his absence had led to the arrests. "I should've been there," he said again.

A well-dressed man, clearly the manager of the establishment, walked toward their table. Jonathan, who sat looking toward the front windows of the building, his back facing the other diners in the restaurant, noted the confused expression on James' face, and reached into his jacket pocket, silently placing the tin container that held his Freedom Papers on the table. Then he rested his palms flat on either side of the plate in front of him, waiting.

James looked from the tin container to the man walking toward them and then back to Jonathan, a sick feeling rising from the pit of his stomach. When he had received Jonathan's summons to meet at Starkweather and Shetley instead of Spouter Tavern as they usually did, he had been so preoccupied with his own mistake that he had barely given the change in venue any thought. It was only now, with the patrons of the restaurant leering at them and the staff bearing down on their table, that he realized Jonathan had intentionally requested a meeting in a part of town where men of his color and class had never been welcome.

"Why did you want to meet me here, Jonathan?" he asked, the coil of guilt in his stomach giving way to anger.

"I wanted to meet you here," Jonathan said, his voice flat, his eyes never moving from James' reddening face, "to tell you that the last of my crew was released from custody this afternoon." He was repeating what he had already said, reiterating a fact James already knew, because the conversation they had been having was not the reason he had called their meeting. Jonathan wanted James to witness the indignity of what they both knew was about to happen.

When the manager reached their table and politely suggested the captain might be more comfortable in a tavern on Water Street, the only thing that stopped James from flying into a violent rage was Jonathan's curt command.

"Don't," he said with such force that James froze in place, watching helplessly as the manager reviewed Jonathan's papers.

"Shall I call the authorities?" the waiter asked, frightened by the tension mounting between the manger and the two men at the table.

"There's no need for that, sir. I was just leaving." Jonathan stared at James as he spoke, collecting his papers and rising from the table. He plucked his hat from the peg on the back of his chair, nodded in polite submission to the manager, and walked toward the door of the restaurant, disappearing into the night.

James paid the bill and exited Starkweather and Shetley, but when he got outside, Jonathan was nowhere to be found. James headed away from the civilized center of town toward a row of pubs and boarding houses. He entered the Spouter Tavern, but Mrs. O' Shaughnessy, who had long since forgiven him for his fight with the dockhand in August, took one look at the expression on his face and sent him away, giving him a bottle of whiskey and strict instructions to find somewhere else to drink it. He wandered the back alleyways taking large swigs from the paper-wrapped bottle, trying to forget what had happened in the restaurant. After a couple of hours, he found himself on the docks of his shipyard.

He sat down, leaning against a large piling, dangling his legs over the murky river. The tides were receding, pulling the noisy current back toward Fishers Island Sound. Crickets called mournfully from the marsh grasses. *Polaris* floated in her slip, tall and dark against the thin, October night.

From his position at the end of the dock, James could see the low skyline of the shipyard, its long line of buildings and offices, its cooperage where watertight barrels were made, and, beyond that, the old barn owned by the Burrows family. As a child, Jonathan had slept on a straw pallet in the cramped attic space of the barn. Mr. Burrows had locked him in each evening to prevent him from wandering free, but Jonathan and James had loosened a board in the back corner of the barn so they could enter and exit without anyone knowing. When darkness fell, Jonathan would place his lone lantern in the attic's dormer window, a signal to James that the cooperage was empty and the coast was clear.

The boys would climb trees in the forest north of the river, dropping rocks and sticks into the Whitford Brook, imagining them enemy warships or pirate fleets. When Jonathan was too tired or hungry to run through the woods, they would play card games in the attic with a deck they had fashioned from folded leaves. The small, uninsulated space was freezing cold in winter and stifling hot in summer, and the walls sloped so low the boys could only stand upright in the center of the room. When Jonathan couldn't sleep, he whittled pictures into the boards with a rusty nail. Carvings of tall ships covered the wooden beams, their intricate lines mimicking the rigging and sails of the boats traversing the river outside his small window.

Jonathan owned only one change of clothes, a small, tin plate for the food Mr. Burrows provided him, and the homemade deck of cards he kept hidden under his straw pallet, so James often brought him books from his family's extensive library to help him pass the time. One rainy evening, while Jonathan was lost in a copy of *Robinson Crusoe*, James found an old piece of cloth that had been tied with twine and tucked beneath the attic floorboards. He opened it, quietly sorting the bones, buttons, and shells inside into neat little piles.

When Jonathan reached the end of his chapter and looked up to see what James had done, he jumped across the attic in anger, wrestling his friend to the floor and pushing him down the rickety stairs which broke beneath their combined weight. The fall snapped James' arm in two separate places, and Jonathan had to run to Alden House to get help.

After James' bones had been set and plastered by the local surgeon, George, who had been genuinely surprised to learn his nine-year-old son had been sneaking out of the house at night when he was supposed to be asleep in his room, demanded to know what had happened. James had lied to his father, telling him he had slipped down the stairs by accident. He would have carried the lie with him to his grave to keep his friend from getting into trouble, but Jonathan confessed the truth about their argument, revealing the location of the loosened board that gave him free access to the outside world.

"Do you realize what could have happened if James had fallen on his head or his back instead of his arm?" George had asked Jonathan.

"Yes, sir." Jonathan's eyes had fallen to the floor. "I didn't mean to hurt him. I'm sorry."

George's anger with Jonathan had faded more quickly than his anger with James because Jonathan had caused the injury by accident but James had lied about it on purpose. George had frantically broken the lock on the barn door to get inside when he had learned his son had been hurt, so he brought both boys home to Alden House where Mary served Jonathan three bowls of warm porridge and tucked him into a soft, clean bed in one of the guest rooms.

"It's called a nkisi bundle," George had told James when the two of them were alone, "and you shouldn't have touched it. Jonathan likely inherited it from his mother or grandmother. It's a spiritual item used to maintain his connection to his ancestors across the sea."

"I didn't know."

"Now you do," George had said, his voice stern. "And I expect you won't forget it."

When morning dawned, George had no choice but to march the boys back to the barn to explain the night's events to Mr. Burrows. The cooperage owner struck Jonathan with a piece of wood from the broken staircase, and the boy tumbled into a stack of half-built barrels, blood spilling from his ruptured eardrum. George tried to intervene, explaining the accident had been an unfortunate result of a harmless boyhood tussle, but Mr. Burrows dragged Jonathan into the street, beating him for damaging the stairs in the barn and for daring to attack the son of the shipyard owner. When George realized his continued pleas for mercy would go unanswered, he forced his son to watch the brutal assault.

"The next time the two of you are tempted to cause mischief, remember that your friend will always face consequences far more severe than your own," George had said when James had tried to look away from the beating. It had been a powerful and heartbreaking lesson, and, for the first time in his young life, James had understood that although he and Jonathan were both growing up on the banks of the Mystic River, they were not really from the same place.

George, who understood the difference between keeping a secret and telling a lie, never told Mr. Burrows about the loose board in the back corner of the barn, so, after James' bones had healed, and after Jonathan had grown accustomed to the partial loss of hearing in his left ear, the two boys resumed their friendship as though nothing had ever happened. Jonathan had taken his nkisi bundle with him when they ran away to sea five years later, and he still kept it, tucked into the top drawer of his desk in the captain's quarters on *Polaris*.

James had never touched it again.

The barn behind the cooperage was dark now. The attic space where Jonathan once slept housed nothing more than the iron nails and wooden hoops needed to craft the shipyard's watertight barrels. An unseen whip-poor-will sent its call into the night, and James stood up, pouring what was left of the whiskey into the river and tossing the empty bottle onto the rocks. The alcohol hadn't helped him forget what had happened at Starkweather and Shetley, so he decided to go home, hoping sleep might grant him some release.

It wasn't until he passed the threshold of the library and saw Arabella, curled beneath a blanket reading a book, that he realized exactly what kind of release his mind, and his body, needed.

James stopped in the doorway and watched her. She was absorbed by the novel she was reading, an advanced copy of a book by Currer Bell that he had shipped directly from London. She had not bothered to turn up the gas lights, and she leaned close to the pages, scanning the words by candlelight. When she heard the floorboards creak, she looked up and smiled. A tide of carnal yearning, hot and pulsating, flooded his body. He balled his fingers into fists in a half-hearted attempt to quell it.

"I've missed you," she said, knowing only that he had been away on business because he had not yet told her about his repairs to her mother's cottage. "Elinor said you were having dinner with Jonathan."

He did not want to talk about Elinor or Jonathan. He did not want to talk. He crossed the room, plucked the book from her hands, and tossed it to floor.

"James," she said, noting his uneven gait even before she smelled the whiskey on his breath, "are you all right?"

He was flushed with heat despite having spent several hours drinking on the banks of the Mystic River, and he removed his jacket, dropping it over her discarded book. He slowly rolled up the sleeves of his shirt, first the right and then the left, his eyes locked on Arabella. The thorny roses on his forearm looked like shadows drawn by the ink of night.

“Stand up,” he said, his breath ragged, his eyes following the tempting horizon where blush-colored cotton met soft, glowing skin.

She untangled herself from her blanket and rose to her feet, her body tingling beneath his intense gaze. When he pulled her close to kiss her, she smelled the damp autumn air that clung to his hair and skin. He stumbled as he straightened himself to look at her, his eyes glossy in the candlelight.

“James,” she said again, “are you all right?”

“I’m fine.” He traced the lines of her throat with his calloused fingers. “Everything is fine now.” He threaded his fingers into hers, running his thumb along the intertwining bands of her silver ring. “Everything is fine now that I’m with you.”

“Your grandmother is upstairs,” she cautioned, reading the desire in his eyes.

“And *we*,” he said, pulling her closer, “are downstairs.”

He had never taken her in the house before. They had always found other places to be together out of respect for Elinor’s wishes, but tonight, he needed to drown himself in Arabella, and he didn’t care where he did it.

“I want you,” he whispered, the tone of his words hoarse and possessive. He tugged the hair at the back of her neck, tipping her face upward, forcing her to meet his eyes. They were as dark as the clusters of wild blueberries which grew in the northern woods. His lips hovered over hers. “I *need* you. Here. Now.”

He kissed her, a slow, demanding kiss that sent shivers down the length of her body. She tasted the sour tang of alcohol on his tongue. He tugged her hair back once more.

“I can’t be gentle,” he warned, “I *won’t* be gentle.” His heart raced with thoughts of what he wanted to do to her. His chest pounded beneath the white linen of his shirt. “I won’t be gentle if you have me tonight.”

His fingers glided over her collarbone as he spoke, and her heartbeat quickened as she tried to reconcile the softness of his touch with the harsh honesty of his words. She trembled slightly, biting her lower lip. Every muscle in his body jumped and tensed at the sight.

“Arabella?” he asked, half question, half command.

She blinked, and he was reminded of the night he had witnessed a lunar eclipse over the Indian Ocean; her long black lashes moved across the green of her eyes just as the earth's shadow had moved across the moon. He had waited for the moon's light to return then, and he waited now, breathless, until she nodded her head, almost imperceptibly. Then he pounced upon her, crushing her body with his, pushing her deeper and deeper into the recesses of the dark library.

She tumbled over an end table, and the candelabra that had given her just enough light to read clamored to the floor, spilling hot wax on the carpet. She would have fallen on top of it if James had not been holding her so tightly, dragging her around the couch, pushing her against its high velvet back. In the sudden darkness he was little more than a hard silhouette of muscle and bone bearing down on her.

"Undo your buttons," he said, tracing her lips with his thumb. Her hands obeyed, fumbling to loosen them, and James, impatient, moved her fingers away. He grasped the thin fabric and tore it in two, revealing the wool chemise layered beneath.

"James!"

He ignored her outburst, ripping apart her undergarment and baring her skin. "I'll buy you another dress," he growled, tugging the sleeves from her arms so she stood topless before him, the shreds of her gown held in place at her waist by the cinch of her skirts. "I'll buy you a thousand dresses, Arabella."

He hoisted her up, sitting her on the rolled back of the couch, lifting her skirts so she could hook her legs around his waist to balance herself. He bent her backward, his hands beneath her shoulders as he covered her neck and chest with rough kisses, his stubble leaving a trail of red and purple scratches on her tender skin.

Without warning, he lifted her into the air again, spinning her around in his strong arms and placing her feet back on the ground. He pushed her toward the innermost corner of the library where a large desk rested against the wood-paneled wall. He wedged her between his groin and the top of the desk, and the sharp metal knobs on the front drawer pressed into the back of her thighs.

"I want you, Arabella," he said, grinding against her so she could feel him, hard and throbbing. "Tell me—tell me you want me, too."

The vein at his temple pulsated beside the white slash of his scar. He pulled at her hair with one hand, stroking her chest with the other, and the competing sensations stirred her into speechlessness. She felt his need travel through her like lightning, igniting a smoldering ache in the center of her body.

"I want you, too," she said, her voice a whisper in the dark.

"Turn around."

She stilled, reduced to breath and heartbeat.

He spoke again, louder and more forceful than before.

"Turn around."

She slowly turned her back to him, and he embraced her from behind, sliding his palms over her curves, relishing the soft feel of her body against the hard lines of his own. She raised her arms and looped them around his neck, threading her fingers through his hair as his lips, his tongue, his teeth marked her skin. When he reached down to twist the fabric still covering the apex of her thighs, she arched against him, moaning inaudibly.

"I need you, Arabella," he groaned, bending her over the desk, running his hands down her back. "Tell me you need me, too."

Her heart thumped against the hard wood as he gathered the folds of her skirt in his fists. She hesitated, frightened by the tone of his voice, unable to twist her body so she could see the loving expression in his eyes.

"Tell me," he demanded.

"I need you, too."

The sound of tearing fabric ripped through the air once more.

"James!" She flattened her palms against the polished mahogany of the desk and pushed herself back up to a standing position, but he pushed her down again, one heavy hand pinning her to the desktop while the other lifted her shredded skirts up around her waist, exposing the creamy, white flesh of her backside. He pressed his fingers into the raw, red marks the desk drawer knobs had left on her delicate skin, and she trembled.

"James—"

It was the only word she seemed able to say, and it wasn't enough to stop the progress of his hands as they traversed the back of her thighs, squeezing and caressing the naked flesh just above the grip of her stockings. They crawled, slowly, torturously, close to the cavern between her legs before they paused. She cried out at their sudden stillness, her body shivering with expectation.

"Arabella?"

It would be his final question, his final warning. If she wanted him to stop, she needed to tell him now. But she didn't want him to stop. She had never imagined he would bend her over a desk and hold her down with his powerful grip, but still, her body longed for the heat of his touch. The world around her faded into a handful of intense sensations: the rustle of leaves outside the open window, the crackle of flames licking the logs in the grate, the earthy scent of leather books lining the library shelves, the painful press of her breasts against the varnished wood of the desk, and his fingers, his *fingers*, poised at the tops of her thighs, waiting, impatiently, for her command. She wanted him, she *needed* him, to tear her apart and put her back together again.

"Yes," she sighed, granting him permission as she rested her cheek against the desk and curled her hands around its edges to brace herself.

He made a low, animal sound and gently brushed her hair away from her forehead. He gazed down at her face.

"I love you, Arabella," he said, circling one of her wrists with his fingers and angling it behind her back so she couldn't move. "I love you."

"I love you, too."

In one swift motion his knee separated her legs and his free hand slid into hallowed space between them, first one finger, and then two, stroking, circling, sliding, in and out, back and forth.

She closed her eyes, borne away by the wonder and fullness of it all. She tried to press her body backward into his, but he held her wrist so tightly, she could not stir without pain. She could do nothing but lie still, absorbing the ebb and flow of an ancient tide beyond the power of her control.

Just as she began to shatter, he released her arm, unbuttoning his trousers and kicking her feet to spread her even further. He placed both of his hands beneath her hip bones and angled her upward, burying himself in her over and over again.

The desk groaned and creaked beneath them. A bottle of ink that had been perched on the corner tipped over, splashing its dark contents across a stack of loose papers. Even the bookshelves next to the desk shook with the fervor of his rhythm as she clenched around him, crying his name, no longer caring if anyone heard her. His movements continued long after she had peaked, and when he finally found his own earth-shattering release, the feeling was so intense that he lifted the front legs of the heavy desk up off the floor. They crashed back down with a loud thud as he draped himself over her prone body, panting like a horse that had just finished a race.

It was a moment before he could stand. He stumbled backward and poured a glass of whiskey from the decanter on the bookshelf to calm his still racing heart. He turned to offer her a sip. She was still lying on the desk, her face in her hands, her back rising and falling as though she was crying.

"Arabella?"

He dropped his glass to the floor and rushed back to desk, panic rising in his voice. "Arabella—did I hurt you?"

He pulled her gently onto his lap, and she reached for the shreds of her dress, trying to cover her nakedness. He pulled his shirt over his shoulders, slipping it around her.

"Please," he said, stroking her tear-stained cheeks. "Please, Arabella. Tell me what's wrong."

"Nothing's wrong," she whispered. "You didn't hurt me, James." She could barely speak. She rested her head on his chest.

"But you're crying." He had wanted to dominate her, to possess her, but he would never forgive himself for harming her. "Arabella, please, tell me what you need."

"I don't need anything." She reached up, tracing the hard edge of his jawline with her finger. "I'm fine. Everything is fine now that I'm with you." She listened to the thump of his heart. It was strong and sure, like the ticking of a clock. Without it, she thought she might float away.

He cradled her until she tried to stand, and then he lifted her in his arms, not wanting her to cut her stockinged feet on the shards of his broken glass. He carried her down the hall and up the curving staircase to her bedroom. He removed her tattered clothes, wiping her skin with a cotton cloth he had dipped in a bowl of rose-scented water. He found a nightgown in the drawer of her dressing table and tenderly pulled it over her head.

"Stay with me," she said, as he lowered her into her bed.

They had never spent an entire night together under his roof before. Her room was her only private space, and apart from the time he had placed the wax-spattered book on her night table, he had never violated it.

"You need to rest," he said.

"Then rest with me."

He smiled and climbed into her bed. She snuggled deep into the nook of his shoulder, her fingers tracing the swirls of the triskelion tattoo above his heart. He held her until the soft, sweet sound of her sleeping breath filled the room.

"*Grá Mo Chroi. Cara M'anama.*" He spoke the old words into the still of the night, relishing the sound of them. He had taken her in the library, he had bent her to his will as though she was his to command, but he would give her everything he had and everything he was in return. "My heart, my soul, and my body" he whispered quietly, not wanting to wake her. "They all belong to you."

VII

Only a few hours passed before a bright morning light flooded the bedroom. James felt Arabella's absence even before he opened his eyes, and he lifted himself up on his elbows, squinting toward her as she stood by her dressing table arranging her braided hair over her shoulder.

"Come back to bed," he said, dropping against the pillow. A wave of nausea washed over him. He wondered exactly how much whiskey he had drunk before smashing the bottle on the rocks.

She sat down on the side of the bed. "You don't look very good," she said. His cheeks were flushed and there were dark circles beneath his eyes.

"Shh," he mumbled, pressing a finger against her lips to stop her from talking. Every sound was like a nail being driven through his skull. "Come back to bed."

"I need to straighten up the library before your grandmother goes downstairs." The toppled candle, the tumbled furniture, the broken glass they had not bothered to sweep away came back to him in flashes of clouded memory. He pulled her closer.

"Don't worry about it," he said. "If my grandmother realizes what we've done, it'll give her a reason to pray." He managed a teasing smile. "My grandmother loves to pray."

He brushed her long, thick braid away from her shoulder, intending to draw her back into bed with a kiss, but his eyes fell on the trail of red marks she had been trying to cover with her hair. He sat up at the sight of them, ignoring the pounding in his head. His eyes filled with concern as he examined a deep, purple bruise encircling her wrist.

"I'm fine, James," she reassured him, "which is more than I can say for you." She kissed his cheek and pulled the sleeve of her dress down over her injured wrist. "I have to go. Please, don't let your grandmother find you here."

He nodded, pushing away the blankets. When she stepped into the hallway, he groaned and pulled them back over his head, searching for the peace of a dreamless sleep.

It was three days before James saw Jonathan again. He had known their meeting at Starkweather and Shetley was only the prelude to an uncomfortable conversation, and he had been waiting for Jonathan to summon him to Spouter Tavern so they could get it over with and move on.

He was walking home through a misty rain after a long day of work at his shipyard office when he saw a lantern flickering in the windows of the captain's cabin at the back of *Polaris*. It was the old signal they had used as children, and James knew it meant two things: Jonathan was ready to resume their discussion, and he wanted to do it on his own territory. James turned down a worn, rocky path, following it to a sandy bank on the side of the river where he pushed a wooden skiff into the water. He rowed out to *Polaris*, climbed the ropes that had been thrown over the ship's side, and made his way to the cabin in the stern.

James had spared no expense in constructing *Polaris*, and the captain's cabin was appointed with luxuries usually limited to larger vessels. The wood paneled walls, carved from teak, had been stained a rich, deep brown to reflect the glowing light of the oil lanterns hung from the ceiling. There was a private sleeping bunk, a cushioned seating area, and a large desk, bolted to the floor. The walls were lined with bookshelves, and Jonathan had filled them with star charts, nautical maps, and adventure stories he had borrowed from James' library. A tall jar of sea glass collected from shores around the world stood on one of the shelves. Boxes of tobacco perched on another.

James delivered a perfunctory knock before opening the door. Jonathan was sitting at the desk, a bottle of whiskey and two full glasses within arm's reach. The amber liquid sloshed back and forth as the ship rolled in the river's currents which had been stirred by the outer bands of a storm raging a few miles off the Atlantic coast.

"It took you long enough to row out here."

"It took you long enough to send the signal."

Jonathan gestured to a high-backed leather chair he had pulled up to the desk. James felt like a misbehaving child who had been called into the headmaster's office at school. Before sitting down, he pulled a bag of gold and silver coins from his pocket and dropped it onto the desk.

Jonathan glared at it.

"It's for the crew," James said penitently. "For their trouble."

"You think this is about money?" His voice was as terse as it had been at Starkweather and Shetley.

"No." James ran his hand through his dark hair, which was still damp from his journey across the misty river. "I can't change what happened," he said. "I'm just trying to make up for my mistake."

"I didn't call you here to talk about what already happened. I called you here to talk about what needs to happen moving forward." The captain leaned back in his chair, surveying his friend.

"It was one mistake, Jonathan. I lost track of time."

"Is Arabella still living in your house?"

"Yes."

"Then you've made more than one mistake."

A thick tension curled between the men as Jonathan crossed his arms over his chest and tilted his chin to the left, readying his good ear to hear the details of James' explanation.

"What happened to your crew wasn't Arabella's fault. If I had been there with the necessary paperwork when *Polaris* docked, no one would have been arrested."

"Let's review the events of the last three months," Jonathan said, shaking his head at James' attempt to gloss over the details of the situation. "You met this woman in the woods north of town while making one of *my* deliveries.

Then you struck a deal with William Stafford that not only resulted in the dissolution of his debts but placed his daughter *inside* your house."

"I only hired her because my grandmother—"

"The next time I sailed into town," Jonathan continued, ignoring the interruption, "William showed up at your house to visit his daughter, *someone* threw a rock at my head as I sat in your window, and my cargo was deliberately set on fire. Then, after I gave Arabella a date for *Polaris*' arrival, a date recorded nowhere, a date no one else knew about, her father and his friends just happened to be waiting on the docks to search my boat for contraband, a situation we could have easily handled if you hadn't forgotten about it because you were busy fixing *her* mother's cottage!" He counted each point off with his fingers, his voice growing in volume as he spoke. "Arabella must have given the information about *Polaris*' arrival date to William, and that means it isn't safe for any of us to have her living in your home. You *know* that, Jimmy."

James shifted his legs beneath him, letting out a long breath he hadn't realized he was holding.

"If Arabella told her father about the thirtieth—"

"*If*?"

"If Arabella told her father about the thirtieth," James repeated, trying to remain calm, "she didn't do it with the intent of harming us. We never told her to keep the date a secret, and she doesn't know anything about our business, Jonathan."

"Do you admit she's in contact with her father even though the terms of your arrangement forbid it?"

"She's not in contact with her father. She saw him, once, at her sister's wedding, and you know I had no choice but to allow her to attend. They were alone in the garden for a short time, and I couldn't hear everything they said to each other, but it didn't end well, and I'm sure she wouldn't have shared the information if she had known what the consequences might be. She would never do anything to put you or your crew in danger."

Jonathan pushed his chair back from his desk and stood up.

"You're making excuses for her," he said.

"I'm not—"

Jonathan picked up the chair and slammed it back down against the floor in frustration. "The last time I was in town all you could talk about were your suspicions regarding William Stafford's daughter. *She* was harvesting herbs by moonlight, *she* went into your office after you forbid her to do so. *You* are the one who brought all of this to me, *you* are the one who was ready to throw her out of your house—"

"I know, but—"

"We delayed all of our shipments so that *you* could determine where her loyalties lie! And now that you have the answer you're ignoring it!"

"I'm not ignoring it." James stood up. "But things have changed since the last time you were in town."

"What has changed?"

"I know her better now."

"Jesus Christ," Jonathan said, realization dawning on his face. "You slept with her, didn't you?"

James didn't answer, and the captain's sharp intellect read his silence like a book.

"Jesus Christ, Jimmy. You're *still* sleeping with her."

James nodded.

"What the hell is the matter with you?" Jonathan stepped from behind the desk and grabbed James by his collar, shoving him backward across the cabin. "She's not some island girl you can sail away from after you're done with her! She's not some girl you met in a New London brothel! She's William Stafford's goddamn daughter!"

"I know—"

"William will kill you. If William finds out what you're doing, he'll kill you, Jimmy. Or worse, he'll make you marry her, and then he'll have his hooks in your shipyard and your family fortune after everything you've done to prevent that!"

James loosened himself from Jonathan's grip, angry because he knew everything his friend was saying was true. "William won't find out," he said stubbornly, "and if he does, it's *my* problem, not *yours*."

"Not my problem?" Jonathan shoved him again, this time with such force that James' shoulder knocked into the bookcase, and the tall jar of sea glass spilled across the floor. "Are you really stupid enough to think that you being forced to marry *William Stafford's* daughter is not *my* problem?" He jacked James up against the wall. "Are you really stupid enough to put our entire business at risk just so you can enjoy a good fuck?"

A moment of complete stillness elapsed before James brought his fist back and landed it square on Jonathan's jaw, sending the captain sprawling across the room. Jonathan's legs knocked against his desk, and the whiskey bottle rolled onto the cabin floor. The quartermaster, hearing the commotion from his position on the main deck, burst through the door with several members of the crew and pulled James off of Jonathan.

"Is everything all right in here, Captain?" the quartermaster asked as Jonathan calmly lifted himself from the floor and straightened his jacket.

"Everything's fine," he growled. "Hold Mr. Alden against the wall." James let out a string of obscenities, but allowed the men to push him back toward the opposite side of the cabin. He was the owner of the shipyard, but Jonathan was the captain of *Polaris*, and a crew would never follow a captain who showed any sign of weakness. Jonathan was going to make an example of him, and James was going to have to let him.

Jonathan hit him so hard blood spilled from his mouth. Then he hit him again. And again. James grunted as the captain's fist split his lip and broke the skin above his eye. Jonathan hit him three more times, each blow forcing James' neck in sharply angled directions. Jonathan shook his bloodied fist before lifting his foot and kicking his friend deep in the abdomen. James dropped to one knee, doubled over in pain.

"Get out," Jonathan said to his quartermaster and crew.

"But Captain—"

"GET OUT!"

The men scattered. James brought his fingers up to survey the damage to his face. One eye was already beginning to swell shut. "Jesus, Jonathan," he said, spitting out a mouthful of blood and attempting to stand upright.

Jonathan wrapped his handkerchief around his fist and shrugged his shoulders nonchalantly. "You know better than to challenge me in front of my crew." He walked back to his desk, picking up the half-spilled bottle of whiskey from the floor as he passed by. He sat down and poured two more drinks. He waved his open hand in invitation, and James gingerly crossed the room, lowering himself into the chair. He downed the whiskey, wincing as its bitter syrup mixed with the metallic taste of his blood. He poured himself another, his hand shaking. He leaned back, trying, but failing, to find a comfortable position.

"You love her, don't you, Jimmy?"

James nodded. "I love her."

"Jesus Christ."

When Jonathan spoke again, he had cleared the anger from his voice.

"Does she know what we keep in your office?"

"No."

Jonathan plucked a coin from the bag James had thrown on the desk. He rolled it over his fingers in his practiced rhythm. The turtle inked on the back of his hand seemed alive with the movement.

"I'm going to find a new distributor for my shipments," he said after a few minutes of silence.

"No, you're not."

"You can't sleep with her and work for me at the same time, Jimmy, not with her father actively trying to destroy our operation."

"I read the report regarding the search of *Polaris*. There was no mention of the secret spaces in the hold, which means no one discovered them." He swallowed the whiskey in his glass, hoping it would dull his pain. "And your lumber was set on fire in the shipyard, which means no one knows we store your stolen cargo in my office at home. Arabella can't tell William what she doesn't know. So, we start making our regular runs again, but we use unpredictable intervals, and we don't share *any* information with Arabella. No more tests of her loyalty. We keep her completely in the dark, for her safety, and our own."

Jonathan's coin traveled over his knuckles, the silver flashing like a fish. He shook his head, unconvinced.

"And when she's naked in your bed, batting her eyes at you?" James tensed at the captain's deliberate provocation. "Are you really telling me you won't give her the answer to any question she asks?"

"She loves me, Jonathan. She isn't going to ask me anything about our work because she isn't spying for William. I'm sure of it. I can keep my relationship with Arabella separate from my work for you."

"And who'll face the consequences if you can't?"

James pressed his palms over the lids of his swollen eyes, watching colors explode in time with his throbbing head. He couldn't blame Jonathan for being cautious. What James was proposing was reckless at best, but he knew, in his heart, that Arabella would never betray him. If he was careful, if he maintained his focus, everything would be all right.

"Finding a new distributor poses a bigger risk to you than letting me continue," James said. "No one knows the woods north of the river as well as I do. We'll do a short run with a full load of cargo delivered to my office six or seven days from now. No one will expect *Polaris* to be back so soon. You can sail in under the cover of night, and even if William sees you enter the river, he won't be able to convince the watch to search your ship again after his last search turned up no evidence."

James stood up. "Talk to your contacts and send me confirmation of the date and time. I'll handle things on my end."

Jonathan dropped the coin onto his desk and stood, regarding James with a skeptical expression. Romantic love was a dangerous game. It made men vulnerable. It gave them something to lose. The last thing he wanted was to see his friend get hurt.

"It was one mistake, Jonathan," James said. "I won't let it happen again." He was halfway across the room when Jonathan spoke.

"Jimmy—"

James didn't turn around, but he stopped, his hand resting on the latch of the cabin door, waiting.

"Promise me you'll be careful."

James glanced over his shoulder, saluting as he used to do when he sailed the rough Antarctic waters under Jonathan's command.

"Aye, aye, Captain.

Part Eight

Behind the Door

"We have the receipt of the fern seed;
we walk invisible"
(Henry IV Part 1)

Polaris departed and returned to Mystic seven days later, entering the river under the cover of a cloudy night, transferring its undocumented cargo from the secret spaces deep within its holds to James' locked office. Three days after that, James carried the packages through the northern woods, delivering them in the quiet hours between midnight and dawn while the residents of Mystic, their doors locked against legends of the *Dullahan*, were fast asleep. The entire process repeated itself in another week's time, with Jonathan pushing his clipper through a treacherous autumn squall and James navigating the forest beneath the pitch black of a new moon to ensure their clandestine cargo was delivered as scheduled.

The cool October air painted the landscape with color; autumn's early patches of orange and yellow gave way to deep shapes of red and russet brown. Arabella needed her soft, grey healer's cloak to protect her from chilly river breezes as she harvested the last of the herbs from the kitchen garden.

James found her one afternoon, surrounded by cannisters and bowls filled to the brim with bright red rose hips. The scrape of her ceramic mortar and pestle stopped each time she consulted her grimoire, replaced with the whisper of incantations, the old words ringing like silver bells. Not long ago, he had accused her of performing witchcraft in his kitchen, but now the tap of her knife on the counter, the lines of concentration on her face, the scent of oakmoss and wildflowers mixing with the nutty aroma of the rose hips; it all felt like coming home.

"What are you doing?" he asked, leaning in the frame of the doorway as he watched her.

He had been out late the night before, making his deliveries for Jonathan, and he still smelled of the autumn forest, a smoky, sweet scent of decay. He walked over to her and brushed a curl from her forehead, picking a stray leaf from her braided hair. The tips of her fingers had been stained red by the fruit, and her hair was damp with steam from the kettle she had set to boil on the stovetop.

"I'm making rosehip tea," she said. "Your grandmother has taken a liking to it, and if I mix the ingredients now and divide them into sachets, there will be enough to last until—"

Her voice trailed off. James nodded. He had noticed the mottling of his grandmother's skin, the whitening of her hair, the unnaturally long pauses between each of her labored breaths.

"Well, there'll be enough to last until next autumn, when the roses yield fruit again," Arabella said gently.

She returned to her chopping and mixing, humming the tune of an old Scottish ballad as she worked. James had refused to tell her about the cuts and bruises Jonathan had left on his face, though she had bathed them with raw honey to alleviate the swelling. All that remained of them now was a dark shadow around his left eye, its greenish-brown tone made more prominent by the white line of his scar.

He cupped his hands around her hips, turning her to face him, lifting her onto the table and upsetting the bowl of rose hips. The bright red seeds tumbled across the wood as he kissed her, the invisible cord of their mutual desire winding itself around them like a tendril. She yielded to him, letting him part her thighs so that her dress stretched, taut and seductive, across her lap. He raised the hem of her skirt over her ankles, her calves, and was slowly inching it toward her thighs when she placed her hands on his chest and pushed him away.

She shook her head. Elinor was resting upstairs, and the sun still hung low in the afternoon sky. The kitchen windows faced the back of the house where, beyond the herb garden and stables, the river walkway was heavily trafficked by shipyard workers returning home after their day's labor. "Someone will see us."

He slid her to the edge of the table, pressing himself into the space between her legs. If society discovered their secret, so be it. A part of him wished for it. He no longer thought a forced marriage would be the worst thing in the world.

He trailed his lips up to her ear, his low whisper kindling her desire.

"Let them watch."

The last week of October dawned crisp and cool. Maple trees cried scarlet tears. Gusts blew in from the sea, their voices as mournful as the baying of the hounds that led the fairies' Wild Hunt through the cloudy skies of Scotland. The veil between the worlds stretched ever thinner, and the Native spirits which gathered on the western bank of the Mystic River appeared so clearly to Arabella in the cool evening light that she sometimes mistook them for living people. Once, in the threadbare membrane that stretched tight over Elinor, she saw the cloudy face of George Alden, waiting to welcome his ailing mother home.

With Elinor's permission, Arabella had decorated the mantle in the parlor with brightly colored leaves and vines, bowls of ruby-red apples, jars of burgundy rose petals collected from the ground beneath Mary's rose bushes, and a small dish of soil mixed with the bones of a saltmarsh sparrow whose broken body Arabella had found beneath the oak trees in the yard. On the last day of the month, James lit fires in each of the fireplaces, filling Alden House with the sweet, hickory scent of burning wood. He had helped Arabella hollow out pumpkins instead of turnips as her family had done in Scotland, and, after Elinor had turned in for the night, James had pulled Arabella down onto the hand-knotted Persian rug in the parlor, circling his arms around her as they watched their pumpkin lanterns glow.

James had learned the story of *Jack of the Lantern* from his mother. Mary had loved sharing her Celtic traditions with her sons, sending Thomas and James out to make innocent mischief on All Hallows' Eve, knowing her cautionary tales about headless horsemen and keening *banshees* would keep them close to home. They always returned in high spirits, their cheeks chapped red from the cold, their stomachs hungry for the syrup-covered griddle cakes their mother would fry in a pan and keep warm for their arrival.

Arabella told James about the Porters' celebration of *Samhain*, the final harvest on the Isle of Skye, the one that reaped the souls of the dead instead of the grains in the fields. The Porter women had lighted candles in remembrance of their ancestors, leaving the flames burning all night to guide lost souls to their resting place beyond the veil. They had roasted nuts on their hearth, baked treacle scones, and dropped silver coins into rich, dark dough, the tokens bringing love and luck to those who found them in a slice of bread. One of Arabella's great-aunts had been gifted in divination, and she had taught Arabella to peel the skins of apples in one long cut, casting them behind her to predict her future.

James listened with curiosity to Arabella's tales of *Cailleach Bheurra*, the veil-wearing, deer-herding, hag-goddess of winter who began freezing the land with her magical staff on the evening of Samhain, and he told her frightening stories of his winters at sea when ships stranded themselves in creaking blocks of ice, their tattered, salt-stained sails billowing in the stiff wind. He spoke of tropical ports where disease-eaten corpses rose from their graves to cool themselves in blood-red tides, and he described the strange, wailing sounds that traveled over flat waters in the dead of night. Most terrifying of all, he said, was the vast Pacific Ocean itself, a sea without memory, rolling over wrecked ships and drowned sailors whose stories would never be told. He drew her closer to him with each new tale, allaying her fears with his kisses, and, although the two nuts she had set by the fireside popped and cracked in opposite directions, a sure sign of romantic trouble to come, James and Arabella stoked a white-hot flame between them, letting it burn until long after the candles in their pumpkin lanterns had extinguished themselves in columns of smoke.

The intensity of her first winter on America's shores surprised Arabella. On the Isle of Skye, winter brought wet winds and boggy moors, but it also gifted the islanders a soft, beautiful light that painted the east with pink clouds each morning and ribboned the north with purple streaks each night. The *Cailleach's* frosty breath settled across the vegetation in thick glittering clumps that sparkled like diamonds beneath the rising sun. Winter in Scotland was a time for reflection, a time to wander the land in search of Great Northern Divers, Mountain Hare, and Red Deer, a time to rejoice in returning home to the peat moss warmth of the hearth.

In New England, winter arrived like an unexpected house guest, unpacking barren winds and frigid temperatures with such alacrity that even the Alden rosebushes, which had continued to bloom throughout autumn, dropped the last of their leaves in capitulation. The geese, which had formed V-shaped streaks across the late October skies, suddenly disappeared, and the downy woodpeckers, which had tapped out the songs of dying summer, stilled themselves, retreating deep into the hardened trunks of trees. The blue-green waters of the Mystic River turned as grey as the clouds above, and bitter winds roamed the flat, tidal lands like packs of spectral wolves prowling for prey.

It was in the desolate chill of deep November that America celebrated its own harvest, a holiday born of the pilgrims' pride for surviving the harsh conditions of a new world. Elinor taught Arabella to dress and roast a turkey, to boil winter squash with potatoes and onions, to mix maple and cranberry syrups for tart relishes and desserts. They baked pumpkin pies and ginger cakes, boxing them as gifts for the shipyard workers ahead of the holiday. Arabella recorded Elinor's ingredients and instructions in her grimoire, transcribing them next to Catriona's spells for stirring gratefulness in the human heart, weaving the Aldens' harvest recipes into the magical history of the Porter Clan.

Elinor sat at the kitchen table, watching Arabella write on the yellowed parchment, sipping a cup of rosehip tea. It was all she had ingested that day, for her appetite had disappeared as unceremoniously as the geese had vacated the winter skies, and she had little interest in eating any of the food she and Arabella had prepared. Still, having no daughters or granddaughters with whom she could share her domestic traditions, she was touched to see her recipes added to the Porter Family Grimoire. She reached out to trail her wrinkled fingers through Arabella's stray curls, something she had never done before, and Arabella looked up in surprise, blinking away a vision of Caitriona.

"Elinor?" The old woman's eyes were misty, and when she took another sip of her tea, her hands trembled. Arabella scanned the veil over her head. It was stretched thin, but it still held, firmly covering the portal to the world beyond.

"Do you love him, Arabella?"

It was a simple question, though it sprang from three months of deep rumination. Elinor's initial fury with James, ignited by her desire to protect Arabella's reputation, had transmuted into worry when she learned how the Porter women boldly thwarted patriarchal tradition. Love, unbound by societal rule, was a volatile and dangerous thing, and Elinor couldn't bear the thought of her grandson's heart being broken after she was gone.

"Yes," Arabella said, tucking her quill into the crease of her grimoire. "I love him."

Elinor was a practical woman who believed in the sanctity of marriage, but love, at least, was something. She poured another cup of tea from the pot on the table, passing it to Arabella.

"George and Mary love one another," Elinor said, studying the air in front of her as if it were a portrait. "On summer nights, they sneak outside to dance beneath chandeliers of starlight."

The change in the direction of conversation was so sudden that Arabella worried Elinor's mind was wandering through time, losing its grip on the present as she slid toward the final weeks of her life. But, when Arabella took a sip of the tea she had steeped from the hips of the Alden roses, she realized George and Mary's waltz was a memory pressed deep into the flowers themselves. The incantation she had placed upon the tea had allowed Elinor to see the plant's precious memory unfold before her eyes.

And Arabella had seen it too.

On the Saturday after Thanksgiving, Arabella awoke to discover a large box near her bedroom door. A note had been written in James' hand:

Put this on and come downstairs.

Inside the box was a velvet dress so soft and green it looked like it had been cut from the leaves of African violets. Silver thread and clusters of purple gemstones wound themselves into a thistle pattern that swept around the full skirt. Beneath the gown was a pair of long, silver gloves, a box containing thistle-shaped eardrops, and a small container filled with diamond, amethyst, and emerald hair pins. Arabella stepped into the skirt and fastened the row of tiny buttons lining the back of the dress. She braided her hair, using the crystals to pin the plaits high on her head, revealing the soft, sloping neckline of the bodice.

She glided down the stairs, wondering what adventure James might have in store for her. He was waiting in the parlor, clean shaven and dressed in his finest clothes. He slipped a black silk cloak trimmed with feathers over her shoulders.

His carriage was tied to the hitching post on Greenman Avenue. A coachman was whispering to the horses. James escorted Arabella into the cab, leaning forward to smooth her voluminous cloak over the seats. Before she realized what was happening, he slipped his silk handkerchief from his pocket and tied it over her eyes, obscuring her view.

She immediately raised her fingers to her temples to unknot it, but he caught her hands in his and brought them back down to her lap.

"No touching." He shushed her with a deep chuckle. "I have a surprise for you."

"James, I can't see anything," she protested.

"That's the point." He laughed as his nimble fingers tightened the knot. "This carriage is traveling to New London on business. It will make a stop before it arrives, and when it does, you'll find me there, waiting."

"Why don't you just ride in the carriage with me?" she asked, clinging to his hand as he pulled away.

"Because we'll be out past nightfall." She heard the caution in his voice and was reminded of the difficulties their last evening trip had caused. "My grandmother is telling everyone at Saturday services that you're spending the day in New London visiting a family friend. I'm heading out in the opposite direction to keep rumors at bay, but I'll circle back around to meet you." He kissed her, and the surprise of his lips against hers made her jump.

"Do you trust me, Arabella?" he whispered, his words tickling her ear. She nodded. "Good. Now, for once, do what you're told, and don't remove the handkerchief." Another kiss, teeth gently grazing her bottom lip. "I'll know if you try."

The warmth of his body disappeared. The door creaked closed. The coachman flicked his whip and clucked his tongue. The horses began their slow trot, hooves clip-clopping over cobblestones. Arabella's world became a dizzying array of sounds: the squeak of the carriage, the swish of its curtains, and the sweet, patient jingling of the horses' harness bells.

She ran her hands along the velvet cushions beneath her, bracing herself as they gained speed. The wheels rolled over the wood of the drawbridge. After a while, stone roads gave way to hard-packed dirt, dampening the sounds of the horses' trot. She lifted her hands to the handkerchief more than once, wondering if she could lift it just enough to make sense of the shadows dancing across her eyelids, but each time she remembered James' warning and chose to leave the blindfold in place. Her body tensed with wild expectation as she wondered when the carriage would reach its destination.

They took a tight turn and traveled uphill, the coachman purring and whistling at the horses as they passed over uneven terrain. When they finally slowed to a stop, he dismounted and began talking. Arabella strained to hear, but his hushed conversation was drowned out by whispers of the trees. The carriage door clicked, and a gust of wind howled into the open cab.

"James." She sighed in relief as the calloused hands she would recognize anywhere closed around hers. "Where are we?"

"Patience, Arabella." He lifted her down from the cab, placing her feet on a thin layer of fallen pine needles as he issued instructions for the driver's return. The horses whinnied and stamped. She imagined their misty breath curling into the cold November sky.

She felt his fingers inspecting the knot at the back of the handkerchief. "Good girl," he said, and she heard the smile in the deliberate, low tone of his voice. He left the cloth in place, leading her up a steep trail lined with stones and briars. "That's it," he said, encouraging her as she complied with his directions about where to place her feet, "just a little further." His hands gripped her waist to steady her. "I promise I won't let you fall."

Leaves crunched beneath them. The air was scented with salt and smoke. November breezes chapped their cheeks. After twenty minutes of slow, tedious progress, James slipped behind her and released the knot of his handkerchief. She blinked at the sudden brightness slanting through the barren trees.

They were in front of her mother's cottage, though it was no longer the dilapidated structure she had first seen three months ago. It stood clean and sturdy beneath a blanket of grey clouds, a warm, marmalade-colored light spilling from the windows. James had carved and hung a paneled door at the front entrance, and he opened it to invite her inside.

A roaring fire burned merrily in the stone hearth which had been meticulously cleaned and fitted with a mantle shaped from a large piece of driftwood. Whale oil lanterns of various sizes and shapes lined the mantle, their light flickering over piles of eastern oyster shells, white slippers, red-ribbed scallops, and channeled whelk that had been gathered from the shore. James had sanded and painted the walls, hung white sailcloth curtains on the windows, and built new furniture, a table and chairs, an armoire and night table, a new bed, piled high with soft pillows. The rusted iron crane Catherine had used for cooking had been polished to a shine, and a cauldron of bubbling apple cider dangled from it, releasing a golden scent of cinnamon and nutmeg into the air.

"I couldn't salvage the furniture or linens," he said, carefully studying her expression. "Your mother didn't have many personal items, but I saved everything I found. It's stacked it in the bottom of the armoire so you can go through it when you're ready."

Arabella looked toward the armoire. It was surrounded by a faint, misty glow. Her mother's grimoire was calling out to her. James would not have known what it was, but he had saved it for her, and she felt a sudden rush of gratitude that he had not discarded Catherine's damaged possessions. He had given her mother's cottage new life without forsaking the troubled past from which it had been born. He had left the scars which told her mother's story.

"You won't be able to visit in bad weather," he cautioned. "Once the snow falls, the pathway becomes impassable, but we can return in the spring if you like, so you can tend the garden."

James walked over to the night table and picked up an octagonal box he had crafted and decorated with swirls of tiny white seashells and purple *wampum* beads. He opened it, and a tinkling tune filled the air, an old, slow sea shanty he had learned on board the *Shepherd*. He had created the musical mechanism inside the box, carving holes and knobs into a cylinder and adjusting the teeth on a vibrating comb until the box sang the tune he desired. The pieces moved in unison, a golden spinning wheel and carding comb enchanted by fairy magic.

"May I have this dance?"

He extended his arm, and she placed her gloved hand in his. There wasn't much room for dancing in the tiny cottage, so he pulled her close and spun her in a circle. She rested her head on his shoulder, closing her eyes. If not for the rustle of silk and velvet she would have believed she was back home on the Isle of Skye, surrounded by generations of guiding Porter spirits.

"Do you like it?" he asked after the music box had plinked out its final notes. "The cottage? The dress?"

"I love it, James. All of it. But why did you do all this for me?"

"I would do anything for you, Arabella." The sincerity in his expression faded into an embarrassed smile. "Besides, I believe I owed you a dress."

He unclasped her cloak, folding it over the chair, stroking the velvet of her bodice. Rivers of blue veins crossed her alabaster skin, and he intended to journey down each one, slowly, methodically. He wanted to cherish her. To worship her.

He spun her around, undoing the line of buttons on the back of her dress, his movements soft and tranquil, like a perfect gentleman.

"Will you finally admit I made you swoon?"

He was lying on the bed, propped up by piles of pillows. She faced him, leaning against his raised knees, her body covered only by the bedsheet. The once roaring fire had reduced itself to a crackling glow.

She rolled her eyes at his question, but smiled, basking in the memory of his restrained tenderness. He had pinched the fingers of her silver gloves, sliding the silk down the length of her arms. He had calmly released dozens of crystal pins from her hair, watching as her braids swept, one by one, against her collarbone. He had carefully folded each item of her clothing as he disrobed her, rolling each of her stockings down with such languid deliberateness she almost collapsed from anticipation. And, when she had finally stood naked before him, the fire warming her backside, he had dropped to his knees, taking her hand in his and gently lifting one of her legs over his shoulder.

Her body had been trembling by the time his lips had touched her, and she had wrapped her fingers in his dark hair, trying not to let his ministrations carry her away. "Please, James—" she had sighed, when she was certain she could take no more, but he had only smiled up at her before returning to his sweet, unfinished task, his tongue pressing harder in response to her growing cries.

Now, she traced the triskelion above his heart, her expression thoughtful. The three interlocking spirals swirled outward like the whorl of a channeled whelk, the sweep of a falcon, the flurry of a whale, each one endlessly rotating around a fixed center. She knew triskelions represented the unbreakable connections found in sets of three: spirit, mind, and body; past, present, and future; Father, Son, and Holy Spirit; Maiden, Mother, and Crone, but she wondered if the symbol had some nautical meaning. "Will you tell me the story of this tattoo?" she asked, sliding her finger over the thick, dark lines.

He sighed, preferring a report on his performance to a conversation about his past, but her gentle movements were sending waves of gooseflesh over his chest, and the lantern lights were flickering through the hazel swirls of her eyes, and he knew he would answer any question she asked if only it would keep her in bed with him a moment longer.

"My mother embroidered this symbol onto our blankets when Thomas and I were children," he said. "An Irish Traveler in the Old Country once read her fortune and prophesied she would give birth to three sons who would always be connected by the strength of her love. I was almost twelve years old when she fell pregnant for the third time. She was convinced the baby was going to be a boy."

"Was it?"

He nodded, shifting uncomfortably in the bed. "He was so small. He never cried. He barely even moved." He cleared his throat. "After my father and Thomas died, I was lost for a long time. I had to stop sailing. I had to take over the shipyard. I spent months wondering how my life might have been different if my mother had lived, if the baby had survived, if my father and my brother had never gotten into that carriage. I got this tattoo to remind me I was once part of a family. I was once one of three brothers united by our parents' love, even though I'm the only one left."

She flattened her palm against the inked triskelion on James' chest, feeling the strength of his beating heart beneath it. She thought about the stretch of years when her own aunts had died, one after the other. She understood the loneliness that comes from losing family. She knew the pain of being left behind.

"It's a beautiful tribute, James."

He half-smiled at her and then laughed to rid the room of his sadness. "My grandmother disagrees. I don't think she realized I could get tattoos on land. She made me promise her it would be the last one I ever got." He took

Arabella's hand, turning the silver ring on her finger. "Now, I've answered your question, so it's only fair you answer mine. Did I or did I not make you swoon?"

She giggled, her fingers trailing invisible triskelions down the inked slope of his chest and over the hard muscles of his abdomen. "Well, I asked you about your tattoo because, in my faith, the triskelion represents the sacred motion of the universe," she explained. "What we put into the world spirals outward, coming back to us threefold." Her swirling fingers followed the trail of dark hair that disappeared beneath the edge of the bedsheet. His muscles tensed beneath her touch.

"The truth is," she said with a coy smile, "you did make me swoon today, and now, that swoon is going to spiral back to you."

She sat up, letting the bed linens fall away from her body.

"Arabella—"

She placed a finger over his lips. "Shh," she whispered, winking at him. "Patience, James."

Her lips followed the trail her fingers had forged, her tongue sliding over the salt of his skin, finding its way beneath the linen sheets. He fell back against the pillows, resolved to let her have her way with him until the carriage returned at its scheduled time to usher them back to reality.

December brought the first snow of the season, a light dusting of powder that fell over the bare branches of Mary's rosebushes, coating them with sparkling light. Soon chunks of ice appeared in the river, and the marshy banks on both sides of the drawbridge froze solid so that boats traveling to and from the Alden Shipyard had to navigate a narrow current in the center of the waterway.

Winter's long days filled Arabella with a growing melancholy. Her own grandmother had died at Yuletide, choosing to slip through the veil on the longest night when the passage was thinnest. Arabella's fairy gift always intensified at the dark time of the year, and specters who barely registered in the corners of her eyes throughout the summer now appeared to her in earnest. Even from the safety of Alden House, she saw ghosts and spirits walking along the river: Natives running from Mason's ravaging flames; red-coated soldiers, their bayonets slung over their shoulders; gaunt children tumbling in and out of the holes in the veil as though they were playthings in the sky.

Arabella had expected Elinor's condition to deteriorate as the membrane between the worlds thinned, but she found herself profoundly moved by the impending loss. When she had accepted her position at Alden House, she had not anticipated growing so close to its residents, and she sometimes felt like she was losing her own grandmother all over again. Elinor was slow to get out of bed in the morning and eager to retire at night. She existed on minuscule bites of bread and cups of rosehip tea, and Arabella sometimes heard her conversing with her sister who had passed away several years before. When they had last gathered for a family dinner, Elinor had mistakenly called James by his father's name. He didn't correct her, but he poured himself an extra glass of whiskey, letting the food on his plate grow cold.

As Yuletide neared, Arabella decorated the mantles with evergreen boughs and bright holly berries, a colorful change from the dried gorse and bronzed heath she had gathered each December in Scotland. The weekend before Christmas, James chopped down a Balsam Fir, dragging it home from the northern woods so he and Arabella could adorn it with clove-studded citrus fruits and long, white tapers. They lit the wicks ahead of Elinor's arrival home from Saturday services, and the old woman happily settled herself in the pine-scented parlor, watching the candles burn themselves down to wisps of white smoke.

On the day of the winter solstice, when the earth stood still, Elinor did not get out of bed. James was busy unloading *Polaris*' shipment of lumber into a large shed at the northern end of the shipyard, so Arabella baked gingerbread loaves and sugar cookies shaped like stars, reciting rhymes about the return of the light over the batter and dough. When evening arrived, she left a plate of baked goods on the table for James' late return, retreating to her room and lighting a rosemary-anointed candle in Catriona's memory. She used the light of the candle to read her new copy of *East of the Sun and West of the Moon.* When she had told James it was her mother's favorite fairy tale, he had tracked down a Norwegian edition, had it translated into English, and bound its pages in leather to match the books in his library. Arabella traced the gilded sun, moon, and stars that graced the midnight blue cover, reminding herself that light and hope would always return, remembering that the earth would always tip toward spring once more.

She was so warm and cozy beneath her blankets that she did not hear the frantic rustling and commotion taking place downstairs. When James thundered through her bedroom door without his customary knock, she sat straight up, suddenly alert.

"Arabella," he said, an edge of panic in his voice. "I need your help."

The man sat on the leather sofa, one hand dangling toward the table covered with maps and charts of the northern woods. The curtains on the window had been drawn shut, and a dim fire smoked in the grate. Arabella had hesitated on the threshold of the room she had been so long banned from entering, but James had pulled her into his office, pleading. "Please," he said. "We don't have much time."

Now she knelt on the floor beside the feverish man, trying to find his pulse. Beads of sweat lined his furrowed brow. His teeth, bright white against his dark skin, chattered uncontrollably. Every few minutes his body convulsed, overcome with fits of coughing that left him short of breath.

"How long has he been suffering like this?" she asked.

"He had a fever when he boarded my ship five days ago." Jonathan emerged from a shadowy corner of the room. "His condition has grown steadily worse."

"This man needs to travel ten miles to the north before daybreak," James said, "and he needs to do it quietly. Can you help him?"

"This man can't travel, James."

"He must." He left no room for negotiation. "He's a fugitive from a southern plantation. If anyone finds him before he gets to safety, he'll be returned to a life of misery. I can't let that happen."

Arabella turned to look at the man, realizing *he* was the stolen cargo Jonathan had been accused of transporting. *Polaris*, the ship named after the steadfast star that glistened in the northern sky, smuggled human beings toward freedom.

She wiped perspiration from the man's forehead with her sleeve. She removed his sweat-stained shirt. She directed James to gather her grimoire, her apothecary bag, a bowl of clean water, and fresh linens. She applied sage-soaked compresses to the man's forehead and the small of his back, alternating them with strips of cloth dipped in cinnamon oil to warm his blood and sweat out his fever. She set a pot of water to boil over the fire, brewing a fragrant meadowsweet tea to soothe the man's lungs. She rubbed his chest with a warm, mustard seed plaster and coaxed him to chew on willow bark between his labored fits of coughing. James paced back and forth, trying to hasten the man's recovery with his impatience, but it was only gradually, through Arabella's healing knowledge, that the rhythm of the man's breath was restored.

"He can't travel ten miles tonight," she warned when James lifted him to his feet. "His fever is breaking and the meadowsweet has stilled the tremors in his lungs, but he doesn't have the strength to walk that far on his own."

"Then I'll lay him in the back of my wagon and travel the main roads for as long as I can."

"The main roads are ten times more dangerous, Jimmy."

"I know, but I don't have much choice. I have to leave now if I'm going to get him to the next station in time. If he still can't walk by the time we reach the woods, I'll carry him on my back." James slung his rifle over his shoulder.

"Wait—"

"I don't have time to wait," James said, cutting off Arabella's protest. "I promise I'll explain everything to you when I return, but I need to leave. Now."

"Please, just wait a minute," she begged, struck by a sudden premonition, as powerful as midsummer lightning, that the night was going to end in tragedy.

James clenched his jaw in frustration but stopped his forward progress, supporting the man against his chest as she rummaged through her apothecary case. She quickly mixed an elixir of quince seeds and honey, pouring it into a glass vial. "Drink this whenever you feel a cough coming on," she said, closing the man's fingers around the vial. She placed one hand on his shoulder and one hand on James.

Goddess of darkness, Goddess of light,
Protect these men as they travel tonight,
By earth, air, fire, and sea,
As I will it, so mote it be.

She chanted her rhyme in the old language, the new language, and the old language again, each word a talisman to keep the men safe on their journey. Jonathan tilted his head to the left, listening to the strange, lilting sound of her voice.

"My healer's cloak, in the kitchen," she said when the energy of her incantation had taken hold. "The grey one I brought with me from Scotland. Let him wear it on the journey. It will keep him warm, and it's stitched with a mixture of herbs that will help hide him from view."

James glanced at Jonathan who was studying Arabella with a curious expression.

"Let him keep my cloak even after you reach your destination. And please, be careful James."

James shifted the weight of the man against his shoulder.

"I will."

"Where are they going?" she asked, turning to Jonathan after James left the room.

"North."

One word. But it carried the weight of the world.

Arabella had heard tales of enslaved men and women forced to walk for miles through hostile American terrain, hoping those they trusted would not betray them for monetary rewards. She had heard stories of their terrifying nights spent surrounded by predators, their hungry days spent crouching in rat-infested barns.

"Are they in danger?"

"Yes."

Jonathan pulled a thin strip of wood from his jacket pocket, igniting it in the flames of the fireplace and lifting it to his pipe. Soon, the sweet, pungent scent of his tobacco eclipsed the sulfur perfume of her spell. He puffed calmly, each practiced movement at odds with the tension lingering in the room.

"What will happen to James if they're caught?"

"It depends who catches them." His stared at Arabella as he spoke, his dark eyes flaming in the firelight. "If it's the law, he'll be fined and put in prison. If it's someone unsympathetic to the cause, he'll be beaten, stabbed, or shot. I've seen men branded with hot iron, an SS for slave stealer on the back of their hand." He blew a ring of smoke into the air. "It's nothing compared to what will happen to the Black man."

"Why didn't you go with them?"

"Because at this point in the journey, especially on the open road, they'll both be safer without me."

"If the open road is so dangerous then why didn't you try to stop them? Surely they could have waited until the journey was safe."

"The journey will never be safe." He placed his pipe down on a small dish atop the mantle. Red and orange embers spilled onto the ceramic, brightening momentarily before they simmered down to ash. "And there's nothing I can do to stop Jimmy when he makes up his mind," he said, the lines of his face hard and dark. "If there was, you wouldn't be standing in this room."

A moment of awkward silence, so visceral Arabella could have grasped it in her hands, stretched between them.

"What's that supposed to mean?" she asked.

His only response was silence.

She turned toward the office door. Jonathan reached it first.

"Sit down," he said sharply, motioning to one of the leather sofas. When she refused, he closed the door, locking it from the inside with a large iron key.

"You can't keep me here," she said.

"I can." His voice was unsettlingly calm. "And I will."

"Jonathan—"

"The success of tonight's journey depends on secrecy, and no one in Mystic, apart from me, and now you," he lingered on the word just long enough to illustrate his displeasure at her involvement in their business, "knows about it." He took a step closer to her, his expression resolute. "I'll do whatever is necessary to keep you in this room until Jimmy returns, and if you force me to lay my hands on you, which I will do, Jimmy will kill me. He'll kill me, Arabella, and he'll have to live with that for the rest of his life, so if you care about him, at all, you'll sit down and wait for him to come home."

"Do you think I'm going to tell someone what's happening? Do you really think I would put James or that man in danger after everything I did to help them tonight?"

Instead of answering her, he leaned against the wall by the door, his casual pose disguising his alert tension, his countenance as deceptively still as the frozen earth itself.

She regarded him for a moment, considering.

Then she lowered herself onto the couch to wait for James.

He returned in the dusky light of morning, beneath a cover of grey clouds so thick they looked like smoke. He nodded at Jonathan, and the tense lines of the captain's shoulders relaxed for the first time since Arabella had entered the office.

"Is the man all right? Are you all right?" she asked, searching his body for injuries. She had a thousand questions, but he stopped them with a kiss. His lips were cold and dry from the bitter winds, and his skin, reddened by his trek through the forest's fog and mist, glistened with moisture. He placed his rifle on his desk and removed his jacket. He unloaded the pistol tucked into his belt and released the strap that secured his hunting knife to his thigh. He rolled up his sleeves, reaching toward the dying fire, trying to cool himself and warm himself at the same time. The grandfather clock in the hall struck eight, its muffled chimes penetrating the stillness of the room.

Jonathan's eyes flicked toward Arabella before landing on James.

"Do you want me to stay, Jimmy?" he asked.

James shook his head. "There's a storm on the horizon. If you want to weather it on *Polaris*, you should row out now. I'll handle things here."

Jonathan gathered his jacket and hat and clapped James on the shoulder. "Send word if you need me," he said. He bowed gallantly in Arabella's direction before exiting the room.

James took Arabella's face in his hands. "Thank you for your help," he said, his frozen lips slow to form words. "You saved that man's life."

She brushed away his gratitude, searching his eyes for answers. She had been summoned to heal a man escaping from slavery. She had been locked in James' forbidden office to await his return. She had stayed awake for hours, worried about their safety, frightened by Jonathan's stern demeanor.

"You want an explanation," he sighed.

"I think I deserve one."

He nodded and walked over to the far wall of his office. The thorny branches of Mary's frozen rose bushes tapped and scratched the window, stirred by the winter squall blowing in from the mouth of the river. He moved a heavy piece of furniture, rolled a corner of the plush Persian rug away from the floor, and loosened a few of the boards. He lowered a whale oil lantern into a dark space that had been dug into the hard packed soil. A small bunker, littered with candle stubs, straw, and wooden pallets, revealed itself in the flickering light. It stretched beneath the twisted roots of Mary's rose bushes. A series of tightly jammed wooden beams were angled into the dirt to keep the space safe from collapse. It was a secret room where freedom-seekers could rest *sub rosa*, hidden from a world that sought to harm them.

James told Arabella all about the Underground Railroad, a covert network of safe passage designed by free Black people to usher the enslaved to the north. There were secret routes and waystations spanning from the deep south to the Province of Canada, and when James had inherited his father's shipyard, it was Jonathan who had proposed they join the emancipation effort, transporting men and women from the hull of his ship into the hands of more experienced conductors who would determine the next steps of their journeys. It had taken James months to build a new ship lined with hidden compartments, to dig a bunker beneath his mother's rosebushes, to alter the governing structure of his father's shipyard so that no one who worked in the offices would have access to the schedule of Jonathan's deliveries. Since then, the hull of *Polaris* and the room beneath the rose bushes had become small places of refuge for those running from the tyranny of plantations.

Arabella thought about the intermittent sounds she had heard coming from James' office, the thumping and low moaning she had believed to be the work of ghosts, the haunting strains of a lullaby she had believed belonged to Mary. It broke her heart to think of a young mother sheltered beneath the earth, humming tunes to comfort her crying baby, singing songs to soothe her grief for the children who had been so cruelly taken from her. Now she understood why James had wanted people to stay out of his office. With the thick curtains drawn and the door shut against intruders, his guests could rest on the couches and warm themselves by the fire instead of crouching for days in the darkness and dirt.

"Why didn't you tell me, James?"

She had long-since rationalized away the accusations of his criminal behavior, but his cryptic interdictions had remained a barrier between them even in their most intimate moments. She couldn't understand why he would take such pains to hide what he was doing when she could have aided him by offering his guests the same kind of comfort and companionship she gave to Elinor.

"I couldn't risk you sharing the information with anyone."

"Do you think I would do that?" Tears glistened in her eyes. "Does Jonathan think I would do that?"

James let out a long breath and sat down on the couch. He was tired and sore. He needed food and sleep, but he motioned for Arabella to sit down beside him.

"There are many people, good people, who turn a blind eye to slavery because it happens in places they've never visited, but Jonathan and I have seen the plantations in the West Indes and the American south. They're horrible, Arabella." He swallowed before continuing. "The network we work for is run by Black and Indigenous people. It's far bigger and more powerful than anyone in Mystic would imagine, but it's fragile because it relies on complete secrecy. It would be devastating if information fell into the wrong hands."

"I would never share information that could hurt the people you're helping, James," she said. "I think what you and Jonathan are doing is heroic."

He shook his head. "It's not heroic. My name, the Alden name, protects me from everything short of being caught in the act of housing or escorting an escaped slave, and, because *Polaris* is registered in my name, it protects Jonathan and his crew in ports up and down the east coast, or at least it did, until the day your father had our ship searched for contraband."

She leaned away from, trying to discern the meaning beneath his strained tone.

"If my father had anything to do with the search of *Polaris*—"

"I read the report, Arabella. Your father requested the search."

"Well, that's only because he thinks you and Jonathan are smuggling stolen property. He thinks you're breaking the law. If we tell him the truth—"

"We are breaking the law, and it's a law that needs to be broken." James stood up, pulling her to her feet, trying to impress upon her the enormity of his need for her discretion. "You have to promise me, Arabella. Your father can't learn anything about what happened in this room tonight."

"But I'm sure he'd understand. If he knew you were helping people instead of stealing property, it might quell the tensions between our families and—"

"William knows exactly what Jonathan and I are doing." His voice rose in anger, as it always did when he spoke of her father. "He's known since the day we fired him from the shipyard. The only thing he hasn't figured out yet is *how* we're doing it, and he sent you to work for my grandmother in the hopes you would provide him with that information."

The green embers of Arabella's eyes smoldered with indignation. "Are you accusing my father of supporting slavery?"

"Don't defend him, Arabella—"

"What would you do if I accused *your* father of such an atrocity?" she demanded.

"*My* father was an abolitionist!" His heart rose in defense of his family name. How it had come to this, the two of them arguing over their fathers' ideologies like they were children? "My father may have been too gradual and too measured in his approach to equality, and that may have caused several arguments between the two of us, but he believed in freedom. Your father believes in oppression. The oppression of Black people, Native people, poor people, even women! Why are you so quick to defend a man you hardly know?"

"Why are you so quick to condemn him? You don't know him either! You were a child when you ran off to sea!"

"I wasn't a child when William tried to unite our families in marriage so he could position himself to take over our shipyard. I wasn't a child when he used my dead father's company to forge deals with domestic and transatlantic slave traders that lined his own pockets. And I wasn't a child when he convinced my grieving grandmother to grant him control of our family's financial holdings so he could steal the Alden fortune for himself."

"Elinor told you he did this?"

"Elinor doesn't know! Jonathan and I discovered what he was doing when we returned home from the Antarctic, and we put a stop to it. There was no point in upsetting my grandmother with the information, not after everything she'd been through."

"There must be some mistake," Arabella said, matching James' furious tone, searching the recesses of her mind for a reason, any reason, which might mitigate William's unforgivable actions. "Maybe my father was desperate. Maybe he needed the money to provide for his family—"

"Which family?" James asked. "The legitimate wife and child that lived on Gravel Street? Or the whore he kept locked away in a cottage unfit for animals?"

A wave of anger, so powerful she thought it might lift her from the floor, welled up in Arabella's chest, and she slapped James across the face. The loud thwack of her palm was followed by a deafening silence.

The shape of her hand bloomed red on his cheek, its sting alerting him to the callous nature of his words. "I'm sorry," he said, lowering his voice to a whisper. "I'm sorry, Arabella. I shouldn't have said that."

"Does it make you feel powerful to call my mother a whore and my father a monster? Do you think it will make me love you more if you can force me to love them less?"

He reached out for her, wanting to lighten the load of all he had revealed, but she pulled away from him. "Please," he pleaded, "I'm exhausted, and I'm not explaining things the right way. If I get some sleep—"

"I'm tired too, James," she countered, wanting an explanation more than she wanted rest. "I stayed up all night worrying about you and the man you were helping. Jonathan kept me locked in this room with him. Did you know he was going to do that? Did you know he wouldn't trust me enough to let me leave?"

A new strain of anger crossed his face, sharper and more intense than anything she had seen before. "Did Jonathan hurt you?" He clasped her shoulders, demanding an answer. "Did he hurt you?" he asked again.

"No. But he was angry with me for helping, and I don't understand why."

He released her, exhaling in relief, and when he spoke again, the tense knot of his voice had loosened. "I'll talk to Jonathan, Arabella. I know he can be intimidating, but you have to understand—what we're doing—it's personal for him. He grew up enslaved, and when you told William about *Polaris*' arrival in September—"

"What are you talking about?" she interrupted, her heartbeat beginning to quicken.

"I told him it was all a misunderstanding. It was more my fault than yours because if I had been there, like I was supposed to be, the crew wouldn't have been thrown in prison—"

"Why does Jonathan think I told my father about *Polaris*' arrival date?"

James opened his mouth to respond but closed it again.

"Why does he think that, James?" she asked.

He rubbed the blue-black stubble of his beard. There was no way for him to tell her the truth without hurting her.

"You were the only one besides us who knew the date." He whispered his confession, hoping the humble sound of his voice would dampen the pain his words were sure to cause. "We fed you that information to test your loyalty, to see if you would tell William what you knew."

"You risked people's lives to test my loyalty?"

"No." James was trying, unsuccessfully, to justify what they had done without angering her further. "We ran the September shipment with nothing but lumber. We knew that if you shared the date with your father, he would be waiting with the watch to search the ship."

"But you never told me to keep the date a secret! If anything had happened to Jonathan or his crew that night it would have been *my* fault! All because *you* decided to perform some twisted test of my loyalty!"

"No." He was explaining it all wrong. He couldn't find the right words. "Jonathan came up with the idea before I truly knew you and—"

"Don't you dare blame Jonathan for this!" Her voice was shaking, her eyes flaming with wounded pride. "Jonathan isn't the one who said he loved me! Jonathan isn't the one who called me his *Grá Mo Chroi*, his *Cara M'anama*! *You* are the one who lied to me!"

"I didn't lie to you." He pressed his hands into his bloodshot eyes, willing her to understand. "I kept a secret from you. Those are two different things, Arabella."

"Don't you realize that by keeping all of this a secret from me you only put the people you're helping in more danger? What if I had told my father about the noises I've heard coming from your office? What if he had guessed you were hiding escaped slaves in your home? If it's true he supports slavery, it would have been *my* fault your work was discovered! It would have been *my* fault if someone had been hurt!"

James squinted, his eyes reducing themselves to sharp blue lines of light.

"When would you have said something like that to your father?" he asked, his voice deathly quiet. She met his question with a defiant stare, and he lifted an accusatory finger in her direction. "You promised me that apart from your sister's wedding you would have no contact with William while you lived in my house."

"You're not the only one who can keep secrets," she said, taking satisfaction in the look of devastation that crossed his face.

William had come to the door of Alden House shortly after Anne's wedding, bringing Arabella a bouquet of flowers to apologize for his poor treatment of her. He had sworn off drinking, claiming the rum had gone to his head, and she had forgiven him. In spite of everything James had told her, in spite of everything her mother's letter had said, she had been visiting her father and sister at Newbury House for tea once each fortnight since, slowly building the relationship she had crossed the Atlantic to foster. She had never suspected her father's casual questions about *Polaris* were anything more than polite conversation. She had never considered that both James and William, the two men who claimed to love her, had been using her for their own gain.

"You lied to me, James," she said, not caring in that moment that she had lied to him, too. "Love is not a lie."

She picked up her grimoire and moved toward the door. He grabbed her arm to stop her.

"Arabella—"

"Let go of me!"

She shouted the words with the strength of Catriona's honeyed tongue, and James buckled against their force, releasing her against his will, unable to prevent her from running toward the backdoor and out into the brewing storm.

He knew where she was going even before she did. Her feet guided her along the path they had taken when they had walked home from her sister's wedding. She wore no cloak over her tartan dress, and its muted colors blended with the swirling white flakes falling from the sky. He had followed her out the back door without grabbing his own coat, and his shirt was soaked through with sweat and precipitation. He stayed twenty paces behind her, unable to penetrate the forcefield of protection her words had manifested, but he called her name into the howling winds, begging her to stop, to turn around, to listen.

If she heard him, she showed no sign of it.

She slipped on the icy gravel of the riverwalk, tearing her dress on the jagged rocks. He thought he would catch up to her before she located the hidden footpath worn into the woods, but she turned onto it with enough confidence to make him wonder exactly how many times she had used it to visit her father and sister at Newbury House. The eastern white pine and black birch trees of the native forest provided some cover from the falling sleet, but the ground was rocky and uneven, and the winds whipped the barren branches to a frenzy. A New England cottontail tumbled from the dense thicket, its long brown hair damp with snow. It scampered down the footpath, beckoning Arabella to follow.

The path eventually opened onto Spring Hill Lane, its newly constructed homes standing tall against the squall. The wind rushed across the open patches of cleared land, and Arabella pushed against it, her eyes locked on the warm light spilling from her sister's parlor windows. She had no idea if Anne would welcome her inside, but the pull of her blood had brought her here, and she pounded on the door. It was Alan who answered, his eyes growing wide at the sight of his sister-in-law's torn and bloodied dress. He took her inside, calling out for his wife while his servants stoked the fire and brewed a pot of tea.

James stood at the bottom of the hill in front of the house, watching. Smoke drifted from the chimney-top, rippling against the blowing sleet and snow. Anne floated down the stairs, a look of alarm on her face. She pulled a knitted shawl from around her own shoulders and wrapped her sister in it, leading her to a room at the back of the house. At least Arabella had found shelter. She was no longer in danger from the storm. But James could not bear to leave her, so he stood, a frozen sentinel, his feet anchored in a pile of snow at the bottom of the Newburys' sloped front lawn.

He steeled himself against the bitter cold, remembering how he had chipped great blocks of ice from the iron chains of the *Nymph* when he had sailed through the tumultuous Drake Passage. Surely the temperatures in the Antarctic had been lower than they were here in Connecticut, but he felt colder now than he ever had aboard that voyage. He stood motionless for almost an hour before the door of Newbury House opened. Alan emerged, his collar turned up against the frigid air. The two men walked toward each other, their footsteps carving green patches in the thin layers of accumulating sleet. When they met, halfway up the lawn, Alan offered James a thick wool coat.

"The storm is getting worse," he said, "and you know I can't invite you inside. Go home, James, before you catch your death of colds."

James' lips were blue. The tips of his fingers were red. Wet snow glistened on his hair and shoulders, trailing down his exposed skin in rivulets of refracted light. He made no move to accept Alan's offer of warmth. He said nothing. He only looked past Alan, trying to get a glimpse of Arabella inside the house.

Once, when James had been young and angry at the world, he had started an argument with a much older and larger man in a port town tavern. He couldn't remember the context of their disagreement, but he would never forget how viciously the experienced boatswain, whose muscles were as thick as ropes, had knocked him to the ground, holding a rusty knife against his windpipe until Jonathan somehow convinced the man to set him free. James felt like that now, like he was being pinned against the earth, like he couldn't move, couldn't breathe. An unbearable amount of weight pressed the air from his lungs, reminding him he was much smaller and more helpless than he wanted to believe.

"I need to talk to her, Alan," he said, the words slicing his frozen tongue in two.

Alan and James had known each other since they were boys. Alan had been a timid and quiet child, a target for schoolyard bullies, and James had often defended him, sometimes getting into trouble with their teacher and his father because he refused to explain why he had blackened an eye or bloodied a nose. Alan had always been thankful to James for keeping his persecution a secret because he was ashamed of the fear he had felt when older boys pushed him around the classroom for sport, but now his wife's sister had shown up in tears at his front door, her dress and stockings ripped to shreds, and James was standing on his front lawn, the raised imprint of Arabella's hand still bruising his cheek. Alan didn't know what had happened between the two of them, but he was not going to allow it to progress. He gently brushed the snowflakes from James' shirt and placed the coat over his shoulders.

"Go home," he said. "I can't have you standing out here and staring in my windows all afternoon. You're scaring my wife."

"I'm not here to see your wife."

"There's no one here you'll be seeing today."

"I need to talk to her, Alan."

James was not going to leave without explaining everything to Arabella, without making her understand why he and Jonathan had done what they had done. At the very least, he needed to secure her promise that she would say nothing to her father about what he kept in his office.

"Arabella doesn't want to talk to you," Alan said, his tone landing somewhere between sympathy and authority. "Go home, or I'll be forced to call the watch."

James turned to look at Alan for the first time since he had emerged from his front door. His eyes narrowed. His jaw grew tight.

"Arabella is under my employ, Alan, and I need to talk with her. I'll wait here, outside, until she's ready to see me, but if you, or your wife, or anyone from your household, tries to leave your home and alert the watch, I'll go inside, and I'll find her before the authorities arrive. Trust me when I tell you that you don't want that to happen."

Alan swallowed uncomfortably. He was a scholar and a businessman, and the last thing he wanted was a confrontation with a man who had honed his fighting skills while sailing the seven seas, but he was duty-bound to protect his wife and her kin.

"You need to leave James," he said decisively. "Now."

"And if I don't leave?" James asked quietly. "What will you do then?"

Alan was no longer a child frightened of schoolyard bullies. He pushed James, who had to shift one foot backward to absorb the force of the assault.

James had not come to Newbury House looking for a fight, but connecting his fist to another man's jaw was a sure way to alleviate his frustrations. His voice coiled in warning.

"Think very carefully before you touch me again, Alan."

There was a moment of hesitation before Alan gallantly pushed James a second time. James slid backwards on the icy slope of the front lawn. In seconds he had regained his footing, and knocked Alan to the frozen ground, unleashing a torrent of heavy blows on his face and body. Blood spurted from Alan's nose, leaving a trail of bright red dots on the white snow. Alan raised his hands in defense, managing to land a few lucky blows of his own.

"Stop it this instant!"

Anne had run out into the storm, clutching a shawl around her tiny frame, her golden hair pinned meticulously atop her head.

"Stop it, James! You let him up! Now!" she yelled, her voice a mixture of fear and fury.

When he saw Anne, looking as small and as vulnerable as she had when they were children, his urge to fight left his body, and the memory of why he had come to Newbury House flooded back to him. He stood up, spitting blood. Alan groaned in pain, holding a handkerchief against his broken nose. James helped him back to his feet.

"You *beast*!" Anne shrieked, pushing her small frame between the two large men. "You *heathen*! Do you think this is a whaling ship or a tavern? Do you think this is a house of ill-repute?" She stamped her foot on the snow covered earth, her posture conveying a righteous superiority. "This is our home! And you need to leave it now!"

"I need to talk to her first," he said. "Please."

"What did you do to her?" she hissed.

James grabbed the back of his neck, taking a step toward the street to stop himself from saying something that would escalate the situation. He let out a deep breath, droplets of blood from the cut on his lip splaying into the frigid air. He circled back to face Anne, who had pulled herself up to her full height in anticipation of his inevitable return. He was not going to leave without speaking to Arabella. His heart was tethered to hers, and he was distraught with his desire to see her.

"I didn't do anything to her," he said, knowing it wasn't true but wanting Anne to understand he hadn't physically harmed her sister. "This is all a misunderstanding. I just need to talk to her, and then, if she wants me to go, I'll go."

"She doesn't want to talk to you! She's going home to Scotland!"

"That isn't true," he said, shaking his head. "Anne, please—"

"She told me she *never* wants to see you again!"

She threw Arabella's ring at James' feet. It landed in the snow.

Intertwining diamond bands reduced to a symbol of nothingness.

"If you don't leave right now, I'll scream until my neighbors call for the watch, and then you'll be thrown in prison where you belong!"

He dropped to his knees in the snow, picking up the ring that had been his promise to Arabella. The lawn tilted and spun. He closed his eyes against its undulation, praying he was suffering from a whiskey-induced nightmare, but when he opened them, he was still kneeling on the Newburys' front lawn, his clothes still stained with mud and slush and blood. He gripped the ring as though it were a life buoy thrown out to save a drowning man.

"Anne, please—"

She started to scream, her shrill voice eclipsing the howl of the winds, and something beyond James' own power to choose forced him to his feet.

He stumbled backward down the hill, struggling to breathe as a sharp pain rent his heart to pieces. Alan followed him, trying to cover him with the wool coat for his long journey back home, but James faded away into a flurry of snow.

Part Nine

Home, 1848

"Get you some of this distilled Carduus Benedictus,
and lay it to your heart"
(Much Ado About Nothing)

Elinor Alden died on a cold, January morning shortly after the turn of the year. She never recovered from the languor that settled upon her on Midwinter's day, and she had spent the Christmas holidays in bed, drifting in and out of fevered sleep. Each time she had awoken, she had asked for Arabella, and James, who had seen in the yellowed shade of her skin that she was not long for this world, and who had not wanted to add his argument with Arabella to the list of his grandmother's final worries, made excuses for her absence.

"You just missed her, grandmother. She's been watching you sleep for hours."

"She's in the kitchen making you some rosehip tea. I'll send her up to see you soon."

"She's run away on a whaling ship. She'll come home in four years, covered in tattoos."

Elinor had nodded her head and patted his arm, trying, even as her soul slipped away, to soothe the unnamed pain lurking beneath her grandson's forced smile.

The shipyard had closed for the week between Christmas and the New Year, and when it reopened, James had not returned. Instead, he had stayed by his grandmother's side. When he heard the death rattle at the back of her throat, he took her frail hand in his, holding it until her breathing stilled and her body grew stiff and cold. He held it until the last embers in the grate of her bedroom fireplace burned themselves into thick, black soot. Only then did he send word to the shrouders who descended upon his home like the plague, their long faces drawn and somber, their quiet voices calm and steady. They closed the curtains, stopped the clocks, covered the mirrors in black crepe, and placed bundles of laurel and yew branches by the doors.

Arabella felt the passage between the worlds open the moment Elinor's spirit let go of its grip upon her body. The veil above the old woman had been stretched thin for so long that the threads where it finally split were frayed and uneven, but they floated gently over her, welcoming her as she crossed the threshold to the beyond. Arabella was looking out the window of her sister's house when it happened, and a slant of pearly light tilted through thick bands of low-lying clouds. It was Elinor's light, flying upward toward the heavens, streaking the dull sky with the mark of her soul's beauty. Arabella closed her eyes, listening to the soft ticking of the clock on the mantle, the quiet clacking of the maids' knitting needles, the hushed voices of Anne and Alan talking to one another in the next room, all sounds of the earthly plane that Elinor would never hear again. Tears, hot and wet, spilled from Arabella's eyes.

She knew it would not be long before workmen walking down Greenman Avenue would see the black cloth tied to the porch columns and begin spreading news of Elinor's death. She drifted upstairs to the Newburys' guest bedroom where she had been staying, pulling her family grimoire, the only thing she had carried with her when she left James, from its hiding place beneath the bed. She flipped through the pages until she found the section labeled *Incantations for the Dead.* She chose a particularly beautiful blessing and rehearsed it, saying it over and over until the sacred words anchored themselves in her memory.

She returned the book to its hiding spot and gathered what she needed to perform her ritual, long strands of brown thread, the exact color of Elinor's eyes, silky blue ribbons she found in her sister's sewing box, and herbs from the pantry; salt for protection, rosemary for remembrance, lemon balm to ease sorrow, crushed hawthorn berries to mend hearts broken by grief. She placed the thread, ribbons, and sachets of herbs in her pockets, wrapped herself in a thick, wool shawl, and slipped outside into the grey afternoon.

It was hard to believe the sunken garden behind the kitchen was the same space where her sister had been married only five months before. The snows from the solstice squall had melted, leaving a rime of frost on the grass, and the majestic trees, which had been strung with flickering lanterns for Anne and Alan's wedding, stood bare, their sharp branches etching wispy patterns into the cloud-covered sky. Arabella walked to the far corner of the yard and chose an old, black birch tree, its web of roots poking down into the hard soil as far as its branches spread upward toward the sky. She sprinkled her herbs around the circumference of the tree and knelt to loop three pieces of brown thread over and under the exposed, knobby roots, making wishes for the flight and repose of Elinor's soul. Then she tied three blue ribbons to the branches of the tree, making wishes for James as the rules of her ritual demanded. *Roots for the dead and branches for the living, my child,* she heard Caitriona say through the winds of her memory. *You must never forget to pray for those who are left behind.*

Arabella recited the incantation for the dead three times in the old language, three times in the new language, and three times in the old again, her mouth moving slowly in the cold, her words rising in columns of mist as her breath met the dry, winter air. A phantom breeze blew down from the north and caressed the tree, making the brown thread and blue ribbons flap like winged creatures taking flight.

A corresponding flutter rippled deep inside her abdomen, and she sank to her knees on the frozen ground. She held her breath, waiting. After a few moments, she felt the sensation once more, a tiny bubbling, barely noticeable, like water tumbling over the stones that lined the shallows of the riverbank. Her fingers, already red from the cold, began to tremble as she realized she had carried more than her grimoire with her when she had run away from Alden House. She had also carried a new life within her, one born of her broken union with James.

She lingered in the cold until the setting sun painted the lawn with soft purple hues. Streams of salty tears flowed down her cheeks as she thought about the child quickening within her. She had left the man she loved because he had lied to her and used her, and now she would be forced to raise their daughter alone as the Porter traditions so cruelly demanded. In trying to escape her family's lonely fate, she had succumbed to it. The sun dipped behind the line of trees, ensconcing her in darkness, and she only returned to the light and warmth of the house when she felt her sister's eyes watching her from the kitchen window. Anne asked her why she was crying, but Arabella shook her head, refusing to answer.

By the next morning, news of Elinor Alden's death had reached Newbury House. Arabella pretended to be surprised by information she already knew, tracing the faded indentation of skin on the third finger of her right hand as Anne conveyed the details. She understood now that the mark left by James' ring would never fade. It would be a permanent reminder of the love she had lost, a physical manifestation of the scar that snaked across her heart. How naïve she had been to think she could rid herself of James by asking her sister to return the ring.

"Arabella, are you listening to me?"

Anne had explained the plans for Elinor's wake and funeral procession, suggesting they visit the dress shop to purchase new black mourning ensembles.

"I'm not going," Arabella said. Her voiced sounded weak and far away, as though she no longer had any use for it.

"But, you have to go. Everyone in Mystic will be there," Anne said. "Even our father will have to pay his respects, Arabella. What am I supposed to tell him when he asks me where you are?"

Arabella had begged Anne not to tell their father she was staying at Newbury House, and Anne had reluctantly agreed. The Stafford family had not gathered together since the middle of December when Anne had last arranged a clandestine afternoon tea. William had told his daughters he would be traveling on business over the holidays, and he had brought early presents for both of his girls, handmade soaps scented with lavender and wrapped in gilded paper. Arabella had left the soap in her sister's guestroom because she hadn't wanted James to question her about it, but, after taking refuge at Newbury House, she had thrown it deep into the woods. Its lavender scent, meant to elicit forgiveness, had made her feel sick to her stomach.

"You were Elinor Alden's nurse." Anne was trying her best to reason with her sister regarding her social obligation to attend what was sure to be the largest funeral in Mystic's history. "No one but Alan and I know you've left Alden House. Everyone will expect you to be at the wake. What am I supposed to say when people ask me about you?"

"I don't care what you say." There was nothing Anne could do to convince her sister to return to Alden House, and Arabella could not fathom how James and William, whose hate for one another ran so deep it had destroyed her life, were going to mask their mutual disdain from the crowd of mourners. "I can't go, Anne. I won't. Please don't try to make me."

James' lonely vigil over his grandmother's body, which had been laid out in his front parlor according to the detailed instructions Elinor had written prior to her death, lasted for three long days. He watched, silently, as hundreds of mourners, who came from as far away as New York, Massachusetts, and Rhode Island, passed through his parlor to offer their condolences on the passing of the Alden matriarch. He stared blankly at them as they shared platitudes about God's divine will. When William, Alan, and Anne paid their respects on the third day, just before the burial, James nodded at each of them, refusing to meet their eyes. He was clean shaven and dressed in a formal mourning suit, a thick black band circling his left arm, dark shadows staining the skin beneath his eyes.

"What did you do to my daughter, boy?" William hissed, leaning close to James when he shook his hand, pretending, for the sake of the other mourners in the crowded parlor, that his hostile inquiry was an expression of comfort. Anne had waited until the moment before they entered Alden House to tell her father that Arabella had taken refuge in her home, hoping her careful timing would keep him from reacting with shock at her sister's noticeable absence. James kept his eyes downcast as a surge of anger welled up in his chest at the sound of William's voice. His breath stilled and the muscles around his scar pulled taut.

"Father, please, not *now*," Anne pleaded, dragging William away when she saw James clench his teeth to stop himself from responding.

"I'm sorry for your loss, James," Alan said after Anne managed to steer her father back outside. The two men stood alone beside the casket.

James looked at Alan. The bruises on his face had faded, but the bridge of his nose, which had been knocked slightly off center by the force of James' fist, remained crooked. James knew Alan would carry that scar for the rest of his life.

"Thank you," he said, his voice thick and low. "Arabella?" There were a thousand questions in the name, a thousand wishes that their shared grief for Elinor might transcend the hurt they had caused each other, a thousand prayers she might forgive him for the unforgivable mistakes he had made.

"She's not coming." Alan's words were clear, distant, final, but he clapped his hand on James' shoulder, a gesture of sympathy for the myriad of losses the man had suffered.

Elinor's casket, which James had carved with roses because there were no fresh blooms growing in the garden, was removed from the house through the death door, an opening cut into the side of the parlor that no living person had ever used to enter the home. The casket was placed on a hearse drawn by six of the finest black Alden steeds, and it seemed that every man, woman, and child in Mystic followed the procession as it wended its way toward the Alden Family Tomb at White Hall Cemetery. James walked alone, directly behind the hearse. Then came the wealthy landowners, merchants, sea captains, and politicians, their wives and children trailing behind. Next were the shipyard laborers, textile workers, farmers, dockhands, and sailors whose livelihoods all depended, in one way or another, on the Alden businesses. Jonathan and his crew were there, maintaining a respectable distance, the captain's discerning eyes scanning the crowd for any signs of trouble from William.

Women were not allowed to attend the graveside service, so Anne paced back and forth in front of the cemetery gate, hoping James and William would do nothing to cause a public scene. Gossip about Elinor's missing nurse was steadily growing among the women, but Anne held her head high, pretending not to hear.

When the service ended, the mourners gathered for refreshments in Elinor's honor, the wealthy men at Starkweather and Shetley, the working class at Spouter Tavern, the women and children in the homes of Seventh Day Baptist parishioners. Toasts to Elinor Alden's memory rang out long into the night, but James did not partake in any of the celebrations. He did not return to Alden House, which he had locked when his grandmother's body had been removed. He did not row out to *Polaris*, where Jonathan sat waiting for him, a lantern burning in the windows of the captain's cabin at the back of his ship. Instead, he took a room in a boarding house on Water Street and closed the door.

James' sorrow ran so deep that Arabella felt it as though it was her own. She knew grief compounded over time, that the loss of his grandmother had stirred up wounds he still carried from losing his mother, his father, and his brothers. *Do you love him, Arabella?* Elinor had asked her. It had been the old woman's way of asking Arabella to be there for James when she died, and even though his lies and deceit had freed her from fulfilling her promise to stay by his side, the part of her that she could not control, the part of her that would always love him, ached at the depth of his suffering.

Although she had refused to attend the wake and funeral procession, Arabella prayed the goddesses would lend their comfort to James. When darkness fell, she carved sigils of safe passage into a white candle, cast a circle, and lit the wick for Elinor. She watched the flame of the candle dance, thinking of the child growing inside her and wondering how much time she had left before her father arrived at Newbury House demanding an answer for her absence.

"I'm sorry, Arabella," Anne said in a panicked voice when she finally returned home. "I had to tell Father you're here. I said it was all *his* doing," Anne had refused to speak James' name since her sister had shown up on her doorstep in tears, "but Father wants you to explain what happened." Anne feared her delay in telling their father what little she knew of the situation had only made him angrier. He had continued to demand explanations from Anne who could only report what Arabella had told her on the night of the solstice storm; she never wanted to see James Alden again.

William appeared in the doorway, his tall, lithe form casting a long shadow across the parquet floor. He removed his hat and bowed in his daughters' directions, stumbling a bit as he straightened. He had been drinking with the shipyard lawyers and merchants who had attended Elinor's graveside service, reminding them how prosperous life had been when he had been in charge of running the import schedules at the Alden Shipyard.

"Leave us, Anne," he said.

He sat down in one of the chairs flanking the fireplace, motioning for his youngest daughter to do the same. The light from the hurricane lamp on the small table between them flickered over one side of his face, making his scowl appear more severe.

"So," he said when he was sure they were alone, "the whole town is discussing your disgrace."

"What are you talking about?" Arabella asked.

"You know exactly what I'm talking about." His voice was a slow snarl in the dim light. "You agreed to act as Old Ellie's nurse on my behalf, and today, at her funeral, I learn that you've been turned out of Alden House." He leaned close to Arabella, his sour breath hanging in the air between them. "What did you do?"

Arabella moved back into the cushions of her chair. "You can't have expected me to go on living with James after Elinor's death," she said. "He has no need for a housemaid."

"Don't lie to me, girl." William's voice, sharp as a knife, was barely more than a whisper. "Anne told me you showed up on her doorstep two weeks *before* Old Ellie passed, and you've refused to explain why. If James dismissed you unfairly, I can hardly make him answer for it if you refuse to speak of it, and if you're the one at fault for losing your position, which is the more likely scenario given your silence, then James can nullify our agreement, force me to pay him what I owe, and add six months' worth of your keeping on top of my debt."

He coiled like a snake about to strike, drawing each word out as if it was its own sentence. "I'll only ask you one more time. What did you do?"

"What did *I* do?" she asked, standing up. "I did what you asked of me. I worked for the Aldens for six months, and now my employment with them is through. Any outstanding debt you owe James is *your* responsibility. It has nothing to do with me."

She walked toward the doorway to the hall, and William rose from his chair, grabbing her arm as she passed him.

"Don't walk away from me," he spat, pushing her back toward the fireplace and shaking her violently.

"I thought you had your mother's charms," he said, his voice frighteningly low so no one in the house would hear what he was saying and come to her aid. "I thought you could get me the information I needed to finally punish James Alden for his crimes. I thought, if nothing else, you could lure him into bed and force him into marriage, or at least demand a financial settlement from him so the Stafford wealth and influence could be restored, but you have failed me at every turn!"

"Is that all you care about?" Tears of pain and anger spilled down her cheeks as she tried in vain to pull away from him. "Taking money and power away from James?"

"*He* is the one who took money and power away from me! Dismissing me from his family's shipyard! Replacing me with men who are beneath me!" He continued to shake her, twisting her arm with enough force to snap the bone in two. "You came to America looking for a father! Well, I'm the father you found, and you'll learn to serve me and my interests whether you like it or not. If you're too dull to hold the attention of James Alden, I'll find another man willing to pay me handsomely for your *healing* abilities."

He dragged Arabella toward the door like she was a piece of his property. She realized he meant to take her away from her sister, away from Newbury House, because he knew she would be easier to control if she was isolated, just as her mother had been. For six months, she had tried to win his favor, she had hoped to gain his love, she had made excuses for every crime he had committed. But Arabella wasn't alone anymore. She carried a life within her. It fluttered inside her, even now, its movement as soft and as strong as the stroke of a raven's wing, and she wasn't going to let her father threaten it.

She wrenched her arm away from William, lifted the hurricane lamp that shielded the sigil-carved candle she had lit in Elinor's honor, and threw it against the stones of the fireplace. Shards of glass and hot wax flew across the room. Anne and Alan burst through the doorway, expressions of shock on their faces.

"What happened?" Anne asked. "What's wrong?"

Arabella ignored Anne and stepped toward William.

"You know what my mother was—"

"Your mother was a witch and a whore!"

Anne gasped, and Alan moved in front of her, trying to shield her from William's language with his body.

"And you know what my grandmother was—"

"An *old* witch and an *old* whore!"

"So, you should know what I am," Arabella said, ignoring Anne's growing hysteria. "You should know what I am capable of doing if you push me."

She took another step toward her father and his face began to tighten and release in wary tremors as he thought, for the first time in many years, of Caitriona Porter. Catherine had told him stories about her mother's strength and power, her vast knowledge, her fearless resolve. He had seen Caitriona, only once, when he and Catherine had ducked behind the corner of a building to avoid her, and that one sighting had been enough to stir an uncomfortable fear in William's heart. All the kindness William had found so easy to manipulate in Catherine was missing from her mother's visage, replaced by a hard, stone-like potency his charm had no chance of penetrating. As William had watched the Porter matriarch walk down the cobblestone streets of Portree, her grey cloak flapping behind her like a wizard's mantle, he had decided, then and there, to cut his losses and abandon the beautiful girl he had been dallying with. Now, he only wished Catherine had had the sense to get rid of the child he never wanted before it had drawn its first breath.

"*You* are the reason my mother ran away from her ancestral home and family," Arabella shouted, as a look of horror passed over her sister's face. "*You* are the reason my mother was so scared and so lonely she accepted your violent attentions as the only form of love she thought she deserved. But *I* am not afraid of *you*." Her breath sparked like sulfur dust, the power of Caitriona's honeyed tongue rising within it as she slowed her words so he understood the weight of each one.

"I was raised by Caitriona Porter on the Isle of Skye. *She* gave me her vast knowledge, *she* gave me her sacred strength, and if you *ever* lay your hands on me again, it will be the last thing you do."

The air around Arabella flickered like distant starlight. William's eyes widened at the sight, and for a moment, Anne thought he was about to turn and run away. Then the moment passed, and he hurled a wad of saliva up from his throat, spitting it at Arabella's feet.

"You think you can survive in the New World without your father's protection?" He made a noise halfway between a snort and a laugh. "I'll enjoy watching you fail."

He turned to his older daughter, determined to punish her for her role in helping Arabella escape from Alden House. "If you give your bastard sister shelter against my wishes for even one more night, you'll be as dead to me as she is."

He turned to leave the room, only pausing on the threshold when he heard his name, not *Father*, but *William*, spoken in a commanding tone that could not be ignored. He swung around, his hand raised, ready to physically reprimand Arabella for the insult, but she stilled his assault with a question he hadn't anticipated.

"Did you bury my mother's body beneath her evening primroses?"

Wiliam blinked, thinking for a moment he was looking at the shade of Catherine Porter's ghost instead of their living daughter. He and Arabella had never once spoken about her mother's cottage or the garden behind it. The girl had always been so grateful for the scraps of attention he had offered that she had not dared to broach the topic of her mother with him. He had never mentioned Catherine's death to anyone, had never breathed a word of her last request. He had waited, patiently, for Mystic's memory of his mistress's pathetic life to fade away, and it had. Arabella's arrival was the thing which had reignited the old rumors he had spread to keep Catherine humble and under his control. He didn't believe in witchcraft, not really, but how else would their daughter know about the cottage and the garden and the evening primroses Catherine had planted? He had underestimated the Porter women. He felt as though his knees might buckle beneath him.

"I'll only ask you one more time, William," she whispered, her voice so low he had to lean toward her body to hear her, though it raised the hairs on the back of his neck. "Did you bury my mother's body beneath her evening primroses?"

He looked into Arabella's eyes, noting how they were woven of the same threads of green light as her mother's. He had loved those eyes once, despite all the trouble that had come of it. He did not speak, but he nodded once in confirmation. Then he placed his hat on his head, and left the room. Alan followed him to escort him to the door.

"What happened?" Anne asked in a small, sad voice as soon as the women were alone. Her face was blanched of all its color. "What did you do to make father so angry?"

"I'm sorry, Anne," Arabella said, though she wasn't. She had held her tongue about every horrible truth she had learned about William since she had arrived in America, hoping that her father's actions would prove James' accusations against him wrong, and she hadn't realized until now what a toll that self-imposed silence had taken on her. She was tired of hiding her questions, tired of hiding her faith, tired of making herself smaller to conform to the rules of what a woman should be.

"You don't have to apologize to me," Anne said. "But you must make amends with father. He's upset you didn't go to him when you left Alden House, but if you tell him you're sorry for what you said and did tonight, and if you promise never to talk to him like that again, he'll forgive you, I'm sure of it." Anne took her hand to encourage her. "You didn't really mean those things you said about what your mother and grandmother were, did you?"

"Did he?" Arabella released her sister's hand. "I will never apologize to him for what I said and did tonight."

"Please, Arabella, you must be reasonable! You can't stay here without his blessing and you have nowhere else to go." As much as Anne enjoyed undermining James' authority by inviting her sister to her house against his wishes, she would never openly defy her own father. "I know you want to go home to Scotland, but you can't return in the middle of winter. There are great sheets of ice floating in the Atlantic!"

"My mother had a cottage by the sea on the outskirts of town, somewhere between here and New London," Arabella said. "If Alan will let me use his carriage, I can load it with supplies to sustain myself until I can return home to the Isle of Skye in the spring."

Anne had heard about Catherine Porter's run-down cottage when she was a child. She remembered how the boys in school used to dare one another to visit the witch's home, and she remembered how her parents had warned her against ever going near it. After Catherine had died, people said the land was haunted by her angry spirit, and the meager dwelling had been left to rot.

"An unmarried woman can't live alone in a cottage by the sea," Anne said.

'I lived alone in a cottage by the sea before I came here," Arabella countered.

Anne took a deep breath, trying to appeal to her sister's sense of logic. "The cottage and the land it sits on must belong to our father. What will happen if he finds out you're staying there? What will happen if he confronts you again?"

"I'm not afraid of our father," Arabella repeated. She doubted William would show his face at the cottage, and even if he tried, she knew how to cast spells to protect a home from harm. Catherine's cottage was small and isolated, but James' repairs had made it habitable. "Please, Anne," she said. "Please. I don't want to come between you and our father, but I need your help one last time."

Anne and Arabella had not grown up as sisters. They had not whispered secrets to one another in their childhood nursery when they were meant to be sleeping. They had not shared their impatience with schoolwork or competed to wear the latest fashions so they could turn the heads of Mystic's most eligible bachelors. They had not even known of each other's existence until they had reached adulthood and discovered that the differences in their upbringings stood between them like the immoveable stone walls that divided New England property lines, but none of that mattered now. Anne had always wanted a sister, and she was not going to forsake her.

"I'll tell my husband to ready the carriage."

Alan, Anne, and Arabella packed through the evening and into the night, and by the time they reached Catherine's cottage by the sea, the sun was a tight red ball of fire peeking over the frosted horizon. Alan had easily located the isolated land, which made Arabella wonder if he, too, had persecuted her mother in his boyhood. He left the carriage on the side of the road to walk the women up the rocky pathway, his lantern light gilding the dried thistle husks that swirled around the home's perimeter. In the shadowy dawn, the house looked dark and empty. A flock of sea gulls cawed, and behind their song was the far-off tumble of water rising and falling around the rocks lining the beach.

Arabella placed her hand on the knob of the wood-paneled door and pushed it open. Alan set to work making a fire from the stack of logs James had placed in a large metal basket by the mantle. Soon it was glowing merrily, replacing the chill of the empty cottage with warm, crackling light.

Anne watched with interest as the fire worked its magic, casting a homely glow about the room. Finely turned furniture and soft, clean bedding materialized from the darkness. Although the cottage was small, far smaller than even the smallest room at Newbury House, it was clean and curtained, and Anne had trouble believing it was the same shack where Catherine Porter, the Mystic Witch, had resided so many years ago.

"Are you sure no one lives here?" she asked.

"I'm sure. When James—" Arabella's voice hitched. "When he first brought me here, it was destitute. He rebuilt it for me so I could tend my mother's garden in the spring."

Anne studied her sister's expression, wondering exactly how much had transpired between her and James Alden. "If *he* knows about this place, then you aren't safe here. What if he comes looking for you?" She shivered, remembering how James had broken Alan's nose and left a trail of his blood on the snow.

"He won't," Arabella said. She knew in her heart it was true. "Our life together is over."

Alan left the women to unpack while he made the first of several trips back down the icy pathway to gather the rest of the supplies. Anne's maid had assembled a case of household items, and her cook had packed three months' worth of food. Anne unloaded crates of salted fish and cured meats, baskets of apples and dried fruits, strings of onions and root vegetables, jars of honey, sugar, salt, and elderberry wine. She piled them in the corner that had once served as a makeshift pantry. Arabella stood motionless in the middle of the cottage while her sister worked. She stared at the incandescent glow rising from the armoire James had built to house her mother's belongings.

"Do you remember my mother, Anne?" she asked quietly.

Anne stopped unpacking and turned to look at Arabella, following her gaze to the armoire.

"Yes," Anne said. "A little."

"Why didn't you ever tell me about her?"

It was a question that had gnawed at Arabella since she had first learned her mother had not perished at sea. William, Anne, James, and Elinor had all known about Catherine's time in Mystic, but not one of them had voluntarily told her anything about the mother she had always wished to know.

"There wasn't much I could say about her, Arabella. Not without hurting you." Anne pulled at the buttons on the sleeves of her dress. "When I was young, children used to tell terrible stories about her. They said she stole babies and turned men's tongues blue. When I grew old enough to make some sense of the rumors about our father and your mother, my mother told me Catherine Porter had cast an evil spell over him. She said nothing he had done was his fault."

"And you believed all of that?"

"I don't know." Anne sighed, as though it had happened so long ago it hardly mattered any more. "He's my father, Arabella," she said because she had no other way to explain her loyalty to the man who had caused her sister so much pain. "I know you don't have many good memories of him to counter the bad ones, but I do. He's always taken care of me. And sometimes, when he wasn't drinking, he was kind."

Alan finished unloading the carriage and told Anne it was time for them to return home. Arabella watched the bouncing light of their lantern recede down the path until it disappeared into the lightening skies. When they were out of sight, she closed the front door and opened the armoire, eager to inspect her mother's things. The scent of smoky peat and dried thistle, as clear and as crisp as a Scottish winter, washed over her, welcoming her home.

Inside the armoire, Arabella found several of Catherine's old dresses, simple frocks dyed in the soft green and blue hues of the Porter plaid, their bodices laced up the front, peasant-style. When she pushed them to the side, a necklace dropped from one of the pockets, falling to the floor like a silver fish. Its pendant, identical to the one Arabella wore around her neck, identical to the ones her grandmother and each of her aunts had worn, had been stamped with the Porter family seal. Arabella brought the cold metal to her lips. She wondered if her father had taken the pendant off her mother's neck before burying her beneath her evening primroses, or if her mother had voluntarily ceased wearing it before she had died, its sacred meaning a grim reminder of the life she had renounced.

Not wanting to lose it, Arabella placed the pendant in the music box James had made for her. She ran her finger over the swirls of shells and wampum beads covering the octagonal surface of the box. James had told her his crewmates aboard the *Shepherd* had crafted similar gifts for their sweethearts back home.

She lifted the lid, and the golden wheel spun against the comb. She waited until the tinkling sounds of the sea shanty slowed to a stop before she closed it and placed it back on the night table next to the bed.

The shelf in the armoire held boxes of candles, black and white, and baskets of dried sage, their stalks wound together and tied with thread for cleansing. She snapped open the metal hinges of her mother's apothecary case and found more bundles of loose herbs among stoppered jars filled with potions, their contents, separated by time, coating the glasses with thick films of grimy color. Arabella sorted the bad from the good, discarding the broken bottles and moldy things she could no longer use, keeping what could be salvaged. She closed her hand around vials of juniper, rue, and pennyroyal, knowing that if she steeped them together and ingested the concoction, it would restore her courses, severing her final connection to James. After a few moments, she placed the vials back in the apothecary case and closed the latch.

She opened the thistle-stamped cover of her mother's grimoire, flipping through the yellowed pages. A sharp corner of paper sliced the tip of her index finger, and she brought the wound to her mouth, absentmindedly licking away the blood as she perused recipes, notes, and incantations. She lingered over illustrations of herbs and flowers from the New England shore, imagining her mother's quill moving across the parchment. A drop of blood and saliva from her injured finger fell onto the paper, and her mouth rounded in silent surprise as a hidden spell emerged, its words appearing on the page like magic.

Caitriona had taught Arabella how to enchant ink that would only appear to those who shared the writer's blood. It was an easy but effective recipe, used during the dark days in Scotland when the practice of witchcraft had been vilified. Wise women who had used their knowledge to help others, talented women who had possessed second sight, beautiful women who had been born with fairy gifts, had been hunted down, imprisoned, and burned alive, all because fearful, ignorant men had falsely accused them of being in league with the devil. The old language had been confined to whispers, the old ways relegated to shadows, and women had been forced to rewrite their family grimoires with enchanted inks that would only reveal themselves when touched by the bodily fluid of their kin.

Catherine had used this type of ink to compose a dangerous spell, one spun of words to bind both hearts and minds. It invoked a magic so compelling and so intrusive that even Caitriona, the most powerful woman in the Porter line, would never have dreamt of using it for fear its dark power might return to her threefold. Catherine must have been desperate to have crafted such a dark incantation. She must have been frightened to have shielded it from prying eyes. Arabella wondered if her mother had ever used it, for claiming dark power and using dark power were two completely different things, and the presence of the spell alone did not denote the intention with which it may have been wielded. When Arabella's blood dried, the enchanted ink faded away, and the parchment looked innocent once more.

A glint of light from the back of the armoire caught her eye, and she moved a heavy box filled with books and bells to uncover a mirror, antiqued and silvered, her own tired face reflected in its center. The ornate frame was heavy, the glass cloudy. It was a scrying mirror. She knew little about the practice. One of her great aunts had been gifted in it, using the placid lakes on the edges of the moors to predict coming storms, but her grandmother had never placed much stock in trying to know an unknowable future. What was meant to be would be whether you knew about it or not, and peering forward in time would cause nothing but pain. Caitriona had chosen learning over divining, and she had demanded Arabella do the same, proscribing a strict course of study for her granddaughter as soon as she was able to read. *Words wield the most powerful magic of all*, she had preached, but Arabella, now curious, squinted into the mirror's cloudy glass.

The mists began to swirl, and Arabella saw herself holding a newborn baby, a boy with auburn curls and emerald eyes. She dropped the mirror in surprise, thankful it did not shatter when it landed in her lap. There had been no boys born into the Porter line for as far back as her clan had kept recorded history. Porter women stayed on the Isle of Skye to raise their daughters and practice their craft, and although Arabella had heard hushed rumors of aunts and cousins who, like Catherine, had left the island and abandoned their birthright, she had never heard stories of fathers, uncles, or baby boys. Was it possible for Porter women to give birth to male children? Would Porter men have access to fairy gifts? It had never occurred to Arabella to ask these questions while her grandmother lived.

The unreliable image in the mirror clouded over once more, and Arabella looked up, glancing through the window where the sky, which had begun to splinter in spirals of ice and snow, reminded her that her present needs were far more pressing than the secrets of the past or her questions about the future. She stood up, took Catherine's grey healer's cloak from the rack, and ventured outside into the cold.

Arabella followed the trail of thistle husks around the cottage, sprinkling salt water to refresh the magical barrier that would keep those with ill intent from entering her sacred space. She drew sigils into the hard soil with the sharp point of a black birch branch, creating Dara Knots in the north, south, east, and west. She recited her spell, the same one she had used to protect Alden House.

Spirits of North, South, East, and West,
I call upon you to heed my request,
Shield me with earth, air, fire, and sea,
As I will it, so mote it be.

Her face and fingers were frost-bitten by the time she came back inside, and she stirred the logs in the grate, holding her hands to the fire to warm them.

The precipitation continued all through the afternoon and into the evening, a light, airy snow that fell like powdered sugar. Cold winds blowing in from the sea spread the snow across the clearing for the next several days. Then came a night of heavy sleet, thick and wet, followed by a string of violent Nor-Easters. Frost bloomed across her windows each morning, and she lay in bed staring at the glittering petals, thinking of the tattooed roses on James' skin.

The stony pathway between the road and the cottage soon became unnavigable, as James had told her it would, so she spent the remaining weeks of January entirely alone, reading through her mother's grimoire, mending moth holes in her mother's dresses, restocking her mother's apothecary kit with fresh teas and potions that might help her secure passage as a healer on board a ship sailing to Scotland in the spring. The turning of the month brought weak but welcome sunshine. The *Cailleach Bheurra* sent a day of clear skies, and Arabella restocked her firewood from the covered pile of logs James had left behind the cottage, preparing herself for six more weeks of harsh winter. She trudged down the path to the beach, collecting snow-crusted rushes, fashioning them into small dolls to place on the corner of her hearth. She baked bannock cakes over the open fire and left a bowl of honey by the front door for Brigid, marking *Imbolc* as she and her family had when she lived on the Isle of Skye.

That evening, she lay in bed, listening to the fire crackle and pop. *Imbolc is Old Irish for "in the belly of the mother,"* Caitriona's voice reminded her, *because seeds of life are already stirring deep in the womb of mother earth.* Arabella rested her hands on the curve of her abdomen. Her baby moved beneath them, a tiny butterfly, already trying to break free of its chrysalis.

"Hello, little one," she whispered, the sound of her own voice strange in her ears because she had not spoken aloud since Anne and Alan had left. Her womb rippled gently in response, like a tiny ocean throwing its misty, white froth to the shore.

Arabella had been midwife to dozens of women on the Isle of Skye, but it felt odd being with child herself. In the fairy stories Caitriona used to tell her, women wished for babies only to bargain them away for lettuce or trade them for straw that had been spun into gold. Arabella had not wished for a child, and several times, during the dark, stormy nights of January when her tears had fallen as fast and as thick as the snow, she had contemplated drinking the juniper, rue, and pennyroyal mixture to bring an end to her pain. Now, with the moonlight shining on the ice and the fire crackling in the hearth, she made a solemn vow never to trade away her child, not even for her own safe passage from sorrow. She supposed *Imbolc*, the halfway point between winter and spring, was a good day to make a promise she would honor for the rest of her life.

By midnight, a new storm had blown in from the sea. Now that she had spoken aloud, for the first time in several weeks, she was possessed by an urge to continue, so she told her baby all about their home on the Isle of Skye. She spoke of Scotland and Mystic, of Caitriona and Elinor, of *Martha's Destiny* and her journey across the sea. She spoke of Mary's pink roses and the purple thistle so important to the Porter Clan. With each passing day, she filled the air of the cottage with stories, and still, she had more stories to tell.

Winter did rage on for six more weeks, as the *Cailleach Bheurra* had foretold, followed by a false spring which melted into a long stretch of cold, damp rain that wrapped itself around the cottage like a cloak woven of mist. Arabella read aloud from her mother's tattered books and recited fairy tales from memory, and although the Porter traditions demanded she never reveal the paternal line, she told her baby all about James, how he had transformed trees into ships that traversed the seas, how he had sailed across the equator and watched the moon drop straight down into the ocean, how he had seen Antarctic ice crystals so intricate in their creation, they had made him believe in God.

Arabella told stories as the sun and the moon and the stars rotated in endless circles of celestial protection around her mother's little cottage by the sea, and her baby grew, like a seed beneath the soil, watered by words, the most powerful magic of all.

The first customer came to Arabella's door in the weeks between winter and spring, just as the sun was sweeping the grey sea and sky into bright, brilliant shades of blue. It was an ash-faced girl, no more than ten or eleven years of age. She had walked the five miles from New London, treading through city streets and coastal woods until she found the cottage by the sea, because she had heard the woman who used to live there had returned. The sailors stationed in New London, whose boats passed by the cottage on their way to the mouth of the Thames River, had seen smoke curling from the chimney.

"Can I help you?" Arabella asked, opening the door. She crouched down so her face was level with the girl's. "Are you lost?"

"No ma'am," the child said, letting her gaze fall to the mud-caked hem of her skirt. "At least, I don't think I'm lost." She looked up hopefully. "Are you the Wise Woman?"

Wise Woman. Arabella was so accustomed to people referring to her as a witch, that the girl's reverent use of the sacred title stirred her heart. The child must be looking for Catherine. James had said her mother had worked as a healer for poor immigrants living in New London.

"My older sister has a terrible cough,' the girl continued, twisting the strings of the apron she wore over her tattered dress. "She hasn't been able to work in the mills, and our landlord says we'll be turned out on the street if we don't pay our rent soon. My mother sent me to find you. She said maybe if I help you with any extra chores you need doing, you'll fix a remedy for my sister's cough." The girl had grown up hearing stories about the Wise Woman who had invited even the most downtrodden into her cottage, brewing cures for aches of the body and sicknesses of the soul in exchange for labor, food, and companionship.

"Did you come here all by yourself?" Arabella asked. The girl nodded her head. How often in America had Arabella been chastised for venturing out of the house on her own, and yet here was a child, small and hungry, who had been sent alone on a long and dangerous errand. It seemed safety was a privilege of the wealthy in America.

She invited the girl into her cottage, giving her a basket of red apples to peel and setting a cup of tea and a tin of ginger biscuits on the table. The remedy the girl's sister needed was a simple one, belladonna diluted with water and sweetened with honey to make the syrup more palatable. When the mixture had cooled, Arabella chopped the peeled apples, showing the girl how to dip them in batter, fry them in bubbling oil, and roll them in bowls of cinnamon and sugar.

"Tell your sister to take a teaspoonful two times a day," Arabella said, handing the girl a vial of medicine and a canvas sack filled with apple fritters. "She'll feel well enough to return to work soon."

The girl smiled and thanked her. "I'm so glad you've come back" she said, believing Arabella was Catherine, the Wise Woman with auburn hair and green eyes who dispensed magical remedies from her cottage by the sea.

Word spread, and soon men, women, and children from the outskirts of New London began making the journey to Arabella's door for salves, teas, and tinctures. Some came at dawn or dusk when they were less likely to be seen, asking for potions to enhance or quell romantic feelings, seeking herbs to increase fertility, requesting talismans to hide them from trouble. They paid what they could, often bartering their time and possessions in exchange for help, the men chopping wood for Arabella's fireplace, the women gifting her gently used blankets and clothes their own babies had outgrown.

The women sometimes stayed to gossip and sew, and their presence comforted Arabella, for she knew she would not see her sister again until the muddy path that led to the cottage had dried and hardened. Anne was not a woman who would traipse through the mud and stain her expensive dresses with silt. It was for the best, because if her household staff deduced where Anne was going based on the damage to her clothes, rumors about her missing sister's location were sure to follow.

The herbs Arabella had salvaged from her mother's apothecary case diminished quickly, so one cool morning in April, she wandered outside and opened the gate to Catherine's garden, hoping to harvest some supplies from the forgotten weeds. She surveyed the unkempt patch of earth. She had planned to leave for Scotland as soon as the spring muds cleared, but her baby was not due until the end of summer. If she stayed in her mother's cottage until the solstice, she could restore the garden and create a stockpile of remedies for her new customers before sailing home to Skye in time to give birth. She could teach the women who frequented her cottage how to sustain the garden, leaving behind recipes they might conjure in her stead.

Arabella raked the matted brown grass. She scraped lichen from the planks of the rotting picket fence. She cleared away weeds from the once orderly rows.

An American robin, her breast bright red in the morning sun, watched from her nest in an apple tree on the eastern side of the garden. Arabella smiled. "Are you expecting, too?" she asked, wondering how many blue-tinted eggs would appear in the nest over the next few weeks. She ran her fingers through her hair, letting a few long strands fall to the ground. The robin flitted down to scoop up the tendrils in her beak, twisting them into her nest of leaves and mud. They glinted like copper in the afternoon light. "Now our destinies as mothers are tied together," Arabella whispered. The robin flapped her brown-feathered wings, warbling a friendly tune.

The sun was already beginning its descent behind the western tree line when Arabella stood upright, stretching her tired arms to the sky. The day, which had started out chilly, had warmed considerably, and she turned her face to the southern shore, letting the sea breeze caress her perspiring body. She closed her eyes, so content she did not notice the sound of footsteps or the noisy creak of the gate.

"Arabella—"

She opened her eyes to find her sister staring at her. The wind had pushed Arabella's dress against the curve of her abdomen. Anne looked from Arabella's face to her rounded stomach and back to her face again.

"You—you're—"

She paused before letting the words tumble out of her mouth like an accusation.

"You're pregnant!"

"How did this happen?" Anne demanded after Arabella had ushered her inside. Anne had instructed her coachman, who had carried a fresh load of supplies up the pathway from the road, to return to the carriage before he could set his eyes on Arabella, though without the wind pressing against the curves of her body, it was difficult to discern her condition.

"You're a married woman, Anne. You know how this happens."

"This isn't funny," Anne snapped, panic rising in her voice. She knew James had given her sister a ring and broken her heart, but she had not realized he had compromised her virtue.

"Is *he* the father?" Anne asked, still stubbornly refusing to utter his name.

"Yes." Arabella sighed. "James is the father."

"Did he—did he force you to—is this why you left Alden House?"

"No. He didn't force me to do anything. I didn't know I was with child until after I left him."

Anne dropped into one of the chairs at the table and Arabella sat down in the other.

"I didn't mean for you to find out this way," she said. She had been rehearsing a speech for weeks, but it hardly seemed relevant now that Anne had pieced together the information on her own.

"Have you told him yet?"

"No."

"He'll do the right thing," Anne reassured her. "He may be a heathen and a beast, but he was raised to be a gentleman."

Annoyance flashed across Arabella's face. "And what, exactly, is the right thing?" she asked.

"Marriage of course. If you marry immediately, we can keep your condition quiet for another month at least. With a proper drape to your skirt, no one needs to know. When the baby arrives there will be rumors, of course, but that can't be helped now."

"Anne—"

"There are advantages to marrying an Alden, Arabella, even if that Alden is James. Your child will have a good name, a good future, and—"

Arabella placed her hands over her sister's, begging her to slow down. "I'm not telling James about the baby, not now."

"Arabella—"

"James has no plans to marry me, and I won't use a child to force him into a union he doesn't want."

"Well, if he refuses to do the right thing then our father will make him! James will have no choice!"

"It isn't doing the right thing if he has no choice."

"Well, he can't make *any* choice, right or wrong, unless you tell him about the baby!" She threw her hands upward in a dramatic show. "You have to tell him, Arabella. This is his child!"

"This is *my* child."

"You can't raise a child by yourself! He's the father and he has a right to know. You have tell him," she repeated in desperation.

Arabella took a deep breath, determined to remain calm. "I'll tell him when I'm ready to tell him. I'll write him a letter after I've returned to Skye."

"You're still going back to Skye?" Anne's expression was full of anguish.

"Yes. Just after the summer solstice." She had already asked several seafaring families who visited her cottage to help her secure passage to Scotland.

"A woman in your condition can't cross the Atlantic!"

"I assure you, Anne, a woman in my condition can cross the Atlantic,"

Arabella said, thinking of her friend, Elizabeth Adams, who had comforted her through the tempest on *Martha's Destiny.*

"I don't think you understand how serious this situation is!" Anne sounded like she was going to cry, and Arabella sighed, looking out the window at the clouds swirling in the bright blue sky. The sea gulls were dropping mollusks onto the roof of the cottage, their beaks tapping a staccato beat as they pried meat from the broken shells. When Arabella spoke again, her voice was sticky and sweet.

"The Isle of Skye is my home, Anne. All the women in my family have birthed their daughters on the island, and I need to do the same." Despite what her mother's scrying mirror had shown her, Arabella knew she was carrying a daughter, and she would not risk telling James before she set sail for fear he would invoke his paternal rights and keep her from returning to her ancestral home. "Please, Anne. I know you don't understand. I know you don't agree. But I need you to keep my secret." She placed her hand on her sister's shoulder. "I promise you I'll write to James as soon as I arrive in Scotland, but you must promise me you won't tell James, or our father, about the baby."

The air smelled of sulfur, and a tingle of warmth filled the cottage.

"I promise," Anne whispered, helpless to deny her sister's request. "I promise I won't tell them your secret."

Arabella spent the misty April afternoons in her mother's garden, tracing triskelions into the soil to encourage the growth of asters, hollyhock, and bunchberry. She sliced her palm with a pair of shears she had found in a small tool shed, letting her blood call forth creeping phlox, marsh marigold, and creamy white lily of the valley. Soon, fiddlehead ferns unfurled in the grass, green moss spread along the garden wall, and golden rue winked in the sunlight. By the end of the month, the apple trees had blossomed. On windy days, their petals floated through the air like pink snow.

Anne visited as much as she dared, trying not to rouse suspicion among her household staff as she packed baskets of fresh breads and bottles of cider to restock her sister's kitchen. Each morning and evening customers came to Arabella's door, ringing the bells she had hung on the knob, seeking tonics and elixirs. The white birch tree on the northern corner of the property, which grew on a small hill where two springs of fresh water met before tumbling toward Fishers Island Sound, was soon covered with spare strips of cloth, each one a wish made by a visitor. Even the most practical of her customers, who came for the sweet taste of her teas alone, paused to tie a ribbon on the tree, for it was believed that a wish made at the well of the Wise Woman was certain to come true.

On the first of May, Arabella woke early, washing her face with morning dew and decorating her windows with rowan, hawthorn, gorse, and hazel to draw down the warmth and light of the sun. As she gardened, she told her daughter how the *Nymph* had once sheltered in a caldera formed by ancient volcanos, and how clouds of pink birds had followed James' merchant ship when he had sailed through the islands of the Caribbean sea. She told her about the farmers on Skye who had marched their cattle over the Trotternish hill each *Latha Bealltainn*, and about the night she and Caitriona had climbed up the Cuillin Mountains to watch the revelers' torches create a river of flame that stretched from one side of their island to the other.

When darkness fell, Arabella carried a few pieces of firewood and a lantern out to the eastern corner of the garden. She wandered through lush beds of low growing vegetation, past arbors of wisteria and Dutchman's pipe, their newborn tendrils curling upward toward the sky. The moon hung low over the horizon, its light silvering the patch of evening primrose that served as her mother's headstone. Night moths, their dark, patterned wings flapping contentedly, brushed against the flowers' mysterious glow.

She built a small fire in a circle of stones, tending it until it burned bright and hot, its smoke and ashes floating through the air, lending protective powers to the garden. Spring peepers courted one another on the banks of the stream, and cool breezes rushed through the sea grasses. Arabella added her voice to the music of the night, singing the old Scottish ballad Caitriona had used to lull her to sleep when she was a child.

O dig me a grave, and dig it down deep
And strew it all over with primrose so sweet

And lay me down easy, no more for to weep
Since love was the cause of my ruin.

The cryptic meaning of the words rolled through her restless mind. Both James and Elinor had described her as *ruined.* Were all women destined to be ruined by love? Was that why the Porters never revealed the paternal line? Had her grandmother's somber lullaby been saining her against the dangers of romance, warning her that she would one day have to raise her own daughter alone?

The moon sailed across the night sky, a ghost ship navigating a star-filled sea, and Arabella cast her circle, acknowledging the north, south, east, and west. She loosened the plaits of her hair. She undid her laces and let her dress fall to the ground. Sky-clad in her mother's protected garden, she closed her eyes, swaying to the tune of her family's lullaby as her daughter tumbled in her womb. She traced tiny triskelions over her abdomen. White stretch marks mapped her skin, scars which told the story of the child growing inside her, a child who already knew the steps to the Beltane dance.

She heard the far-off ringing of bells and opened her eyes. It was then that she saw them, the silver lights of fairies twirling around her fire. She had seen the fair folk only once before, on the Isle of Skye, as she had crossed the Fairy Glen on the eve of Samhain with Caitriona. Fairies were known to feast in the glen, but although Arabella had often heard the bells that meant the good neighbors were near, she had never seen anything more than shadows cast by the craggy cone-shaped hillocks. Then, that magical night, her grandmother had taken her hand and pointed toward a group of sandstone boulders clustered beneath the hills of Uig. Suddenly, Arabella had seen what had been invisible to her only a moment before; a feast of epic proportions, the fairies' ethereal bodies glittering like fallen stars. It had been Caitriona's powerful second sight combined with her own that had enabled her to see the miracle, and now, as Arabella watched the fair folk swirl in the coastal fog, she knew it was her unborn daughter's second sight that had revealed what would have remained invisible if Arabella had been alone. She pressed her hand against the curve of her belly. Her baby moved deep within her.

When she looked back up to the sky, the fairies had faded into the tapestry of night.

By June, New England had drowned itself in color; explosions of bright pink peonies, wild red columbine, and spidery yellow witch hazel erased grey winter from the landscape's memory. Fresh blooms of Scottish thistle spread around Arabella's cottage in their lavender swirl of protection; Catherine had planted it everywhere, among the herbs, along the stony path leading to the front door, across the swath of grass between the cottage and the picket fence. The sweet, musky scent of Scotland permeated the air, and Arabella gathered bouquets of thistle to place on her mantle, her table, her bedside, not caring that the prickly leaves sliced open her fingers.

She spent her days working in her mother's garden. When it rained, she steeped herbs and flowers into teas and tonics, packing and labeling them so the women who came to the cottage seeking help would have what they needed long after Arabella departed for her island home.

Anne visited the day before the summer solstice, struggling to carry a large traveling case up the stony pathway herself because she had told her coachman to wait by the road. Although they had let out the waists of Catherine's old dresses, Arabella's growing figure was becoming harder to hide, and Anne didn't want anyone, not even the loyal coachman who had kept her trips to the cottage a secret from the rest of her household, to learn about the pregnancy. She was terrified about what would happen if news of it reached William or James.

Anne helped her sister pack a few shawls and dresses for her Atlantic crossing, folding the gently used baby clothes from Arabella's customers into a neat pile. Arabella wrapped both of her grimoires in Catherine's grey healer's cloak and placed them in the bottom of her traveling case.

"Do you want to take this with you?" Anne asked, holding out the shell-encrusted music box that always rested on the bedside table. Arabella opened it and removed her mother's thistle pendant, dropping the necklace into a silk money purse Anne had filled with coins for her travel expenses. She snapped the music box shut and returned it to its spot on the nightstand, blinking away a tear.

"Are you sure you want to leave? Alan and I can go with you to talk to James if you've changed your mind."

Arabella shook her head.

"What about father?" Anne asked tentatively. "He's the reason you came to America."

"I have nothing to say to him." Arabella had not seen or heard from their father since the night she had left Newbury House. William had returned to Anne's door the following evening to ensure she had complied with his order to no longer offer her sister shelter, but after that, he had refused to speak of Arabella, only mentioning her name to curse her and her mother whenever he drank too much rum.

When the traveling case was fully packed, Anne rose to take her leave, promising her sister that she and Alan would be back in three days' time to escort her to New London in their carriage as planned. They would stay in a hotel in the city until the merchant captain, who had agreed to employ Arabella as his ship's apothecary, was ready to disembark.

"Do you promise you'll write to James and tell him about the baby?" Anne asked, lingering in the open doorway. She hated James for what he had done to her sister, but she had grown up with him, and she had once been betrothed to his brother. It felt wrong to keep so great a secret from him.

"Yes. I'll write to James."

A halo of mosquitos buzzed above Anne's head and she swatted them away with a silk handkerchief.

"And I'll write to you, too, Anne." Arabella said. "I promise."

The afternoon sun burned hot in the sky long after Anne left, and at twilight's first blush, Arabella changed into her thin muslin nightgown. She wandered into the backyard, trying to escape the humidity of her cottage.

Frogs called out from the marsh grasses, their tongues rippling through the thick air. Arabella walked down to the beach, the place where she and James had first come together. Waves gurgled against the shore, scattering tiny shells on the wet sand. She waded into the gentle surf, watching the sun begin its slow descent toward the western horizon.

One by one, stars appeared in the sky, followed by constellations, and the bright, broad back of the Milky Way. Arabella reached into the night, tracing its patterns with her fingers: *Hercules*, the hero who knelt in the sky, his club raised in victory over *Ladon*, keeper of the golden apples; *Lyra*, Orpheus' majestic harp, hung in the heavens to commemorate the tragic beauty of his songs; *Sagittarius*, half-man, half-beast, shooting his arrow into the darkness; and *Maske*, the great white bear who wandered through the evening, stars shining on his fur like drops of tallow.

As the universe, so the soul. A thousand stories of love and loss were written in the skies.

James had taught Arabella how to measure the angles of stars against the horizon, using them to tell the time, so she tried to mark the passing hours by the *Big Dipper's* slow rotation around steadfast *Polaris*. Water churned at her legs. Her daughter stirred, moth-like, a tiny timepiece inside her womb, ticking out the weeks with her strengthening flutters and kicks. Soon, the two of them would be home on the windy moors of Scotland. The Isle of Skye beckoned, but the thought of leaving Mystic, of never seeing James again, made her stomach cramp with grief.

She cradled her abdomen, trying to breathe through the uncomfortable sensation, but instead of subsiding, it only grew worse. She arched her back, thinking she could stretch her body away from the ache, but a twinge of pain made her double over, and she fell to her knees.

Cold ocean water splashed over her nightgown. A gush of warm liquid trickled between her legs. She drew in a sharp breath as she realized what was happening.

Her baby was coming.

And it was too soon.

She crawled up the sand on her hands and knees like a turtle, going as far as she could between each fresh surge of agony. She had not expected to give birth until the end of August. She had not boiled water or tied knots into thick pieces of rope, cutting the length between each one to summon an easy labor. She sank onto her hips and rounded her back, panicking as another contraction ripped through her. She needed to get back to her mother's cottage. If she was going to deliver early, if her daughter was going to be born in America, she at least needed to give birth inside the magical circle of protection cast by her mother's thistles.

When she reached the edge of the garden, she pulled herself up on the picket fence, but a new cramp twisted her from navel to spine and sent her back down to the ground where she crouched, stiff and breathless, until the tightening passed. She resumed her slow crawl across the lawn, and by the time she reached the back door of the cottage, the thistles' sharp prickles had torn the flesh from her hands and knees.

She pulled herself inside, clutching at the bedclothes, straining to lift herself up onto the mattress. She had delivered more than a dozen children on her own. She had witnessed the births of dozens more, helping as her grandmother and aunts ministered to the pregnant women of Skye, but delivering her own child without anyone to help her seemed an impossible task. Caitriona had always gripped the hands of laboring mothers, reminding them to be strong, but Arabella had no one to hold her hand and whisper advice. She did not feel strong. She felt weak and afraid.

She cried out as a fresh tremor tore through her abdomen. The iron scent of blood tainted the air, and she wondered if it was coming from the cuts on her hands and knees or from the throbbing place between her legs. She thought of James' mother, dying in agony from the complications of an early birth, and her heart fluttered rapidly in her chest. "Please help me," she sobbed. Only the wind replied, howling through the eastern white pine and black birch trees growing on the northern side of the cottage.

All through the night, Arabella shivered as swells of fever and pain crested white and hot in her belly. In the darkest hour, just before dawn, she saw the membrane between the worlds begin to pull apart, its gossamer threads untwisting to reveal a pattern of light as sharp and as bright as a field full of stars. She smiled, thinking it was her baby bursting through the veil, but then her body tightened again, suspending her in aching torment. The blinking lights in the tear of the veil rearranged themselves into the shape of a woman, grey hair piled high atop her head, her aged body leaning on a jeweled cane.

"Elinor?" Arabella's face was red with fever, and she moaned as another wave of pain rolled through her. Elinor's spirit, calm and collected, invited two more shades forward, and Arabella saw Mary, as young and as beautiful as she was in the portrait which hung in James' parlor, and Catherine, her auburn hair and green eyes a perfect match to her daughter's. They both gestured toward Arabella, smiling and moving their lips to speak, but their words were swallowed by the loud buzzing sound of the open veil.

"Please help me," Arabella cried again, forgetting to relax and breathe as she used to instruct her patients to do, forgetting the names of the goddesses she had invoked to help countless women through childbirth, forgetting her spells and her prayers of protection, remembering only her suffering and her fear and her loneliness. "Please, please help me," she sobbed.

The veil flickered and the shades were gone.

Arabella collapsed against the bed. She closed her eyes, sailing toward a black hole in the sky. Her limbs stiffened and convulsed, moving in rhythmic spasms against the mattress, carrying her past her pain. She floated away from her body, drifting toward the tear in the veil, slipping toward a place of rest and comfort and peace. Just before her vision went black, a soft touch at her sweat-drenched temple pulled her back to earth, and she screamed into the emptiness of the cottage as the pulsating throes of her labor returned to her threefold. Phantom fingers stroked her matted hair away from her face.

And what is the pain, child? It was her grandmother, speaking to her from beyond. *You feel the pain in your body, but it's only temporary, like the wind. You must endure it. You must move through it. Pain is part of the process. It is there to help you usher your daughter across the veil and into the world of the living.*

Arabella felt Catriona's hand in hers as another contraction ripped through her. "Please don't leave me," she sobbed, curling her chest around her cramping belly and pulling her legs up on either side of the bed. She was certain both she and her child were going to die, and she wanted her grandmother to carry them across the veil where they would no longer feel this terrible torment.

Your daughter will soon be here. The voice in her ear was soft and sweet, like the words of a poem. *Isn't it strange that something so beautiful must be pulled into the world through pain? Hold fast and have faith, my child, for from this strain of sorrow, you'll discover the greatest of joys. Now, you must be strong. Push.*

She did as her grandmother commanded, pushing until she felt the head and shoulders crown, reaching down to catch the baby that tumbled through the opening of her womb. She pulled the infant to her chest.

The child's skin was wrinkled and wet, her body bruised and bloodied.

She was the most beautiful baby Arabella had ever seen.

She turned to show her baby to Caitriona, but the veil was already knitting itself closed. The sole witnesses to her child's creation faded away, disappearing across the threshold in flashes of dancing starlight. "Please don't leave me," Arabella cried again.

But the buzzing noise of the open veil dwindled into silence, and they were gone.

The first rays of morning sun filtered through the windows as the baby curled her tiny fingers around Arabella's. It was the summer solstice, a year and a day since she had floated her wreath of willow branches down the Mystic River, a year and a day since she had first met James Alden. She gazed down at their daughter, perched on her breast like a tiny bird, her hair as black as a raven's wing, her eyes as blue as the clusters of wild berries that grew in the American woods. She traced a swirling symbol of protection on the child's damp forehead, the back of her hands, and just above her heart, noting the crescent shaped freckle that winked in the hollow beneath the folds of her chin. The baby was small enough to fit in the palms of her outstretched hands.

Goiltai, Geantrai, and Suantrai; James' deep voice welled up from the recesses of Arabella's mind. *Laments, celebrations, and lullabies. All the songs in the universe are composed from these three strains.* A thousand babies had been born to a thousand mothers on this solstice day, each one singing a unique tune crafted from the joys and sorrows of human love. She stroked her daughter's hair, so black it was almost blue, whispering the words of her family's somber lullaby.

O dig me a grave, and dig it down deep
And strew it all over with primrose so sweet
And lay me down easy, no more for to weep
Since love was the cause of my ruin.

The baby, not understanding the meaning of the words but comforted by the music, rooted and began to feed. Mother and daughter had a few precious hours alone together before three women, regular customers who had journeyed to the cottage for new teas and tinctures, jingled the bells on the front door, letting themselves inside as was their custom. When they saw what had happened, they rushed into action, eager to help the Wise Woman who had helped them in her turn. They tied and cut the umbilical cord. They washed the newborn's skin. They boiled water and prepared meals, singing their own families' lullabies to help the weary mother rest.

Years later, when the three women told the story of that warm, solstice morning, they spoke of the red-breasted robins which gathered at the windowsill to trill the news of the baby's arrival. They spoke of the sulfur-scented stardust which swirled through the cottage air. They spoke of the sound of far-off bells, and the glowing halo of light that settled over the mother and child, two souls marked for certain death, who had been saved by a miracle of infinite love.

James adjusted the rifle on his shoulder, squinting toward the tree line. He was walking through the woods, heading home after his latest delivery, when something raised the hair on the back of his neck.

A branch snapped in the brush behind him. He pulled his hunting knife from the leather holster strapped to his thigh. The Whitford Brook bubbled quietly. Cicadas sang in the bushes. He continued walking, increasing his pace, his senses on high alert.

He swung around at the sound of a voice, but before he could identify his assailant, a heavy blow landed directly between his shoulder blades. He fell to his knees, reaching up toward a sharp pain at the base of his neck. His vision grew blurry, and everything went black.

He was awakened by a rocking motion. At first he thought he might be aboard a ship, press-ganged into hard labor by a crimping tavern owner, but it was not the steady lurch of the sea he felt beneath him. He was swaying side to side, bouncing in a wagon rolling over rough terrain. He opened his eyes. Bright, painful spots of light pierced the holes in the burlap sack that covered his head. He tried to lift his hands to remove it, but his arms and legs had been tied and shackled to an iron ring in the bed of the wagon. When he pulled against the knots to free himself, his efforts only made the ropes tighter.

The wagon rolled to a stop. Heavy footsteps crunched in the gravel. The wood slats of the wagon bed creaked and dipped. A knife sliced through the ropes that bound James' arms and legs to the iron ring. Rough hands pulled him to the wagon's edge, and dumped him onto the stony ground. His wrists were still tied together, and he struggled to stand and find his balance on the uneven terrain. Someone gripped his neck, pulling the burlap sack from his head and flooding his eyes with blinding sunlight.

He blinked at the man standing in front of him, and when the features of his adversary's face swam into his view, fury rose like bile in the back of his throat.

"Untie me, Jonathan."

Anne Newbury took great comfort in knowing she had not *technically* broken her promise to her sister. She regretted giving Arabella her word not to tell James or William about the baby because she believed the only solution to the problem of a bastard child was marriage. Since her sister had intended to return to Scotland, Anne had agreed to keep Arabella's secret, but that was *before*. The baby's arrival had changed everything.

Anne had been shocked when she and Alan had returned to the cottage and found Arabella holding a baby in her arms. "She's beautiful," Anne had said after listening to the details of her sister's harrowing ordeal. "But she looks just like—"

"I know."

The baby's features had been a surprise to Arabella, for every Porter woman she had ever known had shared a set of physical characteristics which signaled their place of honor on the Isle of Skye. *When you crossed the veil into the world of the living, your green eyes looking up at me, your round head already covered with the auburn curls that are the telltale mark of the Porters, I knew a part of you belonged to the island,* Catherine's letter had explained. The moment Arabella saw James' black hair and blue eyes in the face of their daughter, her carefully crafted plans for returning to Scotland had dissolved. She knew her child belonged in the New World, and that meant she was going to have to stay in the New World too.

There had been tears in her eyes as she explained to Anne that she planned to continue living in Catherine's cottage by the sea. Anne had warned her the baby could not be kept a secret if she stayed in America. A bastard child living in the cottage of the Mystic Witch was bound to be discovered. Arabella needed to marry and give her daughter the protection of the Alden name. Anne had begged and pleaded, but her sister had refused to free her from her promise not to tell James or William about the baby.

Undeterred, Anne had begun taking daily walks along the river front, watching for the arrival of *Polaris*. She knew the captain was James' oldest friend, and the only living person who could direct his behavior. Anne wanted to make sure her sister and niece would be protected if James lost his temper when he inevitably discovered the truth.

Polaris kept an unpredictable schedule, so when it sailed up to the main dock of the Alden Shipyard for unloading one morning in late July, Anne had not hesitated. She had marched up the gangplank and demanded to speak with Captain Jonathan Burrows.

"How can I help you, Mrs. Newbury?" Jonathan had cautiously asked after he emerged from his cabin at the request of his stunned quartermaster.

"We need to speak in your quarters, Captain Burrows," Anne had said, adjusting the tilt of her hat to shade her eyes from the sun.

"You can't be serious."

"We must discuss a *private* matter—"

"Do you have any idea what your father and your husband will do to me if they learn you've been inside my cabin unsupervised?" Their familiarity with each other from childhood meant little in the face of the social conventions that separated them. "This is a working vessel, Mrs. Newbury, and it's no place for a woman, so you will tell me whatever it is you need to tell me, and then you will disembark and never set foot on my ship again. Is that clear?"

"Fine." Anne had taken a conspiratorial step toward Jonathan who had instinctively moved backward. She told him about Arabella's flight from James on the winter solstice and about her six-month refuge in Catherine Porter's cottage by the sea. Jonathan tapped his fingers on the railing impatiently. It was nothing he hadn't heard before.

"Everyone in Mystic knows your sister has been staying at that cottage."

"Does everyone in Mystic know my sister has given birth to a child?"

A beat of silence had passed before Jonathan responded.

"Jesus Christ."

He ignored Anne's uncomfortable reaction to his blasphemy, letting his quick mind piece together her unspoken implications. "William doesn't know because Jimmy is still breathing and as yet unmarried. Why are you telling me this? Is Arabella all right? Is the child all right?"

"I'm not a midwife," Anne had replied in exasperation. "They seem healthy, but my sister is lonely and sad."

"Then you should be talking to Jimmy. *She* should be talking to Jimmy."

"I've told her that, but she refuses, and I promised her I wouldn't tell him about the baby."

"So, you want *me* to tell him he has a child who's been kept a secret from him? Do you think I have a death wish?"

"You don't have to tell him he has a child. You just have to bring him to Arabella's cottage so *she* can tell him. She still loves him, I'm sure of it. And I think he loves her too. They just need to *talk* to each other."

"Did Arabella ask you to bring him to the cottage?"

"Of course not. She's as stubborn as he is." Anne had sighed dramatically. "All you need to do is get him there. When Arabella sees James, she'll explain everything. I know she will. Please, Jonathan. She won't be able to keep the child a secret for much longer, and I'm afraid of what might happen if James or my father finds out from someone else. I need your help."

She outlined her plan to take the baby into the garden ahead of James' arrival so the estranged couple could speak privately. "Bring your pistol," she had added when Jonathan, who understood that the best way for James to learn about the child was from the woman he still so ardently loved, had begrudgingly agreed to help. "If he acts like an animal, you may have to shoot him."

"I'm not going to shoot him, Anne."

"Well, someone will have to shoot him if he doesn't do the right thing," Anne had said, adjusting her bonnet and retreating down the gangplank. "And if you won't, I will."

"Untie me, Jonathan," James demanded again as his eyes adjusted to the sudden burst of daylight. His back and shoulders were aching, and he was in no mood for his friend's games.

"Take a breath," Jonathan said, his voice deliberately calm.

James kicked the back of Jonathan's knees, and the two of them toppled to the ground. They wrestled against one another in the rocky dirt for several minutes before Jonathan managed to pull James to his feet and throw him against the side of the wagon.

"Take a breath, Jimmy," Jonathan said again, louder this time. "There's nothing you can do. Your hands are tied, and I've got the higher ground." He held a knife, which he had used to release the ropes, poised between them.

"Are you really going to stab me?" James asked, nodding at the silver blade shining in the sun.

Jonathan raised one eyebrow. "I'm thinking about it."

James groaned and glanced over Jonathan's shoulder. When he saw the purple hue on the ground, his heart began to thud against his ribcage.

"What are we doing here?" he asked.

"You know what we're doing here."

"She doesn't want to talk to me."

"Did she tell you that?"

"Her sister told me. Anne said she's going back to Scotland."

"Anne is the one who asked me to bring you here." He sheathed his knife. "She thinks you and Arabella need to talk."

"Anne Newbury—" James paused, narrowing his eyes in disbelief, "told you to hit me over the head and tie me up?"

"Anne Newbury told me to shoot you," Jonathan said. "The rest of it was my idea." He shrugged his shoulders in apology. "I didn't know how else to get you here."

James looked up the stony pathway. The cottage he had renovated for Arabella was bright and peaceful in the morning sun. He had known she had been staying at her mother's old house, and short of knocking him unconscious, there was nothing Jonathan could have done to make him come here against her wishes.

"Do you run all of Anne Newbury's errands for her now?" he asked angrily.

"Only the illegal ones."

His jest failed to bring a smile to James' face, so he held up his hands to show he meant no harm as he approached his friend. He loosened the knots that held his arms together, bracing himself for the sting of retaliation, but James only rotated his wrists, trying to soothe the raw, red burns the rope had left on his skin.

"You need to go up there and talk to her, Jimmy."

James shook his head. Arabella wouldn't have returned his ring if she had wanted him to pursue her, and he would not disrespect the choice she had made by forcing himself into her home. "She's the one who left me, Jonathan. And you're the one who said I was better off without her."

"I shouldn't have said that," Jonathan admitted. "We've made dozens of deliveries since she found out what we keep in your office, and if she wanted to turn us in to the authorities, she would've done it by now." He kicked at the rocks beneath his feet. "I was wrong about her, and if the last six months of your life are any indication, you're not better off without her. You're barely surviving."

Since Arabella had left him, James' work at the shipyard office, his treks through the woods, even his conversations with Jonathan, had done little to assuage his melancholy. He spent all his free time alone, designing and building new ships, treating the back-breaking work as penance for his sins, hoping the tedious labor would clear his mind so he would be ready to explain himself if Arabella ever decided she wanted to see him. Each day that had passed without word from her had pushed him deeper into isolation, and, on his darkest nights, overcome with guilt and grief, he had wandered by the river, wondering if he should let the water take him and be done with it.

James had seen men drown before; a whaler whose foot had been tangled in the line when a wounded animal chose to dive, a sailor who had slipped from the rigging and hit his head on the deck as he plummeted toward the sea.

Both men had kicked and flailed against the currents as the crew scrambled in vain to help them, but, in the end, when all hope had been lost, they had succumbed to their fates, letting the waves gently carry them to their deaths as though they were children being carried off to sleep.

It had been the memory of Jonathan's voice which had pulled James away from the river on those despair-filled evenings after Arabella's departure. *You've got to move through it, Jimmy,* Jonathan had said more than ten years ago aboard the *Shepherd* when James, strung up in disgrace for refusing to kill a nursing whale, had begged his friend to cut him down so he could throw himself into the sea. James had endured his flogging in silence, gritting his teeth and refusing to cry out even as the lash split open his skin, but the thought of being tied to the mast through the long, dark night while the salt spray settled into his open wounds had almost undone him. *Move through it,* Jonathan had said, *everything will be all right when you get to the other side.* James had listened to him then, moving through his pain and embarrassment, regaining the respect of his captain and crewmates by felling more than two dozen whales before their four-year voyage had ended, but moving through the loss of the woman he loved was proving a much harder thing for him to do.

"If there's a chance the two of you can work things out, you need to take it," Jonathan said, nodding toward the cottage. "If you still love her, if you want to marry her, we'll find a way to deal with William. We've altered our deliveries to keep him at bay before, and we can do it again."

"She'll never forgive me for lying to her," James said. "She'll never forgive me for coming between her and her father. If I go up there and she tells me she doesn't want to be with me—" he swallowed, unable to complete his thought. It had killed him, knowing Arabella had been alone in the isolated cottage all winter, but the fact she had stayed in America had afforded him the smallest shred of hope. If Anne had convinced Jonathan to bring him to the cottage by force, it was likely because Arabella was leaving for Scotland. He had been summoned for a final farewell.

"I don't know how to lose her, Jonathan."

Jonathan shoved him half-heartedly, trying to jar his courage loose, painfully aware of a truth his friend had yet to discover. James was a father now, and his child's welfare was far more important than any fears he harbored over losing the woman he loved. He had to face what was waiting for him behind the cottage door.

"If Arabella can't forgive you, if she doesn't want you to be a part of her life, then you need to let her go. You need to take responsibility for your mistakes and move forward," he said, assuming the gruff tone he usually reserved for issuing commands at sea. "Whatever happens in that cottage today, you can't continue living the way you have been for the past six months." He sighed and placed a gentle hand on James' shoulder. "I'll wait here for you, Jimmy, but you have to go and talk to her. Now."

James had faced many dangers in his life. He had sailed through raging tempests. He had been engulfed by walls of flame. He had stared into the eyes of men who sought to harm him, and he had pierced the flesh of mighty leviathans while rowing over turbulent seas, but nothing had ever frightened him more than the thought of knocking on Arabella's door.

He exhaled slowly, shaking away the ache in his chest.

Then he stepped over the protective border of thistle and walked up the path.

"Hello, Arabella."

She was standing on the threshold, her face frozen in surprise. She was wearing a simple cotton dress. Her hair fell loose around her shoulders, and her eyes sparkled like emeralds in the morning light. Her hands trembled as she gripped the door.

"Hello, James," she managed to say, her voice a whisper. Her fingers twisted the silver pendant at her neck, sending dancing rainbows across the cottage steps. He felt suddenly aware of his disheveled state; his work clothes were torn and dirty from fighting with Jonathan. His hunting knife was still strapped to his thigh.

"May I come in?" he asked.

Her heart dropped at his request. Anne had taken the baby into the garden, but she didn't know how long it would be before they returned. Arabella had tried writing James dozens of letters since their daughter's birth, throwing each one into the fire because no words could justify the secret she had kept from him. She thought briefly of turning him away now, of closing the door and going about her morning tasks, of trying to pretend, for one more day, that the cocoon of isolation she had woven around her mother's cottage would protect her from the shattering that was about to take place, but she stepped back and let him inside.

The cottage looked exactly as James remembered it, though now it was cluttered with the trappings of everyday life; a small fire that had been used to cook breakfast dwindled in the grate, bundles of dried herbs and flowers hung from the rafters, piles of laundry were neatly folded on the kitchen table.

"I was sorry to hear about Elinor's passing," Arabella said, glancing at the black mourning band tied around James' arm. It rested just above the wound he had sustained last summer when he had defended her from rumors of witchcraft.

He nodded and tried to smile. His grandmother had been gone for six months. He had waited through the three long days of Elinor's wake, hoping Arabella would return to Alden House, praying she would give him the chance to explain how sorry he was for hurting her. It wasn't until his grandmother's casket had been interred in the Alden tomb at White Hall Cemetery that James had realized Arabella was never coming back to him.

"I didn't get to thank you for everything you did to help her in the last months of her life." James cleared his throat of its thickness. "She asked about you, after you had gone, and near the end, the only thing she would drink was the tea you had brewed from my mother's roses."

Arabella knew the memories stored in the rose hips, memories of Thomas and James playing in the yard, memories of George and Mary tending the garden, would have comforted Elinor in her final days. She wanted to tell James she had seen his grandmother and his mother, she wanted to tell him they were both safe and together in the realm beyond the veil, but that would require her to tell him about the birth of their daughter, and she could not heave the words from her throat.

"Anne told me you're returning to Scotland," he said when he could shoulder the tension of her silence no longer.

She let her gaze drop to the blue-black stubble on his jaw, to the swirls of ink peeking from the sleeves of his shirt, anywhere but the piercing blue eyes that looked so much like their daughter's.

"James," she finally whispered. "I need to tell you something—"

"Wait." A coil of fear tightened deep in his chest. He had thought he would have more time before she sent him away, before she told him she would never open her heart to his again. If she was truly returning to Skye, he at least wanted the chance to tell her how much he loved her before she left. "Please, Arabella, just give me a minute," he said. "Let me say what I need to say first."

He reached beneath his shirt and pulled a long leather cord from around his neck. The ring he had given Arabella was looped through the end of it and he held it out to her. It swayed between them like a pendulum. He gently grasped her hand and placed the ring into her palm. The silver band was cool against her skin.

"This belongs to you." He closed her fingers around ring. "You can sell it to secure a safe passage across the Atlantic. It will fetch a good price, and you'll have enough money left to support yourself for a long while after you arrive on the Isle of Skye."

"James—"

"I can't bear the thought of you struggling to make ends meet," he said. "I would give you the money you need if you would let me, but I know you won't let me, so at least take the ring. It was a gift, for *you*, from *me*. I want you to have it. Please, take it Arabella."

She looked up at him. She had watched from the windows of Newbury House as Anne had retuned the ring to James on the winter solstice. It had been the only thing Arabella could think to do to get James to leave that night, but the look of despair that had crossed his face when her sister tossed the ring at his feet had devastated her.

"You wouldn't be upset if I sold it?" she asked.

"Not if the money helps to keep you safe from harm." James had worn the ring against his heart since Arabella had left him. "You're far more important to me than this ring is, and selling it won't change the way I feel about you," he said. "Nothing will ever change the way I feel about you."

He brought his hand to her face, running the tips of his fingers over her cheek, tilting her chin up so he could look into her eyes. "I know you don't want to be with me anymore," he said, struggling to keep the anguish from his voice, "but everything I said to you when I gave you this ring is still true. *Grá Mo Chroí.* The love of my heart. *Cara M'anama.* The friend of my soul. That's who you are. That's who you'll always be."

Now that he was touching her everything seemed so simple. The words he had been unable to find on the night she left him sprung from his lips as though they had a will of their own. "I'm sorry I hurt you, Arabella. The secrets Jonathan and I keep need to be guarded for the safety of the people we help, but that's no excuse for the way we deliberately lied to you and tested your loyalty, especially after you trusted your heart to my keeping."

Her took her hand in his, intertwining their fingers as he used to do when they were a couple.

"I've spent a long time thinking about the mistakes I've made. I should have been honest with you, and I shouldn't have kept you from your father, no matter what my feelings about him are. I understand why you left me, and I understand why you want to return to Scotland, but none of that changes the fact that I love you. I will *always* love you." He stroked her hair, pushing it back behind her shoulders, revealing the lines of her throat where her heart pulsed in deep, rhythmic beats. "Always, Arabella. If there's anything I can do to change your mind, if there's anything I can do to fix what I've broken—"

She pulled away from him, her eyes brimming with tears.

"Loving someone and trusting someone are two different things," she said. She knew it was true because she had not trusted him enough to tell him about their child.

He closed the space between them, taking her hand again, needing to feel her skin against his. "I do trust you, Arabella. I never would've asked you to heal the man in my office if I didn't trust you," he said. "I never would've risked his life if I believed you would share the information with William, and I should have made that clear to Jonathan so he didn't have to keep watch over you until I returned. I couldn't find the words to explain all of that on the night you left me, but even if it's too late, even if there's nothing I can do to change your heart, I want you to know how sorry I am for hurting you."

She thought back to that tumultuous night. She had never stopped to consider the trust he had placed in her when he had asked her for her help. She had never stopped to consider that James' test of her loyalty had been his way of protecting the people he was hiding. She had been too upset by what he had said about her father, by what her father's foul reputation implied about her. *You must understand before you can heal,* Caitriona had taught her. *Love is forgiveness and truth,* Catherine's letter had said. James was asking for her understanding and forgiveness, and she needed to do the same.

"James," she said, her hand trembling in his, "I need to tell you something—"

A gust of air from the open window ruffled the pile of laundry she had stacked on the table. James let go of her hand and bent down to gather the linens that had blown to the floor. He picked up a small, white blanket stitched with a silver triskelion. He studied it for a moment and then looked up at Arabella.

"James," she began again, but her speech faltered. His jaw tightened as he looked around the room. A tiny basket with bedding was positioned next to the bed, and a white nightgown, just large enough for a newborn, was draped over the rocking chair. James' eyes, now as cold as ice beneath the white of his scar, returned to Arabella's body, moving over the softened swells of her hips and breasts.

"Arabella—did you—do we—Arabella—do we have a child?"

He knew it was true even before she nodded, and his body went rigid with shock. All the hope he had felt when he had touched her transformed into a rush of righteous indignation. He had been apologizing for keeping secrets and telling lies, and all the while she had been keeping secrets and lying to him. She had given birth to his child, and she had not trusted him enough to let him know.

"I wanted to tell you—"

"You *wanted* to tell me?" His raised voice filled the cottage. "You *didn't* tell me! You *knew* you were pregnant when you left me, and you didn't tell me—"

"I didn't know when I left you," she said. "I was going to write to you after I returned to Scotland, but she was born early and—"

"She?" He looked down at the blanket in his hands, clenching the soft wool in his fists. "A daughter? I have a daughter?"

"*We* have a daughter."

"We have a *daughter*, and you were going to tell me this in a *letter*?" His head pounded with fury. "We have a *daughter*, and you were going to tell me this *after* you took her an ocean away from me?"

"Did you want me to come and find you at the shipyard?" she demanded, spiraling his anger back at him. "Did you want me to tell you about the baby in the middle of the Spouter Tavern?"

"Was I supposed to come to *you*? You're the one who left *me*! You're the one who said you never wanted to see me again!" He was shouting, swept away by the tide of his emotions, unable to comprehend her insistence that she had done nothing wrong. "I would have done anything, anything to get you back when you left me! I would have done anything to help you if I knew you were with child! Would you have even told me about the baby today if I hadn't figured it out?"

"I was trying to tell you—"

"I would have married you, Arabella—"

"Only to keep our daughter from being a *bastard* like her mother!"

She was twisting everything, putting words into his mouth, turning him into the type of man he had never wanted to be. He grabbed her wrists, pulling her body closer to him in a desperate attempt to make her listen to what he was saying. The ring he had returned to her tumbled to the floor, its leather cord snaking along the wooden beams.

"I would have married you because I love you, Arabella. How many times do I have to say it before you believe it! I love you! I would have been there for you!" His voice broke as he remembered the desperate cries of his mother calling out for his father during the death throes of her labor. "I would have been there to help you when our child was born!"

"How would you have helped me, James?" she shouted. "By commanding me not to deliver early? By forbidding me to feel any pain? By locking our daughter behind a closed door so you could raise her as an Alden in America?" She was crying, hot tears spilling down her cheeks as she tried to pull away from him.

The back door of the cottage creaked open and Jonathan entered the room, pushing James toward the far wall.

"You—" James seized the lapels of Jonathan's jacket. "You knew about the child! That's why you brought me here! You *knew*, and you didn't tell me!"

"I just found out about the child," Jonathan said, admonition curling in his voice. "And I brought you here to fix things, not to shout at a woman, so stand down, Jimmy, or I will make you stand down."

Anne appeared in the doorway, drawn inward by the commotion.

"I told you to bring your pistol," she hissed.

"Jesus Christ."

The blanket-wrapped baby rested in Anne's arms, and, as if sensing the mounting tension between her parents, she pushed a tiny fist into the air in consternation. She began to wail, a bright, strong sound that stilled James, spiriting him away from his own feelings of distress.

He released his grip on Jonathan, letting his hands fall to his sides.

Arabella took the baby from her sister. James watched as she rocked back and forth, singing a quiet tune, the old words ringing like silver bells. A tear rolled down her cheek, falling onto the baby's blanket, and the sight of it stirred something deep and primal within him. His fury with Arabella did not fully dissipate, but it splintered into a thousand shades of grief and shame for his own behavior. This was the woman he loved more than life itself. This was the woman who had borne his child. This was the woman who had been forced to seek shelter in her mother's cottage because he had acted more like an animal than a man. Jonathan was right; he needed to rein in his emotions before they ignited into something beyond his capacity to control.

Before you, I never knew such anger and such love could sit side by side in my heart, his grandmother had once told him. Her words made sense to him now. As angry as he was with Arabella, he would never stop loving her. As angry as he was that she was planning to raise their daughter alone in Scotland, he knew he had to support her decision. He could not change the mistakes he had made in the past, but he could make a choice, right here and right now, to do what was right for Arabella and their child, no matter how painful his loss of them might be.

"Arabella," he said, his voice stilted, strained, gentle. "I think we need to talk."

The child's cries had ebbed, and the walls of the cottage breathed around him, expanding and contracting with the rapid pace of his breaking heart. He glanced at Anne and Jonathan before bringing his eyes back to the blanket-wrapped baby. He had no right to ask for privacy after the way he had just acted, but he wanted the chance to come to terms with everything that had transpired without the eyes of his friend and her sister bearing down on him.

"Please Arabella," he said softly. "Can I please have a few moments alone with you and our daughter?"

She looked up at him, nodding her consent. Anne opened her mouth in protest, but Jonathan placed a gentle hand on her shoulder to quiet her. He had promised Anne he would ensure everyone's safety, and he took that promise seriously.

"Do I have your word you'll handle this like a gentleman, Jimmy?"

James winced, embarrassed that his own behavior had forced his friend to ask the question.

"You have my word," he answered solemnly. "*She* has my word," he added, looking into the watery green lights of her eyes.

"Arabella?" Jonathan asked, turning to the new mother, granting her the full authority to make the final decision. "Are you sure?"

"I'm sure."

"Then we'll be right outside if you need us."

Gulls cawed above the roof of the cottage, filling the summer air with their song. James and Arabella stood on opposite sides of the room, an ocean of silence between them. The cottage was only a few paces long, but the space seemed larger and more perilous than the vast Atlantic itself.

James watched their daughter squirm beneath her blanket. Their *daughter*. He was a *father*. The knowledge of it, only a few minutes old, wrapped itself around his heart, changing the very essence of his identity. And yet, he had done nothing to deserve the title. Arabella had carried, birthed, and cared for their child alone, enduring the pain and fear of labor and delivery without his comfort or prayers. And, when he had learned the truth, a truth which should have filled him with gratitude for the miracle she had performed, he had shouted at her, more concerned with expressing his own hurt feelings than with understanding hers, reacting to the fact she had kept a secret rather than contemplating the role he had played in her silence. It was painful, knowing he had missed the baby's arrival, but he would gladly accept the pain if it helped him chart a more peaceful course toward the future.

He stood, still and quiet, his back against the wall, scared that any movement he made would send the tenuous calm between them careening out of control once more. He took a deep breath, flexing his hands, wishing he could grasp a tiller, coil a rope, or tack a sail to steady his emotions as easily as he had steadied his ships at sea.

"Please say something, James," Arabella whispered.

James opened his mouth to speak. He closed it. A few minutes passed before he opened it again.

"I wish you would have told me, Arabella."

"I wanted to tell you," she said again. "I didn't know how."

He nodded, absorbing the weight of her statement, realizing he was at fault for making her feel like she had to face the last six months alone.

"If anything had happened to you—if anything had happened to her—"

His fears were too formidable to fully express, and he looked away, not wanting her to bear witness to his suffering. For the first time since Arabella had met him, she felt the invisible cord that tethered them together loosening, its threads unravelling under the weight of so much deception. Still, they shared a child, and that was reason enough for them to find some common ground among the towering mountains of mistakes they had both made.

She sat on the edge of the bed and unwrapped the baby's swaddling. The child was clothed in a white cotton dressing gown embroidered with patterns of pink roses and purple thistles. Arabella smoothed the gown over her lap and released the ribbon which held the child's bonnet in place. She hoped it wasn't too late for her words to reach him.

"Would you like to hold her?" she asked.

The last time he had held an infant, it had died in his arms, and the thought of moving any closer to the child he had created with Arabella terrified him. He pressed his fingernails into the flesh of his palms. If he walked over to them and held their daughter, it was going to make his inevitable loss of them more difficult to bear. If he remained where he was, his back against the wall, he would miss his only chance to know his child before Arabella took her away.

The floorboards creaked beneath James' weight as he slowly crossed the cottage. He lowered himself onto the bed, his heart beating deep inside his chest. Arabella shifted the baby into his arms, guiding his hand to support her head. The baby, not used to a man's rough touch, fussed against her father's sturdy chest, her rosebud lips rounding into another piercing cry.

He sighed in relief at her vitality, cradling her until she settled.

She looked up at him, blinking her blueberry eyes.

"My God, Arabella," he said when he could speak. "She's beautiful."

"She is. She looks just like you."

"No," he said, though there was no denying the baby's raven black hair and ocean blue eyes matched his own. "She's as beautiful as her mother." He gently stroked the child's face. "The tilt of her chin, the curve of her cheeks, the pout of her lips," he caressed each tiny feature as he spoke, "they all come from you."

She'll break someone's heart one day, he thought, though he stopped himself from saying it aloud. "Is she healthy?" he asked instead. "Are you healthy?"

The anger was gone from his voice, replaced by a sorrow that wounded her more than his rage ever would. She placed her hand on his thigh. "We're both fine, James," she said. "I should have told you. I'm so sorry."

He shook his head. "I'm the one who's sorry, Arabella. I have no right to blame you for keeping her a secret from me, not after the way I acted on the solstice." He imagined himself as she must have seen him that night; a man who had forced her to flee because he could not distinguish her character from her father's, a man who had resorted to threats and violence instead of respecting the time and space she needed to process all she had learned. A thousand regrets for his stubborn pride and fiery temper welled up inside him. The very characteristics that made him a strong and capable sailor at sea had weakened him when it came to matters of the heart, but he was resolved to better himself for Arabella and their child.

"What's her name?" he asked.

"I haven't named her yet." Alone with her daughter in her mother's cottage by the sea, there had been no need for names. Every word Arabella had spoken had been for the baby, and every sound the baby had uttered had been for Arabella, as though the two of them still shared one life, one body. *A name is a powerful thing*, her mother's letter had said, *a magic spell that casts a light of hope upon our darkest hours, a charm which conjures the peace of knowing exactly who we are*. It had seemed an enormous task to name their child, one she hadn't wanted to undertake without James. "Maybe we can choose her name together."

The baby grasped her father's calloused finger. He clenched his jaw, exhaling slowly, trying to find a way through the agony clouding his heart.

"She'll need a name as strong and as beautiful as she is," he said. "She'll need a name before you take her back to Scotland." The words stuck in his throat as he spoke. "And she needs to know my name, in case she ever wants to find me." It was a command and not a request. "I'll set up funds to provide for both of you. Neither of you will want for anything. I won't stand in your way, Arabella, but I won't let you take her from me without *promising* me you'll tell her my name."

"I'm not taking her back to Scotland, James." Her voice was a whisper, but he turned at the sound of it, the tiniest spark of hope alighting in his chest. "And she already knows your name. I've already told her all about you. I wish someone had told me about my father when I was a child, no matter how difficult it may have been for me to hear."

"Arabella—"

"I didn't know Anne and Jonathan were bringing you here today," she said, cutting him off because she needed to finish speaking before her tears made it impossible. "I didn't want you to find out about her like this, but I'm glad you finally know. I'm glad you've finally met her."

"You're going to stay here? In America?"

"Yes."

"And you'll let me be a part of her life? You'll let me be a part of your life?"

"Do you want to be a part of our lives, James? Even after the secret I've kept from you?"

He shifted his weight so he was facing her, holding their baby between them. She was offering him a chance to prove how much he loved her, to prove how much he loved them. He could wallow in his anger and regret about the past, or he could begin building a future, a future that only mattered to him if Arabella and their daughter were a part of it.

"Yes," he said. "Yes, I want to be a part of your lives." He had never been more certain of anything. They would find a way to mend the broken trust between them. They would find a way past the family history that had made their relationship so difficult. He would prove to her that he was a man she could trust. He cradled the baby in one hand and pulled Arabella closer to him with the other. "I want the three of us to be a family. I want you to be my wife." He felt the fog of his despair lifting as he spoke the words aloud. "Say you'll marry me, Arabella. I'll talk to William. I'll find a way to get his permission. I'll do whatever it takes to make this right."

"The baby and I don't need you to make us right." She met his gaze with a defiant tilt of her chin. "There's nothing wrong with us." She was tired of the judgements unfairly leveled against her due to the circumstances of her birth, and she did not want any man, not even James, to rescue her daughter from the same fate only to repress what made her who she was. "The Porter Clan have raised their daughters alone for generations, practicing a faith that has been vilified. I won't deny my daughter her birthright. I won't hide my faith from her. I won't raise her to know only half of her heritage, even if I raise her here in America."

She spoke boldly, as she had when they first met in the woods, and the corners of his eyes crinkled as he smiled for what felt like the first time in months.

"I don't want you to marry me so I can change who you are or what you believe. I want you to marry me so we can raise our daughter together."

"You don't have to marry me to help me raise our daughter, James."

He took her hand in his and squeezed it. "Do you love me?" he asked.

"Yes." The word hung in the air, vibrating like a musical cord. "I've always loved you. Even when I left you, I loved you."

"Then marry me because you love me. Marry me because I love you. Marry me because, together, we will love her."

Arabella had been raised to embrace her independence, but since coming to America, she had dreamed of sharing her life with James, a dream that had grown even more pressing after she had left him. She watched their baby nestle against his chest. Was love really all they needed to heal the pain they had caused each other? *True magic is all around us, soft and unpretentious*, Caitriona had once said. *Our hearts, which are so small we might hold them in the palms of our hands, contain the strongest magic we will ever know.*

There is much in a little, multum in parvo.

Love. Love had always been the answer.

She looked up at him through a web of long, dark eyelashes. "Are you asking me to marry you or ordering me to marry you?"

"Does it matter?"

"Yes."

He laughed then, a bright, clear sound that reverberated off the cottage walls. She would never stop testing him, but he would be a better husband, a better father, a better man because of it. They loved each other; that was all that mattered. He stood up, picking up the ring which had tumbled to the floor. He pulled Arabella to her feet and took her hand in his. The sunlight passed through the leaves of the tree just outside the window, painting his broad chest with dappled light.

"Arabella Porter," he said, his voice deep and slow, "You have vexed me since the night I first met you, half naked, beside the Whitford Brook—"

"James—"

"The least you can do is listen to my proposal."

"This doesn't sound like a proposal."

"I'm getting there." He winked at her, and she smiled, blushing with the memory of the night they had met. She looked from his eyes to their daughter's and back again, bewitched by four round sapphire seas.

"You are the most beautiful, intelligent, and frustrating woman I have ever met—"

"James—"

He tugged on her hand, bidding her to be silent as he continued, "but the moments I have spent with you have been the happiest moments of my life. When you left me, I couldn't sleep. I couldn't breathe. Knowing I hurt you, knowing I was the reason you ran away, it made me feel like I was drowning."

His voice dropped as he slid her ring back onto her finger. "I know you can survive on your own. I know you can take care of our daughter on your own, but if you let me, I promise to protect you. I promise to provide for you. I promise to look after you and our daughter for the rest of my life." He laced his fingers in hers, staring into her eyes. "I don't remember who I was before I loved you. I don't know who I would be if I was forced to stop loving you.

I've been lost without you, Arabella. You are my true north. You are the star that guides me home."

He lowered himself onto one knee.

"Arabella Porter, will you marry me?"

The moment stilled before her. The earth itself seemed to pause in its endless rotation. Centuries of Porter traditions could be unknotted by one word, one choice, one powerful incantation.

"Yes." She smiled. "Of course I will marry you."

He swept her into his arms and kissed her, and kissed her, and kissed her, and the cottage by the sea, which had borne witness to so much despair, held its breath in joy. And when Anne and Jonathan walked back through the door, they found the new family spiraled together in a circle of love.

Mother, father, and child.

An unbreakable set of three.

Part Ten

Skye

"If this be error and upon me proved,
I never writ, nor no man ever loved"
(Sonnet 116)

Arabella never learned the details of James' negotiation with William which had taken place at Newbury House, with Anne acting as a buffer between the men before William demanded she leave the room so he could speak with James alone. Anne had reported what little she had been witness to with dramatic relish, telling Arabella how their father had refused to shake James' hand and how James' scar had burned hot and white with anger. When Arabella, who didn't want James to sacrifice his family's fortune or put his business with Jonathan at risk to gain her hand in marriage, asked him about the meeting, he refused to speak of it, saying only that she was worth far more than anything he had given, and reassuring her that he and Jonathan had taken steps to secure their operations from William's interference.

Their wedding ceremony was to be a modest one, but Anne insisted, for propriety's sake, that Arabella and her daughter remain in the cottage by the sea until the day of the nuptials. It took nearly a month for James to reopen Alden House and prepare it for his new family's occupation. He built a cradle for his daughter, bending the Carolina pine and live oak boards Jonathan imported from southern forests into the curved shape of a tiny ship's prow and carving a triskelion into the headboard. Anne had a wedding dress sewn for Arabella, a white gown with three silk roses stitched above the bustle at the back of the waist.

On the night before the ceremony, Arabella carried her daughter out into the late August evening. The day had been thick with heat, and sheets of lightning flashed across the sky, revealing far-off ships that would have otherwise remained hidden by the ink of night. Arabella opened the gate to Catherine's garden, wending her way through the vegetation until she reached the evening primroses which bloomed, lush and white, beneath the silver moon. She lit a small fire in her circle of stones, placed a bowl of cream beside it as an offering, and pulled the letter she had written to her mother from the pocket of her dress. She read it aloud, her soft voice mixing with the crackling of the flames.

Dear Catherine,

Perhaps I should call you Mam, for that is who you are to me, though, having been only an infant when you left the Isle of Skye, I remember nothing of our life together. Whenever the islanders spoke of you, they whispered of "Catherine's" beauty, "Catherine's" kindness, "Catherine's" empathy, so in my heart, you have always been "my Catherine" rather than "my mam" and it is your name, and not your title, that floats through my mind when I think of you.

I feel your presence here, among your evening primroses, and I am grateful that, however terribly my father may have treated you while you lived, he honored your final request to bury you here when you died. Your garden, which looks to the east, over the vast Atlantic Ocean and toward the Isle of Skye, is a beautiful place. I like to imagine you planting it at the same time your mother was teaching me to garden in Scotland. I like to imagine our flowers, forced from the same seeds, blooming on opposite sides of a stormy sea. I wish I had known you survived your ocean crossing. I wish you had trusted in Caitriona's love for you so you could have returned home. I wish the three of us had had a life together, but these wishes are useless now. Wishing shapes the future, but it is powerless to change the past.

The letter you left in the hands of Hamish McPherson altered the trajectory of my life. I was alone in the world when I broke its seal, grieving the loss of Caitriona, buried by the weight of carrying on our Porter traditions by myself. I followed my heart to America, looking for my family. I found my father, though he was not the savior I hoped he would be. I found my sister, and she has become my confidant and my friend. I found you here in the New World as well, following the trail of breadcrumbs you left behind because you knew I would look for you. I found you inside the letter you left for me in your grimoire. I found you inside your cottage by the sea. I found you in the light of your moonflower garden and in the darkness of your hidden spells. Your absence haunted my childhood, but your shadowy presence has left its mark upon the woman I have become.

Here in Mystic, I have also found the kind of love you searched for all your life, a love that unfurls the bracken, a love that makes the heather blush in streams of scarlet flowers, a love as constant as the moor winds blowing over the hills of Skye. You met the man I love, James Alden, when he was just a boy. He called you a witch and threw a stone through your window, but when his mother died, you comforted him as though he was your own. He is the one who brought me to your cottage, erasing its painful memories even as he preserved all you had left behind. The feral boy you once knew has grown into a shipbuilder and a sailor. He tells me stories of the sea and stars. He protects me without isolating me, guides me without changing me. His words and actions, like my own, are often imperfect, but our intentions toward each other are tender, our feelings for each other are true.

James and I have a daughter of our own now. In her still, small presence, the whole of the heavens finds its reflection. You met her too, on the day she was born, when you journeyed across the veil with Caitriona and Mary and Elinor to witness her soul taking its place in this earthly realm. On that solstice morning, she seemed as delicate and as powerful as a bird in flight, with a spirit so beautiful it took my breath away. I knew, even as I carried her beneath my heart, that she would be born with the Porter Clan's fairy gifts, but James and I have decided to raise her together, here, in the New World, embracing both my faith and his own. My decision to stay in America marks the first time in recorded history a Porter woman has not ministered on the Isle of Skye, though perhaps even our ancient clan was once comprised of newcomers to Scotland's shores. We are all travelers in this life, and the places we inhabit tattoo themselves upon our souls as surely as we leave our marks upon them. I will keep the beauty and magic of our island home in my heart as James and I write the next chapter of our lives along the banks of the Mystic River.

Although you never found your happily-ever-after with William, although you were estranged from your blood family, although you felt forced to go through life in isolation, I hope you know how much you were loved. When I restored your garden, I met dozens of people whose lives were made better by your decision to return to the craft you had once abandoned. For every sordid story I have heard about the Mystic Witch, I have heard three more about the Wise Woman who lived in a cottage by the sea, the one who helped those in need, the one who transformed the mundane with her magic. Beneath every angry expression that ever crossed Caitriona's brow when she spoke of you was her unfathomable grief for the loss of you. Behind every indignant question I ever asked about why you left me was my longing to know you better. We are never truly estranged from our mothers, no matter how far away they may be. I know now that, in your own way, you will always watch over me, because if anything is capable of piercing the veil between the worlds of the living and the dead, it is the strength of a mother's love.

It may seem strange that I am writing to someone who has already passed, for words are the tools of the living, but by studying your letters, I have learned that words, properly wielded, are the most powerful magic of all. I know the words of my letter will reach you, just as the words of your letters once reached me, for the fairy gifts which run through our blood tell me it will be so. When I close my eyes, I can see you reading them in the dazzling streams of eternal light that shine East of the Sun and West of the Moon.

Please tell Elinor I am sorry for not being with her when she passed. Please thank Mary for raising such a kind and noble son. Please tell Caitriona I miss her, I love her, and I think of her every day. James and I will carry all of you with us as we raise our daughter, a child named for the divine beauty of her winged soul. We will not be able to protect her from the pain that comes from living, but we will love her, always, and we will make sure she knows she will never have to walk through this life, or the next life, alone.

As my own mother once told me, even in death, love never ends.

Your daughter,

Arabella

She folded the letter. She pulled a taper from her pocket and held it to the heat of the fire. When it began to melt, she poured its rose-tinted liquid over the space where the pages met, pressing her thistle pendant into the pool of tallow, waiting patiently for the night air to harden the seal into a violet-scented wax. She brought the spikes and swirls of the Porter emblem to her lips and dropped the parchment into the fire. The pages curled and writhed like living things, transmuting into flakes of golden ash that sailed upward toward the sky.

She held her child, listening as the flickering flames and crashing waves composed an ethereal tune. *The notes you choose, the softness of your touch, the rhythm of your movement, the intention of your soul, these things make a song your own, even if its score has already been played a thousand times before*, James had once told her. Arabella looked into the bright blue orbs of her daughter's eyes and released her family's lullaby into the air, turning its somber lament into a strain of joy.

O dig me a grave, and dig it down deep
And strew it all over with primrose so sweet
And lay me down easy, no more for to weep
Since love is the key to my keeping.

The baby laughed, a bright, clear sound that filled the garden, and a silver light spiraled around mother and child, carrying the charred remains of Arabella's letter across the veil before disappearing into the thick, dark fabric of night.

Skye Porter Alden, the first in a long line of Porter women to be born on America's shores, had her father's raven black hair and ocean blue eyes, but she possessed the wild spirit and rugged beauty of her mother's island home, the enchanted place for which she had been named. Like all Porter women, she had come into the world with a second sight, a curious ability, an unsettling quirk that held her apart from the residents of her home town, a fairy gift, her trait was called in hushed tones around the pulpit.

Skye's gift was one of prophecy, a propensity for predicting the likely outcomes of future events based on strange visions and premonitions that rippled through her mind like flashes of midsummer lightning. It was a gift Skye would rail against her entire life, for the blood which coursed through her veins came from a stubborn lineage that valued freedom and choice over predestination, and Skye would mature into a formidable young woman who refused to let anyone, the fairies, the fates, or the gods, determine the course of her future.

Skye spent her childhood safe in the embrace of Alden House, beneath the watchful eyes of her parents and her younger siblings, little boys with auburn curls and emerald eyes, each one more trouble than the next. Her grandmother's wild Irish roses continued to bloom in the garden, and her mother planted so many Scottish thistles on the lawn that Skye could not run through the grass with bare feet as she wished, but always had to wear her leather slippers to keep from cutting her feet on the thorns.

Her parents often brought her to the cottage by the sea where she had been born and where her mother kept a luscious garden, growing foxglove and fennel, rosemary and lavender, fiddlehead ferns and clusters of yellow rue. Arabella taught Skye to read the landscape like a book, and together they harvested fern seeds each Midsummer's Eve, crushing them into fine powders and pouring them into secret pockets they stitched into cloaks, shirts, and blankets. They distributed the items to all those who sailed on Jonathan's ship and took quiet shelter in James' office. The hidden thistle, rue, and fern seed mixture, which had been used in the Porters' grey healer's cloaks for centuries, helped freedom seekers move through the northern woods unnoticed as they followed the *Drinking Gourd* in the stars.

It was on the gentle shore of the beach behind the cottage that James taught his children to love the sea. They played in the tumbling waves and sailed along the coastline, sometimes going so far that Arabella could barely see the dot of their boat on the horizon. When she lost sight of them completely, she would write their names in the sand, whispering them over and over, a magic spell, a prayer to return them safely back home.

Skye's parents had been married in a quiet Christian ceremony, her Aunt Anne and Uncle Jonathan among the few witnesses to the nuptials, and after the paperwork had been signed with no public objection from William, after the wedding cake had been eaten and the guests had gone home, after Skye had been tucked into her ship-shaped cradle with Catherine Porter's thistle pendant resting against her infant heart, James took his bride into the garden. The light of a thousand whale oil lanterns twinkled in the rosebushes, and the river breezes ruffled the ribbons threaded through Arabella's long, loose hair. The setting sun gilded the sky in the west, and the rising moon silvered the sky in the east, and the couple danced into the darkening night, whirling and waltzing until they lost their breath from laughing.

If Skye had been old enough to understand her gift of prophecy on the day her parents had been married, she would have foretold a turbulent future for her family. When the needle of a compass points toward true love, life is never easy, and James and Arabella would face their share of heart-wrenching sorrow as events beyond their control tore America apart at the seams. But, even if the couple had known about the tempests that lay in front of them, they still would have spoken the vows which knotted their lives and souls together, for in each other, they had found their true home.

The village of Mystic, Connecticut, as old as America itself, still straddles the banks of the Mystic River, which continues to flow into the brackish waters of Fishers Island Sound. Some say the village, which has burned to the ground and been rebuilt countless times in the centuries since the Mystic Massacre, is cursed by avenging Native spirits, forced to continually rise like a phoenix from the ashes of its dark history, but the village is not haunted by grief alone. Love has left its phantom imprint along the river as well, hiding in pearly slants of light, echoing in the far-off ringing of bells, wafting through the air like the sweet scent of oakmoss and wildflowers, always just beyond your reach.

The last known member of the Alden family passed through the veil just before the turn of the twenty-first century, but Alden House, tall and proud, still breathes on Greenman Avenue; its roses and thistles still bloom against the clapboard siding still painted the color of a calm, green sea. The house now serves as office space for The Mystic Seaport Museum, a re-creation of a 19th century seafaring village where modern shipbuilders and sailors work along the same paths and waterways as the shipbuilders and sailors who lived almost two hundred years before. Like all museums, Mystic Seaport is a keeper of stories, charting the passing of time like sailors measuring angles of light against distant horizons or mothers counting hours by their infants' hungry cries. Curators who work in the Alden House offices sometimes hear a spectral tune drifting from behind the closed door of the west wing, but whether it is Mary's ghost whispering to her roses, or a departed spirit singing to comfort a child, no one knows.

If you visit the Mystic Seaport Museum and walk along the banks of the river on a hot summer night when the fireflies wink like the flickering lights of a thousand whale oil lanterns, you may see the shades of James Alden and Arabella Porter, still dancing in the damp breezes blowing off the water, still twirling together in an endless spiral of sacred motion, no beginning and no end. And, if you listen carefully, beneath the rushing of the river and the throaty call of nightbirds flapping their feathered wings over the waves, you may hear the hallowed strain of fairy music that directs the couple's dance, a celestial chorus, warbling sweet and low, singing the songs of the sea and stars.

AUTHOR'S NOTE

In the beginning, *Sea and Stars* was a vignette published by *The Fairy Tale Magazine* (formerly *Enchanted Conversation*) under the title *Midsummer Magic*. Arabella Porter was there, the last living healer in a long line of women, roaming through the fairy woods and brewing restorative potions in her lonely cottage by the sea. I will be forever grateful to the founder of *The Fairy Tale Magazine*, my friend and Fairy Godmother Kate Wolford, for prompting me to expand Arabella's story into novel form. Kate's advice and developmental editing helped me move the Porter Clan from a nameless fairy tale setting to the Isle of Skye, a haunting landscape filled with ancient lore and windswept moors, a place which shapes and reflects the wild beauty and tenacious spirit of the Porter line.

Early on, I knew Arabella's journey to find her father's family would lead her to America, but it wasn't until I settled on her destination, the small New England village of Mystic, Connecticut, that *Sea and Stars* truly began to take its shape. Like the Isle of Skye, Mystic is a liminal place rich in history and folklore. The town's prominent role in 19th century shipbuilding and whaling provided the historical context for my story, allowing me to ponder the physical and political transformations that defined America's Antebellum Era alongside the emotional and spiritual transformations initiated by human loneliness, loss, and love. Although I do not live in Mystic, it is my home away from home, and I am grateful to The Mystic Seaport Museum, The Mystic River Historical Society, The Mashantucket Pequot Museum, Seaside Shadows Haunted History

Tours, The Stonington Lighthouse Museum, and The Captain Nathaniel B. Palmer House Museum for grounding me in Mystic's past even as I dreamed of filling it with fairy enchantment.

Although the settings in *Sea and Stars* have been drawn from real life, the plot and characters are all products of my imagination, an imagination indebted to the stories I love. *Search for the Lost Husband* tales (like *Beauty and the Beast* and *East of the Sun and West of the Moon*) have always been my favorite fairy tales, and many of their markers (bold female heroines, beasts with human hearts, ineffective fathers, wealth which grants access to art, a slow unfolding of desire, an emphasis on choice, a violation of an interdiction, and a separation followed by a reunion) serve as anchors for the romance between James and Arabella. *Maiden Killer* fairy tales like *Bluebeard* and *The Fitcher's Bird*, (often considered shadow tales to *Beauty and the Beast* narratives), lend *Sea and Stars* its locked door, its iron key, and its scrimshaw egg, and Celtic folklore permeates its temporal setting, providing the protagonists with a language of connection as the wheel of the year turns. Readers will also find nods to the Gothic atmosphere of *Jane Eyre* and *Northanger Abbey*, the ocean adventures of Odysseus, the highland tales of Sir Walter Scott, the fairy poetry of John Keats, the hallowed words of William Shakespeare, and the contemplation of freedom, sin, and redemption explored in John Milton's *Paradise Lost.* In this way, *Sea and Stars* is a love letter to the literature that is anchored in my heart, and I am grateful for my teaching and writing positions at Central Connecticut State University, *The Fairy Tale Magazine*, and *Eternal Haunted Summer* which gift me long days in the company of such inspiring works.

My journey through the world of publication has taught me that stories are not told through words alone. My amazing cover artist, Holly Dunn of Holly Dunn Design, breathed life into Arabella, surrounding her with Celtic knots to symbolize her past and Alden roses to symbolize her future. In doing so, Holly not only helped me tell the story of *Sea and Stars*, but she also made me believe my words were worthy of a beautiful and meaningful cover image, and I can never thank her enough. My fairy tale friend Alison Weber, the artist who created exclusive illustrations for my debut novella *Selkie Moon* and an early reader of *Sea and Stars*, enthusiastically emailed me with ideas for character art, further helping me envision the artistic potential of the scenes I had written. Like Arabella's enchanted rosehip tea that helps memories unfold in palpable form, the art created by Holly and Alison transforms my inky words into images crafted of light, shape, and color, and I am humbled to have their work grace my story.

Being a writer can feel overwhelming at times, and I am grateful to my friends and fellow writers, Lissa Sloan and Lynn Patarini, who have guided me through the endless hurdles of publication, and to Rebecca Buchanan, the Editor-in-Chief of *Eternal Haunted Summer* whose novellas and novelettes never fail to inspire me. I am also grateful to Kristen Baum DeBeasi, the Editor-in-Chief of *The Fairy Tale Magazine*, who leads a talented community of readers, writers, and poets known as the Fairy Godparents Club, a group which gathers to celebrate the magic in everyday life, a group which has become my fairy tale family. I can't imagine a world without their friendship and support.

I am also thankful to all those who championed my decision to write a historical romance with shades of fairy magic. In the academic circles where I spend my days, romance is often dismissed as a formulaic genre that reinforces outdated gender roles, while fairy tale and fantasy are relegated to the realms of children's or popular literature. But I am a hopeless romantic, and I believe sharing stories about the transformative magic of love, in all its varied forms, is a noble and worthy pastime. I am forever grateful to my husband and sons for filling my life with so much love that it spills over onto the pages of my notebooks and works its way into my writing.

Finally, I am grateful to you, dear readers, for being the keys which unlock the varied meanings of *Sea and Stars*. Like most romance stories, my novel has a score that has been played a thousand times before, but each time my words harmonize with a reader's heart, the tune unfolds anew. Thank you for adding your notes, your touch, your rhythm, and your intention to the incantation I have set down. Thank you for being part of my story.

To me, stories are as constant as the pull of ocean tides and as vital as the light that maps celestial darkness. They are my way of understanding and connecting with the world, my way of turning even the most somber of life's laments into strains of joy. I hope you have found as bright a light in your version of *Sea and Stars* as I have found in mine, and I hope, one day, we will harmonize together again.

Kelly Jarvis works as the Contributing Writer for *The Fairy Tale Magazine* and is a Recurring Columnist for *Eternal Haunted Summer.* She also teaches writing and literature at Central Connecticut State University. Her poetry and fiction have appeared in *A Moon of One's Own, Baseball Bard, Blue Heron Review, Corvid Queen, Enchanted Conversation, Forget Me Not Press, Mermaids Monthly, Mothers of Enchantment, The Chamber Magazine,* and *The Magic of Us.* Her debut novella, *Selkie Moon,* was selected as a semi-finalist in the 2025-2026 Speculative Fiction Indie Novella Championship.

Visit Kelly online at kellyjarviswriter.com.

www.ingramcontent.com/pod-product-compliance
Lightning Source LLC
LaVergne TN
LVHW091246150826
845673LV00006B/1340